Strange Birds in the Tree of Heaven

STRANGE

BIRDS

in the

TREE

of

HEAVEN

A NOVEL

KAREN SALYER MCELMURRAY

d

HILL STREET PRESS   ATHENS, GEORGIA

A HILL STREET PRESS BOOK

Published in the United States of America by
Hill Street Press LLC
191 East Broad Street, Suite 209
Athens, Georgia 30601-2848 USA
706-613-7200
info@hillstreetpress.com
www.hillstreetpress.com

Hill Street Press is committed to preserving the written word.
Every effort is made to print books on acid-free paper with a
significant amount of post-consumer recycled content.

Text and cover design by Anne Richmond Boston.

Printed in the United States of America.

Library of Congress Cataloging-in-Publication Data
McElmurray, Karen Salyer, 1956–
Strange birds in the tree of heaven : a novel / Karen Salyer McElmurray
p. cm.
ISBN 1-892514-24-9 (alk. paper)
I. Title.
PS3563.C35966S7 1999
813'.54—dc21   99-22047
CIP

10   9   8   7   6   5   4   3   2   1
First edition

Dedicated to Francis Ellen Salyer
and to the memory of a house we both loved

*The hand of the Lord was upon me and carried me out in the spirit of
the Lord and set me down in the midst of the valley
which was full of bones.*

EZEKIAL 37:1

CONTENTS

PART I

PART II

PART I

ANDREW: AUGUST 16, 1983

Tonight, I sat alone in the woods at the top of the hill looking down through the witch hazel branches at her. I could look into the kitchen, see all she was doing, shining saucers, setting her house in order. She opened the farthest back screenless window, leaned out. All that way and into the dusk, I could see it, the way her lips moved, praying. I could hear her, plain as day. I cast you out, she shouted, her voice so terrible I could find nothing in it to call mother.

I hid behind the witch hazel, pressed my cheek to the smooth bark, a lifeline, a savior. Whatever blessless thing she had cast out winged past, touched the top of my head with a kiss and flew at the sky just as the sun went down.

I told myself I wouldn't believe her about anything, about Henry Ward, or the Lord, or witch hazel. How could she send shapes into the dark? How could she know whether blossoms had a scent, or whether love should or should not have an unfamiliar face? I pulled down the highest branches, buried my face in the skinny petals. I wanted them to have a scent, something sharp and biting. I took the blossoms between my teeth and bit through their tastelessness, wanting to believe.

All of my life, here, where things winged, blessed, merciless, are real. Where the world is a cusp, and I am left, holding on to the sharp edge. I am this, I am that, I love, I cannot. I must, I must not. How to name that place in between, the cusp of the world?

Tonight I, Andrew Wallen, who for all my thirty years am but a would-be, a pretender of intellect and spirit and heart, will not try to convince you of anything. I will quote no ineffable truth, no lofty passage from my most secretly read books. I will not talk of the unbelievable, of how to dream, how to escape today unscathed. I will only rarely hold my head to the wind and imagine the unimaginable, the distant and tantalizing scent of the ocean, a lingering sniff that I can savor, warm salt on my tongue.

I maintain that witch hazel has a scent. I've read that it is odorless, colorless, and my mother, from her personal store of wisdom, calls it a flower with no use at all. But I want to believe in ambitions that take us beyond all we think we can be. I want to know that God does not merely exist between the pages of any book, however holy. And that love, sin or none, can walk and talk in a surprising array of forms. But I hold these notions, my most secret self, next to my own heart, like a bundle of postcards at the back of a drawer I show no one.

After awhile, I walked back to the house, stood quietly at the back door into the kitchen, looking at a sway-backed table and newspaper covered walls.

She was warming rinse water in a metal basin at the cookstove. Her nightly ritual, water for the dishes and just enough leftover for a warmed cup with a spoonful of vinegar to purify the blood, and thus, she believed, the soul. She took two thin dishrags, lifted the pan with her stringy-muscled arms. Her, rolled down anklet socks, flowered house dress unzipped at the back. My mother.

I steadied myself against any memory of the hill, until she saw me and I knew she was calm again. She took down a jar of instant from the kitchen cabinet, made me a cup of coffee. I sat, stirring in spoonful after spoonful of sugar while she stood at the sink.

"I guess you'll go out." Her voice, unmusical, low, not a question. Her back, turned from me, straight, unyielding.

"I suppose," I said, studying my hands. "Maybe." I sipped the hot coffee.

"A lot more than supposing ought to go on around here," she said. She dropped a fistful of washed spoons into the rinse water.

"What," I said, "would you suggest?" I spoke quietly into my cup, nothing but a subversive whisper, but still she heard. "An evening of you and me and the Bible?"

Dishes clattered in their water. "You just go on like that," she said. "Just like that. You'll see right soon."

"And what," I said, standing near my chair, holding on to its back. "What, Mother, might I be seeing so clearly?"

"There's a choice," she said, wiping her hands on the dishcloth. "You know that every time you head out like you do." She crushed the cloth next to her, turned to face me. "With that boy."

I went to the stove, poured more warm water into my cup, took another long swallow, felt the roof of my mouth burn. I turned, met the dark centers of her green eyes. Tried to hold onto that look.

"Choice?" I asked again. "When every single prayer you've ever prayed, every blessing, is about, what? Death? Your imminent one, or mine?" I stood, clutching my cup. "End this world, meet your maker. Heaven, hell, and on and on to God almighty himself."

"Son," she said. "Everything will be clear in time." She stepped toward me, touched my cheek with her red, water-wrinkled hand. She was close enough there was her smell of camphor, stale clothes.

"Which time, Mother?" I asked. "Your time or mine? Now or later?"

Now it was she who tried to hold my look, who tried to move after me, smooth my shirt collar, rake back the hair from my eyes.

"Son," she said again. She called after me as I headed through the other room, out the screen door to the porch. "Andrew Wallen," she called. "Wait awhile. Just wait."

I took one more long, sweet drink, set the cup on the railing. I didn't believe her, the way she meant that the hour of the Lord was at hand. The way she always said this was the time of fulfillment, then drank her cups of vinegar, despised each mouthful of her food. Still I felt the damp shape of her hand drying on my face.

I thought about how, since forever, amen, she had been the light and the truth and the only decision. When I was child, there was no choice. She made good the very bread she set out at our table, every fat, white loaf of it. These are the Saturday nights I recall.

Me, by the window, reading some romance about pirates and treasures and the shining sea, a tale I'd sequestered from the Inez public library. A book hidden inside the sacred covers of the family Bible, which she thought I was reading Genesis to Revelations and back. Wash up, she would say, and I'd go to the kitchen where my father would stand at the sink, scrubbing his hands with a bristly brush until it hurt to see. He would wink at me over her shoulder, as if to say such pain was nothing to a man. Then he would sit at the head of the table, ready to pass the steaming bowls. But it was her who prayed, who said, hush now, children, to all of us. The words of the eating prayer began. She spoke softly, but so fast with these prayers I had to listen very hard not to miss a word, words like not thankful enough, unworthy, sanctify and keep us from your wrath Oh Lord our God, Amen. She made me see how I didn't deserve any of it, potatoes, the cast iron pot of tender squirrel bones and gravy. The scent of the food caused a sickness in me. The words made me feel smaller and smaller, made me feel so light and hungry for something I couldn't hold on to the table at all.

Weightless, I was carried out on some breath of air past the table full of bowls of lettuce and grease and fresh green onions, past the sideboard where the bread and butter lay. I drifted out through the keyhole into the huge night air. If it hadn't been for the sounds of locusts and screech owls and the toll of bells from the church across the ridge, I would have floated on forever. Those things caught me and held me down, as if I were a fish in a net, a flutter of moths against a window screen. I knew she gave this terrible power to the earth, the power of holding down. The letting go was lovely and forbidden, so I scraped my plate clean. I knew I could never be as good as she was.

I sat in the cane-bottom chair and looked through the handle of my coffee cup, down to the road beyond the house. This, now, tonight, was the only real choice of consequence in this world. Sooner or later I'd see headlights in the distance and hear the spin of gravel.

If I counted cars long enough, sooner or later one of them would slow down for me. It would be a 1965 Mustang without even a scratch on its finish and Henry Ward would be at the wheel. At this distance from the road I wouldn't be able to make out even one of his features, the eyes so blue they were almost white, the smooth cheeks so freshly shaven I could feel the sting of the aftershave. From the looks of that car alone you'd think everything about him was perfect, his shirt collars white without fail, his cuticles neatly turned back and his mustache clipped long before the hairs hid the corners of his mouth. Henry.

He was, I knew, just one of the high and mighty Ward boys who had taken off from Inez as soon as they knew how, set on change and glory. All I knew of them when I was a child was that they saw different signs of God than my mother or my father or myself. They sat, just like I did, in the Church of the Holiness watching the newly healed dance by. But while I sat looking for the next hymn early, sure the preacher would find me out if I didn't, the three Ward brothers sat with their eyes turned to the stained glass windows. While sunlight came through and turned all our faces blue and amber and gold, they took those colors and put them in their pockets to trade for something else later on. Bill, the second oldest, lit out for Cleveland to sell biblical odds and ends, but somehow ended up no farther north than Carolina and never wrote home except to tell us all about the fortune he'd made in a chicken factory. Alan, the youngest, disappeared one July night after the summer carnival. No one heard anything from him until almost a year later when he sent his family a postcard entitled Moon over Miami and said he'd hit the big time in used cars.

None of those things made Henry so fine to look at. I could see past the slim collars of his suit jackets, past the genuine silver belt buckle set with turquoise, even past the specially steamed and shaped hat he always wore when we went out on Saturdays. I had always known him. I could see right through to his heart, hear how it beat like waves on some distant shore.

Soon I would be able to hear how he shut off the engine and coasted the last few yards into the gravel by the mailbox. He would lean out the window like he always did, give me some signal, one low tone into a half empty beer bottle, a partly whistled line from the Tennessee Waltz. Even in the dark, from the porch, I would see desire in his hands.

I stood on the top porch step, picked up my cold cup of coffee and set every muscle in my body against her, against turning to look through the door into the front room. I held my back so straight and my shoulders so stiff they ached, but I had to steal one look out of the corner of my eye.

She held in her lap that Bible she gave me for my sixteenth birthday. She touched its leather cover as gently as she had touched the cool body of the whippoorwill she'd found in the barn that morning and brought back to the house. I could almost hear the crisp, new pages crackle, smell the fresh ink. I knew without asking what she was thinking. All things hollow and not filled up with holy praise were damned. The words, for one, of all my books and books she called a waste of a mind meant for the Lord.

She stood at the painted shut window and motioned to me, her arms going up and down like some winged thing, ready to take flight. Through the door I could hear her.

"Come inside," she said. "Where it's warm."

Warm. No mother's lap, no quilt on the couch, but air so close and full of sleeping and warnings I never could draw a real breath. Her holiness. A precious thing she kept inside on her lap, a holiness with a shut in scent that reminded me of water stains on the plaster ceiling of my room.

As I went down the steps to the yard I could already feel the breath of her wanting on the back of my neck. Come back, she said. Come back into the house and kneel down and we will thank God forever and ever until our knees hurt.

I made my way carefully past the things in our yard. Although I had almost never touched a woman, I was sure I would remember every part of any face like I knew these things in the dark. On the right hand porch side was the rusted pickup truck, one my father had worked on that very afternoon. Farther back, near the split rail fence, was a pen where he kept that hound he had been disappointed to discover was not a blue tick and eight new pups. But there was always a litter, ten, and before, six. None of them made a sound as I walked past. Then there was Henry's voice calling out in the shadows and his car door swung open.

"Andrew Wallen," he called. "Hurry on up."

I stood still for the briefest time, my hand on the gate latch, thinking I had a choice to make. I turned once and looked back at my mother near the window, her head tilted back. I knew she couldn't see me in the dark yard, yet she searched me out like the hound had sniffed for her pups when my father had once buried them alive in the back garden. Did I, after all, have a choice to make?

"Andrew Wallen," Henry called again. The inside of his car smelled of crushed velvet and some spicy cologne. Music collided against my ears. Henry passed me a cold beer and I popped it open. After all, what choice had there been?

"Andrew Wallen," Henry said. "Where should we go tonight?"

He turned the radio even higher and I settled back, glad not to hear anything but steel guitar sound.

"Anywhere," I said, thinking how most Saturdays took us anywhere you could imagine, to the Starland Skate-a-rama where we sat on the sidelines, listened to rock-n-roll, and watched boys in their tight jeans skate by so close you could hear wheels singing on their skates. Or maybe we'd go to a drive-in movie out in Inez. We never got a speaker but always sat watching the quiet screen, filling the car with smoke from cigarette after cigarette.

"Anywhere at all," I said, and pulled my flannel shirt tight against the cool night air. Not near the end of summer, and already our warm breath clouded the car windows with steam.

Choice? I settled back and sipped my beer, elixir, sweet night's first taste. The beer went down cold as we headed toward Frazier Lake.

~

Choice, that mystery.

As far back as I can remember my dreams were about choice.

In one dream I woke thinking I heard a summer storm. Still in that tenuous place between sleeping and waking, I sat up asking what, what? The sound of storm gave way to the sound of waves, that sound I'd heard from a would-be genuine hardware store seashell. And then, gently, as if the voice rode on the crest of a wave, something said, I have need of you, I want to know you. I went back to sleep, choosing any place other than a huge unknown.

Even tonight, as I stood, waiting for his summons, the whole of night spoke with the same voice.

Andrew Wallen, Henry has often said, hurry on up. And I have hesitated so often on the threshold of that darkness, his car. Night after night, like diving into a black, unknown ocean, his saying, come out, come into me.

~

And thus have so many of the years of my manhood passed. Manhood? And when you become a man, my mother says, you shall put away childish things. No account, says my father, and recites to me a litany of ineptitude, the ways I have failed my manhood's tests, thirty years old, still at home, disability, when I can get it. And my disabled condition, you might ask? Equipment failure, explosion, failure of hearing in my right ear, disability, failure of courage, since. Failure of my life to choose its own path, failure of my heart to speak aloud by the light of day. And thus is the man, my esteemed dead grandfather once said. Thus is the man who faileth to look after. His own household, my grandfather meant. My own heart's desire, I have said.

All of the years I've ever known until this, lived in hollows, near hollows, Mining, Bear, Paint, Wheelwright, Van Lear. Home, house, that place of heaven's dictates, where night after night I have been in the rooms of my boyhood, in those houses with their holiness. Where I have breathed the scent of those boyhood's rooms, a shut in scent, a scent of dark closets, dust under the bed, the dampness of unchanged sheets, a scent of wanting and not having. I have dreamed of what it means to become a man, dreamed of fire and release. I have dreamed of roads beyond all I have known, dreamed of the endless ocean and the power of forever.

Miles beyond Inez, Highway 23, pot-holed from coal rigs, highway of steep-walled sides, the Appalachian mountains. Road where boulders come drifting down in the wake of passing trucks. Highway of wide, graveled turn-outs, miner families selling household cast-offs on Sunday afternoons, sometime farmers hawking corn and pole beans and musk melons.

Highway 23, south, and you go toward Inez, the only close town, past used auto sales, the one regional medical center, the drive-in movie with the giant ripped screen where they show war movies and sci-fi on Saturday nights. And north. A long haul, three hours and there's West Virginia, Huntington, the big time for an occasional Saturday night. Highway 23, with its side roads, some of them asphalt, some of them rutted gravel and dirt, some of them called mouths, mouths of hollows.

One hollow, mine, Mining Hollow, a place I spent so much of my thirty years. Mouth of that hollow leading to a long dirt road going back and back into the hollow itself, no way out at the end but up over the mountain, through bottom land. Long dirt road going past the Church of the Pentecost, past a trailer with a yard full of washing machines, tires, cans, bottles, stray dogs nosing in the debris. In my childhood I thought, hollow, a place to be held, a soft chest, a palm, a space at the base of a throat.

And later, after the first house burned, there was a second, and still I thought, mouth, hollow, end of everything. Swallowed up. End of another road, little hill going up to another gray house, steep porch steps and a wooden swing and the bug light, yellow light over my mother, sitting in that swing. Waiting for me to come home.

Home from all those nights I slipped out to meet Henry Ward. It was forever itself, those nights. Me, escaping the house. Its five rooms. Me, tiptoeing from my room down the dark hall with the light bulb hanging from a frayed cord. Hall, lit just enough to show the family photos. Photos in discount store plastic frames, hung askew from any handy nail. Mother, father, grandfather. The only known photo of my grandmother, the one who danced away from Mining Hollow, a tintype hung up after my grandfather's death. Living room with a torn, red linoleum rug patterned with tulips, plaster statue of a bulldog, coffee can for tobacco spit beside a green horsehair couch. Then down the front steps, avoiding one creaking board. Down the dirt road far enough to meet the car that waited, just far enough away to be hidden in the shadows of locusts. Me, stumbling down the dark road that enticed, road with its quick bursts of summer wind and music, rock 'n' roll and country pouring forth from the open car windows. And Henry, waiting there. Henry, who believed we could go anywhere.

Down county road after road, exploring hollow after hollow, yards stripped down to the coal, trailers strung with last year's Christmas lights, faces watching through old lace curtains. Saying, there they go, that Wallen boy, him and that wild, no good Ward. I sucked down beer after beer those nights, felt music crash against my ears, dared the night to do anything it pleased.

Saturday nights, hand on the radio dial, music promised to take me. Take us anywhere. Highway 23, past coal yards and the train tracks and car upon car of coal gleaming in the dark, past the swinging bridge over the big river, down the main street of Inez itself. Inez. Lit only by a neon sign on the hill above the pharmacy saying, repent, Jesus, saves.

Right there, plummeting down the town's streets, music wild in my blood, we dared to do anything, even with all the eyes, neighbors, other houses watching. I dared to take his hand, kiss that hand, the fine dark hairs on the middle finger. You are an abomination in the eyes of.

Abomination, abomination. Word whispered from the hollow of all the world I'd ever known. Refrain, whispered from the late-night dark houses of the town. I sipped that word like burning moonshine. Saturday nights I closed my mind to it, opened my heart. I rode the shine of notes and love beyond the town, down back roads, down roads where we could jack the music loud as we pleased and lose ourselves. I plunged into all of it, music, touch of hands and lips, and I was afraid. Afraid of now, of forever.

~

A voice hurried after us, caught at the bumper of Henry's car as we careened around the easy highway curves. This voice knew me, like it had for time immemorial. You, Andrew Wallen, it said.

When will you learn.

Which voice? My mother's? grandfather's?

Voice of this night, of God himself, riding like an angel made of coal dust and sin on the bumper of Henry's car. You, the voice said. You who looketh not into your own sinful heart. Why, you are no man at all. Words settling across my chest so I could hardly breathe.

"Andrew," Henry said, and reached across to touch my shoulder. The tiger's eye ring gleamed on his little finger. "What're you thinking about so hard?"

"Things," I told him. I drained my beer, flung the bottle out the window. "The customary things."

"You been thinking," he asked. "About all we talked about?" Henry cast a look at me from the corner of his eye. A look full of clandestine encounters, wayside Huntington motels, the back seat of this very car. A look full of choice. His.

"When," I asked, "would I have been thinking about anything else?"

What I thought of was driving away from Mining Hollow, from that first house. I recalled so clearly the Saturday mornings on which I would ride to Inez with my father to pursue our various responsibilities, sacred or secular. His lips would tighten to a thin, white line when he looked behind us in the rear view mirror. Behind us to Mining Hollow, house of my grandfather, my mother.

When I was a boy my grandfather, Tobias Blue, lived in the very house with us, watched us as we drove away. That old man, my father would say. Let him ride his own high horse for awhile. It was all gone now, that first house of my past, where the loose shutters banged in the wind, where an old man's fingers held back a curtain, where old man eyes watched us, as if in hunger. As if we would purchase solutions to Armageddon and bring them back in our pockets. I'll tell you, my father would say as he revved the engine. A man can't live every blessed day of his life like it was heaven or hell.

All gone now, first house, grandfather. But my mother resurrected the ghosts of all that time, all that we had lost. At evening prayers, at the very moment before my sleep. Why would I tell Henry Ward these things? I uncapped another beer, sipped.

Henry held the steering wheel loosely, tapped his finger to an old song. *When I feel blue*, he sang, *when I want you, all I have to do is dream.*

As highway lights drifted across on his face, I memorized him, like I had done so many times. Memorized, like delectable passages from a book, passages I could take out and repeat in the dark as I lay alone at night.

I remembered that long ago weekday afternoon, how he had looked standing next to the pool at his father's lavish house up at Wheelwright. There was no one home but Henry and the flushed, green light that poured down over the ridge above the hollow his family owned. The light was so keen when I stood at the pool in my bare feet, the ripples of silver and brilliant aqua made the water seem endless, bottomless.

Legs feeling hushed wind down from the mountains, I spread my arms and balanced, undecided, on the edge of the pool. Head tucked and arms crossed, I waited. The day was too well lit, too clean and clear of everything, concrete freshly swept, air smelling of spearmint, silence in my ears like after a bell had rung. Some cloud, any cloud, should have moved that day across the perfectly blue sky. I held my hands in front of my eyes, toward the sun, looked through the shadows between my pale, red fingers and thought, this is the real way the world looks. Then I felt Henry's hand on the sweating skin of my back, until he placed a drink in my hands. It smelled of coconut and sweetened lime. I drank and drank. I moved without breathing along the translucent bottom of the pool, moved without knowing it through the newness of love.

We took a sharp left off 23, onto State Route 1411, the road to Frazier Lake. I rolled the window completely down, leaned out, shouting into the warm, night air. Armageddon, Armageddon, this is the road to Armageddon! I could already see the road's end, lights along the boat ramp.

Henry Ward tossed another bottle out to the roadside and together we called after it—*forever, this is the road to forever!* I turned the radio higher and we sang the song words as loud as we could. *Anytime, night or day, I'm loving all my life away. It's you, my darling, my sweet thing, my all in all. You and no one but you.*

I pressed my hands against my ears, against rushing night wind and words. But still I heard it, that familiar voice of all my boyhood, all the forever I'd ever known. Voice, riding out the night with me, whispering next to my ears, an unforgiving breath. Andrew Wallen, it said. When, oh when will you know?

For a long time, Henry Ward had asked me just that question. When, Andrew. When will you know if it's me or them?

Him, traveling salesman, now, for a chain of clothing stores, leather and lace and exotic comestibles on a back street in an inland Florida city he visits on weekends. But soon, Andrew Wallen, he says, it'll be the big time. He'll rake in the bucks. He'll buy a condo at an unnamed backside resort. And you, Andrew Wallen, he says, will stay there, weekdays. I'll sweep out the tracked in sand, be keeper of a love nest.

I have loved my imaginings of the ocean so long that all scenarios there are real. Fireworks over the horizon, cool sand in the evening and his lover's body all along my own. His body and my body, twin to twin, my leanness, his softness, mere flesh. The sand, filled with phosphorescence. Roman candles shooting trails into the gently crashing ocean. And Henry, later, holding, entering, my fingers tracing the veins along his arms. A world opening and opening with the coursing of blood, an awful and wonderful explosion of longing.

At his condo, I will wash the beach shoes white and line them up on the deck and bring in shells and bleach them and keep champagne on ice. I will cook magnificent dinners and wait by the sliding glass door. I will dream the most ordinary of lives, a family like all others, breakfast, lunch, forever. Some evenings like this will be endless, but I will wait through them, listening for the much loved footstep, the story of the day. I will wait for Henry Ward to come home.

~

Sweet and endless Frazier Lake night of driving and Henry Ward. Bottomless hole into forever, on the edge of drunkenness, balanced uncertainly on the cusp of the world, full of radio music's aftermath and the longing for what will come.

We drove the last mile toward the lake, near Miner's Hat Lodge. At the edge of the road, a large banner had been strung between two ladders. A sign ghostly white in the dim floodlights, which also revealed a packed parking lot, cars from which ladies were descending, dressed to the nines in their most uncomfortable high-heels, their highest teased wiglets. Celebrate, the sign said. Willie May Whitaker, retired, after forty fine years of service for his company.

Here, the choices were three. Standard Mining, the outfit to the north of town, one said to have investments in both solid American made vehicles from Detroit and less credible, manufacturers as faraway as England or, who knows, more sinister places like Asia. Or there was Long Shot Mining, to the south, notorious for providing getaways for high school boys bound on making good in any world other than high school English or shop when, after all, you can teach yourself all you need to know. Last there was Island Creek, owned by the Ward family, up at Wheelwright. Strip mining par excellence. I'd worked there once, with my father, second shift. Nights, I drove a fork lift and scooped out the rich, black insides of hills, pitched the hills by heaps into trucks ready to take them on for washing, sorting, disposing.

We passed the Lodge itself, its second floor banquet rooms lit. I caught a quick glimpse of long tables, white cloths. Kerosene lanterns, for effect. I imagined a speech, the obligatory gold plated trophy. Another sign, nearer the main lodge building proclaimed the name of a semi-famous country singer, the night's entertainment. My father, for his twenty years of service, had been given a quilt pieced with black and white and rose and appliques of miners with head lamps and picks and a cross stitch saying, Well Done, Earl Wallen. That could be my own life.

As Henry and I got out of the car and walked toward Frazier Lake, all the noises of the night so far followed us, converging at the water along the shore. Distant shimmy of the semi-famous country singer's band. Wind rushing through rolled down windows. My mother's voice saying, plain, clear as day. The crash and shake of rock 'n' roll from the rolled down windows of somebody else's car.

It was the lake where the boys go swimming on Saturday nights. I could see out to where they canoe, to the line of trees to the right where I'd skipped smooth stones along the surface of the water. A sliver of moon had risen so I could even see one or two of those boys now, a Jones boy or a Ratliff standing on the concrete platform in the middle of the lake, arms raised high. They were getting ready to dive.

I stepped out of my shoes and stuck my heel into the cool water. The cold was a point of reference, one beyond all sound, beyond the shiver of too many beers in my head. A point of reference between this night, and the next and the next and the one before, the one last year, last August, at the lake side then, too, or somewhere else, a room, a field beside a road, the car seat at the drive-in movie. All of this convergence of now and before, that, and Henry's breath on the back of my neck, sent me trembling like it always did, but I held steady for awhile and looked out toward the opposite shore. I didn't think about the cold waves lapping at my ankles either as I waded in farther, felt the wet weighing down the legs of my trousers.

Henry's finger traced a line down my back, paused at my waist.

"Andrew Wallen," he said. "Where should we go now?"

I turned, stepped out of my jeans, tossed them far into the dark, toward the rocks and cattails at the edge of the water. I stood looking at what I knew, even in the dark, were all the small places, bright as gold flake, in Henry Ward's eyes, the thing in his eyes I had long named love. Then I turned again and waded farther, until the water swept past my waist and sent shocks of cool into my chest. I dove, clean and shallow, into floating strands of moss, amongst slick bodies of minnows nipping, so gently, at my legs as I glided forward toward water that was deeper, seemed farther than I had ever gone before.

~

Where should we go now? As if I knew.

Since, as you've probably gathered by now, I am a kind of wastrel, both spiritually and materially, in this world of mine. Give him fifty cents, my father often says, and he'll find a way to come back with two cents worth of nothing. And it is a fact. Given spare change for trips into Inez I had more often than not, in my boyhood, an inordinate love for purchasing picture postcards of beach resorts I'd never heard of, like Sandy Coasts, or Sea Oats Grove.

My spiritual wasteland was another matter. My mother little knew where my real sacred squandering had long gone. Summer nights in my childhood I often descended from my bedroom window, climbed the hill behind the house and released balloons, ones I'd purchased with my pennies. Into each balloon, as I blew it up, were breathed prayers—give me, send me, love, the sea. More to the point with any of this, as my dearly beloved father might have said, the boy's got no backbone to him. No grease under fire, no gristle.

But choice, that small matter. Take charge, son, my father says. Choose your beds. Lie in them. Heaven or hell, my mother says. Toward and toward the edge of the world my mother has wished me. She has wished me like ashes to ashes, dust to dust. Wished me thinner and thinner, so I might be light enough to ascend, no trouble at all, into God's merciful and forgiving hands.

And where, Henry says. Where should we go now?

The choices of this world are of greater consequence than perhaps any of them realize. For example. Here in this Mining Hollow world of ours we have man on the one side, woman on the other. Here earth, there heaven. Dark, light. Up, down. Here's God. There, the devil, ready, as my mother says, to eat you right up, then spit you back out like so much inedible meat. On this side of choice the suspect but delectable body, on that the soul, that ectoplasmic wonder.

Book-learned notions, my father would say.

As Socrates said, we are not necessarily a race of two choices alone, but three. During my Inez lending library visits, I read in Plato how the sexes were originally three in number. Woman, child of earth. Man, child of the sun. And a third, a union of the two, a freakish creature with four of everything, feet, hands, eyes, ears, and two of what my dear mother might call the unmentionables places of the body. A creature, so Socrates says, terrible yet great. Without such a creature, he says, we cannot begin to understand the power of the heart.

But still. I have seen visions of angels and desolation, of evil and corruption as the blessed and unknown tongues of church say. God, devil. Body, soul. What if what you are exists on the cusp, on the very edge of this world that cannot reconcile the great and mysterious face of love?

This has been my choice. No choice at all, in fact.

Except to lie at some midnight wakeful time hearing the voice that says to me, you, who do you think you are, Andrew Wallen?

Who do I think I am? In all this Mining Hollow world, if I know, I cannot say. If I say, I will not be answered. To know, to be myself, is the most unutterable truth.

Love, I have said into that dark place, my own heart. What truth comes back to me?

~

And so, eyes shut, I glided forward, into the slow water-numbness of Frazier Lake.

There was no opening my eyes until I was hundreds of yards from shore, near a platform. Ahead of me I saw the watery shape of a boy stroking toward me, his hair spread softly behind his head. With the thin moonlight, his reflection was gray, rippling. He could have been me, long ago, though now his only shape was water. About the shape of his mouth there was no question. Longing, his eyes said. I ached for him, his wanting, but I shut my eyes tighter than ever and headed back.

Toward shore the shaking took hold of me so hard breath wouldn't come. Eyes shut, I seemed to draw the water blackness deep inside me, to hear my mother say, no, places of sunlight and pleasure are not real night, but this, this darkness around us all is night itself. That is the way to see God. My arms circled and pushed back until I forgot they were there. My legs were long forgotten.

Henry found me again at the edge of a bank. Red clay lined my palms and I held onto a clump of cattails.

"Andrew," he said. "Are you ready now?"

That and nothing else as I met him, nameless, faceless, at the edge of the dark water. His soft hands stroked water from my eyes. He lay on the bank and lined his body up with mine, let his weightless hand move down my back and push away the wet cloth of my underwear. He was a secret I held in my hand, a softness that came alive between my thighs. Like so many times before, he stopped my shaking. He was breath in my ear. We were heat entering that dark place, pushing into that unknown ocean, ourselves. Later, my face followed the bristly path down his chest, my cheek rested against the roundness of his stomach. *Surely the light of God is sweet*, I whispered, *and it's right to behold the sun*. Like all the times before, I drank him in, the salt sea taste of him.

As if I were drinking in, from all the vast and ocean dark world, a marvelous and awful light.

~

Early, early Sunday morning, after that Frazier Lake night, Henry took me the long way back.

Back along the late-night Inez highway, past empty cars for the L & N and parking lots and coal rigs and church-houses already open, neon signs saying, prepare, oh, prepare to meet thy Lord.

The houses and trailers and dark windows of my road home said nothing to me. My skin was still wet and cool from the waters of the lake, waters I had already breathed far down and sweet, like an all too brief, already passing thought. Stolen moments of loving, nothing but a precarious transformation, baptism leaving my mouth tender, body forever new and strange with the memory of touch.

I sat far from Henry Ward, our hands now not touching. It was time to go back.

"How, Andrew," he said. "Andrew Wallen, how can you go home now? Not choose me?"

We stood for awhile in the shadows of the silver birch near the road. He held me to him once and I looked over his shoulder at the blankness of that house as it slept—that house and all the years before that made me. House full of year upon year, of the memory of a house before that, of my grandfather's ghost calling down to me even now, saying, a man, Andrew, when I became a man I put away childish things.

I stood and kissed him, a man, the man I had touched in yet one more act of what only I, in that house, could call love. I thought, who, who are you now? In that house, the neatly made bed in which I would sleep. Would I have to be unmade again, made and unmade, child into man into child, forever and ever, and where is the place it stops?

Which Andrew Wallen could dream this night beside Henry Ward, lover, already becoming, this night, nothing more than the memory of my desire, remembered and forgotten and yet remembered again?

I looked up the hill at the steps. Was I dreaming even then, or did I see my mother on the porch in the dark, waiting for me, all the answers to me written in the book of life and death?

"Sleep restless, Andrew," Henry Ward called out as he drove away. I stood watching as the car lights vanished in the direction of Wheelwright.

This house, the only one left in the world.

~

How many times as a child had I gone through the back door and the kitchen, then down the hall past my mother's and my father's room? The hall where I was always an infinitesimal body. Hall, windowless, smelling of last night's greens and onions, old shoes, still air.

Even when I became a man, in that hall I was going down a corridor to a forever I could never reach. Going through the spiraling center of a black shell from the bottom of an ocean I'd never seen, a journey full of dark and light and dark, so dark my hands would shake when I reached for the eternity of the light chain. Light, I sometimes prayed at night. Comfort me, show me morning. Or not.

Past their room, I pulled the doorknob hard, turned quietly, eased into the room called mine. Mine, no brother in the next bed, no sister saying, you, Andrew Wallen, I see what time it is. No one but my mother, the feel of her like a glass pressed against the thin wall, listening to my coming home. Thirty years of me and still slipping home before dawn, guilty boy, Henry's touch on my skin a violation, more a sin than any blood-stained shirt shoved under my bed, any trace of taking a woman.

Another time, this night, to hide my misdeeds, smell of alcohol on my breath, smell of no good, she'd say.

The quilt-covered bed. Quilt, star of Bethlehem, blue and black and brilliant red, made of thrift store shirts and dresses, clothes of the dead, star to guide me down, to quiet the sound of the mattress springs. I lay face up, counting the cracks in the ceiling, finding in the chipped away plaster the shapes of faces, hands, feet. Bare room, devoid of all my secret life, my unknown self. Once, when I was younger, I had taped the walls full of magazine cut-outs, pretty Hollywood boys with white toothed smiles, rolled up tee shirt sleeves and brown arms. Now there was nothing, just the stray piece of tape, the lighter shade of wall from a long removed page. Washstand, scuffed wood floor, closet door open to a few shirts neatly hung.

One postcard, stuck in the corner of the wall mirror, an underwater shot of a lagoon and a submerged statue with crown of thorns and nail-scarred hands. Christ of the Abyss, it was called. My mother thought it my one token hint of faith not lost, my last hope. Henry had sent it to me, a souvenir of a trip of his to southern Florida.

The room spun with alcohol, with all the night I'd led. I left the light on so I could focus on the single light bulb. Light chain, long enough, with its piece of twine at the end, to reach my hand, my wrist, where I tied it, pulled the light on, off, on. *You will remember,* I told myself. You will remember that touch is as real as the light of day. Real, Henry's touch. I wrapped my arms around myself, holding close that place of love I'd glimpsed once more this night, glimpsed and left, and left.

~

Safe? What safe place, when even now I heard an early morning wind rise. Wind full of coal and soot, one coming from the town, the house, the mouth of my mother, from God himself. Wind hissing abomination, abomination in the eyes of the Lord.

Abomination is you, now, lying in this bed you call safe, hearing even here the voice of all your past. You shall know one another only in the righteousness of the Lord, my grandfather said. But what have you known this night? Have you known the one and only truth, the single hard truth at the heart of heaven and earth? Have you listened to the voice of God? It says: *Thou shalt not lie with a man as with a woman. To love this way is an abomination.* But I cannot lie with a woman. I have imagined such softness, breast against my lips, then entering the moistness of her. This is a sin against my soul.

And if I lie with no one, forever and forever, with only myself, with only the memory of Henry Ward? What of God will I know then? Already Henry was nothing but a lukewarm taste.

Sin within sin within sin.

Ridiculous, you say, this despair, this interminable talk of heaven, heaven. Mire of consciousness. Give it up.

Consider the plethora of advice. Mother-given, God-given, soul-given.

Get on with your life, son, says my father. Make your bed, lie in it and sleep the sleep of the well-satisfied. Marry or burn, says my grandfather's ghost. Marry, perhaps, a well-meaning girl from Van Lear, one plump and satisfied, with pink nail polish and a propensity for chocolates and afternoon soap-operas. She'd fix me fried bologna sandwiches and scrub my nails when I came home from the mines. We'd pray together and thank the good Lord for our happiness.

The good Lord? Vile affections, he says, the lust that men feel for one another, waste of the natural use of the women we leave behind. Foolish, men's hands that touch, errors of our ways.

And the practical advice of the well-intentioned? Our families only spawn us, then we become men, take up men's ways, make our own decisions, leave behind all our pasts, all our memories, like so much insignificant dust in the wake of a passing car.

Advice of the heart? I held on to the light's chain, lifeline. I lay there, listening, listening to the solitary beating against my pillow.

The voice of God, whispering, says, *If a man lies with a man as with a woman, both of them have committed an abomination; they shall be put to death.* I have read this, have studied the holy apocrypha, broken open the seventh seal, glimpsed eternity.

Which death? How many ways to die?

I closed my eyes and thought of Henry Ward, so far away, sleeping, blanket tucked in, lights from his swimming pool at Wheelwright shining in softly across his face. I could have gone there that instant, tossed handfuls of tiny pebbles against his window. Come down, Henry, come down to me.

~

The echo of footsteps. Her footsteps. Her, turning the doorknob as quietly as I had, only moments before. Her, standing at the foot of my bed, looking down.

Under the light, her black hair shone threads of gray. Thin patches showed pink scalp I could have sat up, touched, tenderly. How fragile she looked, small, unsmiling, from some other time. Her, in a cotton gown once white, yellowed with age, embroidered at its high neck with miniature roses and vines. If I had stood and hugged her, said, mother, said, bless me now in my hour of despair and love, love me, the vines would have been real, thorns would have scratched my bare arms.

Hand of flour and bones took hold of mine, pulled away the light's chain. Left the room black. Beside me I could smell the leather of the Bible she set near my pillow. She sat, humming. It was a hymn, one she once sang to me every day until I was old enough to leave her lap. Precious Redeemer. She made her own song words. *When you become a man*, she sang, *you will put away childish things. You will fear nothing, not even death.*

And I thought, this house, and her, and forever and forever and forever. That is the dominion of time.

Manifestation of the spirit, hand of God revealed.

So gently, she put the thing beside me, laid it the length of me, like a lover. I could nearly taste the metal. Twenty-two. Rifle. Son, you'll feel it kick, my father told me, long ago, when we'd take that same gun to the gully and shoot rats and bottles and tires.

Then I felt the shape of the mouth she pressed against my neck. *Listen*, she said. *Listen to the voice of God.*

Listening to her voice as if I stood before an expanse of dry land, a desert, so far from the ocean I could never touch it. My mother's childhood, a lost treasure, floated in that ocean, beyond reach. Her childhood and mine, turning and vanishing, turning and vanishing, into the bottomless depths of a never seen ocean.

Bottomless depth, what I might become or never become, love or never.

Andrew Wallen, who are you?

Mother, tell me.

Who?

Listening, I took long deep breaths, trying, trying to remember. But as much as I searched after the sharp scent, there was no witch hazel, nothing, not a sign of love, no car at the road, no rocks tossed at my own window, no voice saying, *come down*, down.

Me.

In all the world's immensity, no sound, nothing but moths beating against the window glass, whispers, other than that, no sound at all except for dogs barking in the distance. No consolation. The center of the world was nothing but a bitter wind in the trees, saying, listen, listen to it, your own lonely heart.

And she said, this is it, Andrew Wallen.

It's time.

RUTH: AUGUST 16, 1983

Long ago in the middle of a Mining Hollow night you heard some night bird calling and you thought there, now, it's come.

The longest, darkest hour.

You studied for awhile, wondering if time could be made of pieces of everything like a quilt, a trip around the world from out of a sack full of memory and wishing.

Time and a voice, the one that comes to you, mostly in sleep, and says, Ruth. It says, open your eyes, Ruth, that you might see.

And so you open yourself and lay there and hold your palms out, waiting.

Sometimes that sleeping voice is a woman's, a right pretty voice. It belongs to Mrs. Ward, or Sister Anna, last summer's tent revival preacher up at Van Lear. Or if it's the prettiest of all, Little Mother's, it says, *hallelujah, praise, dance.* And rise in the dark and do the things it says, raise your arms in the dark and move your bare feet in the yard's damp grass and reach, reach as high as you can toward the sky. Not the sky, just the voice, rising and vanishing and leaving you alone and wishing it back.

Or the voice belongs to Earl or Tobias or Saturday night's radio broadcast of Bobby Darin singing, I want a dream lover, so I don't have to dream alone. More likely, of late, it's the voice of that Ward boy, Henry, saying, you all right today, Mrs. Wallen, a question slick as hair oil.

You do just what that voice says.

Other times, there's a voice you don't know at all. It isn't a man's or a woman's, but the same as glass, as faceless as water. It comes in a dream, a dream of fire, one where your lungs are full of smoke and the walls are crashing one by one, but you can't get out. *Read,* Ruth Blue, the voice says, *read the words first, and then we'll see.* And you dream the words, *abide, gather, hold fast.* You dream that if only you could read fast enough, read all the longest words aloud, you would see your own self rise, ash from paper, rise through an open door.

Rise like ash into the sky and into forever and forever, followed by a voice and a song, *I want a dream lover, so I don't have to dream alone.*

The last walls fall, the walls and the ceiling and the floor crash. You can't speak, or wake, the Bible opens and opens, unburned, no last page in sight. The voice doesn't come again.

But most of it, you know, began a long time ago. Began without voices. Began with you.

RUTH: 1926–1936

Time was, come May, 1935, all we did was listen to the radio. Little Mother, who I'll tell you about, had set that radio up in the corner of the kitchen, too close to the cook stove, so the walnut cabinet Tobias, my daddy, had toted all the way from Inez got sooty and dark, like most things in Mining Hollow, far as that goes. Got so with all that coal business, you couldn't find much wasn't singed or soot covered or just plain black as tar. Wind. The front room floor. Your own skin, sometimes.

But the radio. Afternoons, when Tobias was still away from the house and up to the mines and I'd walked back from the school-house, Little Mother would turn on the stories, Amos and Andy or Charlie McCarthy, and we'd listen while we picked through the beans and set them to soak for supper. It was something to be hearing about two men in a faraway city like Atlanta who owned their own business and named it, and how good they had it, so to speak. I was nine that year but before my daddy came home, we'd play like we were both young and hide in the closet and behind the door and Little Mother would run around the house hunting me, saying, buzz me, Miss Blue. Like we were big, important city people. I never could get over how that story had a person with my own last name.

And all that would have gone on just fine, but one night, when it was just after seven o'clock and the story was just about over, we hadn't turned off the radio. Little Mother had gotten behind with the supper. I think it was fried corn she was stirring in the skillet, and the beans not good and tender, with the potato water boiling behind that, and the table still with flour on it, and the wash water for the dishes not pitched out yet and we were expecting Tobias any minute. My mother was a small woman, kindly short and slender, so every dress she put on would fall full and loose. She'd put her hands on her hips and sway a little if Bing Crosby come on the radio. She'd sway and bend just like a wind-up ballerina in one of the music boxes I'd seen at the pharmacy in Inez.

And that's what she did right there in the kitchen with all that supper going on and the potato water boiling away and the radio still on. For a long time I wanted to cry about it when I thought how she took my hands. She had big, warm hands that could hold on to a body so tight you thought they'd never let you go. She whirled me around and around. I was dizzy from it, that and how beautiful she was. How pretty. Buzz me, Miss Blue, she was saying, and then we were saying it at once, a song sort of like, and going around the kitchen table in a dance with our bare feet sliding along the floorboards. We were the radio our own selves, and forgetting all about Tobias.

It wasn't like he did anything or said anything like sometimes, when his fist would slam hard against the wall and he'd say, no. No, and it didn't always matter what it was, whether the bread was fried a little too dark or the lamp lit and the wick turned a little too high. He didn't even have to say a word or do a thing, sometimes, just stand there like he did that night. He had his big work-boots on and his lunch pail under his arm and what I'd have wanted to see was her dancing right up to him, catching hold of me and him both, and the dance we'd have done would have been right across the kitchen, and on out in the front room, maybe, and the night going on, just like that. Full of us laughing.

I believe to this day my daddy had a hundred dances in him, a hundred million, but they was just so pushed way down in him, inside his chest and way down in him in places he couldn't name, they forgot how to get back out. He never did smile much. That was why he stood there like that, heavy as a sack of bones. Just looking at the two of us acting the fool.

And you wouldn't think, I guess, that a body could do much harm by just looking. The way you do sometimes into a store window or a fancy house on the big street in Inez. But my daddy set a real store by things being done a certain way, supper on time, the garden hoed up nice and even in the rows, how fast you could find a verse in the holy book or a hymn. How many times you said his name right, Tobias, with a long "i" in the middle, the way the Lord made his name, he said.

When he set a store by something and it didn't happen the way he had in his mind, it was like the air just plain filled up. Like it was smoke in the room or one of those hot summer days where you can hardly breathe with the thickness of it. I could have broken something, a canning jar or a drinking glass or one of Little Mother's empty bottles she kept from the bluing, just to set up in the window for the color from the sun. Any piece of glass could have done. To cut right through and maybe let something in, some wind, some kind of breathing. Maybe then her face wouldn't have changed like that, like all the light of the world went out of it, just because it was night and my daddy was home and stood looking at us from the kitchen door. We shut the radio off, quick, and we ate in the quiet, that night.

He took to listening to the radio in his own way, mind. But he was most inclined toward how the radio was just one way the Lord had of showing his marvelous wonders. All the same to him, whether he was standing in the door and listening to a wind come up the holler, or sitting, listening to static and the way the stations went and came on the radio dial.

There is a cause, he said. One cause. God. And if he took a shine, the Lord could bring us whole evenings of listening to Kate Smith or Fibber McGee and Molly. A miracle, he said on those evenings, the way God didn't have to do a thing but reach right up there between the sun and the stars and the Kentucky earth and pull down sound and voices and put them, smack dab, into our living room. If the good Lord chose that way too, and Tobias'd done working a twelve hour shift and the air was heavy like I've told you, we could spend whole evenings listening to him finding Bible verses. I'd sit by the radio, staring into the front of it, thinking about how God must have reached out toward of all those voices and songs and, with hands chapped and black with coal dust and a lot like my daddy's, shut those hands into fists and made the evening so quiet you could hear the Bible pages turn. It was a sheer wonder of the Lord, the way the radio waves came and went, the same as other things like winter or spring or love. But I didn't know that way of things for awhile.

Come May, 1935, the radio told us about dust storms in the west. The country, they said on the air, was like death was touching it, the way black blizzards blocked out the sun, sweeping across all those states and counties and little towns like Inez, from west to east.

You, Little Mother, Tobias said. Mind, now, how the hand of God can make its deeds known.

On the radio I heard how dust storms could last for up to seven hours, burying crops and trees and animals and houses. At the center of those storms, they said, were sand devils, some of them hundreds of feet high.

It's a mighty sign, Ruth Blue, he said. A sign of the end of time.

And a time would come, leaving me looking behind me for the cloud of dust, the demon of change that took hold of everything I knew. Like a better time was ahead of me if I only knew how to look hard enough. That better time always seemed it would look like the sun shining through a dusty window, or like light on water. Only I'd never seen that much light, that much water. It would have taken a mighty angel to take me that far above the earth, above the storms of dust and departure and wishing that would be my life. A fierce-winged angel who could take me to a place of enough water and light to settle all that would come, and come again, and disappear in my life.

Years after that time in 1935, I turned on the radio stories. Amos and Andy. There was that part where Brother Crawford says, "I want you to know that my wife is very unhappy," and I thought it all could have made out a lot different if somebody had said that to Tobias.

Then that isn't right, either. He'd have had to have said it for himself. But by that time I was listening for the voice and the touch and breath of sweet God, on my own. On the radio, and not.

~

A right smart number of people have told me that it couldn't have happened the way it did, that day in 1926, the day I was borned. That I could remember so much. So many fine details of things, and places, and times of my life. Like God was there for me at the very start, telling me, you, Ruth Blue, pay good mind now, you'll want to know why, someday. Impossible, people say. But I remember.

The morning I was borned Tobias got the big eye early on, before four o'clock.

He turned to face my mother, whispered, Little Mother, are you there?

She was sleeping, sound.

He pulled his arm from the warm covers and his hand fell, quiet, on her shoulder. It was February, the end of winter, and the world was as still as ice.

I turned inside my mother, facing him. His hand traced her whole shape. Eyes closed, he saw the whole world. Rich veins, mountains, dark tunnels. He didn't see me, my open eyes, the thin distance of sheets and skin and cold air between us. He stroked her, her swollen belly as it rose and fell. He pulled back the quilts, unfastened buttons, rearranged her arms, her legs, inched his thin, cold fingers into her flesh and, without a thought of me at all, put himself as close to me as he could get. He went farther and farther for what he was after, bituminous, anthracite, a closeness he couldn't name. Behind his shut eyes he saw the turn of wheels and going down, darkness, the loading, the rush, back up into the fair air of day.

Then at four, like it was any other day, Tobias got up to eat some of the cold biscuits and bacon my mother had laid out the night before. He went to work the mines.

A long time after that my mother was awake. I can tell you right off that she was a woman who believed in signs, the way a stray hair'd lay on a pillow or the way a whippoorwill would call out, just so, before the sun come up. But that day she paid no mind how icy clouds fell across the sun, how her mouth tasted of metal. Pulling on her wool stockings, she stumbled toward the kitchen. The room danced.

She felt of the cookstove, took note of the empty breakfast plate. She took a swallow of cold, bitter coffee, knelt. As she blew a coal to life, small hands pressed down inside her. My feet pointed and I was ready to dive. The metal taste left her mouth, became a fever, sweat on her palms, her back, quick, shallow breaths. The room spun and turned, faster and faster, as her waters broke. Her wet legs felt like some other body. Back in the other room, she laid down in cold sheets.

My life right at that time was ready for how I was to come to be: a life as rough shaped as a lump of coal, a life set moving by the muscular legs of a tap dancer, told to me by the voice of God like a melody on a radio. My raising up was not words, but hands and signs. My childhood was not brothers and sisters, neighbors or kin. It was myself, and how I grew to believe in visions of love and beauty and how all that can be broken, fragile as glass. Such visions, I learned, can come to a person when they wish and leave without so much as a fare you well.

~

Still, let me tell it right off, my childhood was filled with treasures. I don't mean play pretties, like a fancy doll with a glass head and real hair, the kind you could buy in the big city. I have to tell you that I was raised up strict, in a house with what some would term no beauty at all, but a grayness. But there were things to pleasure me, all the same.

Up Mining Hollow in 1931, the year I was five, there were ashes from the grate, a treasure I played was good-smelling powder for my skin. And sometimes there was my daddy's watch. It was a hip pocket timepiece, the kind that snaps open with a little fastener. Lining the inside top was a photograph—a woman with cold eyes and a thin mouth, my granny. For a long while, my granny slept in the front room in our house, in the iron bed now mine. She was so skinny you could see every bone, and her cheek-bones and chin were so pointy they drew the skin back so you could just about see the blood come up out of it. That skin, and the tiny veins beside her nose, had a violet cast until the day she died. She turned her face to the wall and I was standing right there, and Tobias said, go on, touch her. I did and she was already as cold as iron. I could swear to this day I saw a shape rise up out of the bed. Something violet and quick. And it was like you could look inside her, at the way she was made, all stern and chilly, a heart like a gray stone. Her lips, black with laudanum, turned just as white, and I touched them when I helped Tobias shut her eyes.

My daddy always said beauty was a sacredness meant for death, and that only with God did beauty last. Anyway, it was her picture in the watch, and it was that I would play with, sometimes.

The treasure I hold most dear of all, from that time of my raising up, was my mother. Her name was Stella, but we called her Little Mother, like she was a little piece of something so lovely you'd only take it out now and again, to show it off. Like the precious stone no bigger than half the size of your finger's end, and clear, like a diamond, that I found on the street in Inez one time. Nothing but fake glass, Tobias said. But I kept it special all the same, in a rose-colored cloth bag that I sewed. I slept with it for a long while, under my pillow at night, until I woke up once and couldn't find it anymore.

But Little Mother. I remember one afternoon in particular, when she worked beside our gray house with me behind her. I was no more than six by then, but I'd fetch and bring, to please her. I smoothed the earth she hoed with my bare feet. We checked the garden and the sky for signs: when to plant potatoes, the best time to harvest corn, what supper Tobias might like. I followed her down the back rows of sweet corn and when she stopped to rest in the shade at the corner of the house, I touched the yellow soles of her feet.

The house's shadow was long and cool, a place where I stood from the heat. I played I was rubbing the shadow on my skin like cool water. Then after awhile, when I was thirsty we walked back to the house. Shadows moved up the hill, followed us without a sound. Inside, there was no afternoon sun. The curtains, made from squares and squares cut from used up clothes, were always drawn shut. We stuffed the space under the front door with rags against the heat.

She fried apples for our supper, wiped the drinking glasses clear.

I followed her, asking one question or another. Do you? Could I just?

But she was already doing the next chore, slicing fat back, sprinkling meal, carrying the slop bucket to the back door. I did my best to help with the forks and knives and then tugged at her skirt. She bent and touched the top of my head. My reflection in her spectacles kept me in mind of who I was—a skinny legged child with no place to put her hands. I was thin and dark.

Not now, she said, it's time.

Just past seven, Tobias came back up the road to Mining Hollow. He wore work boots laced to the top, sooty coveralls, but he kept himself like a gentleman. Over his work clothes he wore a suit jacket from the Mission Store, one brushed and mended at the cuffs, and a string tie, homemade, from a scrap of velvet. His shiny lunch pail held gifts for me—once a cross-shaped piece of coal carved, he said, by a blind man.

I ran from the house and he swung me up high, to his shoulders where I looked at the far away ground. While he went on to the house, I pried open a lunch pail as bottomless as the mines, pulling out oily brown paper wrappers, a green apple core. That day, my treasure was a smooth, brown stick, a finger, he said, one a miner had chopped off with a pick and left to dry in the dust at the bottom of a coal trolley.

Leaving me this present, my father slammed through the screen door, called, supper's late. I heard her feet hurrying, how he settled into a kitchen chair, waiting and waiting, arms folded across his chest. When she called to me on the porch, it's time, wash up, I hurried to my place at the table.

God is great, Tobias bowed his head to say, and I looked up at him, how he sat, tall and strong. At his wrists were cufflinks that snapped open, containing clippings of soft, blue-tinted hair, my granny's, inside.

Sometimes the world was like this to me: death inside cufflinks, us inside that house, house inside the world, which God alone blessed. God is great, I whispered, from the bottom of this world where I looked up, feeling smaller and smaller.

~

One summer afternoon, a Saturday, my father came home early, stood with hands on his hips and said, Little Mother, are you ready? We were going to Inez, a six mile walk, coming and going, to the grocers and post office and dry goods and the few houses that made up the town.

Before we left for Inez Tobias helped Little Mother dress. It was summer, but he laid out black stockings, a full, long skirt, a scarf, a shawl. All of her arms all muscle and her sharp elbows and her long strong legs, disappeared inside these clothes. The shawl fell across her face and her loveliness disappeared, too, the color of her lips, a mole in the shape of a star, the blue black hair done up, a braid so tight it hurt me to see. Tobias, a fire pink from the yard in his lapel, took my hand.

On one side, as we walked to Inez, lay the Big Paint River, a wide reach of slow-moving, stagnant water that smelled of mud and summer's peak. It was a river that seemed to hold, as my daddy said, the secrets of the good Lord himself. Into the waters of that river, people cast off what they no longer had any use for—ashes from burning off spring soil, scraps of food, cans and bottles and bones, dead tires and dogs. In times past, the river had carried flatboats of coal and timber to foreign cities far and beyond, north and south. I could go down to its shores and crouch in the rusted tin and cattails, play in the shallows and lay my hands on my apron, leaving hand-shapes and stains of brownish red.

On the other side of the river lay railroad tracks at the feet of the steep mountains. Beyond those mountains, my daddy said, lay a world. He had been there, working the C & O railroad for a time, once going to a nameless fancy northern city to work in a factory that made bullets and boots. I might never see that world, he said. Nor should wish to, for it was like the bottom of a deep well, and no rope nor chain to pull you up if you set out to go there. It was a Godless place, and the angels that visited Sodom had been there twice, once seeing it full of men's sufferings and another time seeing dance-halls where ladies rolled their stockings down and gave of themselves like they were made of cheap perfume and drank gin and cut their hair and put permanent waves in it. And a third visit, he said, would be when the trumpets of the Lord would sound. But that would be at the end of all time. It was bad enough, in Inez itself, that the ladies stood there in long-waisted, short skirts, artificial flowers in their hair.

At the end of Main Street, Tobias went into the barber shop, then on the other side of the street, to trade knives with a certain man he knew. Meantime, we went to Hyatt's General Store, for supplies, flour and sugar and bootblacking. There, Little Mother stood at the front window, laid her palms against the glass. Window-shopping, she said, for all manner of tomfoolery.

We saw compacts set with rhinestones, hairpins threaded through paper drawn with fine lipsticked women, bottles of toilet water that said rose, or Eau du Paris. And there were clean up to the elbow gloves with seed pearls sewed on to the wrists. Boxes of red and yellow and blue square candies called Turkish Delights. Ladies' magazines that said "newest serial" on their covers, with pictures of girls in shirtwaists carrying hand-sized pistols.

Farther back, on a high shelf behind the counter, we saw dozens of hats, for any number, my mother said, of grand occasions. Berets, she called them, were dusted with glitter. Round straw hats were circled with bright ribbons and lined with checked cloth. Turbans were set with rhinestone pins. Floppy hats were for sunbathing and lemonade or tea parties on Sunday afternoons. Through the window, we could see the shopkeeper, Mr. Hyatt, stroke his long sideburns, lift a corner of his mouth, wink at us once, very slowly. He took down a maroon silk hat with peacock feathers, motioned for us to come inside.

Should I, Little Mother said, should I just?

We hadn't even got in the door when Mr. Hyatt sidled over and set the hat on my mother's head. Startled, my mother moved back and the hat slid forward. Then she glanced at herself in a long mirror. Mr. Hyatt tucked one arm behind his back, bowed, pulled a paper fan from his apron pocket. A right warm afternoon, isn't it, he said. My mother, not meeting his eyes, reached for the fan, waved it slowly. The hat feathers rippled. Her shirt sleeves were rolled to the elbow and her hands, I knew, if you kissed them, would smell of lye. But she was so beautiful I just about couldn't look at her at all.

Vain objects, Tobias said, behind us just as quick without the sound of an opening door or shop bell. He slapped the hat to the floor.

No, I whispered, but kept still and watched them.

Little Mother held the broken feathered hat against her chest. The store customers hushed, watching, and Mr. Hyatt stood, waiting to see what would come of us.

Little Mother without a word laid the hat on the counter, stepped back. The white print from my daddy's hand shone.

Keep it, keep it anyway, Mr. Hyatt muttered, pushing the hat back to her.

Her beauty had already gone, just that quick, and she became the mother I knew, eyes on the floor, hair come down and hiding her face. Tobias set ten coins on the counter and we hurried out into the dusty, bright street. The hat stuffed in his back pocket was like a used up paper poke.

Leaving Inez we walked past houses with lit windows, saw families in their sitting rooms listening to radios. Piano music and song words followed us back to Mining Hollow. *I want to be happy*, these songs said, *but I won't be happy till I've made you happy too*. Little Mother hummed this song so quietly I held her cupped palm against my ear and imagined the words coming out of her to me like an echo from a deep, watery well.

~

There were always spirits in my Mining Hollow childhood. Haints, Little Mother called them. Will-o'-the-wisps, glow worms, the dead that walked. Places, round about, where a body could step and be carried to some faraway place, a foreign city maybe, where the church steeples were so high you could climb up and up, sit with bells only the wind could set going for the angels to hear.

My mother's were the ghosts of music. She grew up in Stafford, on the other side of Inez where, when she was eighteen, she played hymns for the Holiness Redeemed, a church in the middle of town. When she played "Precious Redeemer," her blue-black hair fell across her hands and lent gentleness to the least off-key note. People fell out in the aisles, turned and turned like in a clear summer pond, faces up and then up again, the voice of holiness on their tongues.

That Stella, they said, why, she's the pick of the world. The angels done give up music right to her.

When she stayed late at church, alone, her hands glided along the keyboard as she invented the sounds she heard from some far place in her body, the feet, the heart. Sounds bloomed from her thin fingers and floated like petals on water. Songs she had never heard but believed nonetheless.

I'd guess she married my daddy for the sake of peace, or like she told it to me, for the sake of sleep. Because he seemed like a place where sounds could lay down and rest. But when she lay with him, sounds whirled and whirled, so fast the room danced enough I'd feel it all the way to my bed, down the hall. She had no still place, even when she looked out the window at a star, saw it as a fixed place, a tear in the sky with all that light behind it and a black blanket of holes spinning. I'd guess, at first, she turned to my daddy when sounds came like that, wishing for a solid shape smelling of sleep. Then, as the months passed, she lay awake longer and longer, her hands at her sides, palms up, as if the sounds might land there and stay.

For his part, my daddy came to believe the house was haunted. Shapes settled about his bed and he woke whistling songs he knew nothing about. All the music she had ever wished for became a ghost of itself, lost in grayness and long afternoons so quiet she could hear her own breath.

For a good while at Mining Hollow, I reckon because of these ghosts, we didn't keep a radio, and we made do for ourselves. Outside, on such nights, especially when the moon was to set just right, my daddy would sit at the shadowy kitchen table, an open almanac in front of him. The almanac told signs. When to plant in what they called the head or the loins or the feet. When to cut hair. With barber scissors and a comb my mother separated his hair strand by strand. Last she cropped the hair short on his neck.

Then she poured bath water from the stove into a metal tub. Tobias unknotted his tie, let his belt fall with a rattle, touched the steaming water and pulled one foot back.

Too hot, he said, his voice low and asking and Little Mother went to fetch cold water from the well.

She scrubbed half-moons of coal dust from underneath his thick nails as he lay in the tub. While he closed his eyes, my mother stepped back near the window, pulled the curtains aside. Light flooded in. Gray light so still Tobias's bare chest shone clean.

When he was breathing steady, my mother picked up a hand mirror from the table, raised it and looked at her own face. Her long hair, unfastened, curled from the steam. She was again just a glimpse of the lovely mother I wanted.

Tobias also saw her beauty, walked naked across the kitchen floor, water streaming from his bare legs.

You're mine, he said. Do you hear me? You're mine. He grabbed hold of the mirror, flung it, and glass broke and danced at my mother's feet.

She backed away, arm shielding her face, but he struck her with his strong hand. Their eyes met, held, then looked away as she licked a thin stream of blood from her mouth. My heart shook, but what could I say to them with my child's voice and be understood? When he moved away, I pushed glass slivers into a pile with my bare hands. But before the curtains swept down, hiding the moonlight, I saw her. White violet shadows touched her face, her gold spectacles were bent to one side. Her mouth was a bruise. *Bend down*, I wanted to say. *Oh, won't you bend down?* I wanted to press my lips against this hurt. Glass sparkled, disappeared.

Hush, my mother told me, and kissed the fine cuts on my fingers.

Later, almost sleeping, I listened to bath water emptied into the yard, the flatness of nothing coming after, to Tobias calling, Little Mother, come to bed, it's time. Later I dreamed God was a woman without a face, a face only my father knowed for sure, the mouth, her nose, the two eyes. I woke, said prayers for the dark. *You, God*, I prayed, *are most holy, a merciful ghost.*

~

I was good about prayers, even when I was just little. And not always church prayers like, our father above, or how great thou art, though I've done my share of that kind of praying, and more than most anyone I know.

When I prayed, night times, it was to a God out there, in the yard, or right in the house or the back room or in the bed with me. He was like a ghost, but more times, so real and right I could've reached through the dark and touched him. He smelled like the inside of a drawer, and roses.

The first time I believe I saw him, I couldn't have been more than five years old. I was asleep, and something was outside, scratching and scratching against the side of the house, in the shadows under my window. I called, but Little Mother didn't come. There was just the black fall of rain, me lying and looking at the edges of drops down the window. The pillow and the room smelled like me, where I'd fell asleep with a peppermint kiss in my mouth and wet the bed when I dreamed about the cool taste.

I cried until I slid off the covers and felt my way in my sock feet out along the cold wood floor, along the walls, past their room. He didn't see me, but I could see him. It was plumb dark, except for the little red glow of him, smoking a cigarette in the iron bed. I was quiet until the sheets shifted and smoke rings rose white and I saw she wasn't there at all. It was just him on his back in his sleeveless undershirt.

Sometimes it rains all night, he said, and sometimes it just rains. He inhaled, threw his arm, elbow bent, off to the side of the bed, staring at the ceiling.

Then he said again, louder, it's raining, woman, you going to take all night? I eased into the hall, then to the kitchen door, where I could hear her.

She was out in the yard, near the back step, at the well, in her gown, drawing water. The chain whistled and rose with the bucket, so she could get him a drink. I eased the doorknob and went out there too, down into the wet leaves and briars that stung.

Right away, she saw me, and let the bucket fall back and said, mercy, Ruth, you'll catch pneumonia fever out here like that.

Like I was really catching, I held out my hands and felt of the rain, let her lift me up and wrap my legs around her middle. I tasted the rain, too, but it was salt on her face, not full of the good, sweet dark, like I'd thought.

The both of us stood, looking down into the narrow bottom of that well. The water was stirring, like oil was on it, or fish. The voice that come from below and above was inside me and all at once. *Come here*, it said, *now. Come quick.*

I tangled my fingers in Little Mother's wet hair, held on, and watched the blank face of the water as it moved.

~

The summer of 1933 brought the radio I've told you about. I was seven the afternoon I stood in the doorway behind my mother while Tobias trudged up the road, packing a handcart with a used Westinghouse Battery Operated Radio Music Box balanced on top. He pushed back the table and set the radio smack in the middle of the kitchen floor. It was the pick of the world.

For almost a week we only looked at it, Little Mother and me. Every afternoon, before Tobias returned from the mines, she polished the radio's wood and we sat, turning the black knobs. Little Mother wanted the songs she'd hummed to come out of that box, and the ones I wanted were all sung in her voice. When my daddy did hook up the radio, along with Bing Crosby and Rudy Vallee, there was a scratchy background noise which reminded me of how guineas beat dust clouds in the back yard.

Late autumn of 1933 brought winter on early, cold winds whipping through the Inez streets, tugging at the short skirts of the flappers outside the dance hall, bringing on dark by five o'clock. The only lights on Main Street were kitchen windows, the new electric lights owned, Tobias said, by the high and mighty, Mr. Hyatt at the pharmacy, or that one no account lawyer. Not to mention them that took in revenue by means like illegal corn whiskey run in a six county circuit. We huddled up in quilts around the cookstove, seeing our own breath in the cold at the head of Mining Hollow, miles from anywhere, by kerosene light. The only light we needed, my daddy said, was the true light of the good Lord and the stars in the evening sky. We were the last house on a long dirt road, listening to the radio.

That radio told of storms in the dry plains of Oklahoma so terrible men wore masks to breathe. In Kentucky, on the other side of the country, Tobias went to the mines less and less. The Depression set in hard, the mines shut down one by one, and my father stayed up later and later by the radio, listening to news reports about Dust Bowls in the west. Soon he imagined this dust, blowing east as far as Kentucky, destroying our lives.

Tobias got up mornings, after the usual time for work, and our front door seemed wedged shut by a drift of dust as tall as our house. You'll find something, my mother told him when the last mine sent him his papers. There was nothing he could do. He sat by the radio later and later, listening to music, more news of the Great Plains, then the Star Spangled Banner. When the broadcasts shut down, the sound of static followed us to bed, whirled about the house, scratched at the covers over our heads. Kentucky in the wintertime was black fields, frozen to a crust that broke beneath our feet, but still my father believed it was the dust storms caused our lives to be so, and he blamed the radio for bringing them. Soon he brought me home not gifts of coal, but stolen coal to burn.

One night I hid behind the door of their bedroom, heard my father's angry voice saying, woman, you must make do. Scraps of soap, soup bones, I thought, and I held my breath as I peered around the corner. Tobias and Little Mother stood by the open window. Freezing air blew, swirling with tiny flecks of snow. My father wore a threadbare undershirt and his stringy muscles stretched as he held the radio music box against the window sill, heaved it out like a stray animal, like it was done and gone, a stranger with stories he didn't want to hear. I rubbed my chilled arms as he said, Little Mother, you must make do. She put her arms around him and his crying was a dry sound.

The next day the radio disappeared from the yard, found its way into the lean-to by the kitchen steps where we kept the potatoes and canning jars. But the dust storms, even if they never left Oklahoma, would not leave us in peace. Tobias watched the world go by through a haze of winter sunlight and loss. He imagined dust had left the Great Plains, ridden its way on the air to Kentucky, settled in our town forever. Near his seat on the courthouse steps in Inez, eddies of dust spun out from the locust trees in the town square, hurried across the street, settling around his ankles. Long-fingered dust hands plucked at his britches legs, then circled and settled to sleep in his lap. Before long, a dust cloud covered him and he was left looking after the Confederate flag at the top of the courthouse building.

At night I listened to storms ease themselves out of the woods. Wind hit the window glass like handfuls of salt. Tobias told me these woods were haunted. Ghosts, he said. Of miners. Every full moon, he said, they rubbed soft pieces of coal on their cheeks and around their eyes, strapped lamps on their heads and went hunting the woods looking for somebody one time buried alive in mines. Some coal black skeleton could have been beneath any tree.

I told these stories back to myself. I closed my eyes and listened to storms scratch at the window glass. There was grit between my teeth, a powder that left my hair dry to the touch. My gown hugged to my damp body and I was purely afraid.

Late one night while these miners' ghosts roamed, I heard Tobias's bare feet pad down the hall. He stopped in front of my door, faced me, eyes shut. His trimmed mustache was wispy and thin, his bony shoulders shaking. Sleeping eyes open, ghostly shadows lining his face, he motioned, calling me into his sleeping. My mother laying a blanket across his shoulders, led him back to the bed. They whispered until good daylight and I dreamed of the waves and waves of them talking on the other side of the wall. They talked of the deaths of miners, of dust storms and our lives.

Little Mother, my father whispered, are you there?

~

Once, right around that time, I slipped out and followed my daddy. Along the ridge, where he said they lived in the old ways. Farmed. Tapped the trees for sweetener. Raised big families and made their own clothes and made do, he said, without the likes of Inez and coal.

Of course, around that time, he'd taken to looking for life about anywhere that wasn't right in front of him. He'd taken to comings and goings here and yonder of an afternoon, a mid-morning, sometimes of a late night, coming back with his eyes red, his breath sharp with bootleg. He propped his muddy boots on the kitchen table and waited for Little Mother to take them off and rub his feet warm. He looked for no more signs in the almanacs, did not predict the coming of spring, did not speak about the end of time. He'd hold his head up, stare out the window into the night, waiting. Like an angel would come and mark our door and then we'd know.

It was late of an afternoon when I set out following him. It was still winter, so cold I shivered in my thin coat and rubber boots as I walked behind the house and the pond, then up the side of the hill and up the ridge. I hid behind this tree or that clump of sumac, holding my finger under my nose against a sneeze, sure not to make any sound and let him know I was back there.

My mouth went dry and sour tasting as I walked. Wished I'd had me a long drink of water before I'd set out after him, or a taste of left-over biscuit, anything to set my blood against the cold. Still, I remarked turns and dips of the path along the ridge, rocks beside a creek ran over the frozen earth, patches of ice and freezing water. I'd walked the ridge before, sat on the highest place I could find and looked out over the hollow, its road and houses and mouth to the main road to Inez. I kept on behind him, wanting to see what it was he had in that burlap bag he was packing over his shoulder. It swung against his suit jacket while his big boots made tracks.

I came to a place where the ridge path widened, gave into a clearing with a couple of run-down, tar paper shacks. The Esteps lived there, the ones Little Mother called no good bootleggers, lay backs who lived off others and begged their meal and taters, when times were bad.

I got as close as I could, hid behind a well at the corner of one of the houses. Some man I didn't know walked out the woods, wearing coveralls stiff with soot, a hole ripped clear to knee, one front tooth, I could see, half missing and black.

He spat in the yard, said, who's that walking out nowhere on a Sunday afternoon? Going to prayer meeting, Mr. Blue? Or you just want you a little holy water to burn them sins out of you, good and clean? They laughed.

My daddy slung the sack off his shoulder, down into the cat briar and tall crisp weeds. The sack moved, sounded like those doll babies at the pharmacies, the ones you picked up and held back and they cried, mama, a thin, high sound.

Right cold today, the man said, then crouched on his heels in front of the sack, took a knife out of his pocket, tilted it and dropped it, again and again, into the dirt.

Right cold, Tobias said, and untied the sack, spilled it onto the bare earth.

It was cats in that sack, yellow, striped, black and white cats, six of them, maybe more. They were yowling, coming awake out of the dark insides of that bag, some of them taking off fast as you please up the trunk of a dead locust in the corner of the yard, some of them too young to take off, too blind in the weak sun. I knew those cats. I'd held their mama in my lap and played. She understood words I told no one else.

A couple of boys came out of the house, snot running in streams out of their skinny noses. Something metal flashed from my daddy's pocket and he handed the thing on to one of them.

There was the heavy, dead fall of cats from branches of the tree. Cats, dead at Tobias's feet, dead or running, gone wild and scared. And somebody, maybe it was him, said, them breeding like rabbits, worse, a body can't even think, what's a man to do?

~

One hot morning, come the summer of 1934, my mother woke knowing it was a day when she would have to make a choice.

Ruth, she told me, there are signs, here and yonder and back.

She looked at the sky. She said she had seen a flock of songbirds just before daylight, their song as sweet as piano music. Made her want to dance in her bare feet. At the kitchen sink she did the break-fast things and hummed, *I want to be happy*, as if I didn't hear.

Days past, when we'd walked to the mouth of the holler and gath-ered kindling and slack coal to burn, we'd seen wagons and cars full of everything from tin buckets to stray shoes roll past on the main road from Inez, bound faraway north or farther east, to cities with jobs, towns with crops needed setting, odd jobs for good pay. Neighbors with nothing more than a knapsack left Mining Hollow, gone forever, or gone until big cities up north, Cleveland, Detroit, cities with money, made coming back home worthwhile. My daddy, his suit jacket brushed and tie in a careful bow, sat swinging his work boots, kicking against the porch steps, ready to go out to look for the jobs he never seemed to find.

That morning, my mother decided she, too, had to set out from Mining Hollow. Wearing a straw hat with a few clover blossoms pinned on the rim, she set off in search of work, any odd job she could find, from scouring plates at a diner to sweeping the stoops at storefronts on Main Street. She went back home only when her skirt and apron pockets jingled with pennies and nickels and, sometimes, twenty-five cents a day.

This left me home alone with my daddy. I was eight that summer, but old enough to melt lard, fry our supper and put a boiled egg down the toe of a sock to darn it. After I came home from school, we sat across from each other at the kitchen table. Sometimes he split a load of kindling to put beside the stove, but not in the way Little Mother did it, haphazard sticks and slivers amongst the coal dust. He split more than I could burn as I warmed up cup after cup of coffee. He laid the stacks in crisscrosses, made piles in the shapes of triangles and lopsided squares, left just room enough for a clear path close to the stove, facing the steps off the kitchen. Evenings, when my mother was still out working, I got up, felt my way in the dusk toward the door, thinking, Little Mother, where are you? He stood, grabbed my hand. I was what he held on to between the gray house and the road toward Inez.

No, I said, but his grip left white fingerprints on my arm.

At the end of July, he began to whittle. A fine piece of walnut from the woodpile became a chain, one link for each day she was gone from home. As I heard wood being shaved, I already knew well enough where my mother was. If she took off her going to town shoes and her feet were clay red, she had been away suckering tomatoes. If I met her at the door, held her hand to my cheek, felt the fine ridges of wrinkled, white skin, it was someone else's plates she had scraped. Once she came back with a quart of chicken soup in a pail, some left over from the bowls she'd ladled at a CCC sponsored food line.

One evening she came to the edge of the porch and waited awhile, then reached into her pocket and pulled out a folded piece of paper. She held it up, smiling. Her eyes shone and she waved the paper like a fan.

You'll never guess, she said, voice light as a summer wind come up in the yard.

Clouds shifted and light came through, making Little Mother a ghost, her skin shiny as a dimestore pearl necklace. One stronger breeze and she would have been light enough to blow away. Tobias dropped the wooden chain and it clattered to the floor. He slammed through the screen door, yanked the paper from her. Back inside, he smoothed the sheet on the kitchen table and peered closely at it, saw a sketch of a face, a tall round hat, a shiny black cane.

Taps, twirls, waltzes and rumbas, he read, you, too, can teach the best. Little Mother, he asked, what does it mean?

Still smiling, she rose on her square-toed, scuffed shoes, held the edges of her house dress and turned, what she later called a pirouette. With a deep bow, she announced that the Civilian Works Projects Administration had issued hundreds of fliers throughout the southeastern United States offering teaching jobs to the unemployed, in return for relief money and necessary equipment

There'll be classes in Latin, boondoggling and, in our town, tap dance, she said. And what do you think?

I rested my head on my hands and imagined her in a tissue thin dress, swirling and swirling, moving away from me, down the porch steps, grown smaller and smaller in the distance. Just before she vanished, Tobias picked up the wooden chain, drew it, without a sound, across his palm.

Very slowly, he said, woman, you won't. Not while I'm a man and alive.

For the first time that I ever knew, my mother put her hands on her hips, planted her feet, looked straight at him. And why shouldn't I, she asked. Ain't it true it's me putting beans and potatoes on the table, these days?

For just a spell, it was him who grew smaller, the shoulders sinking into his shirt, his hands covered by his cuffs, boots seeming big enough to swallow his big feet. As he grew smaller, his features went so faint I could hardly make them out. By God, he said.

Then he took her, by the shoulders at first, shook her until my own teeth hurt to watch, until he came back to himself. Frightened, she backed away, through the high stacks of kindling. Like she was wiping away the last of a long, sweet drink, she drew the back of her hand across her face, leaving no sign of what she felt. The matter settled, Tobias took a seat at the kitchen table, said, Ruth, some coffee for us.

As my mother stood, coins spilled from her pocket, a handful of pennies, one buffalo nickel. All three of us watched how they shone in the dark, few and far between, not nearly enough to see us through. Tobias, Little Mother said, we must make do.

And so my mother became a teacher of tap dance.

~

After that, she left Mining Hollow before good daylight, with a blue cloth notebook for folks to sign up for free government tap dance lessons. She came back to the house late, cheeks flushed, not seeing either Tobias or myself, like what she saw was the room shaking with a skate or scoot step or a cross-over tap, words I soon knew.

I'd already have the stove going. Smoke settled in layers in the kitchen with Tobias nearly invisible in his corner. Ten o'clock and Little Mother made us a late night feast, she called it—a white cloth spread on the table, the lamp lit, hunks of cornbread and glasses of buttermilk to crumble it in. She ate like she was starved, a milk mustache above her lips.

It's the dancing, she said, I can't ever get filled up.

Tobias would have none of that food. Each bite tasted of gun metal, he said, and reminded him of tap shoes. She made him more, biscuits with syrup, coffee with cream, and he read us the Bible, a chapter a night, stories of women who danced, Mary Magdalene, the woman with seven veils and seven demons. Dancing brought back the music my mother had wished as a girl.

I myself wished so hard for dance then, just about everything inside me and out shook. Long shadows from the lamp shimmied across the floor, vanished out onto the porch. I closed my eyes and moved alongside these shadows and out into the yard where moths beat against my ears like breath, saying, dance and dance. And I did. I raised my arms above my head in the dark, touched my invisible feet. I twirled until my long braids flew and my head spun. I was a stick girl dancing, knobby kneed, pretending to rumba, leaping and clicking the worn heels of my last year's school shoes. Then I heard my mother saying, Ruth, time for bed. Tobias pinched the lamp's flame between his fingers and the thick black cover of the Bible closed like dreamless sleep.

Soon a government document made my mother a legal tap dancer and my room became hers. Like it was our personal secret, she hauled in box after box, once unpacked a large trunk marked "official business": spit-shined black tap shoes, a thick manual showing basic tap steps, hand on hip, the other arm held way out, fingers fanned, feet doing a dancy sidestep. Later the manuals were harder —double taps, buck and wings, even a dance going up and down stairs. Then, to teach her not only the dance steps themselves, but how it felt to dip and turn, they sent her a tin music box. It had fancy rickrack trim and on top were miniature animals, a fox, a panther, a fat bear.

When this music box arrived, my mother hurried into my room, wound the key, set the animals dancing, figure eights, sashays. By the door she slipped on her sturdy tap shoes. She danced a whispery soft shoe. The music box played a song I'd never heard, but she sang with it in a voice as cool as water. *I want to be happy*, she sang, hugging herself as if she were dancing in the arms of someone I couldn't see. At the dressing table she picked up a tube of lipstick, drew her mouth into a bright red bow, kissed her own lips in the mirror.

She was not Little Mother, but Stella, a tall, strong woman, more beautiful than she had ever been in her checked house dress. She grabbed her cane and a top hat and danced a farewell across the room. Tobias came to the doorway just then, rubbed his eyes. We watched her reflection in the mirror. She danced farther and farther away from us, to the edges of the room, to the window, beyond the drawn curtains and out into the clear air.

A second room of our house, their's, became my daddy's. August became September and he whittled in there later and later. That door at the end of the hall was shut tight and I went to sleep at night with the sound of wood being smoothed and shaped. Once, when the door was left unlocked, I slipped through without being seen into what I found was not Tobias's and Little Mother's room at all, but God's.

Crossing the bare floor, I did a quiet tap, but felt shivers down my back. The room was nearly empty, bed pushed to one side, walls freshly whitewashed and bare except for a picture on the wall of Jesus in the Garden, on the night of his doubt. He looked like a statue, skin white as store-bought soap, yellow hair, lamb of God hands. One of my father's wooden crosses was hung in the open window. I tiptoed along a swaying shadow cross, to a high table near the window.

On the table was the Bible, open. I eased up onto the window sill and looked down just as wind blew, fanning the pages. My finger fell on a Bible verse. *And David danced before the Lord with all his might.* Stepping down, eyes shut, I danced with Jesus, held his cool stone hands, felt myself swept across the bare floor. Faceless, Jesus held me close until I was light as a wisp, floating. *Silence,* he whispered, and *eternal dance.*

I often went to my secret place with these notions of God and tap dancing. About a quarter of a mile back of the house, before the hill up to the ridge, was the pond. I could lay on the bank there or slip out of my dress, wade into the slicky mud. Farther in was clear water where I dove down, watched the world go past, the brown speckled fish and broken cattails, the warm and cold. Then I could reach a place where I could hold steady, hold my breath for the longest time and look up toward the light.

Just at the place where dark water ended and sunlight and the outer world began, if I looked hard enough, I could see Tobias and Little Mother, treading water just below the surface. My daddy wore his suit jacket and black velvet tie and watery sunlight flashed off of his polished cufflinks. Behind him, see-through as the tails of catfish, floated Bible pages. My mother, at a good distance from him, wore her tap dance best, a waterlogged feather boa, silver stockings. She reached toward that light, her fingers trailing, her arm raised, as if she were waiting for applause. Gliding forward, I could reach neither of them.

My lungs burned and I raised up, swallowed the good air. God's words blew in the tree leaves. *Beat your hands together, stamp your feet, mourn your fate, this is the dance.* Below me, Little Mother took a deep bow.

~

The night my mother ran away from Mining Hollow, I woke to wood smoke and bells jingling. It had been fall again, and winter, and we had papered our kitchen walls twice over against the cold wind. These papers told us about worker's strikes and roadblocks, heartland farmers gone to relief, western migrants gone by the thousands toward California, good mountain families who sold everything and headed north, toward the Detroit auto factories. The face of Adolph Hitler covered a hole in our kitchen window.

Then, come almost spring, I was ten years old. It was 1936, and my feet grew quicker out of their shoes so I wore them with the toes cut away. My arms were long and skinny and my hands big and bony, but I reached across farther and farther space, toward my mother and daddy, as they grew farther and farther away from themselves. I wanted my hands to hold together all the world I'd ever known.

One late night that spring, I woke, sat up in bed, just hearing. There was no one sound in particular, but if I held right still, I could hear a steady beat, beat, like I'd woke and the house had a heart. There was no moon, and I felt my way down the hall into the kitchen.

Little Mother was standing near the door, her gloves and coat on and a necklace of glass beads and tiny silver bells hung over her collar. At her coat hem, I saw white feathers, her tap dance skirt. Her fine black hair had been cut short and put up in tight pin curls. I could almost see her face. She looked like she did when she was just about to wake up, mornings, saying, not now, Ruth, give me a little spell and let me have my coffee. She was chewing on one corner of her lipsticked mouth, head tilted to one side. She seemed to be waiting.

I had come upon something I was never meant to see: my mother near the wood stove, prying up the lid. It was November and very cold. A fire glowed as she bent and, one by one, watched things from our Mining Hollow lives disappear. First there was Tobias's black cloth purse. She emptied all its coins on the table, lowered the purse, inch by inch, into the fire. His black velvet tie uncoiled into the stove, followed by his suit jacket and then by lengths and lengths of wooden chain. Last of all, though I only saw the sketchiest shape, it was me she lowered into the fire. Hands on her hips, she whispered, forgive me. Flames rose in the stove and she turned up her collar, straightened her shoulders.

I hurried toward her, ran face on into the edge of the kitchen table. A plate and a fork and a knife fell.

Where, I said, where are you going?

I hurled myself inside her unbuttoned coat, smelled face powder and strong cologne, but also a scent I loved, hers, old clothes, the nearly-lost smell of flowers pressed inside a book. Somewhere in the distance, a car engine was running. She had been waiting, and the waiting was not for me.

Tobias, when he came into the kitchen, was half asleep, his beard a two-day growth, his nightshirt gray against his skin, but he saw clearly how my mother's tap shoes gleamed in the dark. Her coat dropped away from my shoulders and I trembled in the cold air. She looked at me and then at him, as if it were a choice between the two of us, and herself. I saw this in her face: if she waited even one minute longer she might never, never leave, that if she did wait, the waiting would be this house and like a shawl, a shadowlike death, it would swallow her up forever.

Ruth Blue, someday I'll come back, she said. You believe that, don't you?

But I had no time to believe or misbelieve because Tobias was blocking her way, shouting, Little Mother, what do you mean by this, and I will not let you, just as she pushed past him and plunged outside. She was running.

I hurried out onto the porch, leaned over the railing, heart pounding, thinking and wanting, wanting to say, no, you mustn't. Eyes closed for the space of five beats of her heart as she ran, I imagined what our lives might have been, two canes, two hats, our feet tapping joyous unison in some town not Inez, not Mining Hollow. No, I said again and felt that word tear out of me, louder and louder, felt it hurl down the road, quick and longing, but not fast enough nor longing enough.

The echo of taps striking sparks against loose stones died away and I felt Tobias's hand on my bare arm.

No, Stella, no before God, he said, just as a car drove off in the distance.

And then, as if he remembered me, he looked into my face in the dim porch light. There was no love in his eyes but, first her, and now me, I was his. As he closed the door behind us, we cast two long shadows across the kitchen floor.

~

After my mother became a ghost, we continued, Tobias and me, to live in the house of her disappearance. You could tell me a hundred times about those that had seen it a lot rougher, lost everything they had. House fires or jobs they'd held for twenty years or limbs in war-time.

Or smaller things, things you'd think wouldn't count, next to life and death. Like how I heard tale of a woman lost a red stone out of her wedding ring in the garden. She'd spend hours every morning sifting through the dirt, digging up whole hills of potatoes and rummaging at the roots of beans and squash, setting all to rack and ruin looking to find that ring. Blamed that for the way her husband stopped loving her, their first year of housekeeping. That little a thing, a stone. Or a cup broke, or a mirror, and seven years bad luck.

My mother being gone was like that. The years of bad luck, I mean. And the way something was broken, lost, in my chest some days, or the back of my throat, or how even the palms of my hands hurt, or the skin on my arms, with the least touch.

When I went to bed at night I tried to find new ways to piece our lives, to pick through what we had, make do. I moved my legs and arms to opposite corners of the mattress, stretched and stretched, imagining how, if I stretched far enough my thinness could find its way along the floor, fill up the empty corners, wrap itself around the house and our sleep. But my growing bones ached as I wrapped my knees in my arms and knew I'd never sleep without dreaming of Little Mother.

In my dreams, she drank cherry fizzes and danced in towns I'd never seen and never would. In my dreams she sent me postcards of Gatlinburg, Tennessee, or the beach in Florida, postcards that said, I'm yours, yours until the Statue of Liberty Charlestons down Broadway. Places so far away and over the ridges and down roads where she sat in black roadsters with their windows down and wore pretty long scarves that flew out.

By day the postcards never came and the rooms of our house lost her smell, her ways of doing. Tobias sold or threw out most things reminding us of her, perfume bottles, vases, anything I didn't hide in the way back of a drawer or underneath a floorboard. Soon, instead, there was the scent of old food, unwashed trousers, shirts, all of which I set myself to work against. I wanted us to go to town clean, our heads held high and people saying, those Wallens, and ain't that Ruth Blue done her daddy proud, keeping house like she does? I sprinkled ashes down into the outhouse's long hole, toted scraps to the side of the yard, dabbed at cobwebs in the kitchen corners, boiled his shirts in lye and fetched water to the hard earth of the garden, where the last of the tomato vines had fallen, baked to a crisp in the last of the summer sun.

Mornings were like this. I'd wake up with my mouth dry, tasting of medicine and an old spoon, swing my feet out, swallow my dreams back. They came to me in scraps and bits, spinning in the early light as I sweetened Tobias's coffee and put milk in. I made my way down a hall tangled with socks and overalls, carried the coffee and biscuits and syrup to his bed. I'd stand and look down at his face, the sleep in the corners of his shut eyes, the beard and dried egg in the corners of his mouth. Words from my dreams came out of my own mouth, spilled out over his sleep. They were pretty words. *Love, now, here.* The words came out in a voice that made my heart hurt, a voice that made me want to cry and say, *you, there, Little Mother, come back.* I dreamed her and heard her so clearly, but I could never, never see her face. I shook my daddy awake, sat in the chair and watched him drink his coffee by the spoon.

Afternoons, when I walked back up the road from school, I saw a house so full, stray arms of my daddy's shirts waved from the windows, calling me inside. Ruth, he'd say. For a long while he called my name from the room that'd been their's, then, later, when he couldn't stand to sleep there from the front room, where he laid himself on the horsehair sofa.

Ruth Blue, he'd say, sipping moonshine from a canning jar. His voice made me think of how I'd once heard God speak with a voice like Bible pages turning, heavy with dust and Jesus.

Ruth Blue, he said. Who do you think you are?

Who he thought I was was Little Mother. As I walked by the sofa, he'd grab ahold of the hem of my skirt, tug at me until my feet danced to get away. He'd pull me by my long hair, like it was her hair, her long braid, or her who'd let the cookstove go cold and got his supper late or who brung him water that was too warm from the well.

With no soul in the world to hold on to me and say, you, Ruth Blue, there, there, I touched my cheek, and felt the sting of his hand, a ghost that had took flight from her face that night now longer and longer ago, a ghost that settled on me, white and stinging, turned blue, a bruise I took with me to school next day, to the school teacher who said, Ruth Blue, what's that, and touched the place.

A piece hit me when I was splitting kindling, I said. Hit me plumb in the face.

You look thin, she said. You eating right?

And sent me back and to him, to Mining Hollow, always Mining Hollow. At night I prayed to God, to Jesus who'd danced me in a picture, to any dream man who might take me, take me, too, away.

~

Finally, it was sheerly lack, the unclean piles of trousers and unwashed cups, the heap of ashes never cleaned from the cookstove, made Tobias search for Little Mother.

With dimes and nickels earned from selling Little Mother's tap dance trunk, and quarters he earned from odd-jobbing, then from dollars and cents from one, then two, then five acres of our twenty to coal mine speculators from up north, he bought a 1923 roadster that took us to high school galas and then to back-road speakeasies, at which he was sure my mother performed. I packed us up lunches and suppers, slices of bread with a hole torn in the middle for an egg and fried in lard, tomato and bologna sandwiches. Into Tobias's sack, to please him, I stuck slips of paper, hand-written Bible verses, *a woman's hair shall not tempt the angels, pitiful women have sodden their children.*

Eight o'clock, and time to be in bed, I was bundled in beside him, my let-out coat too thin in the deep winter air into which I leaned out, watching the cold stars flash by through the trees as we bumped and halted down this road and that.

To the Starland Skatarama, the other side of Inez, maybe. Or to Van Lear, Thealka, any little town with any sign of music, any hint of dancing we could find. Once we drove three counties over to visit a pie supper where a curly headed blonde woman with fat legs painted with foundation makeup sang "My Blue Heaven" for a dollar for a lemon meringue pie. But she was not my mother. At a firehouse fish fry in Wheelwright we watched families and one with a five year old twice my size in a sailor suit who danced to "Tea for Two" while doing what, I knew, was a poor imitation of a scoot step.

Counties, towns, once past the state line. We drove straight east, Tobias with his thin lips pressed into a white line, hands gripping the steering wheel. One night near a little town called Radiant, the sky turned yellow and two balloons drifted across the moon above a speakeasy where, from the door, I saw lights lowered, silver garlands and confetti, couples gliding past, their arms circling one another, the air full of applause. But nowhere did we find Little Mother. Those nights, we drove down road after road until all roads, long after dark, took us back to Mining Hollow.

What my daddy found, instead, was a message, pure and simple. Selling off five more acres of our land, first the timber rights and then the coal, to Pine Island Creek, a company up north, he left me home alone, that time. He used the money for a trip to Huntington, West Virginia, for a tent-revival meeting where it rained non-stop for three solid days and his hands shook so hard his fingers couldn't meet for prayers. This was how he told it to me. Rain poured through the canvas meeting tent, soaked his good Sunday suit jacket. Still he saw each quake and shiver of the preacher as a sign of the Lord. He had visions of angels and demons, of love and loss.

Or what he had, the last he admitted to, were visions of Little Mother. He saw her and a black-haired man drinking steaming cups from a thermos bottle in a parking lot near a train depot. He saw himself in a rag store suit jacket, sipping corn liquor from a canning jar, trying to light a cigarette, but as the train went by match after match died in the rush of air. Or maybe he had visions of my mother, dead, lovely and dead and lying beneath the waters of the pond, back of the house at Mining Hollow. He saw her life as it might have been after her disappearance: shining counters at a soda fountain, or, later, assembly at a munitions factory and a rented room without windows.

He came back to Inez with two things in his pockets—a square of striped tent canvas, and a hand-written license from a revival preacher, sent by the Lord himself. My daddy was forever and henceforth an emissary of the heavens. He also came back with a fever so bad he kept to his bed for weeks where he sang "Angels from the Realms of Glory." I nursed him, fed him bootleg whiskey and honey as he looked toward the front room window, through a patch of canvas cut into an angel shape.

So he became a preacher of sorts, my daddy, and he became Mr. Tobias Blue, who fixed anything, automobiles, door hinges, a soul or two when he went door to door with a pocket-sized New Testament. Give thanks, he said, to the Lord God, sovereign over all who art and who wast and ever shall be. He sat by the stove on winter evenings, wet boots steaming. My feet sped soundlessly over the kitchen floor, fetching warm water, scraping plates.

Some evenings I caught him looking, not at me, but at what he thought he saw, beauty before its time, before God and shadows had settled on me just right. I spent whole evenings watching the way his calloused hands gripped the sides of his chair, pleased, impatient, then angry. I held my tongue and soon memorized forever the sound a hand makes on a face.

One night I woke to the sound of tap shoes circling the house, hurried to the window and the first ice storm. Thinking this must be a sign, I closed my eyes, then caught a glimpse of my mother as she slipped away to the woods, where she soft shoed, humming, over the frozen pond. I followed her, inching carefully over the ice. She vanished into the white winter air where I wanted, so wanted to go.

Just then, I heard the voice, the one I heard so often, come time later. *Come down*, it said. My shoes were wet with snow, wet and heavy, not a dancer's at all, and I held fast to the earth.

EARL: BEFORE THE FACT

Ghosts. Haints, she calls them, and tells a tale about some miner walking through the woods at night with three of his best guitar fingers cut off and dried up and stuck in a lunch pail. Him singing, *when you are in some far and distant land, you can read the writing of my hand, although my face you will not see, please read these few lines and think of me.* Well, I may have added on to that a little bit, but you get my point. All the bellyaching and tale-telling, enough to make anyone want to be a ghost.

Even if I weren't one, for all practical purposes, right now. Ghost. Dream lover, seven years before the fact. Well, let me tell you, she dreamed me about seven years before the fact and it didn't make one bit of difference, when you got down to skin and touch. *I want a dream lover*, she sings. *So I don't have to dream alone.* Her favorite song, Bobby Darin, right at the top of the charts. I want a dream lover, so I don't have to dream alone. Dream lover. From all the times, there at the start of things, that she laid around and nuzzled up next to me and whispered to me, right sweet, you'd think she was the microphone of the good Lord, the original prophet, with all her bookings arranged by God himself. I've known you, Earl Wallen, she'd say. Known you all along. Why, Earl, I dreamed you. Like she made me up or something, a little mystical soup from the heavenly kitchen up in the sky.

~

I came by my ghostliness honest enough, got most of that fine character trait from my own father, Carl Wallen. Right off I have to tell you. My father, Carl Wallen, was a man who believed the world never changed. The world he knew, anyway. That world, the only one he felt safe in, was Venice, Ohio, years before the late spring of 1933.

When the Depression came, you already know what it did to a lot of men—the locked bedroom door, the click as the gun is loaded, the explosion. But not my father. He grew small and vague. He disappeared altogether in the late spring of 1933, returning a couple of days later with three things in his pocket: a key, a new one dollar bill and a pig's heart wrapped in butcher's paper. The bank crisis began in February, and March saw the closing of the Venice First National Bank. The key and the dollar bill were what he had left from ten years as a Venice, Ohio, businessman. He brought the heart into the house that same Thursday afternoon, laid it on the dining room table.

"Boil this for dinner, Sylvie," he said, bending near my mother's chair. He put his hand on her shoulder and whispered in her ear, just loud enough for me to hear. "It'll be strength, with God's grace, to see us through."

I don't remember much from the time earlier than that. First there was Cleveland, 1922. I was four years old then. I do remember summer evenings and a moon as bright as a newly minted silver dollar. Sylvie, my mother, and Carl went walking at night, one on either side of me, holding my hands. We stopped by the gazebo in a park by the lake. Carl smoked cigars smelling of cherries and, when Sylvie brushed gnats away from my face, I heard piano music somewhere in the dark. Everywhere I looked Carl was tall enough to block the sun and I held my breath as he picked me up and swung me hard. As Sylvie bent over me, I could have sworn I'd seen an angel, one from the Catholic church we went to on Sundays.

By 1925 my father had begun to make a good enough living as a bank teller. Sylvie kept house, not a mansion by any means, but comfortable enough, a big brick house on a street lined with chestnut trees. On hot afternoons she swept burrs from our front steps, then sat on the porch glider, sipping lemon fizz. She had the most amazing collection of mail order catalogues and travel magazines stuck just about anywhere throughout the house. I'd come upon them, behind couch cushions, beneath the drinking glasses, even tucked into my clean bedsheet, like she'd been changing the linens and forgotten halfway through, settled herself right down for a look at all those pictures. My mother had taken a fancy that Wallen was an Italian, or possibly Sicilian name, once spelled Wallini, in the old country. But a man like my father was only full of dreams of travel, promises to take her to see how blue the Mediterranean is, not spine enough to put his bottom dollar on any of it.

I wish I could tell you my father's dreams were something fine, big enough, at least, to bet on. I'd like to think he'd speculated on an Arizona copper mine. And I'd have been the first to have forgiven him if he'd simply been a big spender, or skimmed off some profits from the bank and invested in Florida property, even swampland. But no such recklessness, no sir. Instead he'd snap his fat fingers and say, "Shoot, Earl, I saw the nicest—"

And you name it, new tie, kid-skin gloves, perfume, silk flowers, always something he should have gotten for my mother or me. He usually forgot at the last minute. Or dragged in, late for dinner, a few wilted roses or a embroidered baseball cap wrapped up in the business section of the daily paper. Not that I wanted any of that fancy stuff. I don't know what Sylvie thought, in the last of our Cleveland days, about these oversights. By that time she read travel magazines even at the dinner table, looking up only sometimes to study his face. I studied his face too. Somewhere behind his spectacles and those blue eyes I knew he was adding up bank figures and small, lost opportunities.

And then we moved to Venice. Venice, Ohio, a place with the stick-with-it power of little towns everywhere, the fine allegiance to money and country and good American family, in that order. That town made me and them both. Set me on the high road. And sent them both to their deaths, in sleep, three months apart, right after World War II.

Ruth Blue'll tell you soon enough how I'm cut out of the same fabric as Carl. How I'm full of nothing but his pipe dreams, my own brand of sin with his name on it. Still, I promised her. Promised to write her a song called Ruth Blue. One that went, *All my life I've loved like a rolling stone, bound for the highway, far from my home, till I found you in my heart and right from the start, looked down in myself, clean down to the bone.* I never could get that song right, those words like they ought to be.

What I've done is listen all day to her song, Ruth Blue's, thinking if I only listened hard enough and long enough, I'd understand something. What I've done is be a ghost, both before and after the fact. But she'll tell you all about me and love and dreams and God. All in good time.

RUTH: 1941

When I was fifteen, and it was 1941, the nation turned to new dance fads, the fox trot, the jive. But my body did not dance. I went clean, not pretty, and I bound my breasts with strips of sheet beneath my shirt, put my hair in a wiry braid. Mine was a face I couldn't make out when I looked in the mirror for it. If there was a part of me that danced, I kept it secret, closed up, like a box inside a box in the back of a dresser drawer. In the mirror, instead of myself, I saw visions of my mother at a dance marathon. I could hear the rustle of her slip, silk, from a war-time parachute, a gift from that lover of whom I would never know the truth.

I was alone at Mining Hollow too much of that time. Alone with my daddy and the cracked cabinet of the radio we'd set up again by the kitchen table. Nights we listened to wartime news of Hitler and armored troops sent far into the reaches of Russia. Radio gospel played, *oh God, our shelter from the stormy blast, be thou my guide while life shall last.* Preachers who had been missionaries to countries like Bulgaria and Yugoslavia warned us of the wrath of God set loose from the heavens.

It was 1941 and Tobias paced the floor with talk of abominations and the future of the world. Abominations were tears left unmended, pots of soup beans left out to spoil. They were how many times I failed to pray, hard enough, long enough, while the gravy set on my plate, its rich, meaty scent rising while my stomach rumbled.

The future? When the full moon came and with it the blood from between my legs with its scent of salt and something no longer part of me, I already knew how the future might be. In shame, I laid stained rags in the garden, turned the black dirt over them.

1941 was also the first time I let love close to me, the love of a man, even if it wasn't a real love to speak of. It was 1941 and flowers and wakes. Tobias began to cough coal dust into his handkerchiefs, and even when they called him, didn't go back to the mines. Instead he preached the gospel for free, quoted Bible verses in Inez at the barber shop. Coming back to Mining Hollow, late nights, his breath was like whiskey. I listened from my bed while he teetered up the porch steps, slammed the screen door and sang a hymn down the hall to me, they who are victorious cannot be harmed by the second death. I held my arms and legs perfectly still as he yanked open the door, stumbled across my room, held on to my hand so tight my fingers tingled. Together we went out to the porch, looked down into the front yard, his valley of the shadow of death, and praised God, for what I didn't rightly know.

He supported us with odd jobs, hanging tobacco, signs painted, any and every funeral. Accidents and deaths were a sure sign of our necessary grief. Around that time, my father and I mourned dozens of relatives, none of them ours, maiden aunts, unborn children, third cousins from states up north and, after the country entered World War II, paid tribute to soldiers missing in action and heroes who would never come home.

Wearing coats with the biggest pockets we could find, we went to visit the sometimes unknown deceased. I looked down into satin-lined caskets, toothless faces, paid my last respects. To such times, it was many that brung mile high pies with meringue or potato salad or meatloafs. But we brought prayers for the soul.

And came away with treasures. We filled our pockets with dainties, tea cakes and jam tarts. Filled our arms full of clothes from cleaned-out closets and sorted through drawers. Back home, we relished our finds. Ate fineries that left the taste of sour milk. I slipped on blouses or a nightshirt and felt as if it weren't final, the slam of earth into a grave.

Something thin, a shadow on a sunny afternoon, went home with me from these times and I imagined a hand at the laying-in touching my arm, saying it's all right now, there, there. I could rinse away tastes, but nothing could take the scent of chrysanthemums and roses out of my hair. In God's room, in the lamb of God hands of Jesus, I laid funeral wreaths and bouquets, saying take these Lord, my many blessings.

One spring, an overturned boat was found floating, upsided, on the Big Paint River. Mr. Hyatt from the General Store had gone missing although a body was never found. Local radio news speculated over the next few years, first that he'd just gone north. Later, that he'd gone north to invest in a factory that made hats. Finally that he'd gone north to design hats for movie stars who went overseas to entertain the troops. Anyway, that spring, the town buried a shoe box with a handful of river silt laid to rest in it and gave that his name. Rudy Hyatt, Mr. Hyatt's son, followed his father's footsteps towards a death without a body. He was a hero, killed at Pearl Harbor in December, 1941, having never gone to Europe or the Pacific or any of those foreign places he'd wanted.

Rudy Hyatt's funeral was one we were sure not to miss. Tobias and I arranged our mourning—a wide, dark skirt and too-large pumps with scraps of cloth in the toes for me, a used pork-pie hat with a black band and a bow tie for Tobias. Clothes, the hand-me-down rewards of our blessings, God rest their souls, for the departed. As I followed my father to the car and we headed toward Rudy's lying-in, I sniffed the sleeve of my wool sweater. It gave off a scent, a memory of cologne.

~

They'd raised an American flag over the Hyatt's place and its shadow waved as I crossed the yard, climbed the front porch steps. Tobias knocked and Rudy Hyatt's mother, Octavia Hyatt, opened the door wide enough for us to see her standing on a braided rug, tiny feet in black shoes, arms crossed over her plump stomach, saying, well? Everything about her was buttoned up tight, a dark winter dress fastened snug at her throat, sleeves gathered at the wrist, button shoes, the kind ladies wore thirty years ago. She opened the door wider and peered out. She couldn't quite place us. I shook her hand, saying, Blue, Ruth Blue, but stopped halfway, seeing her blank eyes. I was experienced enough with grief to know one touch could mean a look, then a whole face breaking into grief, softly, like chalk.

Well, she said again, looking odd, because who were we after all? Tobias patted her wrist and bent, whispered, *to him that is victorious comes grace*, the verse he'd prepared for the day. Then he shook his head, sadly, as if he knew what it meant, how her house had been visited by the angel of death itself. And maybe, he said, she had heard of us, how we were messengers for the Lord in times of bereavement. She stepped back, opened the door wider and Tobias slipped into the front room. His too large suit hid every angle of his sharp body, the elbows and knees. He went from one to the next, embracing, clasping hands, saying again and again, *to him who is victorious, to him who is victorious*, a prayer that sung me to sleep often enough.

I told Octavia Hyatt how I'd known her son in school, then found a corner for myself. A crowd was gathered around the coffin, Inez people mostly. A plate teetered on the knee of a woman in a black dress scraped-clean, a man with a heavy jaw licked and sealed a new cigar. Behind them was a full table, bowls shiny with food, buttery potatoes, fresh baked pies. Their voices mingled, what a fine boy he was, so full of life, I mean adventure, of course, and don't his photographs look natural-like?

Laid around the house were pictures, one of Rudy at twelve with bony legs and a string of fish. A portrait almost covered by flowers was set atop of the closed coffin. They'd sent what was left of him home in a tin urn engraved with one word, hero, though everyone knew it hadn't taken much effort to be killed at Pearl Harbor. His remains were in the best oak coffin, which they kept shut, not even a viewing, but a sweet odor like face powders was in the chair, even on the palms of my hands after I touched the cushions.

Rudy, as I remembered him from the Inez schoolhouse where I'd gone up till the last year, was one of the older ones, long trousers, a tie, not someone to look twice at the likes of those of us from up Mining Hollow. We'd walked in toting lunch boxes, lard or boiled white sugar sandwiches inside, while he went home for lunch, had his pick of store-boughts: saltines, pickles, tiny canned fish. He brung to class magazine photos, Babe Ruth and his sixtieth home run or Jack Dempsey dancing and swinging. Later on, it was news clippings of all these places. This, he said, is where I want to be, pointing to long, white sand streets lined by palm trees, a shimmer at the other end he said was the ocean.

Later, it wasn't places he wanted, but people to take on. I'll show him what's what, Rudy said as he pointed to a photo of Hitler standing straight as the back of a chair. Or there were groups of them, soldiers, young boys mostly, fine hairs on their upper lips, in uniforms, bayonets slicing the air. That's me, the second one from the left, Rudy said. As soon as he took a notion.

~

Before anyone noticed, I opened the first handy door down a hall, into a bedroom decorated all in white, thick woven rug in white, white curtains. I sank onto the bed, pulled back the spread and sniffed the newly laundered white sheets, run my hands over the fat, cool pillows. Still quiet, I opened closets, looked beneath the bureau to find a shoe box full of more photographs, Rudy, various moments during his twenty-some years. On the tops of the bureau and stacked along one wall were parcels wrapped in brown paper. I ran my finger beneath tape, unwrapped one box, then two. Inside I found everything neatly folded, socks, suspenders, trousers with ironed pleats. Rudy's, for certain, and so I did one last thing in his memory. I searched through a box of starched shirts, finding, finally, at the bottom, a handkerchief embroidered with tiny initials, R and H. I folded this handkerchief into a smaller square, one that fit into my palm, hidden, where I might need it, at the time of grief.

I redid the packages, then eased into the crowd of mourners. Tobias, near the table, was cramming his pockets with food brought for the dead. My mouth watered at the sight of this, at the thought of the slices of lemon cake and tiny homemade biscuits with ham, at the thought of how I'd eat of the sweets and fancy store-boughts until I grew sick. Ashamed of my own hunger.

What the rest of them were looking at was a stout man with a beard in the corner of the room. A stranger here, I could tell from his foreign-looking pin striped suit, his new suede shoes. He was bending over near a three-legged stand with a black box on top, a camera, I soon learned.

The man held a long cord, raised his hand, ready to push a button on a little black box in his hand. Steady, now, he said, and was still, waiting.

Everyone turned to face him. Before the light exploded, they posed side by side in front of Rudy's coffin, looking at Rudy's portrait, his neat air force uniform. All of us held our breaths, waited for the pictures. Was I the only one who heard it, that which was next? It was the sound a shadow makes, one from somewhere far down, a hall, a throat, a heart.

~

The picture-taker was Jules Cameron, a name I heard about in Inez when I went in for our dry goods. Since Rudy Hyatt's passing away, this stranger had stayed on in Inez, doing who knows what, spending whole mornings on the benches in front of the courthouse though he didn't look at all like someone who would just pass the time of day, a bright blue scarf, a tie pin. Arms folded, a straw hat tilted, he watched us and said in a voice, with something stiff and foreign about it, like persimmon on your tongue, a quite pleasant day. I thought his name was like teabury when you found it in the woods, cool and bitter.

An early March morning and I stood outside the picture window of the empty building off Main Street. The building had been one thing after another. Auctioneers, a watch repairshop, even a missionary church for the Jehovah's Witnesses, though nothing seemed to last, nothing bought or sold for long.

I cupped my hands, took a look through the window at dozens of small glass rectangles strung from the ceiling, close enough to catch the outside light. A wagon loaded with bales of hay passed down the road, an automobile cranked to life somewhere. The glass pieces chimed, and I traced my fingers over the letters painted on the window and said the name, Jules Cameron. A name with the music of spoons on empty glasses.

Through the window I also saw a table with papers, open books, bottles of ink, and behind that shelves with jars and jars and long, shiny cylinders. A camera, and bright light that blinded me. And him, stepping out from the black drop cloth. A second later, a face, Jules Cameron's, was inches from mine. He was on the sidewalk right next to me, motioning come in, come in. I held back, thinking of my daddy, of what it was he'd say. You ought to be ashamed, a young girl like you, mercy on us.

But I went on into that world of scents, some of them I knew, the soapy odor of ginseng, a musky smell of furs drying. Beyond that was a light scent, whiskey light and sharp. Room spinning, I saw Jules Cameron. He was stouter than I remembered him, not much taller than myself. He wore the same pin-striped suit and his shoes were off-sized, one with a thick elevator sole.

Tea? he asked, turning toward a stove the size of a hat. I sat in a church meeting folding chair before the long length of the table. Remembering to ask a blessing, I took long swallows of a milky sweet liquid. On the table were more pictures than I could ever have thought up, all in grays and whites and blacks, all of ordinary house-things. These are things that have been left behind, discarded, he said. Who knows who owned them? In a corner of a picture to my left I saw the leg of a chair, then a chair with the bottom caved in, a cooking pot, a coffee mug. In the midst of the pictures there were real objects, a large black marble, an unfolded paper fan, a smooth-edged piece of glass.

And these, he said as I looked up into the dark inside of his unbuttoned jacket, are photographs of the war. Pearl Harbor and Rudy Hyatt, I asked, but he mentioned other names, Denmark, Norway, Belgium. I repeated these names to myself, thinking Gilead, Golgotha, Gomorrah, the only foreign places I knew, and looked at his pictures of the dead. There was a young girl, arms raised, lying down, hair in long, wet coils. Her legs, loose at the knee as if for sleep, were just at the edge of water, and she was laying on bare, sandy ground. Drowned, he said, the first day of the war. He showed me pictures of a dead hand with a gold wedding ring, of a stiff, stockinged leg kicking straight up. The last war picture was of a casket with candles in tall glass holders beside it. A village in France, he said, seating himself on a crate near me. The casket was small and the face inside was a nut out of a shell, face and eyes and drawn mouth, a baby, its fingers laced together.

I saw right away what was wrong with all of his pictures. It wasn't their lack of light. The picture of the cooking pot showed the least fault, rust spots, the wire handle bent to one side, and if I looked close at the baby's face, I saw the least wrinkles around its eyes, little dark hairs on its ears. Light flooded these pictures, white, straight at the sun light. I wanted to hide from these lit pictures, imagined instead the first blackness after a candle is blown out, a closet, the door shut, darkness behind the clothes.

If Jules Cameron had wanted to show me the valley of the shadow of death, it wasn't anywhere in these pictures of light, no shadows in them. It was what I heard when I stood and left the table, walked back toward Mining Hollow, just thinking. A voice I knew followed me saying, *remember, you will always remember what has been left behind, the last moment of breath.*

~

And this, Jules Cameron said on a bright spring morning, later on, when I visited his darkroom, is you. I stood with him in a room completely black except for a thin red light, felt myself falling toward objects I couldn't see and toward a scent sharper than whiskey.

The next thing I recognized was shiny as the moon on the pond at home, and then stronger light from overhead. I closed my eyes, held my hands against my eyes, opened my fingers one by one, and looked down into water, a long metal pan. A face swam up at me, palms raised on either side of the head, against glass. Cheeks gaunt, a neck too long and thin.

It's a photograph of you, Jules Cameron said. Outside my shop window.

Surely not me, that face as flat and white as paper. All the same I stood in Jules Cameron's darkroom, holding that sight of me on a bright spring morning. And just as quick as that picture was taken, there was a day I almost remembered. Sunlight, the pond at home, and me, sitting with my mother. A day so clear. Brilliant green leaves, my mother stroking my hair and looking up and beyond me, into the shrill blue sky. I bent over the water, but before I could see the reflection of us two, a storm moved in and the water went murky, full of clouds. I remembered that day so clear the memory was sharp, so broken it hurt.

And the camera, Jules Cameron said, does not lie. Even if I did, three mornings in April, then May, when I told Tobias I was returning shirts I'd pressed and hems I'd turned for a couple of families in Inez. Making myself useful, I said, and poured coins in his hand, ones I pulled out of a sock hidden beneath my mattress. Coins for the photographs Jules Cameron took of me. Coins for those three mornings I went out to meet him at his picture shop at 5:30, in time to watch Inez wake up.

One of those mornings I stood at the bottom of the hill below the house, started up the hollow. Each time I looked back, the house grew smaller and smaller into the tree line. Nothing but a place of a god made of stone. I took this picture into myself—the shattered window or two, a dirt yard, old tires, broken chairs, tin cans, everything we couldn't let go of because God did not believe in a wasted life.

When I got to the shop, I rapped on the window, afraid Jules Cameron was still asleep, but he had been up an hour already. He handed me a cup of hot sweet tea and, balancing this, I followed him. We turned two streets and took our seats, hidden behind the corner of the First National Bank, where we could take pictures without being seen. He unpacked his black leather case, camera and tripod, sat fiddling with his glass slides while I hummed a song I called collodion.

Collodion, like the radio, a county fair, like Precious Redeemer. It was the way he took pictures. Negatives, he called them, on little rectangles of glass. Negatives that came to life under a clear, bright sun. Shadows turning into faces, into hands and houses. He'd wind his watch, sit counting the minutes and seconds. Now Ruth Blue, he'd say, and cover the new photograph, take it back to its sharp-smelling baths that made the picture sit and stay.

At this early hour, Jules Cameron showed me what he knew about light. He showed me was the clean, white skeleton of the town. He photographed a miner, with it still too early for work, him sitting in clean sunlight on the street corner with a steaming coffee cup. Or some woman sweeping last night's dead moths from her front porch, or nothing at all, a window just washed with vinegar, clean enough to break like a soap bubble and a runny-nosed child looking out. Jules Cameron photographed anything he called fresh or new or just waking up, eyes full of light, new light.

What I showed him was how the missing looked. It was 1942 and at least a dozen Inez boys had gone off to war. I showed him the street, dust rising with any stir of wind, and that woman sitting on the porch glider across the street, looking down toward the railroad tracks.

Look, I said. How all she can see is dust and Inez.

Inez, the one main street of it with the mountains on either side, the horizon in front of her hand, as far as she can reach, that gone too, no matter how far she reached out from where she sat and sat.

At 6:30 the sun rose, slow and heavy. Sweat shone on Jules Cameron's forehead and I touched that, held my damp palm against my cheek. The sun rose and showed the street, faded, yellow-dry. Shadows rose, from the buildings, from our own legs as we stood, stretched. The woman in the porch glider got up, her front door slammed. A shadow crossed her drawn-tight curtains, paused, stayed there. Picture that, Jules Cameron, I said. Photograph that.

~

On a morning in late summer, with Tobias gone to West Virginia for a tent revival meeting, Jules Cameron and I met at the swinging bridge. He'd rented an old canoe and two paddles from a man who sold night crawlers at a houseboat he lived on down by the Big Paint River. We'd spend the day, Jules Cameron said, photographing the old ways.

I watched his red lips and his beautiful, short fingered hands as he drew words in the air—collodion, meaning gun cotton and alcohol and ether, meaning glass plates, meaning the negatives, which were my own hands, held up to the sun as we pushed away from the bank. I looked through my fingers and counted spaces of light, five of them, for each of the days I'd stolen to be with Jules Cameron.

I'd told my daddy about the closets I'd cleaned out for Octavia Hyatt, the ironing I went out to do, the way I'd spent a whole afternoon churning butter for a woman and setting it out in a mold with a strawberry leaf pattern. It took time, I told him, to do such things. I poured more coins into his hands, ones I earned from showing Jules Cameron the truth of mountains and people and their ways. I hummed my song called collodion, sitting in the prow of the rowboat and pulling my weight with my oar, showing him.

This, I told him, is all the world I know of.

We passed a white house set high on the bank amid a bunch of weeping willows. In a swing was an old woman with a checkedy apron, pushing back and up with her bare feet against a porch piled with bushel baskets. Beside the house hung a washing of fresh white sheets. We passed a cemetery behind a chicken-wire fence, two headstones decorated with bright pink flowers, and farther along a church-house, a low stone building with a hand-painted cross reaching high from its roof, Church of the New Pentecostal Truth.

All the world I knew of, kudzu banks and cattails, debris of cans and bottles and tires. All the world an empty coal trestle, spill of coal from a tipple, smell of river water.

Tell me about the world, Jules Cameron, I said. Yours.

And he told me about that foreign country, France. That city he called Paris, at three some morning. The sound of autos and music, blues. Blues, like your name, he said, and bread so fresh and sweet it was like butter melting, and field upon field of sunflowers and the sea so blue. All of it blue.

74

The sound of the L & N, I told him, was something that came to me some nights when I was my most alone, at Mining Hollow. All the world I knew, but looking at it through his eyes, through Jules Cameron's, was like looking through my fingers at the sun, like seeing the spaces between the branches of trees. World beyond world beyond world.

Soon we were so far from Inez I believed that afternoon we'd never turn back. Jules Cameron laid down the paddle, laid himself down, arms under his head, stretched out his legs, the one thick-soled shoe. He struck a match and lit a long cigar with a scent he told me was cloves.

Ruth, he said to me. With the camera there are different impressions, sometimes, of arms, legs, faces. The camera reveals a truth the subject does not always understand.

I leaned over the side of the boat that summer morning. My hands were dark shapes, chipped nails and the one long scar from a canning jar that broke around my wrist. Scarred hands gliding down brown river water and sunlight. With the pictures he took, I didn't think of how, nights sometimes, I'd pull free of my daddy and he'd be after me, setting me spinning with the back of his hand, like I was no more than play animals on top of a wind-up music box. I never told Jules Cameron of these things. I told no one these truths.

After awhile I moved back to where he was, laid myself near him. We didn't speak, had never touched, but I was as close to him as I could get, imagined the sound of his heart, watched the shadows between leaves and the shapes of branches. That day shadows were like the bottom of a copper kettle shone and reshone. They were lit with the possibility of all the world, the whole of it, a world where I might see myself in other towns, floating on other rivers, polishing glass slides with my breath, helping Jules Cameron photograph worlds and worlds beyond Mining Hollow, worlds of which I'd never seen the like.

~

Right off, when I walked back in the house that afternoon, I should have knowed. That the air had a different scent, one tight and sharp, one like whiskey and hours gone by. A scent of waiting. Outside there was still good, late light of an afternoon, but our house never took it in much. The hall past the bedrooms and to the kitchen was already like dusk.

Tobias, I called. You there?

He was. At the kitchen table, a flame was turned too high on a lantern spewing smoke and kerosene fumes, casting light over my daddy, slumped there. The back of his shirt was soaked through, his head turned to one side, his hair black and wet with sweat against his forehead. The radio, turned full up, played gospel voices, yield not to temptation, for yielding is sin, he who is our savior, dark passions subdue. Beside was the empty canning jar, an overturned glass.

I stood a good long while, looking down at him, thinking of the coins I'd spilled into his hands, watching the way his eyes raced with dreams, the frown of his mouth. My chest tightened, breathless, afraid of him, but I reached down, touched his sleeve.

Ask the Savior to help you, comfort, strengthen, the radio said, and I did, thinking for a while of how it could be. Me, rummaging beneath the house, where I knew my daddy kept his jars and jars of bootleg, shoved back in the potato bin, wrapped in a burlap bag. I could have brung a jar back to the table, shook him just enough and held it to his lips and said, here, here, and watched him take his long swallows, enough to put him down, deeper. *Look ever to Jesus*, the song said, *kind-hearted and true, he'll carry you, carry you through*. I could have been that kind, raised him up, let him lean on me down the hall, eased him, put a cover over him. Left him and gone. But Jules Cameron had never asked me, not once.

I stood still, hand on Tobias's arm, shook him, the least little bit. Then more, saying wake up, wake up, and him groaning in what wasn't sleep, tucking his head down in his arms even more. Jules Cameron hadn't asked me to tote his bags and his camera and thin glass slides, to be his help-mate and more than a photograph. (Had never seen me in this house at the head of a holler leaning down near my daddy's drunk mouth and saying, you, Tobias, wake up now, go lay in the bed.)

Please, I said, and shook him, hard this time, pushed against him with all my weight. The weight of me, in that one spot on earth, between all the world of Mining Hollow and the world of Jules Cameron that was not truly mine to have.

Stella, my daddy mumbled. That you? Little Mother, is that you?

Then he was up. He looked me up and down with his red-veined eyes, that truth of me somewhere between my mother and myself. Stumbling, he came toward me, hand raised.

You, he said, where you think you been? His tongue was between his lips, thick and slurred. You think you just do as you please, miss? I've heard tales about you.

I backed away toward the wall and knew that he knew. But what? That Little Mother had left him with some man, some dream lover, a man in a car by night? That I would have left him too, if I'd known how or where or when?

Then he was beside me, pulling my face next to his, those whiskery cheeks, saying, go on, kiss on me like she done on him.

And then I was running from him, gone down the hall, shutting a door with him on the other side, where I could hear him, saying, you, Ruth, Ruth Blue.

~

Tobias come back to himself, like he always did. But for me, after that, it was different. I became another person, like I'd been tossed in the river and fished out, a gutted thing, changed, left to rust like the roadster parked at the far side of the house.

He watched me. Come morning, early or late, he'd already be in the kitchen, shoveling ashes out of the cookstove and waiting for me to stir up the flour and water for his biscuits. He'd come home at odd hours of the day, check to see if I'd swept or hoed or gathered the eggs or the late crop of beans. Nights, I heard him turn a key in the lock to my room.

I knew without asking that he wanted me to repent, of Jules Cameron, of my secrets, of my mother's sins. I still held on to it, that wish to go back to Inez, see photographs of the world. I wished for Jules Cameron. Or not for him, his too-short leg and his thick-soled shoe, but for the light I'd seen when I'd looked through my hand at the sun.

I would not repent of my wish for shadows to have light, for all the world I knew to become all the world I might have had, true as a photograph. So my daddy showed me what I had to do. I became one of the missing.

He took me to my room in the house and pointed to the four blank, white walls and said, yours is the power to turn water to blood. Show me what God has hurled upon the earth. He gave me three cans of paint, red and white and yellow, and a long-handled brush. He shut me in and locked the door. Through that long winter, I made the angels he had one time seen in a tent in West Virginia dance.

That room was small, with only one painted-shut window, and I spent the first day looking out to the yard at how the farewell to summer was already in bloom and wishing for the mouth, the mouth of the holler. This was Mining Hollow, the last house left in the world, fall coming, the dry grass a washed-out brown. I looked through the yard toward the road until sunset, but there was no one. No one thought of me, and so I became who I was to become. As the room grew colder, nights, the windows coated with the first fall frost and I looked out at this world through milk-glass.

Soon I put from me my wish for the road and the mouth of the holler, put away my thoughts of how, toward Inez, steam from the L & N rose and vanished at dawn as the train pulled away, going north. My days were this room, its hours of sun on one wall and dark setting in on the other.

Days were the beck and call of my daddy, the food he'd bring or not, the taste of paint chips and scraps of paper from the walls. What filled me was the voice, the voice at night that came, more and more. I'd lie at night, awake, it floating above me and saying, *your dreams are like unto ashes, a country you have not yet known, a photograph that will grow clearer with time.* Even though the Bible spoke of abominations and all the verses I knew by heart, still the voice told me of the times to come. *Bring no abominations into this house,* it said. *The world must be made as clean as by fire. Your wickedness is an abomination to my lips.* All the years to come were a voice in the dark, the shadow hand of God across the world, the voice of God that whispered, *do this, do, do not.*

Humming collodion I prayed then I took the long-handled brush and painted the room with light. I painted two angels, their slender hands touching, their eyes shut. I painted how their wings unfolded, a face so beautiful it could have been my mother at the center. The walls shook when I laid on my hands. I colored these wings in with rose and painted soft yellow circles in the centers of their chests. Then I laid on the floor and shut my own eyes. I saw how the yellow circles called the angels to life. Warmth, like love, seeped into their long arms and they stood above me, fanning me with their white wings. I opened my mouth and drank cloves and smoke. But when I told Tobias these things, he left me bowls of warm water to drink, shut the door and said, you have not yet seen God.

Then I painted a third angel. This angel was taller than the other two and its hair was as white as an eye. Like no mother at all, it pulled seven stars out of its mouth and held them, one after another, up to the cold window so there was a melted place for me to see out. Later, this thin angel took me out through the circle and down into the woods behind the house, where I found the first skunk cabbages, tore apart their petals and ate the soft insides.

When I went back to the attic again, the bowls of warm water had iced over, my fingers ached from cold. When I tried to hum collodion my mouth was dry. I was hungry but Tobias had only left me two tiny sandwiches with the crusts cut away. I pounded on the door with my bony knuckles but when he opened it all I could see was one of his whiskered cheeks and the glare of his cloudy left eye. He said, pray. I knelt down, but the angels were silent and the snow fell in dry flakes that whispered, *listen, now.*

In the eighth week I no longer remembered Jules Cameron's full, red mouth. My body felt light as air, bones and thin light, a shadow that could rise. I scratched a hole in the window-frost with my paintbrush and looked up at the sky. A winter storm had come earlier but since then the sky had become so blank I had to look down again.

The prayers he wanted were answered. Ice coated the hawthorne trees in the yard. In the dark, I saw the real angel arms, ones brittle and hollow at the center. I watched while the winds flew up and the smallest branches snapped. It was an awful sound. The world was a sea of glass and the crossing to God, without love, was a sheet of ice. But I could not turn back.

~

After that there was time, a pocket watch ticking under my pillow, time against my ear. I kept a candle and matches handy in the dark, for nights in the room down the hall when I'd hear Tobias, a long, rough breath, then an exhale that skittered and halted. Coughing up demons, he'd told me, reeling in with his thin bottle half full. Those nights, he'd throw open the kitchen window, lean out into the dark and rain, shoulders heaving. Nights like that, I held him as his body shook and while he said, God's the resurrection and the light. When he quit and slept, something paler than night lifted from him, floated off into the trees, waiting there until the next time.

It was spring and then spring and the autumn after that when I at last found news that had been kept from me. One afternoon while Tobias was away working for a man in Inez, I reached into the very back of a closet, a top shelf, dust and nothing I'd seen before. I felt back there until I took out a butcher-paper and twine wrapped box.

A box I opened to several slips of paper and pictures, one of these, me in summer. In one photo I wore a straw hat with a ribbon. My stockings were in my hand and I was wading. In another I was sitting by an open window. Light flooded in behind me, wind had blown my hair and hid my face. Both of these, photographs of Jules Cameron's.

I took the letter to my bed. The paper was gray, see-through pages like my fingers could pass right through and come back with a scent, hands, clove cigarettes, the memory of him I'd hardly known. Where he wrote from was France, he said, and September when he arrived there, just in time for the grape harvest. I closed my eyes and imagined the days he described, women starting down the first row, parting wet leaves, conversations, clusters of grapes falling, shadows against the sun, women and children diving for cover under leaves and vines. He described other sounds, bomber raids, the war.

When I opened my eyes again I couldn't believe in some foreign country, France or anywhere else, where planes had the power he described, bodies burning like paper. What I could think on was how Jules Cameron left, without a farewell. I tucked my legs under the quilt, slid the letter beneath my pillow. What I could believe in was being alone in Mining Hollow, the road down from the house and the road toward Inez dark with shadows of coal tipples.

I pinched the candle flame, imagined Jules Cameron looking up toward my window, that last light gone quick as the snap of fingers, then pitch black, like it was the last light in the world. It could have been easy for him to think I didn't count at all, when I stopped going to his shop that fall. He left for good, having completed what his letter called a photographic essay of Inez, miners lined up for dirt pay first day of the month, stock sales and trade for hunting dogs and knives and guns, all the places I'd shown him, all of it and me. I touched my face in the dark, hair, the arrangement of lips and nose and eyes.

~

One night I had a dream of a foreign country. I can't tell why it was strange to me, those same trees, the same sky as at the one back of the house, but with the light so keen I held still until the shapes in front of me got clear.

I was standing in a field that could have been corn, sharp leaves. I pushed my way through and through and there was a scent that made me dizzy, so sweet I could taste it. When I come to a clearing I wet my fingertips, ran them over the itchy, white scratches on my bare arms.

The first thing I saw clearly was Jules Cameron, the legs of his striped, baggy trousers. The rest of him was under a drop cloth, his camera pointed toward a group of five or six women bent over a large metal bucket, their faces hidden. No one saw me, though I moved in front of the camera, slipping past shoulders and elbowing in, staring down with them into the bucket. It was running over with the crushed pulp of grapes, stems, pieces of stems, liquid, purple and clotted. I touched it and my hands had a scent, a little salty, too sweet, and I rubbed my palms again and again against my house dress. No one saw me at all.

Then there was a humming, a sound from very far away, the same as blood rushing, the same as fainting, feeling lighter and lighter. There were bombers overhead, flashes of light and stinging debris, and I was falling forward, shielding my eyes. The earth cracked open, moving inside.

When it was over, I heard the women around me coming awake. I heard whimpers and moans. Oh hold me, they said, hold me, oh beautiful mother of the light. One of the women was near me, laying face down in the crushed, tall grass. She was wearing a skirt patterned with green and blue feathers, tiny burns scattered across it. She pushed herself up and her hands, rolled aside, and I saw what was once me from beneath her.

My arms and legs were set at angles, like a stick person drawn with pencil. She gently stroked my burned face until skin came off on her palms. Get up, she said, don't you know its time to get up? Then there was the first sound since the bombing—a sound of wings beating fast, the sound a heart makes, the sound of a shadow trying to rise, to escape into the blank sky.

I woke to the whiskey scent of Tobias's breath. The scent caught in my throat, like hair. I pushed hair back from my face, and sat up and said, what, what? It was morning already. A fine morning, Tobias said, crouching on his ankles near my bed, his yellow-bearded face inches from mine. In the sunlight there was every wrinkle and his bloodshot eyes. He was my father and I loved and I hated him and he was everything, all there was. He snapped his razor-thin fingers. He wanted his coffee soon, that soon.

~

After that, reaching to the back of the closet, unwrapping the box, pulling out things meant for me, wrapping it carefully and putting it back, became what I did until one day I reached back and found no box at all.

But before that, I found just enough to let me know I had a past, and that there was a world. Once I found a postcard from Niagara Falls with a line or two on the back, spidery letters that could have been my mother's handwriting. Another time, I found a glass piece less than half the size of my hand. A negative, Jules Cameron once told me, though I never completely understood how the world was better seen through a small square of light, an instant in time. The world now had no shape to me at all, or only the shape of air passing through an open window, how the screen rippled and smoothed.

What I saw when I held the glass up to the window, toward the sun, was a shape of myself, smoky and distant, as if I blew very hard against the glass plate, the shape would vanish like dust and float out the window, over the pond back of the house. In the negative I was doing something very ordinary. I was in a doorway, a cup and a spoon in my hand. But I could have been doing anything. What I saw of importance were bones, quiet blood. What I saw was any shape of myself that floated toward the pond, ready to disappear forever, and inside me I saw tiny crosses and the hand of God, palm down.

EARL: 1941

We're almost there, you and me. Me to the part where I'm no ghost anymore, where I'm more than just a wish on the stars beyond the mountains from a lonely girl at the back of a holler back of nowhere. And you? You're bound to get to the part where you say, you, Earl Wallen, why for sweet Jesus's sake did you go and pick her to fall for? Night, day, her, you. You, Earl, why, love, to you, ought to be as smooth as a guitar string, rich as a song at the top of the charts. And to her? Love is salvation.

Saving. That's not how she means it, but it's been the key to my life and times. Coins, people, faces. All that I've tried to redeem from that road going nowhere, my life.

~

Maybe it was from him, my father, Carl Wallen, I first learned it. That fine art, salvation. Save you enough money, son, he'd say, and a man can do anything he pleases. Anyway, that was what he said, before I was twelve and before we lost what we had to the Depression.

At the bank, on Saturdays and Friday afternoons, I pushed a broom down the marble hall past the tellers' windows and spit polished the brass door handles. That bank, for a little town like Venice, was as done up as the mausoleum of a war hero. Marble cherubs stood on tiptoe above the double entry doors and a mural of a reclining lady and a black swan decorated the main hall.

One early Saturday morning my father left me at the bank doors, then disappeared down the street with a black ledger under his arm. Foreclosures, and I knew it. I turned the key in the lock, swung open the heavy oak doors and could already hear the rustle of wings.

Awhile later, bucket and mop in hand, I stood in the foyer and took a glance back over my shoulder at the painting of the black swan. The swan had spread its feathers, tucked them in around the lady. It glared at me with one red eye.

I set a ladder against the tall windows overlooking the back street, heard paper tearing, the spill of coins into a till, combination locks whirring, though I knew the bank was as empty as Main Street at Sunday afternoon nap time. I splashed the glass clean, then stood still as I smelled, not vinegar, but the crisp oily scent of one dollar bills.

Twenty years later, Ruth Blue would tell me what I saw was a vision. Holy spirits whooping their way through the halls of the bank and pretending they were bundles of notes being unwrapped. If there was any Godly vision that day, it was how I stood there in front of a clean picture window, looking down into the streets of Venice, Ohio, thinking about my father, Carl Wallen. Visions.

Well, I envisioned him. As he got up mornings, fastened his gaiters, adjusted the sleeves of his six year old double-breasted jacket, brushed his suede shoes, then settled down to breakfast, two boiled eggs, toast, no preserves. He kissed my mother, Sylvie, goodbye, and smiled as she whispered in his ear, Cleveland, Carl, or Europe, it's more than time. Then he set off down the sidewalk whistling, the rich get rich and the poor get poorer, but ain't we got fun?

I saw him as he opened the bank, sometimes seven days a week, not counting late Saturdays or Sunday afternoons, arranged the five and ten notes with the faces pointing in one direction. I could see right through his spirit body, to all the parts of him I'd never seen before. His heart. It was a well-meaning heart, it never missed a beat, but it had a sheen about it, the gloss of hoarded coins, with none of the metal. How that heart believed the whole weight of the world could be right there, on the other side of the door, and all you had to do was store up your riches, one by one, on the other side. Pile them up, those riches, coins, dollars, a fine, new home. Anything to keep you safe against that world outside. That world of Depression, war, death. As long as you were saving, all the world could beg and moan and carry on as much as it pleased and you could stay inside. Inside your country or town or house or yourself. Safe.

I saw some of this, inside Carl Wallen, that day when I was twelve and standing upstairs in the Venice First National Bank. It took me more years to learn how that was what my own life was made of. The jingle of a pocket full of coins. Get you a job, son, a big, fine car, a house on Main Street.

Then, later, her, Ruth Blue. Save your soul, Earl Wallen. Lay up your treasures in heaven. Her up at her Daddy's Holy Roller church house. Glory be to Jesus, sweet Jesus, she'll say, kneeling down, her thin hands beating the tile floor, all of what you'd expect. Only there's her face. She looks scared, like if she'd admit it, the only thing she really thinks is one big what.

Or him. Rudy Hyatt. The man I set out to save from the past, from the long, black road to facelessness.

~

Where I knew Rudy Hyatt was 1941, Pearl Harbor, where the green ocean stretched on and on. Where palm fronds rustled like pompons at homecoming games and cheerleaders said, hey you, what'll we do, win, win. Rudy had the strongest hands I've ever seen. Big, with a grip you'd remember when he'd walk up and take hold and say, me, I'm Rudy from Inez, Inez, Kentucky. Before long you knew some of his best memories, the last home football game or his final touchdown, or the surest plan in his head, the day he'd go back and take over behind the counter at his daddy's General Store. Just like me, in a lot of ways, except I dreamed of more, of the most expensive Fender I could buy, of songs, the song I'd write to change the world.

Once Rudy Hyatt showed me a photo he'd had taken in Honolulu, himself and some Chinese woman. She was wearing a silk night gown and he said she had feet so small one of them would fit into the palm of his hand. Rudy was from some podunk Kentucky town called Inez. We'd become pals, Rudy and me. What I remembered later was how he had big hands, the hands of a hometown football star.

At Pearl Harbor, a hometown was far and away for both of us, even if with my eyes closed I could still taste it like fresh morning coffee. What there really was at Pearl Harbor was nothing, rows and rows of barracks and a battleship, The Oklahoma, floating off shore like it weighed nothing to count.

Pearl Harbor was an easy enough place to be, after all, if you didn't mind ninety degree heat in winter time and the whine of mosquitoes in your ears at night. We got weekends off like anybody would, had to man the radars one night and check in a few times the rest of the time. Sundays were better than most. We'd get up a poker game, smoke a few cigars, compare Esquire pin-up girls.

That particular December morning, Rudy Hyatt and I had been assigned radar duty the night before at Knaeohe Air Station. We were just training, and I barely knew the difference between a cathode-ray and a heading flash, not to mention an eleventh hour warning. But the responsibility left me singing. On duty until two a.m. then down to the beach, a few whiskeys, a few hands of poker to see us through to daylight. Come morning, and we still couldn't sleep. We'd got into blackjack by that time. We kept slapping cards down like it was the last thing any of us would do.

That was when God hinted he was there, looking over my shoulder to see I didn't bet too much. Only I didn't know God was there by how you'd usually imagine, chill bumps on your arms or any chorus of angels humming hallelujah in your ears. I did hear God, but what I heard was beeps, pretty faint, but regular, like a heartbeat.

"Rudy," I said. "Did you hear that?"

"Hear what?" He laid a perfect twenty-one under my nose, raked in my last two dollars.

I shrugged and cut the cards again. No sleep since Saturday morning, what did I expect? God was back there in Venice, keeping the doorknobs shiny in my father's bank. I'd only just dealt us each one extra card and myself the one-eyed jack when I heard it again, a beep and beep, like radar up at the air station. For some reason, I didn't know why, I felt afraid.

"Rudy," I said. "Are you sure you don't hear anything?"

He hadn't, and how could I tell him what crazy things it was I was hearing? Instead I tipped back half of the last inch of whiskey, made him think it was me. Phoning would be a good joke to pull and they didn't necessarily have to know our names, and we were off duty, anyway.

"Sure, Earl," Rudy said. He just looked at me, his eyes red and blurry. "Whatever you say." He scooped his cards toward him, began to sort them in his big hands.

Of course, when I did call, I got some buddy of ours on the line. I could hear him half-yawn. "Son," he said, "straighten up and get some sleep. Hell, we haven't picked up the sound of anything noisier than a pigeon with a band around its leg for weeks. You boys take it easy."

I hung up and shook the last three drops of whiskey onto my tongue, all the while still hearing it, that beep and beep. I even closed my eyes and imagined flashes, little streaks of lightning crashing down into the black ocean, into the round eye of the radar. I shook my ears to stop the sound, as if they were logged with water.

"Rudy," I said. "Let's play something else for awhile. Anything."

I'll never forget us, two grown men, sitting in front of the open window, watching Sunday morning crash down on the air base. We played, all right. We played crazy eights, war, fifty-two card pickup. Rudy flipped the whole deck across the table at me and the cards sailed to the floor, kings, queens, deuces. We both felt it by then. Nervous, I mean, with no real reason. We were so restless Rudy and then me got up, poured mugs of strong, cold black coffee from the night before. We had nothing to say to each other.

The sun was getting higher by that time. I could already see red bands of it shining through the Venetian blinds on the other side of the room. I felt sweat trickling down my back and heard flies buzzing the bulb over the table.

"Shut it off," I told Rudy, for no particular reason, and he pulled the light chain and I pulled up the blinds.

We watched the sun rise. It came up white and hot about 7:00 A.M. I leaned on the window sill and watched the way light touched the sand the wind had blown across the sidewalk during the night. And then it was like we both heard it, the bleep and bleep of God I'd imagined became a humming that seemed to fill the whole sky.

Rudy called the station again and someone answered, not that same buddy of ours, just some voice, but he shoved the receiver toward me and it was good, almost, to hear fear said and coming from someone else. By then it was 7:55 and there was no turning back.

I may imagine what I remember, but I remember a sky full of shadows and that humming. I'd read in the paper how it was, some foreign city and tall buildings and the crash of them, the sound, the flash of light. From above you there's some bomber going up in flames, nose down to earth like a bird made of ash and fire and nothing. It was going to happen to us.

Rudy grabbed my shoulder. "Come on, we've got to get out of here."

I'd dropped the phone and could hear, faint as that bleep in my ears, a voice across the line. "What should I do? What should I do?"

I followed Rudy out through the slam of the screen door. We were already running. Downhill, 8:15 sharp and the day was asphalt hot, so bright I blinked, then stared straight up into the clear sky. No, that's not right. Not clear at all. I'll have to tell you the way. It was full of waves and waves of blue smoke, spirals and wings of it, and I thought of looking through the slats of the porch awning, way back in Venice, Ohio.

We ran down the wide avenue and I don't remember now when it was I stopped hearing Rudy coming behind me. He was tall, six foot seven at least, with a big belly. His breath came hard. I heard his boots slap and his dog tags rattle.

"Earl Wallen," he said. "Wait for me. Where do we go now?"

I didn't stop. I ran fast down the landing strip, then headed to one side, over hard-packed earth strewn with flower petals. There was still the humming, only now it filled everything up, my ears, the space between me and the gray shape of a barracks I saw in the distance. It was the strafers, then, that humming. They pelted bullets down around me and it was like heavy drops of rain. They bounced, whined. As I ran I imagined voices, dozens of them. They were cheering like it was the final season game back in Rudy's little town only it was me coming in for a touchdown. The only thing I touched was a door handle. I flung myself inside a room.

There was a seaman in a jacket and boxer shorts and a woman with short, bleached blonde hair. She was crouched on the floor near a table, her hands over her head. Her thin, bare legs were caught up in her arms. Then a blast of something huge shook the building and glass shattered back inside, thin slivers of it. The seaman knelt and pulled the woman inside his jacket. I could see how his hands shook. Myself, I huddled in the corner and looked out through the hole the window made, closed my eyes.

There were 2,400 men killed that day. Only instead of seeing Rudy Hyatt, legs kicked out at crazy angles, it was Venice I saw. It was like I drifted out into the morning air, not in my body, mind you, but in some other way, invisible, back to Venice. Back to Venice where I saw my father at three in the morning, slipping up the back stairs of the bank building, using the key he'd saved, opening the door of what had been his old office, before the Depression. I saw him sit at what had been his desk, open the drawers, straighten the envelopes, run his fingers, as if with love, along the columns of dollar signs in a bank ledger and, only when he imagined footsteps, raise his head, open his boy's eyes, and shiver. What did he know about living or dying?

~

I meant to tell you how it was I saw God. It could be that I don't intend anything very certain by that business of seeing something. Maybe I just mean how it took only 110 minutes for all that happened that day, 188 planes downed, eight battleships. Or maybe I do mean a particular minute, a sound, an almost sure sense that you can, sometimes, hear the way the blood goes and then waits, before coming back into your heart. We went on board the Oklahoma, the day after what everyone now calls Pearl Harbor. It had taken six torpedoes below the water line and could have capsized at any time. There were dozens of men we could have rescued, ones trapped in this or that hull below deck. There were SOS taps coming from all over, waterlogged fingers on doors, walls already submerged. It was that moment I'll call God, when I thought to myself, I'm alive.

I said it aloud, twice, my mouth tasting like metal. I tried to make myself see him, Rudy Hyatt, back in that place I'd looked at for the space of just two seconds, back between the barracks and along the airstrip. Rudy lying there, his dead body, face down.

RUTH: AUGUST 16, 1983

Even now, remembering that time of Earl Wallen, you dream of the mountain air, where it comes from, where it goes. Remembering that time is a song. One that goes, *I'm nothing but a memory on the road to the past, I'm nothing but a memory, but I swear it's going to last, you better believe, girl, you better hold on fast.*

One of Earl's old songs that falls through your dreams so you wake, mornings, the words in your mouth.

You dream of lovers, of love as it might have been. You dream of falling women, and how you have been one. Falling from places so high up you almost can't see their faces. One woman is your mother, who swings out and out over the pond at Mining Hollow, lets go of a rope just before it burns her hands, dives, all that finery, her feathers and tap skirts, streaming behind.

You dream other women. At first they have the faces of angels, then they become moths, and then candle flames.

~

Before you wake up, they are nothing but ash.

RUTH: 1948

When I was twenty-two, I lived on milk, coffee and bread so I could be light enough to fall. By night, I dreamed of exactly how I would fall, into love, into the wide open arms of some man whose face I could hardly see. I'd fall from the sky itself, my blood ripe and full, my woman's bones and breasts taking me faster and faster, right into the life of the man I dreamed would save me, make me. By night, when I was falling head over heels into what wasn't really there, that voice took me. *Ruth Blue*, it said, *you, listen good. You will dream the moon at the edge of a line of trees. You will dream the pond back of the house at Mining Hollow. You will dream beyond the pond, up the hill, far and far.*

By day, I wanted to be weightless as air, for the earth to not feel my weight at all. I wrapped my arms around my own shoulders, felt the brittle skeleton beneath my skin.

By day, Tobias kept his eye right on me, my comings and goings. Good morning this morning, fine morning this morning, he'd say by six. Ten o'clock was prayers and sleep. Now and again of a weekday morning I'd head into Inez with him. While he loafed at the barber shop, I'd head down the street with a list of what to do and when.

93

Buy meal and soda, half-sole shoes, be back to the front of the General Store, eleven-thirty, sharp. Still, I found time to imagine I was someone else, at the new Inez pharmacy.

I'd ask for a glass of water at the soda fountain, take long gulps from the cloudy, chipped glass, crunch the store-bought ice between my teeth and think of all the world not mine. I loved the play pretties in the display case, hair rinses and good-smelling soaps, earrings and rat-tail combs.

One day I asked to see a box of face powders, one with a satin cover and tiny scarlet rhinestones. In its mirror I touched the space between my front teeth, I combed my coarse hair with my fingers. Voices slid down the gray formica counter, right along with the grilled cheese sandwiches and ice cream parfaits. Throat tight, I swallowed back what they said. Strange, the voices said, old maid, strange old maid. What could I care, twenty-two and loveless?

I hid myself behind the dime novel rack, looked through a magazine. Movie star gala, it said. I swept my long hair from the back of my neck, pursed my lips, draped my other hand across my bony hip. I was a spectacle, knock-kneed and sway-backed, pretending I was a movie queen singing to the war troops, Rita Hayworth, Katherine Hepburn, my long hair henna red, my lips drawn to in a kissable pout. I'd have a room with a mirror set with glitter and moons and stars and be somebody else than the me behind a fly-specked pharmacy window, staring down the red dust road out of Inez. Tobias, you might have knowed, grabbed that magazine quick as you please. Led me past the soda fountain, its chromium chairs that swiveled, the swish of wide skirts and whispers of those Inez girls. There's Ruth Blue, they whispered and their nail polish gleamed.

Out front, Tobias fastened the roadster's rusty door and we headed back, spinning gravel, to Mining Hollow.

Ruth Blue, he said, in a voice so calm it was worse than anger, you be careful of what men might do. Why, you don't have the least notion. You'll be a fallen woman, mark my word. You and all those movie stars and those Inez girls and worse.

I imagined what falls, the crooked slash of red lipstick on a mouth, a petticoat strap slipped down an arm, a stocking with the elastic gone settling around an ankle. I imagined what it was men did do, them with their strong fingers, picking up a dropped handkerchief, hooking beneath a fallen stocking, beneath my chin, all the while saying you, Ruth Blue, you.

~

Come spring of 1948, they installed a not-so-new juke box at the Inez pharmacy that played recordings of Bing Crosby and Dinah Shore, forbidden dance songs I wished for. I'd heard there was a music hall called the Starland Skatarama where people skated by day and did who knows what by night, so Tobias warned me. I imagined skating over a slick wooden floor, faster and faster, the smoky air rushing in my face, skating toward a dark place of sin, skating so fast I couldn't stop. At home, at night, on our new secondhand radio, we listened to evangelists and hymns of gospel truth. *Sorrows like sea billows roll*, they sang, *it is well, it is well with my soul.*

That spring of 1948 I wasn't always exactly sure what truth it was the radio preachers were telling me, and I knew even less about the light. We'd gotten electricity a few years back at Mining Hollow, but we were saving, of scraps of soap, odd buttons, lengths of thread too short for a needle, of light itself. Daylight lasted later and later in March, then April, but there was dusk at seven o'clock, then two hours, no more, no less, of thin light from the bulb over the kitchen table.

At night I had chores. I collected slivers of soap in a tin can, added water, and heated them slowly over the cookstove to a paste that I used to scrub the collars of Tobias's shirts. I saved newspapers and lined our walls with them so when dusk came I watched faces disappear in the kitchen corners, movie stars, presidents, the eyes of famous killers. During our two hours of electric light, there were other chores. I polished shoes, scrubbed Tobias's false teeth and dropped them in a glass of clear spring water.

At dark, I lit candles and sat at the kitchen table beside Tobias. We listened to nighttime sermons, the radio voice of God—*have you opened the door, has he come in, will you thank him for coming*? At night the radio faded in and out and sounded scratchy as a wool jacket. Across the voice of God fell dance music, pianos and brassy love songs. The walls were full of shadows, messengers of God, half dark, half light. Late at night, when the radio was silent, I laid my palms together and piped songs between my thumbs. How long ago I'd seen angels dance.

Before good daylight one May morning, I woke and slipped down to the pond back of the house. The sky promised a clear day, just warm enough, so I stepped out of my dress and in my cotton slip waded up to my waist, poked my toe in the cold water. There were oftentimes late nights when I'd leave Tobias sleeping, tiptoe out, ease myself down into this black water, lay there, floating with the reflection of trees and the moon. But so seldom by the light of good day did I feel my own bare self, skin and sun and wind no longer bound to the earth, held up only by light and cool and water.

I waded farther, lay face down on the cold surface of the pond. I held my breath for as long as I could and counted prayers, *God is great, our father, now I lay me, star bright, amen*. I turned, lay facing the sun with my eyes shut. That was when a whistled song floated over the pond, and I put my feet down hard into the slicky bottom. I held my arms in front of me and looked to the right and left, but didn't see anything.

Then I saw sunlight flashing off the chromium hubcaps of someone's car and watched as a man walked out of the trees. He was whistling, no song I'd ever heard, but it made me imagine guitars and how it must sound when one of their steel strings snaps. I was ashamed of my cotton slip wet with pond water, like you could see past it to my white skin and even farther, inside to the place where my heart was.

He was a pale man through and through. Fancy white shoes that looked like spit and polish, hair white-blonde so that I thought I'd meet his eyes and they'd be pale, pink or rose, an albino's, but when I saw them they were blue, hazy blue, the same as looking straight up at the sun with my eyes squinted. He was tall and that made me think pale too, like he could turn sideways, disappear into the woods and I'd have dreamed ever seeing him. But the hand gripping the brim of his gray hat was not pale at all. I thought of hands that knew how to do things, though I had no idea what those things were.

Earl, he said, Earl Wallen, as if I might have expected him. His voice followed me as I hurried out of the water, snatched up my dress and headed for the house.

EARL: 1946–1948

The first time I went to Mining Hollow, it was a May morning, 1948. What I wanted was to challenge Tobias Blue to a poker game with the highest stakes he'd ever seen, that very Friday night. I drove up the head of that old man's hollow, past run-down shacks, yards nothing but a heap of coal dust, past a trailer with some man on a bed in an open door.

I pulled over and yelled out the window, "The Blues' house, you know Tobias Blue?"

Right then, a little girl wearing black stockings with a hole through to her skinned knee said, "It's the last house, you won't find nothing past there." She stuck her thumb in her mouth and stared at me as a I drove on by.

And I did seem to be driving into nothing. The road grew narrower, overgrown with weeds, heaved up with earth and rock from the winter past. I forded a shallow creek, steered along a wide stretch of red dirt, then couldn't see a sign of a road anywhere. I wondered if I'd come farther than the last house, then stepped out of the car, cupped my hands and yelled, you there, Tobias Blue, you up there somewhere? My voice echoed back from trees and boulders and a white sky, the clouds not lifted yet.

I parked near a thicket of trees, not another wide place for it, and then I sat still for a minute, hands on the steering wheel. I stared straight through the trees into a morning fog and I saw a house, a tin roof, a broken down porch railing. Up on that porch, I knocked. Once, again, until at a window, a curtain raised and then fell back in place.

The only path behind the house was overgrown with wild roses and honeysuckle vine and I took it. May, and already that sweet odor. I followed the scent, past thorns and rusted out tin cans, through a stand of trees. Then what I saw was a girl, floating on her back at the edge of the clear water of a pond. A little thing, jet black hair and pale skin, a girl so slight she was like a skeleton of a leaf, her cotton slip transparent with water. Small breasts showing through, full lips whispering. My first thought, go down there, Earl Wallen, catch hold of a cold, wet hand, an ankle, say, speak to me, speak to me out loud. But I stood still and watched her and whistled some song, "The Tennessee Waltz," I think it was.

She turned her head, saw me, and planted her feet on the pond bottom. "Who are you, mister? You got business up here or what?"

She held her arms across her chest and they weren't slight at all, but bones, thin muscles, elbows pointing.

"Earl Wallen, mam," I said, but before I could so much as tip my hat in her direction, she was out of the water, picked her dress up as she ran, just flying toward the other side of the pond.

Months later, Ruth Blue said I'd come upon her secret, hers and God's, that she was praying, little doses of worship tossed up at the sky. But later, as hard as I tried, I couldn't remember anything about it, those red lips moving. Instead I later remembered the white skin that made me feel so cold.

~

Before we get to it, the whys and hows and what-could've-beens that made Mining Hollow my forever as much as it was hers I have to tell you what made me want the world, after the war. The world, not Venice, Ohio, and me full of Sunday dinner ad litanies and sitting out on the front porch with my feet propped up, staring down the road. I could have stayed around Venice forever, running errands at my father's bank or toting bottles at the new soda pop factory. But after awhile, even working for the L & N loading coal wasn't what I wanted. Instead I sometimes jumped a car and rode down the tracks as far as I fancied. I'd lay there with my cheek pressed flat against the wooden bed, watch dark come up out of the woods, brace myself for the buck and jump as the cars took me right along with them. I'd wait around on whatever platform, act like I was a regular passenger, then jump the next one back to Venice. That still wasn't the world, so far away from Carl and Sylvie and Venice I'd never have to say hello or goodbye.

After the war. That was a time with an edge to it, full of ordinariness I still couldn't place, the sound of breaking glass or the scent of leaves burning. I'd headed back from World War II and ended up, without intending to, in my hometown, Venice, Ohio. There was nothing to do at first but sit outside the Kay Lee Diner, calling in order after order of hamburgers and soda pop and waiting for that particular waitress with a certain interested look in her eyes. I guess that's what Tobias Blue would call God, the Lord's will and things and places and people you can't seem to change. But I was set on change, right from the start.

I remember the first morning after I got home from the Pacific, from all those places they'd sent me to, how small everything in Venice seemed. I ate breakfast, neat triangles of buttered toast and tidy poached eggs, with my parents, Carl and Sylvie, and listened to them like I'd never left, or maybe like I'd never even been there.

"Carl," Sylvie asked. "You'd best set those bottles out. Milk delivery at noon."

She moved slowly around the dining room, gathering cups and plates. Something about her looked out of focus to me, even though she'd dressed up specially, so she said. She looked years older, but disguised, garishly young. She wore a polka-dot dress I'm positive she'd bought for my sixteenth birthday supper. Her mouth was a deep, purplish-red, from beet juice, she told me, to save money, and she'd done what some of the girls did those days, painted her legs and drawn a seam down the back. It was the make-up gave her that unfocused look, little red streaks beside her mouth, flecks on her teeth when she smiled, the stocking seams drawn in jagged lines that hadn't bothered to right themselves.

"Carl," she said again. "Carl?"

My father was already busy spreading sections of the out-of-town newspapers he subscribed to across the dining room table. Sylvie sighed. She'd sat up talking to me late the night before, after Carl was asleep. This was his new hobby, she'd said—newspaper clippings of unusual accidents. He subscribed to papers from Cleveland and Toledo and clipped stories. Man killed by thermos falling from tenth floor window, man killed in office by poisonous fumes from unknown source. He scanned a page, then looked up at us, his eyes blurred by his thick, drugstore eyeglasses.

"Yes? Yes?"

Neither of them asked me many questions about where it was I'd been in the last four years, and they asked each other even fewer questions. Sylvie had even given up reading travel magazines at breakfast and instead she studied each breakfast plate, front and back, before she loaded it on the tray for the kitchen. By nine-thirty I had to get out of there, you know how it is, both of them growing smaller and smaller before my eyes, their questions small and point-less and without much expectation of an answer on anyone's account. So I lit out the front door, to see Venice again.

Sure enough, not a block away and I could close my eyes and count every store along Main Street, dry goods, hardware, beauty parlor. I walked past the Venice First National Bank and felt almost as tall as the slate roof. By noon I'd walked the length and width of Venice, drunk five cups of five and dime lunch counter coffee, and nowhere, nowhere, could I find a place to draw a breath that filled me up. My lungs ached for air.

Before too many weeks passed, seems the only place I could breathe at all was Kay Lee's. I'd bought a nearly new Kaiser-Fraiser with some of my war pay, and I spent my Saturday nights circling the diner. Then I'd park and watch who pulled in, their windows rolled down and Doris Day or the Andrew Sisters blaring from the radio. I sat there as long as I pleased, head against the back seat and my feet propped up, breathing french-fried onions and cigarette smoke, thinking of how the ocean had blinded me, distances of it, gray blurring into white, into sound, into island after island. Here, there was only Saturday and 1:00 A.M. and some curb side waitress with her pink lipstick in cute points saying, honey, what'll it be, we're about to close. I soon knew all their names, Maxine, Betty. They each had a cologne, Roses, or Evening in Paris. They'd lean into my car window, say, where you going, after? And I'd say, how's about it? What did I have to lose? I could go home, sure. I could try to slip down the hall, past the front room, just to have Carl's voice follow me up stairs.

"Earl?" he'd say, voice scratchy with sleep. "That you, Earl?"

Then he'd stumble out into the hall and I'd try not to look at the hole in the toe of one of his socks, his loosened tie, his wrinkled business suit. Yes, Carl, I'd think, all right. And I'd follow him back in there, back to the couch where he'd been lying. It smelled sour in there, as sour as someone's sleeping breath, and the window blinds were open just enough to let in street light, broken little bits of it.

"Son," he'd say, in that confidential tone he used with customers at the First National Bank, where he was now a clerk. "I'm glad it's just you and me awake. So we can have us some man to man."

All right, I'd think, saying nothing. All right.

"Limits," he would say. He'd strike a match, light a slender cigar that smelled too sweet, like perfume. "A man has to realize what he can do and what he can't and how long and when to quit."

Empty words, all of them, but they'd twist in my gut, leave me feeling heavy and listless. He'd seem small to me then, shrunken and no account, and I'd suddenly feel embarrassed that his tie was loosened, his undershirt showing, that there were gray hairs on his chest. Limits, he'd say, but all I could think of was Main Street, dim and white under the street lamps, cars spinning gravel past the window, stray dogs slinking off into the shadowy light from head lamps and porches.

And there'd be stories, none of them mine, the mysterious accidents he'd read about that day, the past, what he'd once managed to do, a war he imagined, love. He told me that one again and again. A love story, him and Sylvie back then, way back then. Later, I'd leave him lying there again, hands tucked between his knees, face against the sofa cushions, lips pressing a wet kiss into the sofa. I'd slip past the kitchen where Sylvie was clinking ice into a glass, for gin, I knew, because there'd be less scent on her breath. In my room, I'd lie awake. I'd try to summon up thoughts of Betty down at the Kay Lee, hips to make you shiver. Then, sooner or later, I'd be more and more awake, imagine myself clerking at the bank, in Venice, forever, Carl's stories playing over and over in my head, like some song you hear once too often and want to forget.

Later, I'd go up to my room early and turn on the radio full volume. It was sound, music, that kept me alive. I had an old Fender and I picked notes to songs I liked. Johnny Mercer singing about smoke rings and memories, would drift down into the streets of Venice. Venice, hooked to other towns, towns whose names I didn't know, only by telephone lines.

When I slept I dreamed, not dreams of radios and fast cars that went anywhere you pleased. I dreamed of Rudy Hyatt. I seemed to hear sounds of him, a pen knife hissing down the window screens and letting him in, the rattle of his dog tags. Hey you, Earl Wallen, Rudy Hyatt would say, it's me. Those Venice nights I had dreams, dreams of Rudy Hyatt, a man I couldn't quite remember.

~

I left Venice one September morning in 1947. I wasn't headed for anywhere in particular, not for Inez, then. All I knew was I wanted music any way I could get it, live or radio or me, playing dance halls, headed south. I wanted hours of driving, forgetting, two-lanes, dirt roads, the next town, a town without limits.

And at first, leaving behind Venice and my parents, Carl and Sylvie Wallen, was simple as my guitar and one old leather suitcase. For three days before I took State Route 93, that suitcase was packed and ready. Socks and suspenders on top, beneath that my favorite tie, shirts, one pinstriped suit, and, in last, my Army fatigues, patched, durable, reminding me of just how well I could stay alive.

Then came the goodbyes. One float at Kay Lee's Diner, one last midnight rendezvouz with the waitress, Betty, during which I gave her a rhinestone initial pin, a kiss and a good enough explanation about how touch was no more than just that. If it hadn't been late September, brisk air, those would have been my goodbyes, over and done. But you never knew, Sylvie said, how cold a winter might get, or where you'd get caught out, sleeping in the car, fifty miles to the next town.

"A precaution, Earl," she'd say, and lay a flannel shirt, a scarf, gloves, on top of my open suitcase.

Carl's worries were also the nights I'd be stranded, and it was my car he filled. There was a bundle of cardboard tied up with twine, one piece to slide behind the radiator in sub-zero weather, the rest for who knows what. And there were newspaper articles he'd clipped to warn me—motorist dies when plugs up tailpipe, breathes car fumes. Motorist stranded in car three days after pitching keys from window and locking self in. And the both of them filled my pockets with souvenirs of Venice, snapshots, hair clippings, cancelled postage stamps, claiming the last thing I'd ever want to be was stranded without some memory or other.

As I walked down the steps from the house that September morning, the handle of the suitcase, which was bulging and barely fastened, bit into my palm. I looked over my shoulder at the two of them watching from the open front door. Sylvie was waving goodbye, a dainty handkerchief tucked into her sleeve, and Carl was adjusting his tie clasp. I slid into the front seat of my car and headed south, watched their faces in the rear view mirror and felt no grief at all when they were gone. How could they understand me, leaving Venice for a song? To them, unknown towns were a future as solid as an echo.

Leaving Venice, I found out right away, took some unburdening. Ten miles down the road, I popped the clasp on the suitcase, rolled down the car window. As I passed open fields, I let go of my socks, one by one. Watched a checked shirt suck out into the wind. In a thick grove of trees I tossed out a tie, one painted with a martini glass and a high heel, and after that there were other shirts, trousers, dress shoes Sylvie had polished the night before. I shredded snapshots and newspapers and scattered them, yelled after them out the window, you there, go, until my throat ached. I left myself a wide, empty seat, an almost empty leather suitcase with my dance shoes, my service-man uniform, a good change of clothes jacket. That gave me just enough, if I worked at it, to be a new man.

I little knew, at that moment of casting off the past, how much I'd really left behind. How a few months later, I'd have headed south through more nowhere towns than I'd ever dreamed of—Hanging Grove, Bartlettsburg, Pine Bluff. Towns vanishing into memory, leaving me the sound of cups sliding down a lunch counter, the taste of leftover coffee. How, in one of those little towns, with a name I never could recall afterwards, I received a letter. A brown paper wrapped package with address after address crossed through. Return to sender. Refused. Addressee unknown.

But they found me. A lawyer's office from Venice, Ohio, one rep-resenting the final remains of one Carl and one Sylvie Wallen. Carl, dead of an attack of the heart, not three weeks after I'd left Venice. And Sylvie, following him a month after that. The estate? Travel brochures. Greece, Sicily. A book called *Florence: See it in Springtime*. Gold plated cufflinks and a name tag saying, Carl Wallen, First National.

~

With all my past behind me, I drove through miles of flat land, corn-fields, horizons I never reached, my mouth fuzzy from too many cig-arettes, my fingers tapping time on the dashboard—Betty Hutton, The Ink Spots, Johnny Mercer. Inspiration, I wanted that.

The more I thought about inspiration, the more it just about seemed possible. Me, a rock-n-roll star, showing some little town what was what. Inspiration. Sweet juke box music and a room where pool balls cracked, sequined stockings and a lipsticked mouth that didn't know where to stop.

The tail end of 1947 went by, fall into winter, and me from one job to the next. I knocked on the doors of radio stations, played guitar when I could for anything from a high school dance to a firehouse picnic. Mostly, I shoveled gravel, laid brick, polished forks and knives at a second-rate hotel. Once I even spent a week at a farmhouse, between towns, moved a fellow's cookstove from the barn to the house, did odd jobs. I spent the nights in his extra room, listening to him and his bony little wife make love without a word. But most times it was the road that was quiet, my car windows rolled up tight against the chilly air of an early winter, the radio on full blast.

I drifted, heading always south, x-ing off miles and landmarks on the service station map I kept open on the dashboard. Flat land and pastures gave way to mountains and coal towns, Kentucky, tipples and mountains of coal. Where to now, big shot, I'd ask myself and pull off the road, shut my eyes, drowse to the sound of the windshield wipers, the engine's hum. Where to now, I'd whisper, and before I knew, it was Rudy Hyatt's voice right there in the car with me, asking, where to? And I'd keep my eyes shut, try to imagine him, recall my dreams, every careful little detail. As I kept south, he stayed in my memory, a man without a face.

~

It was Inez, as you know, where I lit down at last. Inez. Not a town I'd have chosen, but one that, as it turned out, chose me. Right away I should have known there was an emptiness about the place. It was January by then. January and five o'clock on a Friday afternoon and the streets seemed deserted.

Or should I say the one main street, a wide graveled one, lined with squat, ugly buildings, most of them cinder block and hardly a lit window anywhere. Yards were bare, with yellowed, wintery grass poking through a sidewalk or two. Not a soul out. The brightest light anywhere, far as I could tell, was from a radio tower. It sat on a long, low hill in the distance. Pale pink and lavender lights flashed—WINZ.

Luck, I guess you'd call it, that my engine stalled just as I passed a place called Pappy Imes's Gas and Go. I pressed the starter, again and again, then coasted the last few yards into the parking lot.

"Hello?" I said as I stepped out of my car. "You there."

I stepped on the trip wire for the service bell and it jangled. I looked hard at the front of the station where there was a drawn shade moving with the cold wind through cracks in the window. That wind picked up fast, set an empty can rolling past my feet, rippled the cloth gas and grill sign stretched across the parking lot. I stepped on the bell wire again, twice more, then made my way slowly around the building, cupping my hands and peering through the cobwebby windows.

"How's about it," I called, rapping on the glass. "You got gas? Peanuts? Or what?"

Then I heard music. Faint piano, sax, lyrics I knew: *dream, that's the thing to do, watch the smoke rings rise in the air, find your share of memories there.* Wind whistled down the street and the cloth sign snapped. I shrugged, fastened the top button on my jacket and raised my collar. Johnny Mercer made me feel lonely, that was all, lonely and chilled on a gravel road through nowhere.

I peered in a narrow window at a back door, saw a long bench, neatly arranged rows of tools, wrenches, sockets, clamps, all of them gleaming. And then I wasn't imagining it, that man, swaybacked and pot-bellied. He yanked open the door with a rattle, glared at me. His jaw was square, jutting, and his skin had that look of black oil so drunk in soap wouldn't touch it. He held a shiny screwdriver and a spotless white rag.

"Want something?" he asked. "We're closed. Don't we look closed?"

"I don't know what you look," I said and stepped closer, one foot inside the door. The room felt warm, smelled of oil and burning coal. "I figure you looked like you were selling gasoline, if you could."

"We're out. Out of gas, out of nabs," he said. "Out and done until tomorrow. Or the next. We're expecting a delivery. And I wouldn't go looking for another station, neither. Ain't one." He squinted at me, yawned, then turned and started to close the door.

It was easy to imagine this Pappy Imes in there alone evenings, the walls hung with tools, with the inky vats of used oil along the walls. Evening after evening, him arranging and rearranging grips and vises, counting and sorting screws and bolts, setting his stock in order for an empty little Kentucky town. And I could imagine me, lying in some motel room, smoking cigarettes, watching weak pink and lavender light. Radio and no one to dance with in a damp, cinder block room.

I inched forward one more step into the room. "Coffee, then? You sell coffee?"

"Boy, you just don't read, now do you?" He reached over, flipped a cardboard sign hanging on a piece of twine. Shut Down. He'd scrawled the words in pencil, in big sprawling letters.

Behind us, the wind scattered winter leaves and a thin, chilly rain had begun to fall. I was just beginning to think that Inez and night were settling so I'd end up with, at best, a cheap bed and a Jehovah Witness bible, or at worst, the back seat of my car, when Pappy squinted again, then snorted—what I took to be a laugh.

"Just no end to you, I reckon." He stepped back, motioned me into the room.

I cleared me off some room in a corner, near a table with a hot plate and a radio on it. There were stacks of auto magazines, stray electrical wires, and I had to find room for my feet in the middle of a pile of oil filters. Pappy poured me a cup of strong, black coffee and I warmed my hands.

"You're not from Inez. Cat drag you in?" he asked. He smiled, with one corner of his mouth and a raised eyebrow.

"I'm headed south, generally speaking. Looking to play a little music, when I can."

"That so? Where you from, anyway?" He sat down on the bench a few yards from me, reached into a low pan and pulled out a handful of bolts that had been soaking. He cleaned them one by one.

"Venice. Venice, Ohio. And then some." I said as I sipped the coffee, studied the walls. It was dim in there, smoky, like cigarettes and engine fumes, but I saw photos enough to make a preacher blush. Film stars, black lace slip straps on perfect shoulders, garter belts sliding up naked legs.

"It's that then some gets you, don't it?" He might have winked, though it was hard to tell with the hefty chunk of tobacco he'd crammed in his mouth. "I've been to then some, myself, though you wouldn't think it from the looks of this place." He spat into an empty milk bottle, studied it. "Went to France once, though that wasn't no picnic in a field of sunflowers, I'll tell you. The war."

"Went to the Pacific, myself," I said, draining my cup. I got to looking at the hot plate, the red glow of the coil wire.

"You could have fooled me. Son, you don't look that old. Mighty young, as a matter of fact. Reckon it's that fancy slicked back hair, or them shiny shoes. Guess the girls like that, say? Girls, I could tell you." He reached under the bench, pulled out a flask, army issue. "Well, if I'm going to tell you about women, we'd better have us a little drink."

He poured me two fingers of neat whiskey, watery enough stuff, but I sipped it slow, then took one long swallow as he told me tales of Parisian hotel rooms and French mouths he'd kissed. With tobacco streaks beside his mouth and his wisps of lank hair, I couldn't imagine him in the arms of any French Valerie or Martine, but three neat whiskeys later the oily scent of the room could have been cologne. The posters of movie stars made me imagine myself in some foreign city, in a cafe, sipping wine from a fancy glass, watching beautiful girls pick flowers off window sills. I imagined their soft breasts, loose shirts, their promises.

"Wouldn't have had no chance at all. Without the war." Pappy tipped his own cup, wiped his mouth across his sleeve. He looked over my shoulder, out to Inez at night.

"Chance?" I asked, even though I knew what he meant. I just wanted to hear it, how much he'd wanted and hadn't had, just like me, how he'd taken any chance he could get to see the world.

"Women. Now that wasn't the half of it, even if I wouldn't take anything for them. Me, stepping off some train in the middle of nowhere, coffee and bread where I could get it. Before I knew, a garter slipped in my front pocket, or a note. Soldier boy, come meet me. Soldier. That was the real truth of it. Son, you can tell me about that one. You and your war."

I did try to tell him, found words like sing and absolute and glory. None of them were the right ones. Sing was too much like the radio and lyrics you want to remember but can't quite, and absolute was more like final, when I'd meant complete, maybe that. And glory was, well, how the war had put me close, that close to God. But calling what I'd felt God and leaving it at that was a door closing, slamming, trapping something you wanted to touch but couldn't inside. Something like light.

But we knew what I meant by soldier, Pappy Imes and me. Light traveling on radar or down the long barrel of a gun. The sing a bullet makes traveling that light distance between you and him or him, the absolute look of confidence you've seen in another person's face changing to surprise, to something scared, but it isn't that, it isn't scared at all. Instead, if you looked, besides the sharp explosion of chest and blood and fear, you saw light, a quick minute of light, lifting off the face of a stranger, the enemy, someone you'd never see again or even think about, light rising to the sky and vanishing. Just like that. Then you'd strike a match, blow it out, make time for a cigarette. I downed some more of Pappy Imes's thin whiskey.

Pappy's droopy eyes were red and content. "Was that all?" he said. "I thought it was about being a hero. I was a hell of a hero. You and me both, I reckon."

The service station settled for the night, oil drums popping, thick silence. But not so quiet I didn't hear a voice. Was it Pappy's? Mine? Or was it Rudy Hyatt's? It was the war, that voice said. The war that made us men.

~

We didn't spend the night in Pappy Imes's Gas and Go. Instead, Pappy scooped out gunk, scrubbed his face and the rings of grime at the back of his neck. He laced a pink tie through his shirt collar, zipped up a scuffed World War I flight jacket. He laid his hand on my shoulder.

"Well, son, what about it? You want music. We've got music in Inez, all right."

Like old friends, we took to the streets to raise cane and promises. To each other of some chance that what it was we'd felt in the war was still out there, waiting to be found. Inez was a town I'd known for only a few hours, but I followed Pappy Imes as if I already knew the streets, the doorways, the women I'd ask. Want to dance? How about a drink for two?

We walked down the wide graveled road, past shadowed houses that weren't so quiet now. Glasses clinked. There was laughter, and everywhere, at my back, tingling at my ears, song words. *Watch the smoke rings rise in the air, find your share of memories.* I stumbled, my legs whiskey light, in and out of Pappy's shadow. We eased past houses, a pharmacy, dry goods, past back yards where bonfires burned, metal and old tires burning, faces in shadows, distant voices saying, honey, you don't mean a word, tell me the truth now. The town gave out, its outskirts trees and a dirt road I felt my way down. Pappy's face, white and grinning, appeared at spots of moonlight, and he raised his fists, pretending to box.

"Have us a fine time, son. A doozy."

I shadowboxed and followed until the shapes of buildings receded behind us and I could just see the steep hill rising above this town I didn't know. The radio tower flashed, WINZ.

"Pappy? You there?"

Then I was calling into brightness, sounds, scratchy phonograph music, high heels on a wood floor. A square block building stood in a clearing to one side of the road. A packed dirt parking lot was full of what got people there—old roadsters, a bicycle, even a horse and wagon. A large sign was just enough light to see by. Christmas lights were strung on wire twisted into the shape of a giant roller skate and into words—Starland Skatarama. Somebody was saying, hey, Pappy, you old fool.

Pappy mounted some wooden steps, called over his shoulder, "Make yourself to home, boy."

A red-head with elbow length gloves caught his hand, pulled him inside to a circle of dancers. Shag, turn, jive, they shouted, dancing the Big Apple. I stood where I was, looking up at the building, which was plain wood, unpainted. Streamers made of butcher's paper hung from the windows. A woman in a backless silver dress picked up one of these streamers, hung it around my neck.

"Come on inside, sugar," she said. "And just feel good." She smiled, her lips chapped, a streak of blood on her lower lip.

She handed me a paper bag. I took a swig from a bottle and it was moonshine, all right, clear and burning in my gut. I held on to her hand, running my fingers along callouses, as we went in. I caught glimpses of her legs, snagged stockings with glued on sequins and cut out stars.

At the door I dropped ten cents admission in a metal bucket and we wove our way through the crowd, past chicken feather boas, cracked patent leather shoes. The dance floor was a skating rink, wooden railing around three walls, scarred wood surface. My shoes slid along and I felt light, unsteady, held my breath against the scent of mothballs and sweat. We passed a tub full of ice and liquor, then a Wurlitzer in a far back corner.

"Got a nickel, honey?" The woman pressed her face close. She had a small moon, outlined in glitter, next to her right eye.

"You bet." I capped the bottle, tucked it under my arm, pulled a handful of coins from my trousers pockets. I emptied the coins into her open palms. "Pick a song," I said. "Anything at all."

While the records dropped, I crouched on my ankles in the corner, near the juke box. I sipped, blew warm air into my cupped hand. It was cold, colder than the afternoon. Women danced by, wearing lace-up boots and thick socks, their shoulders bare. A big bellied man in coveralls poked a fire and waves of coal-heat rose just as the music began.

"You want to dance?" The woman was behind me, her legs touching the back of my head. Cheap cologne, a sharp, warm scent.

"I'm Lolo. Lolo Lafferty," she said. She sipped from the bottle, laughed. "The Queen of the Starland Skatarama, you could say."

The room circled as I felt my way up, holding on to the wall. She slipped under my shoulder, keeping me steady, just as a blast of cold wind slammed open a window across the room. A light bulb on a long wire swayed, and the dancing began again, faster now, *flat foot floogee with a floy floy*, old music I didn't know, music on a record so scratched the sound was an echo, saxophone, drums I felt in my teeth. Hands waved and pretty legs kicked in time and in the middle of it all was Pappy Imes. His fat jaws were a drunk's red, and his belly shook as he clapped, sang, there's a place in France where the naked ladies dance. He caught sight of me, waved, raised his hand to his forehead. He saluted, then took a deep bow.

"Might as well dance, soldier," he shouted. "Why the hell not?"

The woman named Lolo draped her arms around my shoulder, pulled me along in a two step. "He's a regular war hero, ain't he?" she said in my ear. "They put up a banner for him, ever decoration day."

I closed my eyes, leaned into her, into the music. Until wind slammed through again and again the light bulb swung, then swung hard once against the ceiling, with a shatter of thin glass. Glass sprinkled down on us and I felt Lolo press against me, her shoeless, stockinged feet rubbing the insides of my calves.

"Hey, sweetheart," she said. "You're a war hero too, aren't you?" Strands of her red hair caught on my chin. "Now tell me everything."

The darkness reeled, full of the shadows of bodies shimmying. Hero. I remembered myself as one, that day. I remembered me, standing in a line of soldiers and the top dogs saluting us, one by one. A flag kicked overhead. Then as I stood there I seemed to see swarms of planes, and the shadows of wings. Earl Wallen, they had said, calling my name. Their faces were blank and distant.

"Hey, you there, sweetie." Lolo's hand was on small of my back and we were dancing. "You in there, or what?"

I touched her, ribs, rough skin, every little soft place I could find, looked down into her eyes. But there was no use in it, no use in something invisible. I pushed her away from me, pushed my way through breathing and them still dancing all around. You haven't paid for the liquor yet, she called after me, but I didn't stop. I knew the song words now, *watch the smoke rings rise in the air, find your share of memories.* I couldn't listen.

I fought my way for air, fought my way out. When that cold air came, I breathed it long and biting, then raised the moonshine. It ran down, tasteless, and my throat stung. Outside, the night was black, black as nothing, and who knew where the town was? Or if I made my way back, found it, Inez, so what? What would I find? Inez, with the black mountains reaching, reaching into mountains and flat lands, where I'd been, where I was going. Nowhere. Far ahead of me and up high I saw the radio tower, flashing pink and lavender light. Light so sweet I wanted, how I wanted, to taste it. But the black night shook and my hands shook as I tilted the bottle, hearing already that voice I knew too well, saying, welcome home, soldier boy. Welcome home, Earl Wallen.

Like it was a prayer, I whispered back. "Rudy Hyatt, is that you? Show me your face, you son of a bitch. Show it."

Like a prayer, I whispered over and over, and got no answer. It was like a prayer Ruth Blue could have heard, all the way to Mining Hollow.

~

I'd only been around Inez a few weeks and was still sleeping on a cot at Pappy Imes's Gas and Go, just till I figured out my next move, found work for however long. I hadn't asked Pappy or anyone else about Rudy Hyatt yet. I wanted to find out on my own who he'd been, study him in secret. Nights, I reviewed the map of Inez I already had in my head, the streets, the back alleys. Houses quit numbering themselves just beyond Main Street, but I knew every yard and porch swing. I'd memorized faces and at night I thought of noses and mouths and cheekbones, thinking, parent? Father? Sister? Which face was part of Rudy Hyatt's? I planned how often and when I'd introduce myself, get people to say, Earl Wallen is it, them saying my name in a voice like Rudy Hyatt's. Mornings I'd sweep up around the place while Pappy counted nickels and dimes from the candy and spark plugs he'd sold the afternoon before. About ten he'd say, Earl, I'm about ready for me a little fresh brewed, how's about it? And we'd head down Main Street, turning up our coat collars.

"Cold as a witch's tit," Pappy said. "Not too cold to cut loose." The sky was gray as an old handkerchief, threatening snow.

Inside the Main Street Diner, Cowboy Copas was on the radio with "The Tennessee Waltz." Lolo slammed two coffee mugs and a menu down on the counter and turned her back on us. Or turned her back on me, that is. After I'd gone just so far but not far enough, walked out on her, by necessity you'll recall, at the Starland Skatarama. I'd seen her on the street a few times since. She looked different by good daylight, no silver dress or stars, but polished Oxfords and her name embroidered on the pocket of her uniform.

She tightened the strings on her apron and scraped a dozen pieces of bacon onto a spatula at the grill. Hero my eye, I heard her mumble, nothing but a two bit guitar player and a jerk to boot. She served us coffee, a scalding stream of it that splashed drops onto my hand.

"Well, Pappy Imes," she said, not looking at me, "what have you done took up with?"

Pappy poured coffee into his saucer, sipped. "Nothing but another soldier boy, coming home. You know how it is." His boot prodded my ankle under the counter.

She did know about soldiers coming home, so Pappy had told me. Inez had sent dozens and dozens of men to the war after 1941, some of whom came back. Demobilized, they became junkmen or miners or too sick to leave their beds. It wasn't these men that Lola Lafferty was known to comfort. Instead she'd be seen leaving the Starland Skatarama with this or that soldier become traveling salesmen of cleaning agents or not-so-very-good insurance policies. She took long walks with them, bought them bootleg whiskey with her tip money. No one had exactly seen her disappear with them into the room she rented above the diner. This was a secret life of hers, as secret as she could keep it in Inez. Waitressing, she kept her hair done up in one of those mesh hairnets ladies wore. Not a hair wisped around her eyes or ears and I thought, there, that's her secret life for her—bright red hair, kept neat as a pin.

"Just what this town needs. Somebody with a crooked-neck guitar and a tin cup panhandling in front of the ten cent store."

Lolo wiped fast circles with a cleaning cloth. "What'll it be?"

We ordered the dime breakfast special, an egg, two bacons, toast, and while she fixed it I studied where I was. Pink and gold flecked tile and red checked tablecloths. Lolo had stuck a plastic daisy or two around. Mid-morning and we were the only customers, except for some old guy with a huge belly sitting by the stove near a table in the back corner. Pappy got up and went in that direction. They were discussing news—when it would rain, or had either of them seen so and so's boy, working up to the mines washing coal with only one hand, lost at the Battle of Selerno, or did they know who'd lost a blue tick hound, or another son, since the war, to a job up north? No one I'd met had mentioned a Hyatt, not even the name.

I watched Lolo work. Her hands were blunt-fingered, freckled. She broke eggs, dropped the shells onto an empty plate and crushed them with quick motions, then swept the fragments into a trash can, a neat and compact way of doing. Supposing I had gone home with her that night at the Skatarama, what then? She'd have kissed me, blunt and quick, and my shirt and trousers would have been neatly folded for me, the morning after, on the chair next to the door.

"Sunnyside up? This yours or his?" She set the plate down along with a bottle of tomato ketchup and I just so happened to look up. "Well," she said, in that tight voice that meant, eat it and get on.

I saw green eyes with these little tired shapes that were brown, eyes that made me wince. She held my look, brushed my sleeve with her fingers as she refilled my coffee. I imagined the room I hadn't gone to that night—one smelling of plate lunches and some salesman's cheap hair oil, an empty room, when I had enough empty places of my own to worry about for a good long while.

"Pappy," I said, looking over my shoulder at the two of them sitting. "Chow's ready."

Pappy and that pot-bellied man were sitting hunched over the floor as I walked back. Ten-thirty on a weekday morning and the dice were already shaking. They pinged as they struck the iron leg of the stove.

"Eleven," I heard the fat man say. He slapped his knee.

"Hell's bells," Pappy said. "Don't look like no nick to me. Can't you count?"

Maybe it was because I could still feel the sadness of Lolo looking, enough to make a shiver run down my neck, but my fingers itched for those dice. I could already feel the sevens and the points rolling out.

"Cut me in," I said, and settled on my ankles near them. The pot-bellied man had one eye and the place where the other one had been was a dark red slit. He tore off a plug of tobacco and held it in my direction.

I tucked a few shreds into my lip and we bet all around, ten cents, a quarter, and I covered everything, feeling down the length of my pocket into pennies and nickels from my one night music gigs. Tasting hickory smoke, I picked up the shaker, rolled. A pair of twos. I rolled again, seven, and lost my first spare change. Pappy did better, a pair of box cars and a match. The fat man hit a perfect eleven.

Ten o'clock went eleven fifteen and I heard Lolo tapping a fork on the edge of a plate, clearing her throat, then the scrape as she dumped our breakfast. The dice were bone and their slick feel pushed my hunger back.

Outside a light rain set in and by half past eleven there was a film of ice on the diner windows. The Inez streets were deserted, only a coal truck shifting hard, a far off train whistle. There were a few lunch customers, some skinny woman in men's khaki pants leading a kid wearing a man's overcoat and some house slippers. He watched us shoot for points and naturals until his mother called him, you'd better get yourself over here. They left with a blast of cold air. The one-handed soldier boy from the Battle of Selerno came in and took a stool at the counter, back to us. Mine's shut down early, real bad ice storm coming, he announced to nobody. Between shots I watched him thread his metal hook through a coffee handle, the spill and how Lolo mopped up after him, more gently than I'd have thought.

Fine ice kept falling and the diner windows were thick with it, Main Street through glass and whitish light, the woman and the kid blurred shapes that disappeared around the corner. We switched to three dice, betting pennies on eighteens, and the one-handed boy moved down nearer the stove, still not speaking, back to us, facing the blank window. His metal hook traced shapes on the frosted over glass, buckets, houses, a long, narrow knife. The ice mixed with snow, a whisper on glass that silenced everything but the toss of dice, tobacco streams into a tin, one of us saying, nineteen ain't eighteen, boys, you know that. Match after match, we filled the air with cigarette smoke, with wood smoke from the open stove door, nothing doing in Inez beyond this place and its diner air, smoke and stale food. The radio had snapped dead, Cowboy Copas and Peggy Lee frozen in mid-air. We gambled and time passed.

Lolo, filling our coffee cups, said, "So, boys. How about giving the rest of us a chance?"

The one-handed soldier stood, hooked his jacket zipper and headed out into the ice storm. The diner was deserted. Lolo kept standing, hand on her hip, coffee pot spout down. Ladies I knew didn't gamble, or if they did, it was like my mother, Sylvie Wallen, back in Venice, a careful spread of hearts in one hand and half a cucumber sandwich on a china plate, over tea. Women gambling meant gin and mints on their breath or midnight rendezvous. Us cutting her in would be a little like the Starland Skatarama, I reckoned, and Lolo on a Saturday night secret date. The fat man winked his one good eye and held the dice cup out in her direction.

She took it. "Nobody fool enough to come out in this anyway." She went to the door, flipped a sign to closed. "We can do some serious thinking then."

Just before she slid the chain in the lock, the door rattled and a man stepped in. I ought to be able to tell you about it, that first glimpse I had of Tobias Blue. Telling would be easier if he'd had a gold tooth or a cloth patch or a toothpick in the corner of his mouth, anything a tad bit remarkable to make me think, well now, that's someone to change the course of events. He had thin arms, a plain black suit jacket with the arms too long. Looked like he used to be taller.

"One o'clock and I know you ain't closed up yet." He brushed flecks of ice from his shoulders. His voice was deep, slow, with a kind of whine to it.

"All right already. Hold your horses, mister. Well, if it isn't Tobias Blue, excuse me, the reverend himself." She shut the door behind him and kind of bowed, her bony white legs dropping into a curtsey.

He didn't look at her twice, or at any of us. Just came on in, set his hat down carefully on the counter. It was a broken in hat, what had been a good one once, the kind my father would have worn in his Venice banking days.

"Mister Blue, like usual," Lolo said. She went behind the counter, dice cup still in her hand, held a match to a hot plate. "All we got's leftovers." The coffee pot rattled down. "You want just coffee, or what?"

Tobias folded his hands, nodded, a yes or no or an I don't care. He drank what he got, coffee Lolo warmed just long enough. I'll swear he was the first person I'd seen who drank like it was communion, blew on his coffee, held it in his mouth, swallowed slowly. There was no pleasure in it, that's the truth.

"Lolo," I said. "We cut you in so what about it?"

She stuck the dice cup in her big front pocket and marched back over, unpinning her hair as she went. Red hair tumbled out in loose waves. We rolled again, the four of us, and Lolo shot pretty well, not eighteens mostly, but right well, closer than we could get. Shit, Pappy mumbled. He wiped his hands on his coveralls, loosened his suspenders. My own hands sweated as I felt the nickels and pennies in my pocket dwindle. Lolo's blunt hands grabbed the cup her every turn, tossed. She stared me down as she raked in spare change. Sucker, she was saying, see what you missed that night with me? Luck, that's what. I wondered how much she made those traveling salesmen forget the war when they were just plain took.

The ice storm set in and we were down to some real gambling. We were so serious what Tobias Blue said passed me by, between my turn and Pappy's. He said it twice. "Casting lots against their brethren, while God's house waits, with the wages of sin." He drained his cup, but didn't look our way.

Lolo kind of laughed as she said, "Mister Blue, another refill?" Pappy opened his pocket knife and scraped down his coveralls leg, rolled lint between his forefingers. "Come on, Tobias, what's the harm in a little sporting?"

I, for one, wasn't thinking about God, that's a fact. I was thinking of what craps had just won or lost me, that fifty cents I'd made in a country music joint forty miles north, a quarter I'd found on the street, my kind of empty pockets. Sin, the man said? He kept drinking his coffee.

"Out with it, Blue," Pappy said. "We know you're antsy as the rest of us. Get on over here." He held out the dice cup, shook it.

I had to look twice when Tobias Blue, hat under his arm, did a half turn on his stool, scratched his cheek. "Even they cast lots, in the days before the son of man," he said. He winked and we made him a place.

We were gambling and I couldn't quit that afternoon in a land of sin and ice, and it was plain Tobias Blue played to win, win what I didn't know at first. He picked up a dime and bit it, said, well sir, then cleaned up. He rolled sevens and elevens almost every time and his shiny suited arms raked in the last of my guitar coins, Lolo's tip money, spark plug nickels, even one oily dollar bill from the fat man who soon rubbed his one good eye and said, nap time, boys, I'd better get on home. Even Lolo threw it in, put her waitress apron back on as new penny after penny slipped into Tobias' jacket pocket.

Past lunch time and the storm stilled to a washed-out sun. Shapes melted and froze again on the iced windows. Lolo put back on her apron, turned the closed sign and before long a customer or two drifted in, stamping their wet feet. Slabs of bacon sizzled.

"Come on, son," Pappy said. "We'd best get on back to work." He buttoned his coat, waited for me at the door a minute, but I stayed on.

Don't get me wrong. It wasn't his prayers I wanted, some old bag of bones in a hand-me-down suit, a hole in the road preacher. I could smell the whiskey through his pores. And it wasn't his brand of God I wanted, no sir, I'd had my share of what I'll call God, took it when it came to me. Why I stayed and lost everything I had to Tobias Blue was sound.

I'd never seen a man play to win like Tobias Blue did. He played and won, but for every toss he asked forgiveness, his and mine. He scooped the dice into his big-knuckled hand and blessed them before he threw. After the storm diners clattered plates and knives, but I could hear how he'd pray, a little whispered thing, right before the dice flew out, a long clean slide against the wall, sevens and elevens and sevens. They cast lots, he'd say, wiping his hands on a handkerchief, making them clean. Even the host, them that were instructed in the songs of the Lord, they cast lots. I lost my leather belt, then a pin-up of Rita Hayworth from my wallet, even a tooth made of abalone from a girl I'd met in the Pacific. There wasn't much left for me to lose, except what mattered most, my Kaiser-Fraiser, my guitar.

The next time I threw a twelve, I handed over a rat-tail comb. Tobias turned it end to end in his leathery looking hands, ropy veined hands with cracked, stained nails. "Mighty poor wages, I'll say. This all you got, son?"

All but key rings and guitar picks, but I kept on playing. That was when what I began to lose was sound. The more I tossed, the more the dice were a sound, some other sound I wanted to be quiet for, listen to. Burger's up, Lolo called from the grill and shovels screeched on the sidewalk outside, breaking ice. Hush, I wanted to say. Let me listen.

"They're yours, son," Tobias said, handing me the shaker. He crouched on his ankles, took out a pocket watch, spat on the cover, polished up and down his sleeve. "You going to take all day?"

I was losing but I was trying to remember sounds that were so far away I could hardly remember them at all. The dice whispered in their cup and I remembered ocean, war time, the slap of cards. Rudy Hyatt's dog tags rattling, his big feet slapping as he ran. Ran where?

Tobias paused and looked at me before his shot. I stared into mean eyes that looked like dull black glass. "You got troubles, son? What's your name anyway?"

"Earl Wallen," I said and shook the dice cup again. This time I heard dog tags rattle and I saw Rudy running, ahead of me, never looking back. Three in a row I rolled the dice, a point and no match, a point and no match, a point and no match. "What's it to you?"

"I know troubles when I see them and that's a fact. You pray, boy?" He slipped a tiny Bible out of his left pocket, a bedside motel model. He licked his index finger, riffled through the pages.

"Not unless I need to," I said, still wanting to say, hush, let me hear. The memory sounds were quieter, sand shifting, humming too far off.

"Do you good to call upon the Lord," he said. He held the dice in one hand, the Bible in the other, opened pages out.

"Look," I said, "I didn't ask for any sermon. Just craps. All right?"

My palms itched for the dice, but I grabbed his Bible anyway, squinted at it, anything to make him hush. I read the first words my eyes lit on—and fire came down from God out of heaven, and devoured them.

I don't know how to tell you how it was. How as I read word by word, fire and devouring, the sounds vanished, the sounds of Rudy Hyatt and a day I needed to remember so bad I could taste it, a taste of sulfur. Vanished. No, the sounds burst into flame, one by one, like words and ink and paper catching fire, falling in and in, into blue and ash and nothing, until there was nothing left of sound. Nothing but the hiss sun could make on damp asphalt. Come on, Earl Wallen, I told myself, bit the inside of my lip hard enough to taste blood. Come and wake up and smell the roses. You've been had, that's it, some boozing preacher taking you for all you're worth. What's this foolishness about sound? I had been had, the last shot, the end of the game, my last two cents in his pocket, not mine.

"What are you after, son? Something, that's for sure." Tobias was putting his hat on. He set the dice cup down beside the stove, scratched and stretched, then came beside my chair. He picked up the Bible when he leaned over near me. "God hears what you don't."

"Maybe I'll have to ask him for a few pointers for the next game," I said, but I felt purely cleaned out. He adjusted his hat, checked his pocket watch. I watched him go, out into the brittle, already melting ice of Inez, and I counted my losses. Empty pockets, thin wallet, and sound, a sound somehow so distant it was just the echo of a shout. He walked fast, for an old man, in the direction of what I later learned was Mining Hollow.

"Come on, Earl, you haven't lost your best friend," Lolo said. She laid down a plate with a two pickles and a burnt grill cheese. "It's just a game. What did you expect?"

~

The days after that I didn't waste time, I asked questions. Who was Rudy Hyatt? What did he look like? Tell me a story about him, I asked, any story at all. I talked to the owner of the Inez Pharmacy, to messenger boys at the grocer's, to people in the street. He was well off as a child, they said, had everything given to him on a silver platter, gourmet food right off the shelves of the general store, that is until that accident with his father. Fancy dreams about all those foreign places. What kind of food, I asked. Oh, things in cans, expensive things, don't eat them myself. Accident, what was that? Some story, I don't know, something with a boat or was it a swinging bridge?

Dreams? To be a soldier. Countries? I couldn't tell you, Paris maybe, I'm just a common person and I don't keep up with foreign countries much and it hurt me to read the papers during the war, you know how it is, even the radio, you never knew what they'd tell you next. What did he look like? Let me see, blonde hair, big boy, always was, but his face, well, I'm not too sure, how do you expect a person to remember something like the color of somebody's eyes? Mother took it awful hard, I know that much, funeral was a big to-do, considering the number of them since then, what with Inez sending one hundred twenty-three of our boys over there, a town this size, you tell me.

"Rudy Hyatt?" Lolo said when I asked. She frowned. "Not somebody I had much truck with. Used to live the road over from the Pharmacy. But his mother's funny turned. You won't find a sign of him there, I double guarantee it."

Funny turned, a tiny woman with a nose like a bird's beak, hair tinted Easter blue, little bird legs, a plump stomach in a too-tight skirt. I spent some time on the her front porch, hands in my pockets, staring at the maroon curtain across the glass door, heavy glass with a beveled edge. Maybe I'd never have knocked at all if she hadn't pulled the curtain back a few inches.

"I already have someone to mow, thanks." Her voice was muffled by glass. She waved her hands, no.

"It's about your son," I said, then repeated myself in a louder a voice. "Your son, Rudy."

The maroon curtain fell back, covering the space through which I'd seen her, and I stood waiting a long time, until the door eased open, with a sound like bells pealing.

"It's an automatic device," she said, smoothing her apron, a white one, with small lilac dots. "My late husband ordered it in, all the way from Huntington, when we were first married."

She still stood in the doorway, the house dark behind her, smelling of bread and maybe it was roast beef. "What is it you've come about? Do I know you?"

"No, mam. I'm Earl Wallen, just come to town. It's your son I'm here about. I knew Rudy pretty well and I thought we could talk for a spell, if you're up for it."

She smoothed the apron again, and her thin, blonde hair, over patches of light pink skin. Closer up she looked like a Kewpie doll, rouge and powder and long eyelashes. "I've got an engagement at three, and I'm not quite fixed up for it yet, but I suppose, just a for a little while. I suppose it wouldn't hurt."

We went down a long, maroon hallway, over soft rugs and embroidered cloths on tables, past a shelf with dogs on it, toys with white and lavender hair and glass eyes. I stepped on another bell, a cord across an entryway into the sitting room. There were shades of purple in there too, a braided rug, a scarf on a wine-colored horsehair sofa, a needlepoint picture that said, dear God, bless this home. "Sit down," she said. "I guess you should." She stood near a wing-backed chair, straightened some arm rest covers. "Well? What did you want to tell me about?"

I sat back on sofa, traced lines along the scratchy fabric. "I don't know what Rudy wrote you, mam, or if he did. I don't expect he'd have written you about everyone he met. But him and me served together for awhile. At Pearl Harbor."

"No," she said. "I don't guess I recall a Wallen. Earl Wallen, that was your name, wasn't it? His letters were about his duties, his assignments. My son was a very important man, you know."

"Yes, Mrs. Hyatt, I do know, about those duties, I mean. I could tell you a little about it, if you'd care for me to, radar and decoding and ..."

"I don't think that will be necessary, Mr. Wallen. My son was a very important man, a Navy man, and I don't think he would have liked us to discuss what it was he did. It was, well, it was confidential, you might say. His letters told me so." She was still standing by the wing-backed chair. She straightened the arm covers again, patted a cushion.

"About those letters, Mrs. Hyatt. Maybe that's a place to start. It's just that I've got these questions, or notions you could call them. About your son."

"Notions?" Her hand paused mid-pat.

"Memories would be a better word. At night, it's memories, or sounds, or something like that. Your son. If you could tell me one thing, just one thing about your son."

"What could I possibly tell you?" She was closer to me, in front of a coffee table. There were lots of things sitting, a paperweight with snow, a feather fan, a jar colored stone. She began rearranging.

"His voice, what was it like? Is there a picture you could show me? Or one of those letters you could maybe read to me?"

"I don't know how to tell you this, Mr. Wallen," she said, bending close to me, across the coffee table. The pink skin looked fragile, lined, and her eyes were frightened, a bird's. "But I don't keep memorabilia. My son was a very important man, a good man. What else is there? What else but trouble?"

"If you could just tell me," I started to say, but the house was suddenly filled with bells, a clock chiming on the far wall, the bell at front door as it must have opened, a light voice calling, Gertrude, that you back there, I'm here early, her ladies' engagement.

"Mr. Wallen," she said, "Earl, wasn't it? You'll really have to excuse me, I'm sure you'll understand. Some other time?"

Down the maroon hall, the phrase echoed, a good man. There was no doubt about it. She was right. A good man, but unseen.

~

I didn't let it go. That night, late, I snuck back to her street, knelt behind a forsythia in her yard. I don't know why I went, with what provocation, what voice woke me on my cot at Pappy Imes's, a voice that said, Earl Wallen, go look.

What I saw was a light in an upstairs window, pink light behind sheer curtains, then a light in lower room, then a light on the rear porch. She was dressed in a furry bathrobe, slippers, brush curlers in her hair. She scurried, her arms laden with a large box, a shoe box, a hatbox, something with a lid she unfastened and set gently on the ground by her feet. One by one, she laid the contents in metal trash can, what looked like letters, newspapers, other paper bits of this and that I couldn't see. Then she fumbled with something, a lighter maybe, something from her bathrobe pocket. Smoke rose into the cold air. She warmed herself by the small flame, for a long time.

Later, after she was back inside and the last light, upstairs, was dark, I walked over and sorted through what was left. Ashes, mostly. But here and there were corners of photographs, small charred squares and strips. I held an ear, an eye, in my palm. There wasn't much, not nearly enough to tell if what I held were fragments of a big, blonde man, a good man. And later still, as I walked back to the Gas and Go, it just so happened that I looked east, in the direction of what I soon learned was Mining Hollow. When I looked in that direction, what I remembered of Rudy Hyatt was as soundless and white as ice.

RUTH: 1948

Draw a card for Jesus, Tobias called it, the next times I saw Earl
Wallen. Friday and Saturday nights the two of them played poker at
Mining Hollow. Tobias had met Earl at the diner in Inez and what he
wanted was two things—service-man drinking money, or to win
back what he was sure Earl Wallen had lost a long time ago, his soul
in the heart of God.

Those evenings they gambled for who got the higher stakes.
Money, of course. And radio time, too, when they took turns jumping up from the supper I fixed to change stations. In the middle of
Earl's favorite, "Little White Lies," Tobias tuned in to a broadcast of
baptizings at the Lick Fork Missionary Baptist Church. As I washed
the supper dishes and sliced bologna for sandwiches for the next day,
I listened to voices rise and fall, sultry ballads, eternal hell and fire,
The King of Swoon, the King of Heaven. In between their battling
the airwaves, they played cards, rook or hearts or poker, with the
winner to get the last song, the last prayer before the radio signal
died down to a static after the National Anthem.

I fetched them coffee, apple brandy, whiskey, and their quarreling
got louder, a glass crashed against the wall, cards slapped down on

the table, became voices I couldn't tell apart, full house, flush, the power of almighty God, the glory to be of rock-n-roll. They hardly noticed when I slipped off to bed. To them I was nothing, the slightest sound, careful footsteps, the closing of a door.

One evening while they were at their cards, I was out on the porch, washing my hair in the dark. I was leaning over the wash pan on the railing, combing, feeling my hair fall strand by strand into warmed rainwater. Then there were light footsteps behind me, tiptoed footsteps, I later thought, and a finger tracing down the back of my neck, down my towel-covered shoulders. You're as pretty as, Earl Wallen whispered, but I didn't give him a chance to finish. I turned, towel edges held together at my throat, and the pan fell, rainwater splashing between me and him, down my skirt and on my bare feet, on the long legs of his trousers. That'll fix me right up for laundry for a week, he said, laughing, and pulled out a handkerchief, held it in my direction. It fell, a square of white he'd touched, as I ran, through the slammed screen door, past Tobias shuffling the deck of cards and saying, Ruth where you off to, tell me, what? All the time I ran I heard him, Earl Wallen, still laughing, and felt my wet skirt cling to my legs.

As I tried to sleep that night, I pressed the pillow against my ears and listened to them out there, shouting and spinning the radio dial. I told myself neither of them knew anything about God or songs or me. I shut my eyes and listened hard for the voice at night. *Ruth*, it said, *come here, come down.* It was a voice as rich as moth's wings. But as I fell, softly and softly, into sleep, into this song-full voice, I heard that other voice, Earl Wallen's, saying, pretty as. I touched the wet ends of my hair. Pretty as what?

~

That night, I dreamed of myself scrubbing the walls of my daddy's house at Mining Hollow, but they stayed gray with coal and soot. I washed shirt collars again and again, but my knuckles only bled with what would not come clean. *The residue of wickedness*, a voice said. Tobias's lips spat brown tobacco into an empty jar beside the bed. *What names will you see in the book of life*, the voice said. *What face, true as a photograph?*

And then the dream was of falling, head over heels. It was a well, or a long stairway, or the front porch steps. In this dream I couldn't see my face. My thrift store skirts billowed and wrapped themselves over my head as I pitched forward, then forward again, with no rail to grab hold of, no helping hands. But even with my skirts covering my head like someone about to be hung, even with the cloth over my eyes, in my mouth, muffling what I heard, I knew where I was. Mining Hollow, always Mining Hollow.

A dream of Mining Hollow, completely dark, no sound. The only light anywhere was fireflies, but not flying up, light and full of light. They were shells, husks, hundreds and hundreds of them littering the ground. The air had the smell of insects trapped inside glass jars, come the first humid, heavy air of a summer night.

Voices crossed and recrossed this air I was in and all of them told me what it was I should do to stop falling. *Up and back*, the voices said. *Start, stop, stay still, completely still.*

Because I was dreaming, I kept moving, falling, head over heels. At the bottom of the steps was Earl Wallen and he was pale, as pale as the day I first saw him, pale as the sheen of a knife blade.

I fell toward him, arms opening and opening. Ruth Blue, he said. Silk ribbon songs slid past my ears. Nighttime gospel and the holy word of my father's radio. Earl Wallen and a song with a bite like moonshine. When I stopped falling, Earl uncovered my face and I took a long, burning drink.

EARL: 1948

I stayed on in Inez. It was never like I planned to call Inez home, one more podunk town not that different from the one I'd grown up in. I got used to it, that's it, the particular smell of Inez sulfur water, snow on the edges of the streets, mounds of snow scattered with coal dust. Next Friday, I told myself, penciling in map routes I'd take southeast to Hatteras and soft shell crabs, or southwest to Knoxville, then Nashville, and some gig in a cowboy bar. At night, in the back room at Pappy Imes's, I composed the lyrics I'd use—*one locked suitcase and a Fender guitar, red dirt road, you're like a lover, no way you'll have me back*. But three weeks and four passed and I stayed, trying to put by for a rainy day, so I told myself. Spring wasn't far off and Lolo Lafferty always had my black coffee waiting at the diner, with a spoonful of dark cane syrup and a red lipsticked kiss on a paper napkin, for sweetener.

I wasn't the only one to stay put for awhile. Across America, people were spending their evenings listening to the radio, not to the theaters of war, now, but to soaps with stars like Stella Dallas and her daughter Lolly-Baby. On "Stop the Music," Mr. and Mrs. Hubert of Philadelphia won $35,000 worth of free gifts, everything from five years free hairdressing to a free Paris vacation. Anything seemed possible, that sons might be missing in action, not dead, that hands could grow back, that four war years could be unremembered with a spin of a radio dial.

Pappy Imes kept putting me up, most of that winter. He was sort of pleased to have an ex-soldier to swap stories with and so he nickeled and dimed me for odd jobs. I was no mechanic, but I made as much as I could of my career as a wartime radio operator. I even rewired a battery operated valve set he'd had when he was a boy. We listened to Czechoslovakian accordion music, the "Voice of America," and to the Washington, DC, trial of Axis Sally, the "Vision of Invasion" soap opera star who'd scared the troops to death before D-Day.

It wasn't until the middle of February that I began to see the natural signs of a man needing his own time of day. At first there were just hints here and there, say, a customer's oil filter on too tight, me doing my damndest, and Pappy over my shoulder the whole time pointing out which way the threads ran. Then it got to where he took a magic marker and outlined the shapes of all the screwdrivers and sockets on a peg board in the shop. I'd see him eyeing the empty spaces before I'd even had a chance. He finally took to heading to his room before nine in the evenings. The Betty Grable calendar would disappear from the shop wall and behind Pappy's shut door I'd hear whiskey and ice and Glenn Miller's trumpet sliding a mean octave higher. I figured it was time I found my own place if I was going to stay in Inez.

Must have been gambler's luck that brought me the room I got— a large walk-in closet, free for odd jobs, right in the Inez radio station, WINZ. I set my suitcase, open, against one wall and my guitar case against the other. No windows, but I did have a sink with the rear view mirror from a 1935 Dodge Six bolted above it, plus the bottom half of a kid's bunk bed. The top half of the bed was loaded down with tubes, transmitter wires and hack-sawed parts of an old antenna. Nights, I smoked cigarettes and imagined smoke rings were radio waves rising through the bed, through concrete, radiating beyond the mountains that surrounded Inez.

Odd jobs meant fetch and carry and fix, and I called on all I knew from my wartime days, and then some. One of my first jobs meant repairing the neon letters on the radio antenna on the outskirts of Inez. That night, late February, the temperatures had dropped sharply again, and I stood at the base of the low hill, warming my bare hands in my pockets. Wooden steps led up the hillside, and on from there, metal rungs stretched past Z and then N and then I and then to the slants of lavender that were the burnt out W. At the top of the stairs I unlocked a metal box, flipped a switch, and the tower went black with a sizzle of light.

I rolled a cigarette, studying where I was and where I'd climb and how. Head thrown back, I saw the shadow of the antenna reaching and I thought, so, Earl Wallen, you're up here and going up, a thousand watts at your fingertips. I wondered how it would feel if I touched a live wire, the tingle in my teeth. Or careening down, grabbing at empty air. Did shouts make a sound as you fell? I strapped my tools on, climbed into the murky sky, rung by rung, hands aching from cold and metal.

As I climbed, I remembered this man, a lineman for the new telephone company who'd worked in Venice a few weeks. My buddies and I had admired him, the thick-soled boots, how he strapped himself to the pole and pulled himself, spike by spike, toward wires that had hummed with power, electricity and small talk, when we'd crossed the street underneath them only moments before. We didn't see him after those weeks and we imagined an accident, one of the lines snapping, him grabbing the writhing end of it, sparks zipping past his face like sparklers. He'd probably been a hero, we imagined, and they'd probably sent him on to some other, even more powerful job, underground cables maybe, or, better yet, cables under the ocean, linking us to foreign country after country.

Near the top of the antenna, at the bottom of the W, I paused and figured which neon tubing I'd replace, which wires to splice, which fuses to check. Below me were Main Street's windows, and scattered houses behind that, and far to my left, boats and lanterns on Frazier Lake, and voices in the trees at the base of the hill I was on, voices, flashlights, beagles let loose, baying at whatever moved. On a wild hair, I held on to the antenna, hand by hand, pulled off my jacket and my shirt and let them fall behind me. Then I shouted at the red signal light on top of the tower, as loud as I could—Earl Wallen, you can be whatever you choose.

I imagined what I might choose, those brand new 45's spinning my name, my voice on the radio. All up and down the tower I imagined spirals, white smoke rising, radio waves. I felt the power of them, on my fingertips, up my arms, across my bare chest. You can forget anything, I thought—Rudy Hyatt, sounds you don't want, anything, anything at all. I held on and leaned out into the cold air.

Actually, my rise in radio world was pretty damn slow. By late February, Inez's thin asphalt streets had broken into potholes, mud and more mud, and my basement bed-sitter was a damp hole. Mold crept up my guitar strap, down the soles of my shoes, and I spent more and more time in the studio room. Nights, on the pretext of changing a light bulb or checking a ground wire, I'd watch the nighttime programming. The evening DJ was a tight-assed guy with a scraggly mustache and short, yellow teeth. I hadn't thought much about putting together a radio show, but I thought what he dreamed up was about as imaginative as praise God at vacation Bible school. Still, he didn't say much when I hung around those wet nights.

Some of the evening programming was pre-recorded, wired, reel-to-reel. Some was LP's, but most of it was live, either from Huntington, West Virginia, or right off the streets of Inez itself. Let me tell you some highlights from the average hot lineup for a Tuesday night. Around six there was news. Even in Inez, we heard about the trial of Alger Hiss, Un-American, supplier of military secrets for the Soviet Union. Ought to line them up, Pappy Imes would have said, and I heard the same thing about locals, like the news story of the pharmacist's wife who ran off with a door to door salesman of the latest Hoover vacuum cleaner. After the news, there was Organ Moods, from the Van Lear Baptist Church, hymns like "It Pays to Serve Jesus," or "Loyalty to Christ," broadcast live during a baptism or the Lord's Supper. There were comedies like the Burns and Allen Show, and swap shops, with their own radio jingle—*swap shop, swap shop, where the best bargains are always saved, swap shop, swap shop, do you have something today?* Local talent hunts were sponsored by the Pepsodent toothpaste company and one of these brought Hanna's Incredible Hoola Hoop Show. By that time, I was attending the evening broadcast regularly enough, even had my own folding chair in one corner of the studio.

The evening DJ set aside thirty-five minutes for Hanna's show, which was a mixture of interview and performance. The time slot right before was Evening Melodies and the DJ played a canine rendition of Jo Stafford's "A You're Adorable." While we waited, Hanna's mother, a broad-faced woman with whitish blonde hair, riffled through a fat black notebook, stopping to wet her finger, flip a page, point to a particular passage and frown. Right before broadcast time, she creased Hanna's crinoline skirts and bent her wiry pigtails at the tips.

"We're on, Hanna," she hissed. Her brows were plucked to an almost invisible line of fine hairs, giving her eyes a wide, fearful look. "Now, Hanna. Stand up straight."

Hanna was about ten years old, also blonde, with wide cheeks that had a pasty bonelessness and a broad, receding hairline. "I know what now means, Mama," she said, puffing one cheek out with air, letting it go flat, puffing it again.

She was standing on one patent-leathered foot, leaning on a giant blue ring. As soon as the red light on the console flashed, on the air, she planted her feet about half a foot apart, set the ring against her hip and twisted. There was a rhythmic jingling sound and I looked for the bells, but they were hidden, inside the spinning hoop or somewhere in the folds of crinoline.

"Tonight, listening land," the DJ began, "I'd like you to meet Mrs. Willy May Daniels and her daughter, Hanna. Hanna's been building herself quite a reputation as a performer. In fact, she's way ahead of her time—she's mastered a to date little known art and fun form. It's called the hoola hoop. Mrs. Daniels, what can you tell us about this hoola hoop?"

Mrs. Willy Way, compact in hand, was nervously applying the last touches of some pale white lipstick. She looked surprised, as if she hadn't quite realized the show had started. "Excuse me?"

The DJ flashed a saw-toothed, reassuring smile. "The hoola hoop, Mrs. Daniels. I don't think many of us in radio listening land have heard of a hoola hoop."

Mrs. Willy May frowned impatiently. "It's a hoola hoop," she said, underlining each syllable. She giggled. "All you have to do is twist. Why, my little Hanna has hours of fun with it. Just listen." The hoop twirled on Hanna's fat hips, bells jingling.

"Well, that' fine, Mrs. Daniels," the DJ said, "but I understand Hanna isn't just an ordinary hoola hooper. She's a marathoner. Can you tell us about that?"

Willy May shook her head. "Anybody could tell you that."

The DJ smiled again and I could hear his yellow teeth grind. "Rumour has it that Hanna has been hoola-hooping regularly since July 6, 1944, the Allied invasion of Normandy. Is that true, Mrs. Daniels?"

Willy May composed herself, hands in her lap, lips almost touching the microphone. Her voice sounded whispered and hurried. "I guess you could say that, around that time. Of course, I always taught her the value of repetition before then. That it is very, very important not to waste a single motion. Why, right after 1941, I began saving scrap metal and odds and ends to send to the troops, not a stray cooking pot in my kitchen, no sir. Why, the first gum in Hanna's mouth meant she'd come running, giving me the wrapper."

Behind her, Hanna whirled, the blue hoop whishing, faster and faster. On her bland face was a look of painful attention, but she wasn't looking at her mother, or the microphone, or any of the radio paraphernalia. The bells chimed.

"That's spoken with real patriotic spirit, Mrs. Daniels. But what can you tell us about Hanna? What possessed her to turn your patriotism into a, how can I put this," the DJ paused, "a fun time, with meaning? When did she start hoola-hooping?"

Willy May bit her shiny white lips and glanced at Hanna. "I think it's especially important that we show the country our sense of devotion, don't you? That's my girl. Graceful, isn't she? Hanna, do the deep knee bend, you know the one."

Hanna, hoop still revolving, pointed her shiny shoes to either side, raised her hands, fingers touching, above her head, did a bow-legged bend, her hips still rotating. The jingling never missed a beat.

The DJ applauded politely, then turned to Willy May again, a look of impatience on his face. "Come on, Mrs. Daniels, what's a hoola hoop have to do with war, anyway?"

Hanna shouted, "The letter, Mama, tell them about the letter." She was out of breath, cheeks a sweaty pink. She pirouetted, still hooping.

Willy May laid her cheek against the microphone, closed her eyes, then took a deep breath. "Well, if you must know, I'll tell you, though I, for one, thought what we'd come here for was a performance. Why, my little Hanna has been practicing for weeks. Actually, it was July 20, 1944. Hanna's been hoola-hooping off and on since that day, not July 6. That was the day I heard I'd lost both my boys, shot down. One was a major and the other was a captain, both pilots. Why, they had a record of forty-three enemy planes between them."

Hanna pirouetted, still hooping, but right then her chubby, little girl legs seemed to give out. The hoop fell with a clatter of bells.

"Hanna," Willie May said, jumping up, looking madder than hell. Her eyes were wide, her brows thin lines of pencil. "Hanna, we're on the air. Do you get me? On the air. Thirty minutes, just thirty little minutes." She bent down, whispered in Hanna's ear.

And Hanna began again. The hoop circled her waist, faster than ever. Looking at me, the DJ threw up his hands, then lowered a microphone, right at Hanna's hips. Ten minutes of programming left and we sat quietly, all of Inez, all of radio land, listening to bells spin and a little girl's breath, coming hard and fast. The whirl of blue made me think of a sky, clear, cloudless, a sky from which nothing could ever fall.

"Oh, my," Mrs. Willy May Daniels said, sitting down again. She leaned close to the microphone. "Isn't the radio just real enough to make you think they can see you out there?"

~

In late March, the yellow toothed DJ suddenly took another job at WHNT in Huntington, West Virginia, a promotion to 5000 watts for him, and a fine stroke of luck for me. I applied for the job right away, told them how I'd radioed messages from Tarawa to Kwajalein to Eniwetok, islands across the Pacific, toward Japan. Lost in stories of rain forests and war, they asked me few questions about my plans for nighttime Inez radio.

To tell the truth, when WINZ hired me, I think it was kind of temporary—a favor to them and me both, down and out soldier coming home plays a few pre-recordings of baptisms and communions, gets satisfied with Jesus, gets on his feet, and becomes a highly thought of store clerk. They didn't count on me really having plans, and plans were what I had. I wanted to shake the foundations of Inez, its coal dust, its preachers, its pretty, tight-legged women. I cut Organ Moods and replaced it with a half-hour of just plain sound—recordings of racing car engines, cattle stampedes, trains in tunnels, or my own brand of calypso, rhythm on oil cans I swiped from Pappy Imes's Gas and Go. I bought three discarded mannequins from the General Store, dressed them in tight skirts and halter tops and set them near the console.

I wanted to fill the studio with bodies, make the songs I played felt in the fingers and toes, on the tip of the tongue, on the streets of Inez, in the back seats of Chevrolets, on blankets on the sand down by Frazier Lake. After the eleven o'clock news some evenings I'd even take out my guitar, sit in front of the microphone and transmit the lyrics of Earl Wallen—*come on baby, don't be shy, kick off your shoes and step in, swim, the water's clear and who knows where we'll go or why.*

One night, two hours before sign-off, Lolo Lafferty came to see me at the studio. She took a chair, the one I used to sit in when I was a visiting maintenance man, and kicked off her shoes. They weren't the saddle Oxfords she usually wore, but little wedge heels with a thin ankle strap. Through her stockings I could see her toenails, bright red moons. I finished my ad, breakfast special at the diner, one egg and waffles with syrup, just fifteen cents, then switched to an LP, "The Tennessee Waltz."

"You're wrong as you can be Earl Wallen," Lolo said. She leaned forward, struck a match against the floor, lit a cigarette.

"Wrong? What the hell are you doing here anyway, Lolo? This is purely a professional operation, you might say." *The night they were playing,* Cowboy Copas sang, and I adjusted the tone control, making his voice so smooth you could touch it.

"That may be, Earl, but you're still dead wrong." She blew a perfect smoke ring, then stuck her cigarette through the center of it.

"What do you want me to do? Play prayer hour five times a night?" I took the cigarette from her, lit one of my own off the end.

"You're mighty jumpy, aren't you? I wasn't talking anything about music, or whatever it is you play around here most of the time. I just meant it's two eggs, not one."

"What was that?"

"Two eggs, not one. The breakfast special. You've been getting it wrong for hours and I came by to set you straight."

Waltzing with my darling, the night they were playing, Copas sang. I shrugged and took a deep drag off the cigarette. "Well that'll make Inez roll over in its sleep, won't it? That all you wanted?"

"Well, as matter of fact, I'm not sure. Maybe you can tell me." She flicked her ashes on the floor, raked them aside with her bare foot. "I was standing at the sink at the diner, about closing time, up to my elbows in dishwater. The radio was on, the strangest thing I'd ever heard, like somebody was beating hell out of an old tin can. Caterwauling, my Mama would have called it. But you know, Earl Wallen, my feet just wanted to dance."

"And you came here?" I said. "Thought you lived at the Starland Skatarama."

Then she was standing next to me, holding my hands, her hands rough and soft at the same time, hands that knew what to do and where.

"Come on, soldier boy," she said, "just dance with me."

She laid her head against my shoulder and I smelled spray net and another scent that made me think of all those men I'd heard about, the salesmen who ended up in her room. The scent was like cheap hair oil and an old comb, and then another scent after that, hers, one to make a man think twice.

We danced through "The Tennessee Waltz," once, twice, and another time, until the telephone on the back wall started up and I let it ring, some radio land complaint I didn't want to hear. She stood on the tops of my feet and we waltzed slow circles, laughing a little, because after awhile the needle reached blank space and fell off, scratching. I cut to a pre-recorded broadcast, and we kept dancing, in and around the microphones, a waltz still, and then faster and faster, my shoes scraping time and her hips swaying, her body saying what, not a few years later, Joe Taylor would say with the blues—*you wear low dresses, the sun comes shining through.* Ten years later what I felt that night with Lolo Lafferty would be rock 'n' roll.

I'd like to tell you that after that night, everything was fine and dandy, that I became a star, that Lolo quit the diner and had her hair done up nice, that I got a new car with a radio every year afterwards and that we went where we pleased. But you know and I know that's not the case. It could have been.

For awhile, in the weeks that followed, even Rudy Hyatt was just some man, an average man, in my dreams. He knew how to do things, fix car, watches, ham radios. Sometimes he was standing underneath my bedroom window, in the dark. He was young, baby fuzz on his upper lip, cigarette perched, unlit. I dreamed his every little motion, the match bent back from the cover, the flame pinched with his bare fingers. Other dreams, he was a lot older, gray haired, shorter. He led some snot nosed grandkid by the ear right across my front yard, yelling, you'd better get on home. I wish he'd stayed an ordinary man, stayed in my dreams, a man so ordinary I wouldn't have thought twice about him by the light of day. A conversation I had one night changed all that.

~

I was in the studio alone that night and I let the phone ring while I switched reels and played the recording of the news I'd made earlier. I had the headphones on to monitor the sound and just slid one ear back to listen and say into the telephone receiver, "WINZ, nighttime's the right time to change your listening ways."

The voice sounded flat, whispered, but sort of familiar. "You have not yet seen God," it said.

"I'm sorry, mister," I said. "You must have the wrong phone number. Lick Fork Missionary Baptist has two threes and we have one, otherwise the number's exactly the same, so try again."

I was ready to hang up and get back to business, when the voice said, again, "You have not yet seen the Lord, that's plain."

"What is this?" I glanced at how much of the reel-to-reel was left, pulled off the headset and listened hard to the phone. "This a crank call, or what?"

"How is it," the voice asked, "that you see God, when you see Him?"

"I don't have the least idea what you're after."

"Describe God to me. You must have said a prayer sometime, don't fool me. Describe Him."

I laughed and cleared my throat. "Well, now, if you're going to just about insist on it, let me see. I'd say God was a jive joint on a weekend night, and some woman in spike heeled shoes, no, velvet spike heeled shoes. And you're dancing, and some voice says to you, put your hand there, no now, you can do better than that, lower down, squeeze. That, mister, since you asked me, is God."

There was a silence, and I switched to a prerecorded sports broadcast. "Woman?" the voice said then. *I saw a woman sit upon a scarlet colored beast, full of names of blasphemy, having seven heads and ten horns.*

"Horns?" I said. "Only horns you're going to interest me in, mister, is Dizzy Gillespie and a shiny new trombone."

"I'm telling you, son, before it's too late. You have not yet seen God."

I leaned back, propped my feet up on the desk, lit a cigarette. "All right, mister, since you're so high falutin sure of things, you tell me. What's God look like?"

"The Son of Man has golden hair, eyes a flame of fire. To look upon, the Son of Man is like jasper. There is a rainbow around his throne, and his throne is an emerald."

I laughed. "Only gems you're going to get me excited about are in a radio transmitter. You know they use quartz crystal for those things?"

There was a sigh on the line. "You don't know a thing about it, about God."

"All right, already," I said. I was getting fed up. "God, then. God's one of those nights where, you know, you slip into your room kinda late, you've had one too many. Maybe you're renting a room somewhere, say over somebody's shop, or the back room at some old lady's house. So you slip in, quiet like, don't turn on the light. You feel your way around the edges of the room, corner to corner to corner, stumble against this thing, your toe hurts fit to scream, and then you find it's a guitar, yours. So you sit down right where you are, old lady or not, and you play the hell out of that thing. You keep the light off, mind you, just for her, but there's nothing like it, notes like sparks off your fingers, just flying. Now that, mister, is God."

The voice changed tones, got angrier, louder. "Those songs you play, they're an abomination. The radio is an instrument of the Lord and for how you play it, God will pour his vials of wrath upon the earth."

"So that's it, mister, why didn't you just out with it? One more crank call, I knew it. This is my station, every evening six to twelve. You don't like it, swing your pinky and find a station you like better. Isn't that what the war taught us, why, we can do about what we please." I slammed the phone down hard.

It was much later, after I'd already signed off for the night, after I was lying in my bunk bed, a cigarette going and a pre-release of Vera Lynn singing "No Love"—and she didn't mean no flowers or candy—in my head, that it came to me, whose whiny voice it had been on the phone. Tobias Blue's. One old hypocrite who'd broke the mold when they made him, that was for certain, I thought, lying there smelling used oil and gasoline and thinking about him and cards. He had me forty bucks in the hole with my service money, and Friday nights I headed out there, to Mining Hollow, determined, every time, to win, God or none.

~

And so every Friday night for weeks, I went to Mining Hollow for poker with the old man. We played seven card stud, high-low, draw, spit in the ocean, Black Maria, whatever we dreamed up. The stakes were nickels and dimes, but more than that. Tobias Blue wagered his Bible would win, my soul already pressed between the pages. For me, it was the body that couldn't lose. Sometimes in my mind that body would be some woman dancing in a red dress, Lolo Lafferty maybe, our bodies so close, moving to some ragged out blues on the radio, moving so we were one body, a body that rocked, shook with the music, music that lifted right off our skins like sweat, moved out into the night air like radio waves, became a body of its own, Rudy Hyatt's, a whole man with a face, as if the war had never happened.

While we slapped down cards those Friday nights, Ruth Blue sat out on the porch swing. Through the open screen door I'd hear the creak and sway, and crickets roaring from the trees. She sat out there until it was pitch black, until Tobias called her in.

"Daughter," he'd say, "we're in need of some coffee."

Or more light, or a plate of toasted white bread. She was a mousy little thing, and she did what he said, running for this or that.

"Mister?" she'd say, and stand about three feet away from my chair, a tomato sandwich on a plate.

"Go on, lay it down." I scooped up the cards and made a place. "I sure won't bite," I said. "Least not too hard."

But that sure wasn't the way to make her laugh. She'd slide the plate down next to me and be gone before I'd looked twice. I'd feel her watching me from the other side of the room, but I was never quick enough to turn, catch what was in those nervous black eyes of hers. Only once did she touch me, an accident, a cuff and a bare wrist against my hand, but she pulled away like I was on fire. On fire for her was the last thing I was, her sneaking down the hall, shutting the door to some room, inch by inch, not even the click of a lock.

Those Friday nights I always lost, as hard as I bluffed. I went back to WINZ flat broke, lay and listened to the sounds of the Inez streets outside. Inside me music buzzed and hummed, ready to become song lyrics that would take me further South, along lines and lines of map after map, until I wrote the song, the one, that would change the world forever. But I always headed back to Mining Hollow.

Headed back, until one night when I parked the car at the bottom of the bank, looked up through the trees toward where I now for sure knew his house lay. The night was as black and nervous as her eyes, Ruth Blue's, and I suddenly saw her as she must be, inside that house, kneeling on the other side of her closed door, ear to the keyhole, listening to us ante and take. Winning her would be easy. I'd win her and show her old man who God was, all right. God, the sound of me with his daughter behind a closed door.

Love, I'd say when she asked me. Love? You'd better ask God about that one, Ruth Blue.

RUTH: SUMMER, 1948

Come summer, 1948, Earl Wallen kept on coming back. To see me, though my daddy knew nothing about it. I'd be in bed while they dealt cards and passed a bottle Earl'd brought in his jacket pocket, until before long Tobias's head went down, like it did, on the kitchen table. That's when Earl would give me a little sign, a whistle outside below my window, or a line or two from a song. *Ruth Blue*, it'd go, *if you're so true, true and as good as your word, then come down to me now, please me, you, and it'll be grander than you've ever heard.* I'd slide out of bed and throw on a coat over my nightgown, tiptoe past through the kitchen, and out.

We'd meet up at the pond, where we'd do the finest things. Skip stones over the black water. Hoot back at the owls and whippoor-wills. He told stories about himself, asked me things and I listened. Felt the strangeness of new questions in my mouth. Who are you, Earl Wallen? What brung you here, out of nowhere? He was a soldier, had been one, came from Ohio, some town called Venice, and he was never going back. No ties to keep him there anymore, no kin, no responsibilities. He'd come to Inez, not a place he'd picked exactly, but one where he heard music in his head, hummed it, felt it, sorry

144

and no account or not. He wanted to be a local singing star, country, or rock-n-roll, it was the same to him, he just wanted to be someone and knew he could. I sat close to him, traced my finger around the small gold stars he had on his shoes. Star shoes, he told me. I listened and told him no stories about myself. I wanted everything about me to be new, with no beginning or end.

At first, we never so much as touched, not a hand or shoulder, though sometimes strands of my hair snagged against the sleeve of his service jacket. And sometimes I saw reflections of us in the pond water. Wind and light bent our shapes so close we could have been holding on tight.

There was a revival at the Lick Fork Missionary Baptist Church that summer and Tobias did some preaching on Tuesdays, Thursdays and Saturdays. I imagined he wouldn't miss me at the church house on those particular nights, because I had seen often enough how the Lord took him in. He led communion, passing out squares of unsalted crackers and tiny cups of grape drink and his eyes would look the way they could, shiny and full of sin and glory. He talked to the crowds that came from Inez and I knew well enough how he didn't look at anyone in particular, least of all me. His sallow face flushed and his voice rose, higher and higher, until it became an unknown tongue and he was only held there, part of us, by the way his long index finger pointed at whatever person sat in the middle folding chair in the last row in the tent. I made sure it wasn't me. I spent those evenings with Earl.

Then, one Saturday night, Earl drove me three counties away to see Mae West and Cary Grant at the drive-in picture show. Earl's short shirt sleeves were rolled up high, his hair slicked back. He kept one hand on the steering wheel, one arm along the back of the seat and I thought I had never seen a prettier man, how all those lights beside the gravel lot at the picture show made his white hair shimmer. We parked way back, near the chicken wire fence beside the main road toward Inez and right away I didn't know how to act. I'd never been to a drive-in movie. I fumbled with the speaker, the long, coiling wires, turned the volume knobs so high the Rinso White ad blared, so high-pitched and off-key, I pressed my palms tight against my ears.

Never mind about that, Earl said. He rolled the car window down, tossed the speaker out as far as he could. That's not why we came anyway, he said, and laid his calloused hands against my hair. It was the first time I'd been kissed and he kissed me, narrowed his pale eyes and tilted his head back, studying me, as if this, or this, or this were just the right spot, until his thin, cool lips settled, gently, beneath my right earlobe. Air tingled in my ear, like tiny, invisible hairs on the surface of my skin. Do you mind, he asked. What I called to mind was nothing at all, only how our mouths fell in and in to each other, tasting of thirst of strangers we felt but couldn't quite see, in the shadows, in the light of a picture show.

Later, we walked down to the concession stand for cokes and ice. Look, I said as we walked, will you just look? But after I'd said it, I wasn't sure what I'd meant. As we crossed the lot between parked cars and speakers, the movie screen swayed with light and huge faces, car beams high and bright in the distance. The night moved around me, it towered around me, bigger than the whole, huge world and all I'd ever known or been. I kicked off my shoes and stood on the tops of Earl's feet. I was as close to the real God as I ever wanted to be. I'd been picked up and carried off by something I didn't know the name of. I could fall back to earth at any minute, but I shut my eyes as Earl began to dance.

EARL: SUMMER, 1948

Ruth didn't know it, that night at the drive-in movie, but the listening audience for WINZ had plummeted to an all-time low. LP's played by the late-night Balladeer, Earl Wallen, reminded Inez of how music could take you anywhere, if you let it. Shake you right out of your good Sunday shoes and set your feet tapping hot jive on the parlor rug. Make you hear tom-toms and a saxophone and see the sleek skin of a woman in a low-cut dress. Make you breathe smoke and sin. You know the score. Wrong time, wrong place. Desire and rhythm in a little town, five years too soon.

I played Nat King Cole, the Orioles singing "I Know It's Too Soon," Louis Jordan singing "Early in the Morning," sent base notes out into the streets, made them tap at respectable windows of fine, radio-listening homes, made them float above beds and send dreams of the blues, low and mean, into the hearts of Inez First Southern Baptist churchgoers. Until those same churchgoers, led by a now and then street corner preacher named Mr. Tobias Blue smashed recordings of black artists on the courthouse steps. Those big wigs at WINZ took me aside, said to me, come on Earl, just tone it down a little, that's all, how would it look if we had to fire an ex-soldier?

That night at the drive-in Mae West crooned and swaggered in her tight, black dress, her diamonds catching the camera light. On the other side of my car seat, eyes fastened on the picture screen like she'd never seen anything so fine, sat Ruth Blue, hands crossed in her lap, the hem of her baggy skirt pulled down over her knees. I'll admit it to you up front that when I reached across to her right then, just as Mae West took a drag off her long cigarette and said, when women go wrong, men go right, I had a plan. I'd win her. Win her and woo her, put my mouth against hers and edge my tongue between the lips of that mouth that looked too small to kiss. I'd be the music Tobias Blue and Inez and those tight-assed ladies with their Sunday hat and button-up gloves have bad dreams about. I'd enter the body of one of their own, be like a double scotch with no ice finding its way into her blood, find just the right spot to touch her so she'd be like the reed of a clarinet just wetted and blown on so soft it would vibrate with a song, one low-down and good.

Mae West took a long drag off her cigarette, blew a perfect, round smoke ring and I reached far across the seat, laid my hand on top of Ruth's. She jumped liked I'd spliced the speaker wires and laid them against her bare skin, so I held back a minute, just let my hand rest there, waiting. After I felt her breath slower, felt her unclench her fingers, I moved, turned her hand over, traced one of my own fingers, making circles against her palm. Mae West's smoke rings rose and settled above Cary Grant's head, just as I scooted over, draped my arm around her, touched her hair. It was kind of coarse, smelled like rain and earth, as I pulled her toward me, put my mouth over hers.

I had a plan, that whole time, while we necked and I touched her, the shoulders, the back of the neck, nothing too friendly, too far. I kissed her, danced her a mean "lindsey" in the parking lot, thinking all the time of how I'd win her. Her old man, that boozing and card-dealing and God-mouthing old man, he could smash all the records he pleased, could burn ads and schedules and interview sheets right off the daytime DJ's desk, could set fire to the whole damn station, for all I cared. I'd write a love song, one I'd call Ruth Blue and play there, right in her heart.

~

When I took her back to Mining Hollow, there was a part of me, well, more than just a part, that hoped her old man would be home already from his preaching and carrying on and wherever he'd been that night. I stood with her for a good long while, down at the bottom of the yard. Checking the oil, I said, and raised up the hood of the car, flipped on the flashlight and shone it down, admiring my own handiwork, the polished clean engine and her, standing there until I put my arm around her again. Pulled her toward me, against my hip and off her feet, stood back and swung her and that long skirt, around and around. There was a good half-moon and enough light for me to see her face, the way she looked up at me, happy, won to me already.

Then, from way inside the house, I heard the sound of glass breaking, then a thud like a boot kicking and then the front door, crashing open. I set Ruth down and peered around the side of the car. Just as I expected, Tobias in all his glory was standing out on the front porch, waving his King James edition around in the air. I could smell him from where I stood, old sinner, walking bottle of rot-gut whiskey.

Ruth pulled back from me, a scared little girl with her legs in her rolled down ankle socks just shaking, ready to set her flying toward the steps and into the house.

"Earl," she said, stepping back into the shadows of the car. "You ain't never seen it like this. Earl, he'll say it's now, right now."

"Now?" I asked, and hadn't the least notion what she could mean. Now could mean anything in that house, him jerking the tablecloth off in the floor, plates smashing, saying supper's not enough and more, right now, or him, belting down whiskey fingers, seeing who knows what crawling out of the walls.

She grabbed hold of my arm, tucked herself beneath my shoulder. The both of us looked up at him in the porch light. His grayish dress shirt was unbuttoned to the waist, his undershirt hanging out over his trousers. He stumbled against a loose board in the porch, raised his arm and I saw it, the book in his hand, the Bible, it had to be, and even that looked too heavy for him. I could tell he was already lit, little medicinal doses of bootleg lacing his coffee since breakfast, chasers while he dealt himself solitaire. No telling what he thought he saw at that minute, Jesus in a chariot, or his own yellow whiskers in the mirror.

"God has come," he shouted. "Come to bless this house."

I should have snuck off with Ruth right then and there, took her into Inez to the back row at the late-night matinee and seen how he liked looking at just himself for an hour or two. And I would have, too, if, well, if one or two things hadn't happened I'll call strange. Signs, Ruth whispered beside me. Tobias leaned over the porch railing, his head down, the Bible held out to us.

"Come to bless this house," he said again, the words thick, slurred. "Nothing but a house made of air."

It could have been a sign, what he said, that and how right then a cool wind sprang up as we walked up from the road. It came from behind the house, or through it, or from inside it. Glass panes rattled, the raggedy white curtains blew through the screenless windows, and the Bible fell from Tobias's fist, landed softly in the tall weeds. I thought I could hear the pages ripping in the wind, or imagined it, how the loosely sewn binding unstitched and unstitched, setting loose the gospel truth. Pages whipped past our ankles in the moonlight. Ruth let go of me and darted here and there, gathering sheets, and I caught them as they curled against my trouser legs. I couldn't help myself, later on I even read a verse or two, like you do when you open the Bible to just some place, to check your fortune. *Lover and friend hast thou put far from me*, that page read, *and mine acquaintance hast thou put into darkness*. The wind blew and pages blew past us and I was changed forever, if I'd only known it.

Right then, I crumpled the paper and stuck in my pocket, flung open the door of my Kaiser-Fraiser. I leaned in, pressed the starter, set the engine humming, and then switched on the radio. I wasn't having any of it, no midnight hocus-pocus, no cheap motel room Bible, none of it. My arm circled Ruth's waist, my hand cupped hers, tight, and right there in the yard we danced. Or I danced, dragging her, tripping and halting over the dark, uneven ground. We danced our way across words, *doom* and *mystery* and *abomination*, *darkness* and *judgement* and *wrath*, danced to Patti Page, "With My Eyes Wide Open I'm Dreaming."

"How do you like it?" I shouted. "Like it any better than you did the blues? I'll be dancing on your grave, and that's a fact."

The way he acted, instead of a little bag of bones, she could have been the Queen of the Starland Skatarama. He came charging down the porch steps. Well, feeling his way along was more like it.

He said, "There is no man in heaven, nor in earth, neither under the earth, who is worthy."

We kept on dancing, damn his soul. I held her hands and twirled her, even when he'd come down the last step and was making straight across the yard. We danced until by the lights of the car I caught a glimpse of us, a reflection of me and her, in the bumper. We seemed to dance farther and farther away, grow smaller and smaller, in that dim reflection. And it suddenly came to me, what I was, her soldier boy, her salvation, come to take her away from Mining Hollow. Whether she admitted it or not, I was supposed to be her personal angel with a sword, her truth and crash of thunder and lightning.

The little spot of rouge she'd daubed on just one cheek stood out like a slap. What did she want me to do? Tell her God was probably up there, given a little luck, hair and clothes bright as a new dime, eyes half shut, taking his ease, but sure to come and get her and me both, once I gave the word. Or tell her, all right, so I'd even seen God a few times myself, though it wasn't like her and her daddy meant, all pious and committed and shouting praise. Or tell her I'd take her away from Mining Hollow, now and forever, just for a song?

What I knew of her was this and that, evenings while she fetched and carried and we dealt cards. Kisses with closed mouths at a drive-in movie, an hour here or there beside a pond by moonlight with a mousy thing in baggy clothes who hung on my every word like a life-line. A Bible-toting father and enough prayers of her own, I'd seen them, enough to bless the popcorn and soda pop at the picture show.

And still I held her and danced her, felt her backbone, her thin arms wrapped around me. Felt the need coming out of her pores, full of all the scraps and pieces of her life like the ashes and corners of burnt photographs of Rudy Hyatt I'd found when I'd stood behind Mrs. Hyatt's house.

All of what I knew of her winding around me like smoke, a fire catching hold. Fire of love? Not that. Fire of anger? That, maybe. Looking at that old man set my teeth on edge, enough to make me know I'd win her. Fire of anger for her own sake, days later when I saw her, the short, rough cut of her hair and she told me how Tobias made her kneel with him, cropped her hair and told her to beg for forgiveness. Gold, he whispered at the back of her neck. And silver. You'll be damned for worshipping such things, he said.

Fire enough so when I looked at her, her face, it was like a photograph burst into flame and in its place I saw the face of Rudy Hyatt, then the face of my father at his bank on Sunday afternoons, then a face, face I couldn't name at all. Just a blankness, a hole in the air where a face had been that felt like the center of my own chest. A hole I'd tried, all my life, to fill up with a song. *Sweet and light, dark and bitter,* a song I'd now call *Ruth Blue.* Just as Tobias rounded the corner of the car I let go of her, leaving her standing between me and him. She stood blinking her eyes in the sunlight, standing between me and him.

"You will," she said, a simple statement, a fact, a belief.

Will, I thought, will take her away, will take her, will. All I had to say was yes, but I held my tongue, even when that old fool was standing right beside me, hands on his hips, staring right at her, saying, "You've danced in the house of the Lord."

Before he could finish, she took off running, up the hill behind the house, toward the dark woods and the pond, that house made of air right at her back. I should have gone after her, said, hey you, Ruth Blue, who do you think I am? A savior? But her question, will you, echoed back to me, and still all I gave her was silence.

RUTH: AUGUST 16, 1983

You remember how you woke from dreams that left your mouth dry, tasting of an old metal spoon. You swallowed these dreams, but they floated to the surface of you by morning light, came spinning to your lips. Came out of your mouth, caught hold of your hair. You thought *God, God and dream lover, dream.* You kept your eyes closed until you saw the real God, his face the sun, his feet pillars of ice you fell down to kiss.

Then the peaceful mornings, after they'd gone and you didn't have to be up at the Wards till afternoon, how you'd be standing at the kitchen door, looking down the road, in the direction of Mining Hollow and the house that burned. Or you'd be looking over beyond Abbott Mountain, at the ten o'clock white sun rising, rising and burning its light down through the screen and right into me. Into you, skin, throat, lungs, heart. You closed your eyes and felt the reaching up, you, weightless air, you drifting on forever on one pure thread of light.

A shadow like tree branches or clouds or airplanes came out of the sky, right over the burning sun. A shadow, wide, dark net that caught and held the precious house and husband, son. Caught and held down. Without any word at all, you knew what the voice of God said right then. It said, *listen.*

RUTH: 1948–1953

Love, come November, 1948, was a window coated with ice through which I saw my past, given up once and for all. Love was Earl Wallen who, since Tobias had found us out, contacted me only in secret, tossed a handful of pebbles against my window as a sign to come down, meet him. We left notes at the black oak wrapped with barbed wire at the mouth of the hollow. *Baby,* his note one time said, *I ain't got nothing, never had, but the sight of you done stole my heart, done took my soul for good or bad.*

The night of the first snow I was already asleep, sounder than usual, when I woke as quick as if someone had jabbed me twice between the ribs, saying, Ruth Blue, Ruth Blue. There'd been no plan with Earl to meet that night, but I opened my eyes like I'd been splashed with ice water. I tossed and twisted in the sheets, couldn't lay still.

My mother had once searched the sky for signs, and I searched now, went to the window and peered down to the yard, wishing for Earl Wallen, his whitish-blue eyes. Not a thing, no sign, just slate-gray sky, the first large, wet flakes of snow. I shoved my feet into my shoes, went anyway, eased open the front door, slipped down the porch steps. I kept close to the shadows in the side yard, took a deep breath, held the edges of my coat tight.

I was standing right between two worlds. Only a few hundred yards to the thicket of trees, then a little bit on from there to the pond, where Earl and I often met, a world where moonlight would be as warm as Earl's hands. And on the other side of me, the house, windows, Tobias. I could almost see his face, looking down at me from my bedroom window, a face hid by glass and ice. At that minute he could be finding me out, the turned back blankets, the cast off night dress. Come back, he said, though all I saw was the shadow mouth, the cloudy eyes. How alone he was, prayers circling him like moths looking for the least light, rooms with the smell of shoes, of him.

The inside of my nose felt the sharp cold and I held my palms against my bare ears, hatless and bare of my long hair. Old man, I said aloud, feeling the cold pierce me like joy, like fingers running through my short hair, everywhere, everywhere. Old man, I'll leave you soon, leave Mining Hollow forever. I set out to choose Earl Wallen, that world, and all I didn't know.

~

I wasn't a fallen woman, but during those next few weeks, I was a woman I'd never been before, one with the sour-sweet taste of possibility on my tongue.

Two nights after the night of myself between worlds, I set a jar of the finest moonshine Earl's money could buy beside Tobias's bed. On top of that moonshine floated oils that sent visions and rage, that racked my daddy's body with misery, sent him off to his bed where I sat with him, reading him verses and singing him sweet songs. *Thou hast turned my laments into dancing*, I sang, *thou hast stripped off my sackcloth and clothed me with joy, that my spirits may sing psalms and never, never cease.* When his head tilted back and his breath came heavy and rough, I packed myself a pillowcase with my two good dresses, a brush and a comb and a nightgown left by my mother, so many years before.

Come those next few weeks I slept on the top half of the bunk bed in Earl's rented room in the Inez radio station, once we'd cleaned off the boxes and old 75's and a tangle of wires and metal. He kept an old record player on a workbench near the door, played the same record again and again, Joe Williams and "It's You or No One." *How did I guess*, the words said, *that the long loneliness was past, I merely looked at you and I knew that I knew.* The long loneliness, the hours of silence and nothing but the call of owls and mourning doves from the trees at Mining Hollow. The long loneliness. I slept in Earl's rented room, my hand trailing out of the covers.

Earl slept below me, and times came those nights, when his hand reached up and mine down and our fingers laced and held on tight. He drew pictures with his little finger, up and down the inside of my arm, sharps and flats and base notes. I lay, knees curled, inside most of the covers he owned—a long winter overcoat, a threadbare army blanket—and wished for more, for the warm inside of his mouth, the warm palms of his hands. You're clear and clean, Ruth Blue, he said, clear and clean and untouched. He drew whole notes and staffs and chords on my arm. He drew plans for our lives.

Hands under his head, Earl lay that long way from me and described for me the home we would have, the chain link fence where hedge roses would grow, like they had in his hometown, Venice, Ohio.

He told me of the side of the house, mimosas for good shade, of the screen door that would slam when I came out on the porch to meet him in the afternoons, how the radio would be on loud enough for songs to drift out into the shadows of the late afternoon. Songs and their words, *each time we kiss, now and forever, and when forever's done, it's you or no one for me.* And later, in a year, or two, or five, the song words drifting like air and curtains of lace out the open window, why, they'd be his, Earl Wallen's, songs right on the radio waves, his voice, his lyrics, lyrics that would change the course of music history, the course of memory and human lives, the course of love itself. He touched my arms again, those nights, the soft, untouched underside of my arm, and sometimes and never more than that, his fingertips smelling of aftershave and cigarette smoke, would stroke my cheeks, my upper lip, my breath as I fell asleep. I touched him, he said, with dreams.

Nights in Earl's rented room, I dreamed of that house with its fence and porch light rising, over the street and the mountains, light so clear it was like music. I also dreamed, some nights, how I got up from my sleep and went to the hall outside and to the radio station window. In the street I saw him, my daddy, standing under the streetlight, waiting and saying the worst he could. Saying nothing at all.

~

It was like waiting for a fist to slam against a table, for a body, dead heavy with drink, to fall into a bed, that time of no word from my daddy. Every time a door shut in the station down the hall from Earl's room, I knew good and well it was him, toting a shotgun and a warrant, so Earl said.

If I'd stood between two worlds that night at Mining Hollow, we both stood there now, letting be. Like the match before it lights the wick, the holding in before a good, deep breath lets out. Earl called that time a bluff. Time of a hand dealt, the deal's called, and let's see who raises who now. I like it better when he called it a time of getting to know. What it really was, was a time like before you lose what you love most, and you remember it later, and want it back and can't. I'd have held onto it for the longest while, if I'd known.

After a month passed, and still no sign from Mining Hollow, Earl said it was now or never, that he was going back to ask for my hand. Hand, he said, and made out like I'd be the best deal he'd ever got, a house full of love, four of a kind with me and him and the two pretty children we'd raise, a royal flush with me the queen of his heart. He spit-shined his shoes, shaved twice over, close and clean. He let me straighten his maroon tie, one he'd bought in Hawaii, during the war, he said, one painted with two white flowers and hula dancer in a thick grass skirt.

He left me alone in his rented room where, for the first hour, I paced the floor enough to make a track. In the wake of the dust I raised, I found a broom down the hall, swept and tidied and squared the corners of the blankets on Earl's bed. I set his cufflinks in a neat line of the bedside table, emptied his ashtray and polished it, wiped away coffee rings from the window sills. *Oh may I be happy*, I hummed while I worked. *Oh may I be blest, in a neat little cottage with the one I love best.*

I waited for Earl until eight o'clock, then sat by myself in the dark, humming, *oh may I be blest,* but the song sounded hollow by ten o'clock, then eleven. Outside the closed door to the room, I heard keys rattling, doors closing. I was in Earl's room on the sly, but the evening DJ knew, and kept it to himself as long as Earl did him a favor, now and then. Dusted LP's or fetched him a plate from the Inez diner or made good excuses for where he was, an evening now and then, when his wife called up and he wasn't there.

Then a knock come on Earl's door. Hey, Wallen, you in there, a voice said. It was the DJ. I held right still, listening. He knocked again, harder, and said, Wallen, buddy, I've got to high tail it on out of here. I've got a few, you know, errands. He held still, waiting, then cleared his throat, thinking who knows what about what Earl and I were up to behind that closed door. Ten minutes of ads, he said then, and the new recording, and you're on, buddy.

I still kept quiet, let him think what he would until footsteps shuffled down the hall and a door shut and the DJ went on. Outside, a car sputtered to life and headed off on the road past the WINZ sign.

I felt afraid, thinking of how many times I'd seen a look in Earl Wallen's pale eyes, the look that said all he wanted, the music he'd send out over the radio, call-ins and requests for songs for the lovesick and the ailing, the songs of his own he'd write and play late at night, so they made people dream of cities they'd never seen, seas to cross to Hawaii and other foreign countries, kisses they'd never kissed. Earl, the Late Night Balladeer, bound for wonderful times. And now not showing up because he was at Mining Hollow, dealing cards for spit in the ocean and asking for my hand in marriage.

I was afraid of all that, and afraid, too, of how long the hall seemed, once I opened the door and headed that way, toward the recording studio where I'd sat some nights with Earl, when he was on the air.

Lifebouy, Lifebuoy, let it be your joy, an ad said as I stepped into the room, sat at the office desk and put on the headset. *Your joy, our employ, to make your romance keen.* I knew some of how it was done, microphone, console, transmitter, a tangle of wire and metal that made me quiet when I'd sat with Earl a few late nights. Now I watched the last of the wire in the reel-to-reel run down and glanced at the clock.

Twenty-six after, four more minutes until there was what Earl said every radio announcer feared most, silence over the airwaves, dead air space. People, still awake in their living rooms all over Inez, coffee cups filled, them waiting up, hands on the dials of their sets, and nothing, nothing but me, Ruth Blue, saying, well now, you don't know me none, but here she goes. I put my hand on the microphone overhead, held it there. Three more minutes, and what I felt wasn't dead at all.

Laying on hands, my daddy called it, what they did at revival meeting when they called upon the Lord, and touched foreheads or ailing backs or limbs and felt the power just ride on waves and waves of air between heaven and earth. One minute and an inch above the microphone and it was like touching dust or rubbing hard and back and forth on a wool blanket and raising your hand and feeling the itch between. Between me and the microphone was power, the song not sung yet, news untold, weather that could happen or not, the faceless radio voice in kitchens and back rooms that folks waited on, night after night. One minute left and it could be me.

I cupped my hand around the microphone, looked down between my fingers, took a deep breath. WINZ, I said, like I'd heard Earl say. Station identification, check-in, he called it. I whispered the letters into my hands as the last seconds ticked off and the wire ran down. WINZ, I said again, clearing my throat. Listening land, I said.

Later, Earl told me that in those last few minutes in his car as he drove to the station, what he heard was a song I sung, me, Ruth Blue, in a voice stumbling and shy. *If I'm feeling blue*, the song said, *all I have to do is come home, come right home to you.* It was a song full of night sounds, a back porch, tree frogs singing in trees peaceful and dark, the sound of a heart and the way Earl would breathe into my hair as he held me. I don't remember that, the singing.

I remember my hands, cupped there around the microphone. I remember the sounds that came back to me. How Mining Hollow spoke to me out of a microphone mouth from a radio station.

I heard Tobias and Earl, sitting out on the front porch steps and talking. I listened to their low voices, heard words like promise and sometimes and for awhile. Glasses clicked and matches struck. Tobias slapped his leg hard, laughed, as they bent their heads together and Earl told him what must have been a story, a long one, maybe a story about his air force days. Or one about his boyhood in Venice, or his days on the road in his new Kaiser-Fraiser.

I heard about myself, discussed and agreed upon, same as a piece of land with the mineral rights sold, as a car that ran good. I heard myself given for marriage like a new pair of shoes that felt fine in the toes.

You're mine, Earl Wallen said to me, then. He was behind me, pulling my hand away from the microphone. He bent down, face flushed and wild, breath liquored and yet sweet as he kissed me full on the mouth. As he, the Late Night Balladeer, told all Inez who and what I would become next in my life. Wife. Raised up in love above all the rest of the world, like a song made of notes so light they could float on forever.

~

Even when I was standing in front of the mirror in my bedroom, on my wedding day, Tobias said I would be sorry, that my marriage was damned from the start.

You're a painted woman, he said, and I thought of the side of a circus truck I'd seen in Inez once, the painting of a girl in a leotard with a parasol, her eyelids a deep, powder blue.

I gave you space, he said, to repent of your ways, and you repented not. He watched me outline my lips with deep red lipstick, a gift from Earl. I will cast you, he said, and them like you. Out into the world of sin and sorrow, except you repent.

I scattered red petals in my short, black hair as he whispered in my ear. *You and yours, your children and those you love, all will meet with sorrow. I am he that knows and I will give you according to your ways.* You don't know, he said, what it is hands can do.

But a lent thing was something to be proud of. On my bed that morning I found a gown, one the color of milk just turned, its lace collar and cuffs a tattered lace. I picked it up, gathered to me its smell of mothballs and old roses. I drew the scent into the ache in me, hearing her, Little Mother singing, *I want to be happy, but I won't be happy until I've made you happy too.* Her gown, kept who knows where, pushed back in a box under the floor, in the far corner of a closet, beneath a floorboard. I gathered the wrinkled, moth-eaten folds, pulled the ghost of my mother over my head and walked down the hall of the house and out into the whirling leaves and wind, just as a storm came up over the ridge.

Earl wasn't down at the road yet, so I stood there, shifting my feet in the too-tight pumps I'd got for a bargain at the General Store. Beige pumps with roses on the toes, and ankle straps, and heels that sank into the red dirt. Earl Wallen, I said to the air, hurry on up.

When it was him at last, I pulled the car shut to the good, clean scent of him, aftershave and hair wax. He'd cut his hair since I'd last took sight of him, so short the scalp was pink and tender and I reached over, touched him, that way of doing already mine. I took one last look back at the house windows, the curtains pulled shut, quick, Tobias watching me leave Mining Hollow.

How pretty I felt. Pretty and the beads at my throat cool and good as I rolled them between my fingers during the service in Wheelwright, justice of the peace's. No sign from my daddy, no family of Earl's from anywhere in the world. Just the two of us, and the justice's plump, aproned wife. She met us at the back door, with a tray of powdered sugar wedding cakes and paper cups of punch and, for me, a bunch of flowers, mustard and dogwood and pinks.

All the while, rain was soft on the roof, light and passing, and the justice said, we are gathered here. Dearly beloved in the sight of the Lord. And for just that little spell, I was the dearly beloved, hand on Earl's arms, a thin band of gold put on my finger. He kissed me, took me, Ruth Blue, his mouth tasting of tobacco and the question he asked, what do you think now, Ruth Wallen?

After the service was over we hurried out to the parking lot, the justice of peace's wife showering us with rice and giving us hard candies and fliers that advertised good motel rates on the other side of Wheelwright. Smile, she said, and took our picture, and later on, Earl got copies for us, two dollars for a blow-up one, me next to Earl, next to the Ford, the both of us leaning in to the open door, ready for all that was to come.

I settled into the front seat, said, Earl, where should we go now?

Our honeymoon, he said, and I thought of a moon rich as honey, and full of gold and light, shining on us as far west as Mammoth Cave and underground, deep black air and bats and me in Earl's arms, as far east, miles and miles, to Wilmington and the ocean I'd never seen, my shoes and socks in my hands and a bag of shells collecting between us.

Earl switched on the radio and to the words of an old song, "Man With the Mandolin." I put my head on Earl's shoulder, next to the lapel of his jacket where he wore a carnation. All that sweetness, but my daddy's words danced with the leaves down from the hill, through the open window, settled in my hair behind my left ear. Like preachers did, I cupped my hand there and listened. No sound. I sat watching the traces of lightning, the huge drops of rain on the windshield.

I should have knowed, the minute Earl started the car and headed out of town, what was about to happen. I expected us to go anywhere, in the direction of Inez, and miles down the new paved road they'd built, to highways beyond and far beyond the red dirt road at the mouth of Mining Hollow where we stopped, pulled over. I reached across and touched his cheek.

Earl, I said, where are we going?

He smiled at me with that thin mouth I'd kissed and kissed. It's a wedding gift, he said and took my hand. Your father's said we can stay with him, just until I get on my feet.

Beneath my own feet, a vibrating, as if I could feel clean in me the soft rumble of the motor of Earl's car, or more than that, the rumble of the storm, starting again, more powerful this time. Lightning and thunder building and building, coming over the ridge, coming behind us, moving the car forward, forward into Mining Hollow. Earl, I said, what do you mean?

I saw it, deep in me, I saw it, that dream house with its white fence, the black dirt of the yard that I would turn and sow with seeds, with my own seeds, my own hands. The way shivering notes of music, Earl's music, would float out through the windows that were ours, ours alone.

It's just for awhile, he said, a month, maybe two, no longer than that. That at the most.

I already had my hands on the car door. The car was still moving, slowing down for ruts and heaves in the road. I was quicker than that, the car door already swinging open, me out and landing on my knees and then up, already running. Running, back to the mouth of Mining Hollow, down the red dirt of the road that was to go all the places I'd imagined, any place I'd imagined, any place but what I'd always known. The tiny heels of my wedding shoes caught in the stones and earth, but I kicked them off, went on, went on running, in my stockinged feet now, through the line of trees, into the deep woods of locust and pine, into the shadow of the bramble, the branches weighted with rain, and the black clouds moving in, moving in with a rumble of thunder I felt in my legs, in my chest.

The rain went harder, steady, and I tasted it, dusty and lukewarm but still like winter, as I turned my face up toward the black, huge sky. I felt it in streams down my back, soaking into the wedding gown, into my slip, soaking down to my bare skin, down to the empty place inside my rib cage, full of nothing but words and words, *you'll be a fallen woman yet*. And I was falling, growing smaller and smaller, the sound of the glad day slowed like a record on the wrong speed, airwaves, dead space.

Then he was behind me, the rough cloth of his good suit, his cheeks against my neck. His cheeks were fresh shaved that morning but already rough with whiskers. I shivered, warm and cold with rain, with running, with stopping now, my arms folded against me, hugging myself and him all at once.

It's not for long, he said. Don't you believe me? Just until I play my first song, the one I'll call Ruth Blue.

~

Ruth Blue, Ruth Wallen now, I closed my eyes and watched myself being lifted, wet clothes and all, light as a bundle of straw, and carried into the only house I've ever known. Earl carried me through the kitchen, down the hall past Tobias's room, that door shut tight, another wedding gift, our privacy, this one night, though I could feel him lying in there, listening to how our footsteps echoed. Earl carried me into my own bedroom, a room not mine anymore, but what he whispered, ours. It had been prepared for a marriage feast. There was a low table, one yellow candle, plates and food spread out on a wide green handkerchief.

There was apple cake, freshly killed venison and bowls of hard cider. I drank and ate the two squares of venison Earl cut and placed on my tongue. Right away I knew the meat was tainted, I knew the blood hadn't been let soon enough. It tasted strong and wild, it tasted of death, but I swallowed anyway and then lay back on the mattress where Earl was sitting. Again I closed my eyes and tried to think about nothing else, about nothing else but how his body could almost be the same as mine, thin, long muscles, skin, warm blood. We lay side by side, wet clothes touching, touching knee to knee, shoulders, hands held. I wanted us to stay that way, so quiet I could hear the way tiny bats beat against the window screens. But the candle flame sputtered and dimmed and darkness dropped, suddenly, like a cat, settled, humming, on top of my stomach.

Earl Wallen turned toward me and draped his knee across my body. I felt the heat of him press and press. I wanted to gather him into me but something without a shape moved from my stomach, to my chest, then tangled itself in my hair. I held my breath as Earl moved his body across my own. I looked up and saw the way ragged-winged moths scratched and scratched against the light bulb.

Warm me, I said, but something dark and alive picked me up and carried me out through a shatter in the window. I slid along through the outside air, faster and faster, was soon so far from myself I hardly felt the quick pain between my legs, hardly saw the way the pupils of Earl's white eyes were wide and dark with this thing called pleasure.

The dark thing at my throat carried me up until I touched the edge of the mountains around Mining Hollow. I looked back and saw a body that wasn't my own any more. I saw a bed, the one safe place that used to be mine, now belonging to my husband. Everything, Mining Hollow, Earl, myself, was heavy with the weight of a nameless thing, with having, with wanting to have, with not.

Earl leaned up on his arms and looked into my eyes as I fell down hard from the place I had gone, back to this house, this forever and forever. Outside the room I heard Tobias. He coughed an old man's cough and then shuffled down the hall, toward the kitchen. What now, I said, what now, feeling the words come from me like a scream, but I couldn't. Earl put his hand over my mouth and said, hush, as if this was a kindness.

EARL: SPRING, 1949

Rudy Hyatt, when I knew him back at Pearl Harbor, could ride those waves. And I mean radar. He could tell you about oscillators and frequencies and modulated output signals. That boy had a heart made of quartz crystal.

The surprising part of it all was how he could ride the real waves, ten-footers, body-surfing Powder Point when we had a free Sunday afternoon. All six Eastern Kentucky landlocked feet of him rising with the crest and sliding in toward shore, his long arms held out and pushing back sea foam and his head held high above the salt. Him shouting, you there, Earl Wallen, mercy sakes alive. I'd never seen the like, that much life and those big hands taking in waves and waves of an ocean he'd never seen his whole life till then.

And I could have ridden waves too, airwaves, rocked around the clock, written songs to change America. I believe that. Only by 1949 America wasn't ready for a small-town Ohio boy too big for his seersuckers who wanted to ride waves of change and rock around the clock before the clock was even wound yet. Come 1949, Americans had seen enough change to last for good, wanted to spend their nickels and dimes to buy their sweethearts roses, a buck ninety-eight for twenty-five. And war? It was over there again, where it belonged, in the dark, suspect world of Asia and if there was sin, the scientists, they were the egg-heads made a bomb to beat the band, and Alger Hiss? Crucifying him was the country's salvation from the Commies, while Bible sales soared and nice girls hid their desire with boned girdles and crinolines. Touch a woman's breast and hope for more? Get a life, buddy, and watch how that padded cup springs back in your hand. Bad dreams of war, the South Pacific? No war zone, but a bad memory of war turned into big screen romance, even if everyone didn't get to be happy. Mary Martin washed Ezio Pinza right out of her hair. All America tuned in the radio dial to enchanted hours of music about home, church, love, marriage, even death.

Back at Pearl Harbor, Rudy Hyatt went on about the mail order bride he was gonna get sometime, a Hi-wah-yun one, he said in that Eastern Kentucky way of his, the long i's and the slow syllables. She'd have tiny feet and dance at home in the evenings, swaying and dancing in the dark just for him who'd reach up under her hula skirt because she'd wear nothing at all underneath. Other than that, she'd be a good wife, sweet as Doris Day. But I'm ahead of myself. That was me, about eight years later, when I married Ruth Blue.

By now you know my motives. Get back at old man Tobias. Be Johnny on the spot for poker on weekends. Mainline to cheap whiskey and fine bootleg. Corrupt the young and see what she wore under all those baggy skirts. Or maybe it was none of that. Maybe it was that I wanted a mail order bride all to myself. A mountain nymph, her daddy dead in a few years, with a house she'd inherit where she'd meet me at the door and take my shoes and make me supper with light bread and fried bologna gravy and tell me, how fine you are all right, Earl Wallen, sweetheart, dear. Put down your inherited cufflinks and your travel books and welcome home.

All of it's true, and not a bit of it. What I know of 1949's how songs came to me, waves and waves of words. And I tried, like Rudy Hyatt, to ride the big time, the highest crest. Songs to change America, with me bound for glory. Only the words that came out of me were all the same. *True, you, new, few, love, above, fine, mine.* A fine bunch of drivel with about enough heart to make Nat King Cole clear his throat and say, you kidding me, or what? I wanted the sound between a bullet hitting pavement and the racing of a heart. I wanted the face of a man I'd left lying on an airstrip at Pearl Harbor. Song of sorrow, comfort, loss, make me, break me, deal. The world of glory would not crack open, deal me a fistful of truth, a song to make your teeth ache, blues, the blues.

She had it already, in her very name for Christ's sweet sake. Ruth Blue. Blue, the color of a song I wished I could write. Blue of ice on a pond in winter, sky so blue it sings, blue of the center of a flame. None of them the right blue, that blue I could never write in a song. A blue like looking through a keyhole and seeing a world of sorrow I couldn't begin to find at the tip of a pen, in the lyric of a radio song. *Sorrows like sea billows roll,* she'd sing. *It is well, it is well with my soul.* What was that, I'd say, what you're singing? And she'd just smile and say, that? That old hymn? Or she'd pray for me.

Ruth Blue turned Ruth Wallen turned song, a song if I could name it, a song I'd call Ruth Blue.

RUTH: AUTUMN, 1952–1953

Come fall of 1952 I was pregnant with Andrew and the weight of Earl's hand on my stomach at night was a frenzy of notes I now knew better than myself. *You, Ruth Wallen*, they said to me. *Let me in.*

I had learned many things about what my father had meant by a love of gold. Whether he meant the gold stick-on stars on Earl's shoes or the gold records he dreamed of framing and hanging above the wood stove in the house, it was all the same to me. I fell asleep with him whistling "Good Night Irene" into the pillow and woke to the sound of ice breaking in the wash basin, him singing musical show tunes at the top of his lungs.

He wouldn't go to work in the mines like most of the men in Inez, but instead dreamed of writing songs to change all of us forever. He filled our house with song words that crashed in the air around the supper table. Be quiet, I'd say to him as he flipped the radio dial from orchestra music to country diner songs. Before long Tobias and Earl became the same to me, the same voices, saying, Ruth, do this and that, their shadows crossing each other on the kitchen floor.

At first it was the music brung them together. Tobias came back late nights from whatever odd jobs or evangelizing he did, took off his work boots and his socks, sat sipping the glass of buttermilk and cornbread I'd bring. I'd flip on the radio dial. An hour or so later, Earl himself would rush in the door, back from his part-time job at WINZ. He'd kick off his fancy, pointy-toed dance shoes, send them flying toe over heel. He knelt by the radio while he impatiently spun dials and fiddled with the antennas, knelt just like it was prayer-time. Then the three of us would wait for the moment we'd hear him, Earl Wallen, his voice.

He'd make it personal, those little moments on the radio, personal as they'd let him. He'd say, it's me, Ruth Blue, me right to you, right at your fingertips. And it was him all right. His voice, but not some moony country song, not blue suede shoes, not even a yodel, like he'd wanted. Instead, it was him reading the weather forecast, or a sale jingle for the grocer's, or just maybe, if he was lucky, singing an ad for a paint sale. *For you who love to flirt with fire*, he'd read, *who dare to skate on ice, a lush and passionate scarlet, like flaming diamonds dancing on the moon.*

Then it was Tobias's turn for gospel and revivals over the airwaves from this or that vacation Bible school. He held his fingers inches from Earl's face, counted off the souls he'd saved, one by one, with his very own preaching.

I went to bed and left them with their cards, their radio and their profitable prayers for the dead. As I tried to sleep, I pressed the pillow against my ears and told myself neither of them knew anything about God or songs. All my life I had listened about God, Tobias's voice, or whispers, shadows, hints, what might or might not have been real.

I wanted to listen to what was a voice as rich as the powder on moth's wings. *Ruth*, it said, *come here, come down.* Yes, I whispered, into the room with its moonlight and light from the partly open door. I fell, softly and softly, into sleep, listening for the melodious voice of the night and my own prayers.

~

Days passed and weeks and still I hoped this time of Earl and Tobias would be a long dream. I would wake up once and for all, roll down the windows of Earl's car and feel the quick air as we drove away from Mining Hollow forever. But all the weeks that passed held Sundays and prayers and nighttimes and Earl's more and more settled breath. I knew this was my life.

By then, Earl, the Inez Balladeer, was a late-night lonely heart's club with radio advice for housewives who'd lost their husbands to the Starland Skatarama or to the gossip on the courthouse steps. Just show him, honey, he'd say, just show him love or a new housecoat or a little bit of leg, and he'll come right back, I guarantee it. He advised blotchy-faced schoolgirls, two-bit waitresses, rich bankers' wives from west of Inez, any and every woman who'd listen to him say, *sweetheart, you've got it, that razz-ma-dazz, why, just go to the mirror and see*. He'd listen, and question, and advise, then sing them a line or two, *don't you feel me darling, I'm waiting just for you, don't you see me darling, my two-door's ready for the road, but if you don't want me darling, my heart's nothing ever but blue*. Any lines from his latest, greatest hit, one a big time Nashville agent was bound to, just bound to hear.

With him out, late afternoons and into the night, that meant the both of them were home, days, and they wanted me more and more. Ruth, Tobias would say, fry us up a little of that corn pone. Ruth, you reckon that cider's done turned? And Earl was no better, not at all, even if his get me a little more jelly for my toast, sweetie, came with a kiss and a promise. My days filled up with their want and want, food, clean plates, starched shirts, clean socks.

Then about five, Earl would put on his red and white bow tie, spit polish his shoes and say, Ruth, honey, comb my hair, won't you? I'd comb, make him a duck tail sleek with butch wax, leaving it gleaming and neat, and never once did I say, once, ever, that the patched elbows of his radio star's suit jacket wouldn't make his voice carry any farther or be any better than it was.

After Earl left, I'd make Tobias's supper, his favorite, hominy and red-eye gravy if we had the fixings, and we'd both sit through the evening programs, the weather, the swap shop, the Moonlight Gospel Quintet. I'd wait for Tobias to yawn, stretch himself out on the sofa, begin to snore. Then I'd get up close to the radio, close as I could, turn the volume down and listen. Listen to the late night balladeer, radio lover, my husband, gone, nights, later and later, not back till dawn sometimes. I crouched on my ankles, laid my ear next to the speaker. *Listen, honey, don't give up, dress yourself up real fine some night, then you'll see,* he'd say. The words hummed into my ear and I closed my eyes. Closed my eyes until I felt Tobias's hand on my shoulder.

A whore, he said, a whore married to one, now isn't that a fine thing? He'd click the radio off and what little I'd had of Earl, that voice miles away in Inez, would fade and leave my ear ringing and hollow. Kneel down, Tobias would say. Pray. We'd kneel and fill the radioless house with the prayers for all the things he wanted. *Make her a wife who rises before dawn, who sleeps last and least. Make him a husband who looketh after, a man, a man who mines the earth. Forgive us for gold and longing.* During these prayers, he never once shut his reamy eyes and he held his bony fingers so tight against my arm the knuckles were pale. Pray, he said, and I prayed with him, a bottomless thing, a want without an end.

Later at night, I lay under the quilts and waited for my husband. Sometimes I'd hear him drive up, come in the door, then stay in the front room with Tobias. I'd imagine the tiny clatter of dice in an empty fruit jar, the toss along the floorboards and how the praise hims and sweet mother yes's would roll off their tongues. Other times I'd lie very still, waiting for the least sound from the front room, a ghost of the radio's voice. There'd be the ghost of an ad Earl had played that very night, for Diablo's Secret Cologne, maybe, with its power to take a husband from his wife or a sweetheart from the arms of a loved one. There'd be the ghost of rock-n-roll beneath the gospel songs that said *praise Him, praise the smallest leaf that's lost, the lost that do not pray.*

Hour after hour, those nights, I praised, listened beneath the covers for the way my heart beat, asking about love. I held my breath to keep that heart steady, held my breath to listen, some nights, for how late Earl's car would pull in, bringing him back from who knows where, his hands, as the weeks passed, smelling of cologne and something musky as cantaloupes ripening. Especially that last night of radio music and touch I later wanted to forget.

One night I lay awake longer and longer, and still Earl didn't come to bed. I made the sheets warm on his side of the bed, listened to the radio sign-off, ladies, gentlemen, another day where you have conquered the air, then the anthem, then static. Tobias's door shut. Last coughs. Creak of bedsprings. Everything ticked the seconds by, the rise and fall of wind, hum of nothing, tires I didn't hear in the drive. I slept, at last, and when I woke again it was to Earl.

He'd thrown the covers back and he lay on top of me. The sweat smell of his dress shirt pressed against my nose, a weight, and he was cold and shaking. I just let him stay like that, held myself still for his tiredness, his even breath. He'd stumbled in this very way, I was sure, in the time before me on the road and at the station. I moved slowly, a shoulder, a hip, careful to hold his head in the curve of my arm as he slept. Ruth, he said, so soft it could have been static, a hiss of air. Ruth. Be still.

He moved then, hips and legs and arms, leaving just enough of him, a knee pressed firm against my own legs, holding me down. Don't move, he said. Don't move a thing. What choice did I have against the weight of him, sweat and knee and a hand pressed with its sweet scent against my mouth? The other hand, button by button, undid my gown, pushed and pulled at my underclothes. He traced one finger then, one soft radio-man's finger, all down my cooling bare skin. This, he said, starting at the pulse beneath my skin, is where I started. Venice, he said, but you don't know that place. I lit out of there like smoke and fire, after the war. This, he said, his finger traveling down my throat, my chest, stopping at my heartbeat, is who I once was. Do you hear it, Ruth Blue? Do you hear it, Ruth?

And I did hear an echo of his off-key voice singing all the songs he'd longed for, the radio hits that hadn't been, the late night melodies he'd once played, just for me. And this, he said, at last, is who I am now, who I've become. His fingers traveled, then, across my swollen belly, stopped between my legs, pushed into me, so that I arched myself, afraid at the cold and suddenness of him, afraid and holding him, afraid not to. Then all of him traveled over me, the knee held me, the trousers unzipped, the weight and weight was quicker and in no time at all he was made of nothing but air, a whistling without a sound, and I took him in. Even then I thought of how I'd made the sheets warm and waited for sound, his sound.

Listen, Ruth he said, and ear against his neck, I listened. Listened to the sound of blood pulsing in him, to the way our two breaths grew quieter and quieter until there was almost nothing, no sound at all but the empty room and all the weight of nighttime around that room, nighttime and mountains and Mining Hollow all around. There was more than that. There were notes, the low, hollow humming of blood, his and mine, and those notes, almost muffled by flesh and bone, played a song I'd once known, a song he'd called Ruth Blue.

It was a song he'd promised me, one he'd played in a two door car along back roads, singing it full voiced to the empty roads going everywhere he might have once gone. Only now radio was television light in Inez living rooms not our own. Radio played inside us, played inside my pregnant stomach, rushed down my legs against his legs, played along my bare feet. It played inside his emptiness too, in his chest, his own empty self, his mouth that would never after that night sing radio jingles or country songs or say it, this, I'll be a radio star, just wait, Ruth Blue.

I've been fired, Ruth, he said, after. Let go. No more radio, he said. It's gone, he said and laughed. Gone like waves of air.

I lay beneath him, waiting, waiting. Soon I couldn't hear the least trace of notes, in me or him. There was his breathing and his sleep.

When he'd been asleep long enough, I moved from under him, out of bed and across the room, feeling the wet of him ease down me onto my bare feet. I wanted water, milk, anything to fill me, stop my legs shaking, take the taste of salt sweat from my mouth.

I felt my way through the kitchen, along the table top, crumbled cold bread and held it to my mouth. Before I could swallow, I heard rustling, a scrape and skitter in the walls, the corner, beside the stove. A laugh. He coughed, one dry cough.

Tobias, in his undershirt and robe, sat with a jar of whiskey in his hand. Repent, he repeated, and took a long drink, wiped his mouth. *I gave her space*, he said, *to repent of her fornication, and she repented not.*

I let the bread crumbs fall, fumbled at the buttons of my gown.

Guess you heard about that radio job, he asked. He took another long drink.

No, I said. Not a word. Nothing, nothing at all. I fastened button after button, quickly. Had he known how Earl had been more than empty in the bed just now and how he'd gone and cried?

I guess he wasn't enough account to keep around, he said, and the whiskey jar clanged onto the stove. Reckon he'll show the mines some account now? Reckon he knows what the good Lord knows about the man who looketh not after his own household? Reckon you'll pray for him? Or are you good enough?

I turned, crashed into the table, into a box beside the kitchen door. I wanted out into the blackness, into the yard and tall night, wanted to reach up and up, beyond Mining Hollow, beyond mountains and clouds and sky, up into the light beyond that, light so thin and clear I could lay back in it, be invisible, away from both of them.

I got only as far as the porch railing, the first step down. It was there the wanting held me, their wanting, the both of them. That wanting, stale and fidgety, wove its way out of the open kitchen door, tapped at my back, circled around me, held on. What was I to them, it said, this wanting. A map to follow only so far, a body hollow as a door to enter and leave? The bitter mouth of God?

I wanted to run across the yard, through the trees, anywhere, anywhere, to the pond at Mining Hollow. But my husband, emptied, wanted the fullness of me, and my father wanted prayers. The wanting held on a little longer, then led me through the kitchen and back to my husband's bed, where I lay at his back and prayed. *Show me*, I whispered. *Show me.*

~

A month later, Earl went to work for Island Creek Coal Company, a ten mile drive, there and back. Six days a week he drove a forklift and loaded coal rigs, tried to forget all the songs he'd ever known.

And because of it, he wanted from me more and more, wanted me to bring back a light he'd lost. The black heart of the earth opened day by day, and he came home, pale eyes ringed in coal, miner's paychecks smudged with coal dust. The fancy gold stars on his pointed shoes dulled and peeled, the chromium on his two door scratched and blackened, his white hair took a yellow cast. He brought home boots full of cinders and skin with a scent of soot and tiredness. Ruth, he'd say, hold me, just that. I'd lay beside him and he'd hold and hold, as if laying any little part of him next to another body would bring light back to the dark of his days. By day, his pale blue eyes squinted in the least sun. By night, he talked about bombs and the sun, mumbled, let me see you, damn you, let me see your face.

Soon the dark around him was so thick and heavy he could see no one, not even himself. The insides of him lost their shine. No more songs, no more whistling up the drive home, no more dance steps across the porch. He held on to me at night, wanting and wanting, and the dark hand in my chest grew and grew until I could hardly breath.

I held on tight to him and me both, to the weight of my belly that kicked, held on to the darkness, like it was pieces of slag and charred kindling I'd found in the road, a dark with a shape, a face in the dark whose features I knew. I wanted, with my own thin self, to find the cracks in that dark, slip softly through them, then out and up into all the light we'd lost. Did that light slip out at night, dance through the trees in Mining Hollow, run back and circle the house, ease back in, then hide in the walls and chairs and picture frames that held Jesus?

At night, as I held Earl, I could almost hear it, that light, a dry thing, rubbing and rustling outside, sliding along the floor, setting itself, hidden, in all the things we owned, the cups, plates, Bibles.

Pray, Tobias said, by day. Pray and God will show you. Mornings he stood watching Earl drive off down the road, sat paring his nails off the front step. Pray, he whispered, as if to himself, as I swept the porch, threw dishwater down into the yard. He went to Inez less and less, spent less time poring over the guns he'd go in to trade, the knives he'd swap and sell, the souls he'd save. He stayed by me in the

177

kitchen as I peeled onions, sorted beans. Pray and pray, he said, as I combed my hair and washed my arms and face, as I waited for Earl to come home.

Pray? Pray for what, I said to him, but I prayed anyway. I prayed words that made no sense. Forgotten. Vanish. Up. I prayed words I thought I knew, or had once known. Mother. Glass. Broken. I prayed for anything, anything to happen, those long afternoons while Tobias stayed by me, whispering his own prayers, coughing his dry cough, shuffling, an old man's walk from porch to back door to me.

I prayed for all the things I might have been, things I knew no name for, prayed for all I had been, all I was not, prayed and thought of the nights and their holding, the days and the praying that was never enough, prayed for a voice that could sing to me in the too quiet blackness, alone, alone. I prayed, for the shine that was no longer Earl, the shine hidden in me at night, that shining light in walls and cups and spoons and me, far down in me.

My heart is sore pained within me, I prayed. *Oh, that I had wings that I might rise and fly away and be at rest.* I will call upon God, I prayed, and he, he will save me, us all. But the voice of night was far down in me, saying nothing, saying nothing in this world. You, it said. You and no one but you.

I prayed and I waited to bear my son.

~

It was an August night in 1953 but dead of winter cold. Without waking Earl, I went into the kitchen, found a leftover piece of kindling, set a fire to blazing in the stove.

From far away, neither above nor below, I heard voices, words of a hymn, rich words, *rich dews of grace come over us in many a gentle shower, and brighter scenes before us are opening every hour.* I felt as light as air, invisible. I rubbed my invisible hands in front of the fire, felt no heat, ran invisible fingers through the flames, felt no burning. I saw the clear blue flame in the wood, heard the steady hiss of pine sap. As this hiss lulled me, I sank with my invisible self into a rocking chair.

Rocking, the fire humming, I sat so long sweat eased down my back, into my eyes. A fever came over me, a sickness, and then I knew this room. It wasn't a room of kitchen and cold, but Mining Hollow, the center of forever, where I would give birth.

Then I was in a bed, lying in sweat and broken birth waters, a bed smelling of blood and salt. In this room, at first, were just the two of them, father, husband, Earl in his tee shirt, sleeves rolled to shoulders, Tobias in his Sunday suit, white shirt gray with wear. They worked against each other, bringing too many rags, bitter tea I couldn't drink, useless boiled water. This birth, this way, their coming to life. In my pain I lay waiting for something, a movement, a taste or sound to break me open, deliver me.

For awhile, later, we walked, one of them on either side of me, slow, wide circles around and around. Earl said, it's a new dance step, the stroll, and I swayed to the rhythm of it, felt the heavy weight of this child rock and settle, not leaving the inside of me. I asked for cool water and Earl brought me a sponge. Tobias squeezed it onto my tongue, a few drops at a time, told me what it was I would be given in this my greatest hour, hour of need and bringing forth. I bit the inside of my mouth against it, but this couldn't help the pain. The Lord will provide, Tobias said, but then Earl, behind him, was saying, a doctor, old man, can't you see, look, are you a fool? From far away I saw the two of them, studying me, me, a body I was no longer in, a body as little mine as a cow, diagramed and laid out to butcher, the engine of a broke down car, the word of the good Lord, marked, underlined, memorized.

Memorized forever, the place of dreams and darkness I was in. Outside the window I could hear a hollow sound, a flute, but Earl placed a warm cloth on my forehead and told me it was the radio. He turned the volume higher, so high the waves and waves of static stumbled across the room, danced around my ears. Too loud, I tried to say to a man in a black coat who sat at the foot of the bed. He reached up, pressed against my belly, said, turn, it needs to turn, and placed a cold bell against my skin. I could hear, not him, but the heart beating, tiny heart in salt water, inland sea, sea of me.

I saw myself walking at the back of the pond at my daddy's house. Saw a horse there, its four legs stretching stiff and up toward the sky.

Eyes glass and silver. *This*, he said, *is the fourth horse, whose name is death*. I plunged into, water, pain, waves of pain. I rode the sound of flies buzzing the room, so loud I screamed again, bit Earl's hand over my mouth, bit down hard.

Later, there was nothing but a sheet between me and my son's birth with them on the other side of it, keeping the sight for themselves, one and one and one, husband and daddy and the doctor who'd come with his bag, all of them surrounding my bed. They held a sheet up high below my waist so I couldn't see my own body as my son came forth. I saw this sheet on a line of clean clothes, blowing back and blowing back. Then I saw a wind, a Holy Ghost, circling and circling, white and spent. *Now*, and *here*, their voices said. *It's time*. My flesh gave way, tore, and he left my body, cried a strange, weak cry. Far away, I saw their eyes, red with lack of sleep, shiny, awed. As though this birth had been all theirs.

What they had not had, had not heard, was the song, a song saying, *want*, and want and want, saying, *oh, listen*. I had learned at last the name of the voice, my visitor by night. Lover, words rich as milk and humming. God's power? How he had long searched for me by night in the shadow of the forsythia by the front steps.

Rich voice, filling me with urgency and reach and before any of them could tell me how or what or why, I, not them, had released him from myself. Like this, God spoke through me, his own sweet song, said, *Ruth, you are the giver of life.*

I took him in my arms and he was mine, the wet, black hair, transparent skin streaked with blood and mucus, son, son. I placed him at my breast, watched while his small mouth opened, ready to suck and suck.

Oh, listen, the voice said. *Clothe thyself in ashes, make thee mourning, as for an only son*. I stroked his cool, wet skin, whispered to him, promised. How the breath, so small and weak, came out of his new mouth. Listen, listen, I said. I held him close, knowing I could forever fill him with praise, forever teach him salvation.

PART II

RUTH: AUGUST 16, 1983

You remember a June hot enough to scorch the yellow grass and make a kitchen breeze useless. Nights, you'd lie awake, listening, wanting the loose roof shingles to blow, the thunder to start, the house to creak and moan with the changing weather.

But those nights were dead quiet, full of waiting. Awake, you pulled quilts over your damp body, listened for your heartbeat to quicken then still, for mice in the cabinets to go quiet. One night you even went and stood at the pond, listening to frogs and snapping turtles, them diving into humid, mossy water. You brought Andrew, lay with him on the dock Earl had made. Held your baby, put your ear up next to his breath.

Next day, after Tobias and Earl both went off, the one to loaf in Inez, the other to the Wheelwright mines, you went to the yard, laid him on the blanket by the steps. You scrubbed canning jars for the blue beans. All above you, new leaves were too green in the burning light against the mountains way back of the hollow, light you held your hands up toward, hands white and wrinkled from water and lye in the fine cracks on your fingers.

You worked an hour or so into the hottest time, felt your stomach rumble, no breakfast, and your head light. It was peaceful sitting there, the jars clear and drying, lightness into your legs and feet, then up again, to the very top of you, hunger moving like you could move with it, right up to the cloudless sky.

Then the pale yellow day got more, and you stood and caught hold of the chair back, knew you'd gone too far this time, that it was possible to float up and up, forever. Orange flags grew beside the house, a color made you taste rust. You looked for a solid thing, handle of the maul against the woodshed, iron horseshoe above the door, anything weighted to hold your lightened body down.

Andrew lay on the blanket and you looked down there, at the fine hairs above his lip glistening with sweat, the plump baby arms and small toenails you'd bitten short. You lay beside him and held him, the hands, streaks of red dirt where he'd reached over. His fists were clinched in sleep and you pried at a thing there. He whimpered and rolled toward you, palm open, and there was something tiny and featherless, a dead bird, pink eyelids shut. A pink that made you swallow against the sickness inside you, take deep breaths of the clean of your son's hair.

You wanted to hold on to him, fold your own hands around his. You wanted to pray. *Let it, oh Lord, let it come to life, let it fly, let me and him hold on an on.*

The voice said, the voice of weeks of heat and no sleep, said, *tell him, Ruth.* Tell him what? No more words. You stared up and up at the yellow sky and you held on to Andrew until he woke and began to cry.

ANDREW: 1962

The summer I was nine my grandfather, Tobias Blue, saw a hole reaching into eternity in the floor of our living room, a hole the size of a man's fist, just beneath a corner of the torn red linoleum. He believed he could cast all his personal visions of sin into that a hole—whiskey when bootleg was sky high, poker when he had lost more than he'd counted on, and any sins at all of the flesh. How, for instance, Ruby Dean, the fat girl from Inez, met certain boys at mowing season and hid with them behind the bales of hay in barns, moaning as they kissed the lush ripples of her flesh.

One afternoon that summer of the visionary hole, he curled up in a blanket on the couch as my mother cooked our supper. In the kitchen, she moved from table to stove as if the food were an inconvenience, an afterthought that she made as transparent as possible. Her foods, milky gravy, watery soups I spooned through for tiny bites of potato, all the scraps we might have thrown away.

That particular afternoon, she stood at the sink for a long while, then moved to the screen door. She looked down the road where the sun was already heading behind the mountains beyond Mining Hollow. Brushing back her short, dark hair, she stared directly into the bright light. Holy light, she said, and looked neither happy nor sad as the crimson shone through the screen door, through her, and onto my lap. Her face seemed to have no eyes, no mouth, only kitchen shadows, in the shape of a face. My mother as I wished for her, cool hands, hair smelling of wood smoke, vanished on such afternoons and I was afraid I'd disappear with her into that holy light.

She walked back to the sink and past my chair, where I caught the blue hem of her dress, that little touch of cloth making my heart ache. Slow down, I wanted to say. Take time. But the hem slipped from my hand like water. Andrew, she said, the Lord Jesus expects us soon.

The couch springs creaked as my grandfather turned over. My mother's paring knife shredded cabbage and she hummed the Lord's praises. The Lord, he asked in his sleep. The Lord?

We stepped into the living room. Knees in his arms, eyes open, he was staring at some dark corner of the floor we couldn't see.

"Ruth?" he asked. "You see them? Secrets of the Lord, secrets no fancy traveling preacher will give you. Secrets. Mercy. Why, they're right here if you want them."

The three of us looked at the bare floorboards beneath a corner of the linoleum, and at the hole, just to the left of the couch. I had laid down many times, put my eye to the hole, and seen red dirt, cobwebs, the last hours of sunlight. You about to fix that, Earl, my mother would say. Or leave it be till winter sets in good? Lately, my grandfather had hidden the hole, stuffing it tenderly with old handkerchiefs, now and then pulling out a sock or a matted ball of twine so that any of us, if we chose, could look down into a forever full of shadows, full of Jesus, whom we could tell everything, give everything, every last secret hunger.

I was afraid and held my mother's hand as tight as I could to keep her from vanishing into this place my grandfather dreamed.

"Can't see in the dark," my father said, behind us. "Can't find supper neither. Aren't you hungry, old man?"

The light switch clicked. He grabbed the blanket from my grandfather, leaving his skinny body looking cold in the bright living room light.

~

At the end of that July, the traveling preacher predicted stepped off the conductor's car on the L & N, bound for Cincinnati with fifty cars full of coal. This preacher was to bring a revival to Inez, one that lasted through the weeks of late July, and then on from there, into an August so hot the patches of tar on Main Street grew soft and stuck to our shoes.

The afternoon Preacher Martin stepped off the train in Inez, he stood in front of the courthouse, brushing cinders off the wide lapels of his gray suit jacket. He took off his black felt hat and pulled out a piece of paper, raked back his blonde hair and took a seat on top of a tall cardboard box. Sun glinted off what I later learned was his right, glass eye.

"I'm Preacher Martin," he said, and cleared his throat. Then he began to read. "The great day of his wrath is come. Who, I say, who shall be able to stand it?" The words rolled off his tongue, rich as molasses, with a high-pitched edge, like a song whistled off a blade of grass.

We were under the weeping willows by the courthouse steps, ready to eat the biscuits my mother had packed when my father rolled up his sleeves, leaned against a tree, arms folded, a doubtful expression.

"Wrath," he said, reaching for a biscuit. It dripped tomato seeds and grains of sugar. "Now what does that rhyme with, I wonder?"

My father was God-fearing, but he believed the spirit spoke to you in places more secret than a town square, in the garage maybe, between the raised hood of a Ford pickup and an engine with trouble.

"Wrath," he said again, taking a large bite of sandwich, wiping his mouth on his shirt sleeve. "Last time I felt that was on the way to Number Nine Mine."

He looked at my mother, who laid her white gloved hands across her stomach. She believed in the unholiness of my father's some-times doubtful and sometimes card-playing ways.

"The wrath of the Almighty, Earl," she said, in that toneless voice with a catch, a voice for mealtime blessings and Jesus prayers.

I made my way through the crowd by the courthouse steps. Women and boys and grocery clerks from the store across the street had gathered and my grandfather, Tobias, was already up there too. His Case knife gleamed as he pared his nails.

"Tonight, brothers and sisters," Preacher Martin said, "let the word of the Almighty speak to you." The strong muscles stood out in his neck, his lean finger pointed at first one, then another of us. "Let the words of sweet, holy Jesus fill you, take you out of your homes, down your roads. Come out to Him, I beg you, for the name of all that must be bathed in the light of the holy Lord."

He paced, making neat turns at either end of the courthouse steps, his saddle oxfords scraping asphalt with a kitchen match sound. "But beware, oh ye brothers of God, oh ye sisters of the earth. Beware even now of the evil in our midst that will hold us back, keep us in our houses. Keep us back from the mystery on high that I have to show you."

His bowed legs quivered. Repent, repent, he said, like a hymn. *Just as I am*, we sang, *oh lamb of God, I come*. People nudged, pointed, as though God himself had just stepped from behind the courthouse, humming, softly, tenderly, clothed in light as clean and new as the neon sign just installed above the door of Wyatt's Pharmacy.

My grandfather moved out of the shadows, stretched his arms above his head, shouted, "Glory, yes, glory!" His hands were held palms up to the sky, like he was testing the direction of the wind or asking God for a sign. His watery eyes narrowed with suspicion as he looked at the Preacher. My grandfather, I had been raised to know, had a personal connection to the Lord. He saw glory for himself, seldom attending any church house to seek the truth he believed well enough on his own.

"Glory," he shouted again, that word his question waiting to be answered.

Behind me there were praises and amens, but also a high, clear whistling, my father's. He was whistling a song as quick and light as the old fifties rock 'n' roll tunes he'd me he used to love. As I pushed my way back through the crowd I could barely see him, standing by the willow tree, arms folded.

My mother leaped up, gloved finger pointing to heaven.

"It's what I see," she said, "what I see!"

"How do you see," my father asked, "any better than I do?" His look was what I felt when I wanted the light in my room at night and couldn't find it. He backed away, dipped snuff into his bottom lip.

I took my mother's hand, looked up the tall length of her. Her eyes were closed, her black hair wet with sweat. Even through the glove I could feel the cold damp of her skin. It's what I see, she whispered.

I stared too, waited for the Holy Ghost to settle on the preacher's shoulders, or on mine. The mid-afternoon sun danced, became a bird darting from behind the World War II soldier's monument beside the courthouse door. It flew in quick, flashing circles, became a motion of wings just the shape of Preacher Martin's fist. He held his Bible high and the pages fluttered in the warm July air, made wing sounds.

There were only two of us, that hot July afternoon, who could possibly have thought Preacher Martin was a pretty man. On the way to the car we passed a storefront window and I saw Ruby Dean, her wide nose pressed against the window-glass. Her face was flushed and the usual perspiration stained the front of her dress. She watched Preacher Martin, licked soda from her upper lip and smiled. I held my mother's hand as we passed. I didn't know it then, but I had already begun to memorize him for all time, his fierce eyes, one as blue as cobalt glass, the loose folds of his clothes, the pale pink of scalp beneath his thin hair. I memorized him, my first face of love, though it was long before I knew this. He was a fierce looking man, but I wanted to go back to him, take a seat, lay my cheek against his bony knee.

~

If any of them had asked me, that summer of the revival, what love meant, where love came from or went, I could have told them. That whole revival summer I tried to store up love like the hungry store up food. At night, love flew against the glass of my painted-shut window. It was like moth's wings, saying let me in, in. I lay still, my hands open and uncupped, ready to catch hold of that love at its most unsuspecting minute. But love escaped me. On the walls of my room and on my bare skin were the shadows of moths. When morning came I saw these walls as they really were—gray and water stained, as empty as I felt. Empty and waiting to be filled that whole summer I later would call the first one I loved.

~

Two days after we saw him by the courthouse, Preacher Martin's revival began. The first night, we pulled into the parking lot of the Denver Church just as Ruby Dean and her father rolled to a halt beside us in their dusty, bug spattered truck. Window down, Ruby Dean smacked her chewing gum and nodded her head to radio music, turned so loud we could hear it above "Just As I Am" from inside the church.

"She's got the right idea," my father said and drummed his fingers on the dashboard.

Ruby eased her legs out of the truck, made her way up the steps, looking back, I thought, at me. She had her usual smile, far away and unsatisfied.

She had the same smile when she met us at the door, the time my father and I drove up to Essa Creek, where Ruby lived. While the two men were out in the yard, talking guns, I sat in the kitchen with her and ate. I was amazed at the house. The walls were papered with cutouts from movie magazines and the radio was up full volume while she danced her way from refrigerator to cupboard, swaying to old love songs like "Blue Tango" and "You, You, You," all the while loading the kitchen table with sweets. I ate more that day than I can ever remember eating, pie, cookies, tarts, fancy tea cakes. We ate while through the window came the sounds of our fathers talking lines of sight, buckshot, scope. I ate until I felt sleepy, glutted with so many pastries their tastes were indistinguishable. Ruby's full lips were coated with powdered sugar. She ate more and more, until her eyes were sleepy and distant, her lips parted in a sugary half smile.

The lights flashed off, on, then off, leaving the church in darkness. She smoothed her enormous poodle skirts and sat two rows ahead of us.

"Praise God," Preacher Martin shouted, and his voice, lightning clear, flashed down the aisles, crept, tingling, onto the palms of our hands.

"Have we all come here to praise Jesus," the Preacher asked us. The congregation said yes, Lord, then there was the sharp scrape of a match. Three candles were lit on the altar, casting shadows on the tall walls. I cupped my hands and raised them, made the shadow shape of a mule, a bird, felt my mother elbow my ribs.

My eyes adjusted and I saw Preacher Martin, even finer than I remembered him from the courthouse steps. During the invocation, I studied his glass eye, blue as a glass marble in the candlelight. And for what blessings shall we ask God, he said. His gray dress suit had been carefully pressed, arranged as neatly as on the body of a dead man at the funeral home. But life came from everything about him, wide, red mouth already full of glory, fist slamming hard against the pulpit. I imagined holding that fist as I crossed some dangerous place, a street, or something harder, the steps to salvation. That fist would untighten in my hand, grow warm and kind. Brothers, he shouted. Sisters. The grace of God has flown out of our midst. The Holy Ghost has departed. And for what blessings shall we ask?

Shall we ask, my mother repeated, just as the overhead lights came back on. Preacher Martin lowered his voice. Are you prepared to meet your Savior? Then he dragged out a tall cardboard box from behind the pulpit. Paper tore with a whispery sound. His bony elbows flailed as he ripped off the last length of wrapping tape, lifted a plastic figure out of the box, set it down gently on the altar.

This, the Preacher said, has comforted me, when I have traveled in unknown towns, when I have felt friendless, Godless. This, I know, is the way I will someday see my Savior. The statue was about three feet high with arms to either side, palms tilted slightly up. The hair was yellow, the skin faded, the bare feet red as clay. The paint from most of one eye had peeled away, leaving the face with a winking slyness. As the sermon began, Preacher Martin's voice rose and fell and rose, his thin fist slammed the pulpit, while the statue slid forward, closer and closer to us. Beside me, my father snorted. Seen one of those in the five and dime, Andrew? My mother glared and he pulled a pack of cigarettes from his shirt sleeve, eased out the pew toward the back door.

The sermon began then, with eating, with strange foods, honey and olives and pomegranates. He told stories of foods known only to God, a long scroll filled with the sacred word which, on Judgement Day, we would eat to taste God's love. I had, when younger, eaten pages from the Sears and Roebuck catalogue and I thought God's words might taste similar, only richer and inkier. On the last day of the world, the Preacher told us, God would give us wine to drink, a sin in any Christian county, but this was wine from the press of wrath, the blood of Christ.

Ruby was staring at Preacher Martin, her eyes wide and dark, just the color of chocolate pie, round cheeks flushed, full lips beautiful, moving in what I thought was prayer. The rhinestone buttons of her dress strained open and I caught glimpses of dimpled, vanilla moon-pie skin.

But food, Preacher Martin continued, is only a sign of the journey God wishes us to take through the human body. We must, he said, journey beyond flesh, bone, mere blood, must realize that all we touch is less than spirit, that to drink the blood of Jesus is to stand at the brink, the edge of the valley of the shadow of death. To love Jesus we must descend, realize the world and the world that is the body cannot last. Signs of the impermanence of the world, he said, were or would soon be everywhere—earthquakes in divers places, unnatural weather patterns, children who were not children. Other signs, he said, we would have to look for harder. We might, for example, believe ourselves to be falling in love, might sit for hours staring at a woman's hair or a man's eyes. We might stare so long we would forget how the shine of hair tempts the angels or that the pupil of an eye is only a passageway, a dark hole through which we are supposed to fall, head over heels, and then on and on from there, into eternity and the embracing arms of Jesus.

The congregation was so quiet not a pew creaked. He told us to examine our palms for the mark of the beast, to search our hearts for truth, but as I tried to listen to him, a love song came to me instead, a song I might have heard at Ruby Dean's house, or it could have come from farther back, from as far back as I could remember, when my father used to sit on the front porch at Mining Hollow with his guitar. I looked at Preacher Martin's beautiful face and closed my eyes, as if in prayer.

Someone danced in the aisles, Bible raised like a tambourine. Oh praise, the Preacher sang, for now the sermon was a song, words faster and faster, words none of us knew. Singing praise, he stepped down from the pulpit, stood by the altar, his arms raised, Jesus with the little children, Jesus crucified. He unbuttoned his suit jacket, loosened his tie. His thin hair clung to his scalp with sweat, with glory. Praise God that we shall be healed. Healed, the blind, the maimed, the crippled, healed, the clear-skinned, the steady-eyed, none of us perfect before God. Preacher Martin held one hand out to us, palm down. So come, he sang, come to the touch of the Lord. The church dimmed again and behind him was the Jesus statue, dull and colorless in the candlelight.

Healed, I thought, imagining the Preacher's hands. Would they be freckled on their backs? Would their palms be warm? Ahead of me, Ruby Dean was sitting forward in her chair. She had loosened the top buttons of her dress, was fanning herself, all the while looking straight at Preacher Martin. I was sure of it. What she felt for the Preacher was not necessarily praise, but love, purely and simply. What I felt filled my chest with something soft as the lobe of an ear, something so forbidden I could give it no name.

~

What, you might ask, was this mistaken world of love? A sin, you tell me, right from the start. Or, worse yet, there is no start. A boy who loves a man will be no man at all. Will be an abomination, a freak, a transgression beyond naming. Not possible, you tell me, that we are created with a seed of love in our hearts, a seed that unfolds with its own secret name, each for each.

And yet all that summer I dreamed of the possible faces of love. At night my hand went again and again between my thighs as I discovered the power of my invisible body in the dark, a power my mother hinted was a sin. The forbidden, touch, that thing men did. A sin, the thing all men did, no less the way I dreamed. Imagining another body beside me, I touched the dark, its cheeks, nose, eyes. Sometimes I pulled back the dark and found the face of Preacher Martin. Or sometimes I touched faces I knew better, boys from town with whom I'd slipped away, after school or during church mornings, to smoke forbidden cigarettes. At night I unbuttoned their shirts, touched their bare skin. After touching myself, I couldn't sleep, knowing there would be morning, and morning after that, and that these ways I dreamed would never have another name. What if I pulled back the face of the dark and found no one at all?

~

Night after night that summer, we went back to the revival, to Preacher Martin and his statue of Jesus, to sermons about the end of time. We were looking, each of us, for the secrets of God my grandfather insisted lay in a bottomless hole in our living room floor. Night after night, my mother sat through Preacher Martin's sermons, eyes closed, seeing a place of her own visions it seemed she might sometime never return from. My father, saying he feared no God in heaven or anywhere in Inez, drove us to the Denver church night after night. During the long sermons, he often sat in the parking lot, radio on in the truck, impatient fingers tapping on the dash as he smoked his cigarettes. Other times I'd see him, all the way back at the church house door, arms folded across his stomach, a look on his face of longing and scorn, as the voices rose with yes, sweet Jesus, yes, with the chanting of the chosen holy in rhythm to tambourines and drums and guitars for the Lord.

I sat, night after night, listening to the invitational words. Come, ye who are weary, Preacher Martin said, holding out his hands. I followed the words right into his warm palms. Come unto me, he said, and ye shall rest. In the warmth of those hands, I shut my eyes, giving a face to the dark in which I had been so many times. I was comforted, until, one night a song began, the song I always called a miracle. That night was when Ruby Dean sang her own song of praise.

~

When I say she sang that night, I mean of course, what I imagined, or what you will, years later. Call it imagination or wishing or even looking at the world through smoke colored glass. What any of us remember of childhood or of the expression on a face or of love in its aftermath. What any of us imagine when our lives are hungry and waiting to be filled. I believe, that night, Ruby sang "Some Enchanted Evening," her voice full of a clarinet and a saxophone from the school band, of sounds from the long ago records my father had owned, the ones my mother tossed into the yard. She walked toward the pulpit, hands held out, waiting to be received. *Some enchanted evening*, Ruby sang, *you will see a stranger*.

Hymnbooks closed, paper fans stopped waving. Even my mother sat forward, listening, her mouth in a tight line. Like it or not, we were all suddenly in a huge room, not church at all, but a high school gym with dim light and blue smoke. We closed our eyes and swayed, slow-dancing. *A stranger*, she sang, *across a crowded room*. I saw myself dancing, breathing the scent of Preacher Martin's clothes, a scent like new leather. As we danced, he placed his hand on my head. I felt my heart shiver.

Then Preacher Martin laid his hands on her shoulders. Her eyes were full of notes, and she sang the radio, the Bible, a love song, *rise up, my love, my fair one, and come away, for lo, the winter is past and the rain is over and gone*. Preacher Martin's arms fell to his sides as he stepped away from her and watched. There was nothing else any of us could do. Ruby was right. Winter and the end of the world had nothing to do with that moment. I shook the sleep from my head and turned to look out the open church windows. It was summer and lovely and the last of the day's heat was vanishing in the cool moonlight. From beneath the window, rose the slow smoke of my father's cigarettes.

That was when the miracle happened. A miracle, or a trick of light, or just a wind that picked up, a summer wind that smelled warm, like vanilla and honey and milk. It scooped Ruby up, held her, suspended gently above the altar and the statue of Jesus. Her skirt blew and her black hair came unpinned, in a long braid below her body, a rope inviting us all to climb up into an invisible lover's arms. The whole thing lasted only seconds, then Ruby Dean was back on earth again. She rubbed her eyes drowsily, looked first at Preacher Martin and then at the congregation. What, she asked. What?

Ruby Dean's love song vanished as suddenly as it had come. The altar candles sputtered and extinguished, leaving the church dark and smelling of burning wax. What happened next in the shadowy light was my mother, standing, whispering, brimstone, wormwood, holy and holy and holy, words that made me so afraid whatever love song I had wanted or imagined broke in my chest, broke brittle as glass, black glass, forbidden radio songs.

My mother pushed past me and stood in the aisle, her thin arms raised to heaven. Oh Lord, she sang, her own awful song, and the light was just enough to reveal her face, the twitch of the mouth, the eyes rolled back, those chilly quarter moons. I saw the way she fell out, her unfamiliar face down, the way she lay, legs kicking some sacred dance all her own, hers and God's, the way she rolled and spit speaking with unknown tongues. I was the one who went to her then, smoothed her dress, hid her thinness, held her down and down, until the terrible power of glory let her go.

The church lights came back on, a harsh, blinding light, and I saw two things. My mother, released now, lay still and pale. My stomach knotted with fear as I also saw the empty altar, with the statue of Jesus gone. Praise God for what he has wrought, the Preacher said. But I could not praise. I imagined the summer night outside, with Jesus walking among the dark trees, not listening to any love song I might whistle, however clearly.

~

When we got back to Mining Hollow that night, I slipped out and went to the woods back of the house, near the pond. My shirt clung to my back with the humid air, but I wrapped my arms around myself and felt cold, then colder as I imagined black pond water and the invisible trees of night, and the mountains beyond that, and the end of world beyond that, a hole in forever no love could fill. I stood at the edge of the pond and looked down and down into my own visions of what might become of us all.

I saw my father, sitting, in the late evenings, tapping his foot as the tree frogs chorused, whistling in time to the night until my mother padded upstairs in her bare feet. When we heard the creaking of the floorboards and knew she knelt in prayer, my father's tapping stilled and the night grew silent, the whistling, then only the upstairs and faraway sound of praying. A shadow settled beneath my father's chair and curled up under his feet. I saw how my father would soon become a ghost, staying gone more and more, down at the bottom of the yard, working on the truck, as long as there was any light at all. Soon he would take on night shifts at the mines.

I saw how some nights, when storms came and torrents fell on the roof I would lie imagining Preacher Martin's hands, touching me in ways that made me ashamed and glad. My mother, coming in later to check on me, opened the door and in the light from the hall, I could see she had drunk prayers rather than love. They clung to the corners of her mouth like spider webs. The longer I looked at her, the more she grew almost, but not completely, invisible, as if she floated on her back, fingers trailing, partly beneath water. She floated in a visionary darkness where love was no longer necessary and little by little, more and more of her vanished, a kneecap, a foot, one finger, until I could see almost none of her, only a wave of black hair and an empty place that felt like falling and falling forever.

~

Preacher Martin left town not long after that revival night. He left on the five o'clock bound north and the last I saw of him was a glint of sunlight in his glass eye as I watched him through the train window. I watched the train until it disappeared into the distance, leaving only a thin trail of smoke. I walked home slowly, thinking of the end of the world.

After that, the only other person, besides myself, who seemed to remember the revival was my mother. Some nights, when both my parents thought I was asleep, I'd slip into their room, stand quietly beside their bed. My father lay on his side, arm draped across her transparent body. Her skin was silvery as water. I could see straight through to her heart, which was just below the crook of his elbow. It was empty as a glass lamp shade, with just enough room for me, and in it was a tiny flame. I bent closer. What I saw inside this flame was the Holy Ghost, ready to race, through her blood, a bird made of fire.

EARL: 1962

By 1958 you'd think a family man couldn't have asked for much more than a TV dinner and the "Lawrence Welk Show" and maybe Peggy Lee singing "Is That All There Is?" Still, it was me, not Tobias Blue, who kept television out of the house at Mining Hollow. It reminded me too much of myself.

Not that I'd have minded an evening now and then with "Howdy Doody" reruns and a TV dinner, mind you. I'd seen TV at the Inez diner often enough. The fuzzy picture and a voice from a commercial saying—*do you arise irked with life, are you prone to snap at loved ones, with our strong, hearty breakfast coffee breakfast becomes a spirited, even hilarious affair!* Hilarious was one word for it.

I wasn't a man now. I was a television shape moving behind snow and interference, a ghost shape from the happy American family, from the blessed Sunday dinner table, spending forever at Mining Hollow.

Up and leave, Earl, Lolo Lafferty would say to me, over diner coffee. And what she wouldn't say was, be a man, Earl, be with me, sugar, looking at me the whole time with those blue eyes and that mouth I knew how to kiss.

A man, I asked? You just show me what that is, Lolo Lafferty.

And sometimes she would.

Your future is great in a growing America, TV said. Be man enough to take charge of yourself, Lolo Lafferty told me. Film stars do it all the time, she said. Go out for cigarettes. Take the high road. If there ever was a time for optimism, it was now—that was television. And on Sunday mornings TV gospel time. A man, they said, who looketh not after his own household, he's worse than an infidel.

Forever, all of it. Work, time card, pay check, back to the mouth of Mining Hollow. Wasn't that what a family man did?

~

I'll tell you what forever is. Forever's like this morning. Five A.M., Tobias Blue out in hall but close enough to tickle my ear with his nose whiskers, saying, rise and shine, boy, rise and shine, there's a man's day's work to do. What little he knew about a day's work would have fit into my into my eye tooth. The day of that Van Lear revival, for instance. I laid still for a long while that morning and kept my eyes shut while he walked on down the hall. I heard him go into Andrew's room.

Beside me, Ruth threw back the covers, letting in a little chilly air. Her bare feet hit the floor and she said, "Earl Wallen, I know you're awake. Can't do a day's work in bed."

I could have told her a lot about what you could do with a day in bed, but I kept my mouth shut and stayed where I was while she snapped and buttoned and tied, covering up every square inch of her holy flesh. Five minutes, I wanted five minutes with her and him both out there and Andrew getting ready to drag-ass down the hall and me laying, alone, thinking.

Through the walls, I heard the creak of Andrew's bedsprings, the knob rattling, then him in the hall, on tiptoe, like he did. He paused outside my open door, just stood there for the longest while. With the sheets over my head, I could feel him looking. He was like that. He'd be on the other side of a door or beneath the front porch steps, any sneaking place he'd think you wouldn't see him looking and whispering to himself. Whispers, or something like it, never a song exactly, just something silly and soft sounding, like if I turned around real quick he'd be giggling to himself. I could feel him whistling right now, little high-pitched notes tugging at the skin on my back, but I laid as still as I could until he went on to the kitchen.

"Andrew Wallen, you get on over to the sink. How many times have I told you? If your hands aren't black as tar. Earl?" she called. "You going to work or going hungry?"

Black. Black as tar, coal dust, night. I sighed and threw back the covers. Records were the only black thing I used to worry about. 1948 and "The Tennessee Waltz" and the first LP's. By 1949 45's were going like hotcakes. What was the song that year? "Forever and Ever?" Then 1950, Red Foley, "Chattanoogie Shoe Shine Boy," and then 1951 and Johnnie Ray and "Cry" and 1952 Rosemary Clooney and "Botacha Me." But by 1952 I wasn't buying records anymore, don't even know why I'd bought them until then. Stacks of them, the latest, greatest top hits and notables and revivals, stacks and stacks and nothing to play them on, nowhere to put them but at the back of some Mining Hollow closet I've reached back into ever and now and then, and pulled my hand back, quick. All that dark and dust and who knows what. Things to make my skin crawl, things I'd better forget, that's what.

Some days I reached back, way back, into my belly, my chest, and I found them, a few words, a few straggly words that might have been a song once, *work all day, work all night, baby come hold me until the morning light.* Those few words were a little black thing spinning inside my chest, spinning faster and faster, spinning so fast my ears rang, saying, *listen, can't you hear?* Lately the black thing inside me has slowed down, slowed to a few scratchy words, an off-key note, to nothing at all, nothing but a bad taste in my mouth.

I pulled on my clothes from yesterday, my work pants so coal dust stiff they could have stood up on their own. At the wash basin I splashed my eyes, inhaled some cold water, blew black threads into my palm.

The three of them were already at the table when I went in there. A skillet with fat slabs of bacon and fried toast was in the middle of the table, but nobody was reaching for any. She'd gone and lit an old kerosene lamp, when I'd made sure, just last fall, that every room was wired right, with my hard earned dollars, too. I slid into my spot and reached for a fork.

"Earl," Ruth said. She laid her hand on me.

Wait. Five-thirty in the morning and nothing to look forward to but a ten hour shift below ground and she says wait and be thankful. I pushed my plate back, crossed my arms.

"Let's hear it, old man," I said. "What little gospels gems do you have for us today?"

Tobias was at the other end of the table, fingering the bowl of scrambled eggs. "Nothing you're liable to listen to till it's too late," he said, without looking up.

Then he cleared his throat and it was like it always was. Ruth reached around her plate, took Andrew's hand, then mine and Andrew took hold of Tobias. I sat, while they bowed their heads, and I pretended to, just at first. I waited until he'd said it, that one word, Lord, then I looked up, watched them, one by one, how it was they prayed.

"Let us be thankful," he said, "for these mountains, for the earth, and for what the Lord has put beneath them." The deep lines beside his mouth moved as he prayed. A mean mouth saying, "But though we pray to the mountains, and the rocks, fall on us."

"Fall on us," Ruth prayed, softly, her eyes open, looking, maybe out the kitchen window at the sun just rising over the mountains at the back of the hollow. Or not looking at all, that was my guess. When she prayed, mealtimes, evenings, Sunday mornings, she kept her eyes wide open, but it was like a cloud came down between her and what it was she saw. The Holy Ghost, she'd have called it.

"Fall on us," Tobias prayed, "but who shall be able to hide from the wrath of the Lamb?"

And Andrew, a long strand of hair across his face, tilted up, toward the little bit of dawn light up the kitchen shadows. Eyes fluttering back and forth back beneath his closed lids. It's visions, Ruth had said, when Andrew's eyes did that same thing, when he was a baby and asleep.

As I waited for them to finish their holy business, I thought, well, yes, falling mountains. The mountains of Mining Hollow falling in and in, leaving who knows what distances, which roads and roads, the places I might have gone.

Tobias held out a bacon slab speared on a knife. "You eating this morning or what?"

I rubbed my eyes, shifted in my chair. It was pretty easy for a man to drift off, with their goings on. The prayer was already over and Tobias had his plate heaped with everything, eggs, torn up toast, dribbles of cane syrup over the whole mess.

"Sure," I said. "Why not?" I dug in.

"Earl?" Ruth asked. She'd put half a piece of toast on her plate, was pushing one or two spoonsful of egg around with her fork. "You off early tonight? Like I asked?"

"Early? You know they've been having us work doubles on that new load. It's Wednesday, we're behind." I peppered my eggs.

"Earl Wallen, you've known for four solid weeks I wanted you to go to prayer meeting tonight."

"If I took off early for every Wednesday night social there was, you wouldn't have bread to butter, now would you?"

"It's plain, boy, you don't know that bread comes from the house of the Lord," Tobias said. He scooped out a big spoonful of jelly, dumped it on another piece of toast.

"Revival?" I said. "Revival? Only thing needs reviving around here is me."

I pushed my chair back, got up and went over to the window, threw it open. Cool, early morning air rushed in. I stayed there a minute, elbows on the window sill, looking out at the light. Revival. My guitar had been under the bed so long, unplayed, I'd be lucky if it had two strings left.

"Earl," Ruth said. She was up now, gathering empty cups, scraping plates. "It won't hurt you to put aside three good hours of your time. For Him."

"Him?" I turned from the window. "Which him are you talking about? If it's Tobias, I reckon eight good years working for Island

Creek to put food in his mouth isn't enough for you? Him, I'll be damned."

At the table, I picked up my coffee cup, drained it. Andrew was still sitting there, picking at his food. He'd cut his toast into neat little triangles, was staring off into space, not listening to a word. "What are you looking at anyway," I asked him.

"They came to our school," he said, his eyes big and dreamy.

"What's that?" I stood beside his chair.

"The Huntington Talent Hawks, they came to our school." He buttered one of the little toast triangles, traced a shape on it with jelly and a knife.

"Who the hell are the Huntington Talent Hawks?"

"Earl," Ruth said, swooping between us. She picked up a plate, some silverware. "Let him eat up. He's poking enough as it is."

"Come on, Ruth. Give the boy a chance. What's this about Talent Hawks?" I knelt close to his chair. "Speak up, son."

He tore shreds of the toast, sort of whispered. "These men, and some lady. They came to our school, looking for talent for a show up in Huntington, next month. They said I could sing. They liked me."

Only singing I'd heard him do was that whistling, tuneless and on and on, standing on one foot and scratching his leg with the other, looking out the window just when you wanted him for something. The last place I could imagine him was in an auditorium somewhere, dressed up in a robe like a choirboy, a suit and tie talent scout behind him, his fat hand held out, monitoring applause.

"Well, now," I said. "Will wonders never cease." I laughed, stood up, ruffled his hair.

It was five forty-five, time and past for me to head on. Outside, I pulled on my work boots, standing in my sock feet for a minute on a thin coating of frost on the front porch. The boots were stiff with coal dust, dust and layer after layer of mink oil. I could still hear them talking through the shut kitchen door. Ruth's voice, high and nervous, something about hurrying on up, and light already, and foolishness, that's what it was. And Tobias. I couldn't catch much, but I didn't have to. Song of Moses, song of the Lamb, the only song.

There wasn't a snowball's chance in hell they'd let him go to Huntington, Huntington or anywhere else, to sing or anything else, but what could I do about it? He'd have to make his own man's way in this world, his own music.

I zipped up my jacket, gripped my lunch pail, started down the steps and looked back, just once. Just for a second, when I got to the bottom of the yard and slid into the car, cranked it up. He was standing there, at the window, watching after me. He'd rubbed a hole on the icy glass, enough for me to see his face, pale and shadowed, the lips pursed, whistling. And then I felt it, for a time no longer than the width of a knife blade. That blackness inside me, spinning, wanting to make a sound, sing.

The front door opened and Ruth stuck her head out, yelled down the hill after me. It didn't take much to figure out what she was saying, even above the sound of the engine. The revival, come to the revival, you'd better, Earl Wallen.

"Revival be damned," I said, and floored it. Off to the mines, like I always did, and what did God have to do with that, I'd liked to have known.

~

I went after all, and not just that night, but to every last whoop and shimmy of that summer revival. Every last holy roller in the aisle attraction. Them shaking pom-poms and saying, *give me a J, give me an E, give me an S U S,* and *what does that spell?* and so on. But I went. Like she'd asked me to. And I even began, from then on, to look forward to those revival evenings, kind of like going back again for bad love or wanting more of the poison on top of illegal moonshine.

Must have been some kind of whiskey craziness took hold of everyone that night of so-called miracles. When Andrew swears he saw fat Ruby Dean fly wearing a poodle skirt and when Ruth swears the Lord handed her a vision like a grilled cheese with pickles on a china plate. The only hide nor hair I saw of God that night looked pretty much like a vacation Bible school project, that Preacher Martin and his cheap-shit statue of Jesus. Which I'll tell you about.

About midway through the night's sermon from that bag of bones glass-eyed preacher called Martin, one to beat the band about angels descending from heaven and standing on the ocean like it was a mirror and the sky being like a body of water opening and everything coming out, woes and thunder and lightning and red dragons, and a child being born to a woman with a crown, and the church hot as hell to boot, so I couldn't take it anymore. So I went on out to the truck and flipped on the radio and sat back to smoke me a cigarette or two. Shelley Fabares came on. *Johnny Angel,* she sang, *you're the one that I adore. Someday he'll love me, that's the way it's gonna be, oh Johnny Angel.* Her voice, sweet as love on a clear night of stars. That song was taking me right out of the parking lot and out of Inez and into a place I wished for, a smoky barroom full of notes and the sound of feet on a dance floor, when, wouldn't you know, there came Tobias Blue. In his shirt sleeves, carrying something wrapped up in his suit jacket, slung over his shoulder like he was old man Christmas. He kicked against the passenger side of the truck.

"You planning to sleep all night," he asked. "Or just all day?"

I stayed put, leaned back in my the seat, eyes closed, feet propped up on the far side of the dash. I didn't answer him.

"I said, you asleep or what?" He kicked the door again, harder this time, on my side. I could smell sweat and mothballs, and with my own eyes barely open I could see his face at the window, the sties on his eyelids.

"Yeah, I'm asleep." I lowered my feet, sat up, turned to him. "Having the same bad dream, too."

He snorted, stepped back from the truck and swung the bundle off his shoulder. It thudded onto the gravel. "You just get your beauty rest then, son. Or maybe you'd rather wake up awhile and help me out on an errand for the good Lord."

He reached for the bottle in his back pocket, settled on his ankles near the suit jacket. He took a long pull, then put out his hand, held it over the bundle. "He that hath an ear, let him hear what the Spirit saith unto the churches; he that overcometh shall not be hurt by the second death."

"What are you talking about anyway, for Christ's sake?" I pushed open the truck door, swung my legs out onto the parking lot. "Spirit? Last time I looked that was your suit jacket."

"Repent, or else I will come unto thee quickly, and will fight against them with the sword of my mouth," Tobias said. He took another long pull, touched the bundle, jerked his hand back like it had been burned.

"I admit that suit jacket's seen better days and all," I said. I knelt near him, held my hand out until he put the bottle in it. I took a nip, rinsed my teeth. "Don't know as I'd go so far as to insult it, though. A man can't complain too much about a halfway decent suit, seems to me."

"Thou has there them that hold the doctrine of Balaam, who taught Balac to cast a stumblingblock before the children of Israel, to eat things sacrificed unto idols, and to commit fornication." He looked downright transfixed, that hand held out, not a tremble in it, either.

The bundle just laid there, of course, though for all his high and mighty carrying on, you'd have expected it to rise and walk or levitate or worse. I held on to the bottle, sipping and considering. Then before he could sermonize as bad as they were doing in the revival, or could object too much either, I reached my hand out and jerked away the jacket.

"Thou sufferest that woman," he was saying, "to eat things sacrificed unto idols."

Repent, or else, he was saying next, but I was none too polite by that time and I interrupted him, before he could move on to power and worship and vengeance and deceiving and overthrowing and the like. I was rolling in the aisles by then, as they say. I hadn't laughed so hard in a good long while. Idol, nothing.

It was a little old ceramic statue, that's what it was. A couple of feet tall. Painted none too well, either, like it had come right out of a rehabilitation center handicraft class, all bright yellow haired and red lipped and little dots in the center of the eyes with the black paint run down onto the cheeks. Jesus, the one from out of the church that rat-trap traveling Preacher Martin had hauled out of a cardboard box and plopped down on the pulpit like it was a saint in our midst.

Andrew swore up and down, later, it came alive and walked out to the pond, and Ruth believed that, too. Jesus, out at the bottom of the pond, singing "Dream Lover" for the fishes. I'll tell you about Jesus, Jesus statues and miracle Jesuses and Jesus of the pond at Mining Hollow.

Jesus lay, face up on the gravel, arms stretched out at its sides and eyes wide open and staring right into the face of Tobias Blue. Idols? If there was ever an idol around Mining Hollow it was how much he wanted everyone to think he was God's right hand man. He'd stolen Jesus, that's what he'd done. Tobias Blue, out to save Inez from false dime store idols.

~

You'd never in a millennium get me to say I ever once enjoyed that no account, foul smelling, bleary eyed son of a false prophet, and a thief, to boot. No way. There I was, eating my meals at his table, sleeping with his daughter night after night, in his bed, under his roof, answering to his God, and watching everything I'd wished for, every song I'd wanted to write, every road I'd wanted to drive down, every star I'd wanted to shine, disappear like water pouring out of a leaky bucket in the dark. Enjoy wouldn't be the song word I'd pick, for certain.

Ruth and Andrew and the whole nine yards of revivaling could stay back there in the church-house with the doors shut and find their own sweet way home. I made my own revival. I laughed until my sides split. I cut loose. I played that night like a Les Paul guitar, played it and him for all they worth. I shouted and hollered, just to please him, like I was took hold of by thirteen demons when I picked up the statue and set it between us in the truck.

"What you think, Tobias Blue?" I said. "Have we got us the key to eternity right here? What do you say?"

He kept pulling at the whiskey, passing it along, though he stayed good and far back against his side of the seat. The statue just sat there, of course, but I'd draped his jacket over its face.

"We got us a devil by the tail. Got hold of a sign of the apocalypse." I rolled the window down, told all of Inez about it, how we were riding the back of the beast, that night bucking and raising cane along with us through the lit streets of town. "You gonna thank me for this, old man? Me and you, saving the world."

He grunted and coughed into his hand, lit up one of my cigarettes, mumbled something about a new song before the throne. So I jacked up the radio as high as it would go. They were playing hits new and old, Clyde McPhatter and the Drifters, Carl Perkins, Johnny Cash, the Platters. All the stars I'd never be serenaded us along the highway toward Mining Hollow as me and Tobias Blue escorted a ceramic Jesus to its final resting place up the hill and to the pond. All his holy this and that and signs of the end of time nothing but a chipped hunk of plaster wearing a crown of thorns.

That's all God was anyway, I thought as we walked along the dock. A hunk of plaster. Nothing at all. The moon was high, bright and white, and I felt heat burn and turn as I sipped from the bottom of the bottle. We were stumbling a little, by then, and I tripped once against a loose board, plunked the statue down. There Jesus was, helpless as a little baby, face up and palms out and empty, stretched out on a dock between two drunk men, while the rest of them were back in Van Lear praising Him up and down and slapping their tambourines and saying, yes, Jesus, yes.

God. I'd prayed, believe it or not. Nights, sitting up, giving Ruth a little longer, give her time, time alone in bed with her Bible with a scrap of cloth marking some place. The gilt edges gleaming in the dark when I slipped in there, under the covers, made me remember the first time I'd seen her, floating on her back in the pond water out back of this house at Mining Hollow. What did I know, that day? These days all I could imagine was how my tires could spin and how fast I could go, if I chose, and how hair, long, red hair, could fly out the window, the damp ends invisible in the night air. Not her hair, not hers, Ruth Blue's.

Lolo's, maybe. Or another woman's. Women running through my mind, reminding me of all I'd never be, all I'd wanted to be and was without prayer for, now. All my prayers were about forever, about eternity. Me walking through the shadows toward our room, thinking of what I'd chosen and why. Our room was quiet, just that quiet. Some days I prayed about guitar strings and songs, but when I struck a chord all that came out was an off-key twang. Prayers about forever and forever. Me awake to all hours, watching the wet kiss her lips left on the pillow, God's kiss, not mine.

God. Sure enough, a slap-dab decorated hunk of plaster stolen from a traveling revival preacher. Tobias Blue handed the bottle back to me and I tipped it once, drained it, feeling the hot whiskey edge down, fast and sure into my gut. My head spun. Just before we grabbed that statue, me hold of its feet, just below the robe, him hold of those out-stretched hands and saying, worthy is the Lamb, and every creature which is in heaven, and on the earth, and under the earth, and such as are in the sea, just before we tossed it heavy and far and fast into the waters of the pond, I glanced down, stared it right in the eye. It looked back at me, winked once, a sly quick grin, a mocking smile on its red lips.

RUTH: AUGUST 16, 1983

The fire, first set loose in you. At Van Lear, where you were Sister Wallen, honored in the sight of the Lord, receiver of visions. You, rising early to oil the offering table, polish the blues and blood reds of the stained glass windows? You, following the preacher, holding the lukewarm pan of water, kneeling by his side and praying as he washed the feet of Inez waitresses and beauticians and rich doctors' and lawyers' wives? *Praise Jesus, sweet Jesus,* you shouted as the church hummed with holy songs, *how great, how great thou art.*

Praise, you shouted, and raised your hand to testify to glory. *How great,* your tongue swollen, vibrating, ready to part your lips for the secret words of angels, the fearful words that echoed in golden heaven's streets. *How great,* and you fell out on your hands and knees, feeling the flush of vision, shake of mystery. *Show me,* you whispered, Sunday after Sunday. *Show me, oh sweet vision of salvation.*

You remember one Sunday, how it started. You were there early to dust the hymnals and mend the pew cushions and sweep the carpet runners. That humming, low, one toned, like breath down the neck of an empty bottle. You looked up at the ceiling and saw hornets, half

210

a dozen, brown and yellow and swarming the lights. More hornets, then a few more, lazing in the hot wind as you went back there, shut the windows, turned, feeling the sharp sting near your ear. You slapped at the place. One of the bodies of the hornets laid in your palm, the brown legs quivering.

Later, you sat real still during the first half of the sermon. During the bulletin and the first, peaceful hymn, the morning light is breaking, darkness disappears, the sons of earth are waking, to penitential tears, you felt your palms burn. Your belly heaved as hornets and humming took you, ate you from the inside out.

Sting of poison to flesh, a whisper, a humming, hushed and stirring and stirring, your tongue and your lips itching to speak the ways of the Lord. You could hear the hymn, far and away, each cry to heaven going, abundant answer bringing and heavenly gales blowing, with peace upon their wings. Your lips parted, your tongue fluttered, an open eye struck, and you felt the foreign words spill, felt yourself falling, forward and forward, arms, legs, shaking, and all around you voices saying, *yes*, Sister Wallen, *yes*.

The preacher knelt beside you, hand heaven raised, in praise of this visitation, spirit of sweet truth. You were lying, face down, in front in the aisle and from very far you saw him and you smelled his minty cologne. He laid his hand on the back of your head and his rough hand snagged and he said, tell us what you see.

And you tried to say how the back windows were open again to the hot summer and how hornets were drifting in and out in the stirring air. He lifted his red face to the ceiling, sweat on his upper lip. His gold ring caught the sun.

You tried to say how the humming filled you and how you could feel its burning sting in your arms and hands and in your deepest self and how you longed, like a thing full of glory, to rise above the church-house, above the hollow of your world, Mining Hollow, this world where love failed.

You remember now this time of fire's first setting loose.

RUTH: 1963-1966

July, full of heat lightning, me slipping off evenings to the dock at the pond, staring down at the way the pond was edging back on itself with heat, a deeper and deeper green smelling of dying plants and fish and a summer that was rainless? I stared down like I could see through layers of decay and years, through all the years passing, one upon another, to all I was becoming, an undoused ember laying at the bottom of that pond. That was a summer when my thirst could not be quenched, when my insides burned and wanted, the voice in me saying, *you and you*, refusing to be still.

~

Mining Hollow was all there was, all there ever was. Tobias, Earl, and Andrew, too, by then. The three of them wanted, wanted how I fetched, did, made, made money, bread, a clean God-fearing home. I did for them so they never should have wanted, not a thing. I ate the fattest part of the meat, drank the last of the soured milk and gave them fresh, scrubbed their shirt collars until my knuckles bled, asked my prayers, for them.

Andrew sat by the kitchen window, looking out and beyond and on, like it was forever, looking at me as if I knew where what he wanted was. Tobias laid in the bed all day, false teeth in a glass and his cheeks hollow, and he called to me, Ruth, Ruth, from that room filled with his pray and pray. Even at night the wanting was never finished, even when I lay worn out, cracks in my chapped hands stinging. Ruth, Earl whispered to me, this is a sad house, a house without the light of human kindness. He held on to me after he slept, tighter and tighter, like he'd take my last breath, the least air, anything light enough to make him rise above the walls, the roof, the mountains of Mining Hollow.

When he held me I thought of all the shadows of the house, every seamless darkness and black place, closets and drawers, old envelopes and boxes, inside sleeves of coats and dresses Little Mother had left behind, inside the shapes of times I couldn't quite remember, inside dreams that came to me right before I woke, dreams that were forgotten by nightfall. And around me, between me and the body of my sleeping husband, was that darkness, too. It was a secret blackness that held me like water at night, silk blackness, beautiful as ink. I could reach out my hand and stroke the face of the darkness like the face of a lover. *Speak to me*, I would whisper, and it would, its shadow mouth full of words, *stay, wait, hold still*. It was a blackness that slid between me and Earl, stroked me, covered me until our two bodies, body of dark and body of me, were one.

I was the thin shadow that kept their house. A house of cards where, after I'd wiped away any trace of dust, the vases I set back slipped from my hands and crashed down. Where I mashed their potatoes, forgot to scrub away all of the red dirt from the garden. Hemmed their trousers and forgot the pins, washed their dishes and left dried yellow egg yolk on the fronts, rings of soup on the backs. Their wants dropped down into the deep, empty inside of me, piling up and up. I looked at the mirror as if it were stagnant water, a face just below the surface I wanted to see. A face that looked like me, but was not.

Earl and Tobias spent more and more of their nights playing to win, playing now for the earth. Strip mines, Earl would say, and pace the room, describing how this was the wave of the future, bales of wire, lights so bright nothing was hidden, bulldozers scraping the earth clean, clean down to stones and roots, to the least ounce of coal. Move it to the left, boys, some boss-man would say, and Earl believed it would be himself, strip mine rich, on the striped bare road to fame and glory.

For Tobias it was deep mines, no better way to harvest coal than down in the mire and guts of the earth, the pit of darkness itself, men with lights and picks and trolleys, no fancy drills or motor cars for him, even if he never went there, never had, in years and years. He'd been there, he said, treading the fine line between earth and hell, safe in the guts of darkness, blessed be the judgement of God. Judgement, Earl would say. Why, old man, it's enough to make me split my sides laughing. God ain't nothing but a sideshow preacher selling snake oil as holy water.

And so they fought through night on night, sipping moonshine, their voices colliding in the front room, *strip mine, deep mine, God of wrath, Godless two-bit wonder.* Their words crashed and struck, sparks that rose and broke around my head.

~

One night, I stayed up after he'd slept, sat in the dark kitchen, lit an oil lamp and turned its flame down low. I didn't bother to get up and blow the embers in the wood stove to life, just sat there a long time, then longer, chills and shivers going up my arms. Then I was listening, listening. Something was moving, circling like moths brushing the ceiling. Then in the stove, a shiver and rattle of sound going up the flue. Then it was down the hall, across the floor, scratching in the walls, at the windows.

It was nothing at all, I told myself, a ground squirrel caught in the ceiling, or maybe more than that, all the quarrel-words I'd heard earlier still striking home to each other, sparking and glowing in the dark. A hand made of the way cobwebs felt in the dark touched my bare arms, stroked my chest, spread its fingers over my heart. I rubbed my dry hands together as I prayed with the hands that had cleaned and held. I called my prayers from deep in me, breathed them out, and they tasted of the smoke of Earl's cigarettes, of the burning clearness of Tobias's moonshine, of all they'd had to comfort them, their sins that had never comforted me. In the lightless kitchen, I could feel the solid kitchen walls, how I'd held them up with my own bones and blood.

Glass jars on the kitchen shelves gleamed in the dark, full of all I'd gleaned and gathered, dry kernels of corn, threads of onions strung from the ceiling. The hands from on my chest felt their way across the floor, touched the kindling box and scrapes of wood so dry I felt them in my teeth. The room was full of hands and dark and prayer words spinning, long threads of time I'd saved like scraps of cloth to mend and patch, years I'd done nothing but abide, hold, praise.

Abide, hold, praise. Dry words I rubbed between my palms. Dry fingers, dry tongue, dry skin, all of me was so dry the thinnest wind through the wood stove touched me and I felt my dry bones bend and break, ready to catch, paper and flame. *A third angel*, Tobias had once said, *will sound, and a star will fall from heaven, a star burning like a lamp*. The bitter dryness of me shaped itself like a bird, tore at the darkness, and light shone through. Andrew had been right. Light, light was everywhere and it was me.

One thin shred of something light as the words of a prayer said and done flew out from behind the wood stove, from the kitchen corners, from underneath the table. No, that wasn't the truth of it. I felt something move, ease, then rush out of me. All those words, *abide, hold, praise*, were a letter hidden at the top of a closet, a photograph I'd forgotten, a paper with song-words. *It's you or no one*, the song said, *how did I guess, long loneliness was past, I merely looked at you and I knew*. Words, songs, dreams on lost paper scraps unfolded from out of the center of me, and I could taste them, their smoke-bitterness. Ruth Blue, Earl had once said, all our lives would be as clean and clear as a song he'd call Ruth Blue. Pray, Tobias had said, and I had knelt so long I was dry and thin and bitter.

My shoulders ached from looking up at a faceless God. The center of me unfolded, a long list of holy words I'd prayed and prayed. The center of me reached up and up toward a tear in the darkness bitterness had made.

~

The fire started, they later said, at the back of the wood stove, where kindling and leaves and pine cones I'd gathered smoldered and caught. That the makeshift wires Earl had rigged wore through with mice and time. That it was Tobias or Earl, or the both of them, liquored and sleeping and the bed sheets afire with their cigarettes. Or me, falling asleep at the table, the lamp crashing down.

None of what was said was the truth. The fire started with me that kitchen night. Dry words of darkness broke through and flamed up, the darkness of all my years of holding and doing. It was earlier that evening, the way sparks snapped between my daddy and my husband, evening upon evening before that, the way anger and moonshine touched and burned. Or it was farther back, the night Little Mother burned in the wood stove all that held her back and ran as fast as she could, farther back, some time none of us knew, when a house began without love.

Our house at Mining Hollow burned as quick as paper, turned to smoke and ash. Flames spread from the kitchen corners, felt their way, inch by inch, across the warped pine board floor. I sat at the kitchen table, watching, as the flames burst from everywhere at once. The yellowed newspapers covering the walls leapt into fire. News stories about the Great Depression, faded news photos of Theda Bara, Errol Flynn, Clara Bow, ignited, vanished. The walls were licked with orange and blue and flames grew in the glass of kitchen jars, in the panes of windows, and the air was filled with breaking.

Still, I sat, held on tight to the rickety table, as all the world I'd known crackled and sighed, gave way into fire and smoke that burned my nose, caressed my bare arms with warmth. The kitchen, all the five rooms of all the house around me, sighed and whined, resisted, as the fire took hold, claimed with light all floors I'd scrubbed, corners I'd swept. Years, years of holding down, burst into light so beautiful my eyes stung with smoke and tears to see it. It was light more beautiful than apple wood burning, blue, soft red, pink smoke, rising, rising, soft but shining and full of quick heat.

Crash of the first ceiling beam, giving in of a wall, giving way of a floorboard. Coughing. Behind me, I heard a door slam open, voices, hurry, hurry, a moan that might have been my son. All of this time, I was safe, I was invisible, I was so full of the firelight that I could lift my own thin self and rise, over the roof as it glowed and collapsed, over Mining Hollow as smoke drifted up and out of our hollow and curled into the sky. I was invisible, and like this smoke I could ease through the disappearing rooms of our house, watch mirror glass and windows heat and shatter, enter closets as forgotten boxes of Little Mother's clothes and tap dance books singed and vanished into ash, as bottles of her sweet cologne exploded.

I could wind my way down the smoke-filled hall and see them, Earl, his one arm full of record albums and a free hand dragging our son after him into the yard. Hidden, I could join the wider and wider circles of smoke into the yard where Andrew stood, barefooted and shirttail out and an unsurprised look on his face, as if he'd seen this light, all along.

Invisible, I could crouch low in the choking waves of smoke and watch while Earl grabbed handfuls of anything at all, a coat, a scarf, a miner's light, a dresser drawer, and tossed them through the shattering windows.

Even when Earl pushed his way past a doorway full of flame, when his fingers dug into my shoulders and he said, Jesus, woman, move, move, and drug me, even though I was holding on tight to the rickety table, even though I was filled with love for the shimmer of firelight rising up and struggled to stay put and hold on and see, see the face of God full of holy light, even when I fell on my knees in the yard full of embers and burning, I remained invisible.

Invisible, I watched, as Earl fetched buckets from the well and tossed them, useless drops of water on a flame that had its own power, its own life. Invisible as smoke, I could drift back in, past the crumbling and alight doorways of our few rooms and peer in there where Tobias lay, untouched, sleeping, an empty moonshine jar beside him on a bed circled with blue flame.

A third angel will sound, my daddy had said. *It will sound and a great star will fall from heaven, burning like a lamp. And the name of the star is called Wormwood, and the third part of the waters became wormwood, and many men died of the waters, because they were made bitter.* Falling, the burning star landed in Tobias's open hand, and I watched his bed burst into fire and his eyes open up to heaven.

~

For awhile after that night, Earl and Andrew and I all had our dreams of fire and walls crashing in and voices that wanted to be saved. Then the dreams were something else, calmer, filled with the way light had looked in the sky, long after the smoke of our burning house had cleared away. Earl dreamed again. Of a stone cottage in a town called Venice, where he'd write musicals about diners and coming home from the war. Andrew dreamed of roads and signs, of the ocean he'd never seen, like it was a stone or a brand new penny you could hold in your hand. And I dreamed, after awhile, of how Little Mother had once hummed, *I want to be happy, if you're happy too.* I dreamed of a blank white box that opened and opened, filled with smoke, behind which lay God's face.

That winter, regardless of our dreams, the mines shut down, and we learned to make do. We lived on sweet coffee and bread and dollar bags of clothes from the Mission Store in Inez. The clothes had the scent of mothballs and someone else's hidden closets, and they fit my body like a time I had lived before, 1941, the year of flowers and wakes. We lived very little on the charity of neighbors, although Earl brought brown paper sacks full of hand-me-downs from the Main Street Diner, a few times, given to him by well-meaning coffee drinkers and sympathetic waitresses who remembered him as the Late Night Balladeer, so he said.

We lived the rest of that winter in a miner's shack three hollows over from where we had once lived, spent our last bottom dollar on a no-account plot of land on the side of a hill. Anything, Earl said, that was ours, and not that old man's. Soon, Earl built us a makeshift house out of salvage from torn down Inez shops and storage buildings. We saved his miner's pay, when Island Creek had struck a new vein and called him in.

I decorated our shack with what we'd saved from Mining Hollow. Little Mother's music box, its fox and panther and fat bear scorched from the fire, sat on the wooden electric company spool we used for a kitchen table. I wore what had once been her dance hat, its feathers shorter and singed, as I boiled our coffee on a kerosene camp stove, strained it into thrift store mugs, and hummed. *I want to be happy*, I hummed, my mother's long ago song. Earl's slap-dab arrangement of boards and shingles and two-penny nails was new and bright to me, and my eyes still saw light, bright and blazing, a light so strong it had helped me rise above Mining Hollow, would keep me rising, up and up.

All the rest of that winter, as we stuffed socks and handkerchiefs and rags into the cracks of our miner's shack, I had, and sometimes Earl had, talked of laying to rest the dead. Is my grand-daddy dead and gone to heaven, Andrew would ask, as I covered him with dollar store blankets and thrift store coats, at night.

Yes, I told him, dead and gone.

I did not say to heaven, although that last look in Tobias's eyes had been full of the fire of destruction and the resurrection and all that was beyond. When I tried to speak about heaven, the word stuck in my mouth and would not come out.

Let the old buzzard rest on a bed of soot for awhile and see if anything good hatches out, Earl said, on Sunday afternoons, as he hammered and I handed him nails and paused to look toward Mining Hollow and the yard and the pond Tobias had left me.

I left my daddy alone that winter, but I could not let him rest there for good. His bones and teeth lay waiting for me, and I thought of wet ashes under the frost and how if I touched them they'd feel like slivers of used soap kept with water in a jar.

One overcast day in early spring, when Earl was back on at the mines and Andrew was off to the grades, I went the old way back, along the top of the ridge three hollows over, along paths just flowering with trillium and lady's slippers and the first tender shoots of ivy. I ducked under an old barbed-wire fence, passed a stand of apple trees thick with water sprouts, just as a shower fell. I stood for awhile, munching a small, tart apple, listening to the rain, drop by drop, and then, I was sure of it, to light footsteps. As I started out walking again, they echoed me through the leaves, step by step, until I turned, whispered back over my shoulder, *who are you?*

Who? There was silence, and the light, cool rain. *Show yourself*, I said. No answer. I walked on, faster now, with the footsteps, one step for each of mine, one halt for each of mine. A game, if it weren't for the chills up and down my arms, the light and invisible touch of fingers at the back of my neck.

I came to a footpath, cut across a thick patch of Johnson's grass and wild roses, and then was above Mining Hollow. I cut down to the left, nearest the far corner of what used to be the yard. The footsteps came with me to near the crisp remains of walls and windows and the rotting wood cover of the well.

I sat down on the soot-covered stone that used to be the front step, and looked at all we'd left behind, after the fire. There were tins that had once contained needles and thread and scissors, jars of beets and corn and beans, store-bought cans with their labels burned away. Amidst charred boards, halves of burned chairs, broken glasses and plates and mirror, was the blackened remains of an iron bed, its once-cotton mattress burned to thin layers of ash. That, I thought, was where I'd find the last of Tobias.

Near the iron bed, I knelt, began to sift through the cold, damp ashes of my daddy. I gleaned and gathered, found pieces of all that had been him, cufflinks that I struggled to pry open, a gold tooth, a chain from a pocket watch. There was almost nothing left of the mattress itself, and the pieces of burnt cotton I touched crumbled down into the metal bedsprings, but I imagined an outline, anyway, the long stretch of bony legs down to the bottom of the bed, the one scrawny arm reaching, palm up to God, the other holding on tight to a moonshine jar. I found the jar itself, its canning lid melted with fire, rusted with winter, struggled to open it. At last, I gathered handfuls of Tobias and put him in the pockets of my dress and apron. *Wait for me*, the echo steps and whispers said and my back, and together we set out to the pond.

~

There, like I had once done as a girl, I stepped carefully out of my clothes, holding tight to the seams and edges to keep the ashes in, then walked down through the reeds and cattails to the chilly spring water. I stopped there, whispered a prayer to the water, *shall I not seek rest for thee, that it may be well with thee.* Then I held my dress out, over pond and water and the reflection of early spring light, and said goodbye. Goodbye to false teeth in a glass, to the memory of a hand against a face, to milk gravy and toast, to kneeling and hair and scissors, to the sound of ice and silence. I shook my dress hard and gold tooth and cufflinks and chain flew out, sank without a sound.

As the cool water drenched my skin, soaked my thin slip, gray smoke rose on all sides of me, spiraled toward the sky, then settled like talc next to my skin. I dove down, stayed down and ran my fingers through my hair, rubbed my arms, legs, my cheeks and open eyes under the water. When I felt my lungs burn for air, I kicked back up to the surface, breathed long breaths. The air still tasted of smoke and as I treaded water, I felt a fine coating of slippery, clinging ash. I cast prayers over the waters—*now I lay me, star bright, God is great,* and I stared up at the pale yellow sun. Praying as I'd done was a useless thing, and already I knew the way it would be.

Smoke tainted fingers stroked the water beside me, made circles and eddies that I swam through, back to shore. The fingers drew crosses and words I knew on my back, on my chest. *The third part of the waters,* the words said, *became wormwood, and many died of the waters, because they were made bitter.* I waded through the slicky mud and cattails, sat at the edge of the pond, my hands over my ears.

Pray, Tobias said. You have not yet seen God.

~

Time turned one house into another, one room into the ghost of another. Earl dreamed of a town called Venice, where the least wind could destroy a house, even one made of stone. Andrew woke in the night with visions of the ocean, where he said he'd almost drowned in the taste of salt. I dreamed of a blank, white box, and I was inside it, tumbling over and over through a faceless place I called God. Ours was a house made of cards and kindling, and Tobias, smelling of burning and smoke, took his place at our table. Two hollows over became the same as two hollows back and Mining Hollow was any hollow, filled with all the ghosts of a time I could not leave, filled with fire, fire that blazed up and took hold of me and them.

EARL: SUMMER, 1969

The night television showed them walking on the moon, I remember the warm skin underneath Lolo Lafferty's shirt, the smell of cooking oil and cigarette smoke in her hair. It was August 2, 1969, and I sat at the diner with half the rest of Inez, watching the television over the grill and replays of Neil Armstrong and Buzz Aldrin jamming an American flag into a pile of rocks and dirt.

Two booths over, I heard Pappy Imes snort and say, "Yeah, right. How're we supposed to know if it ain't a Hollywood recording studio and a couple of stunt men? You tell me."

Lolo stood behind me, coffee poised while the astronauts sidestepped the flag, a slow dance. She knew and I knew that I'd scribbled a note on the underside of my empty plate, saying something like, quarter of eleven, salute the moon? It was a signal I gave, that I was ready to go for a late night drive, to Frazier Lake, or to the State Park at the Breaks of the Mountains, that I'd come to pick her up tonight.

"Evening, Earl," she said, impersonal-like. "Will wonders never cease," she said, looking at the TV screen, the long shadow of the flag, the astronauts raising their suited arms, waving to all of America.

I acted like I always did when she leaned down. Like I didn't notice her closer to me, whispering, sure, any time, with her husky voice that still excited me, was so familiar. As she filled my cup, I let my fingers just touch her wrist. She shouldered her tray loaded with the coffee pot and hamburger specials, headed across the diner, her ankle-strap platforms clicking on the checked tile. She had her red hair pulled back with a purple ribbon. Red curls and, more and more, streaks of silver that made my heart ache.

Lately, I'd taken to wearing my Air Force uniform jacket, tie clasp and all, whenever I went to the Inez Diner. The girls in their bouffants and mascara, in for a late-night cherry coke or ice cream parfait, licked their straws and giggled, and I felt a little like I had back in Venice, those months after coming home from the service. But mostly it made me think of Lolo, how she looked at me that same certain way she had, all those years ago. Her, back then, leaning down and peered into the window of my Kaiser-Fraiser and saying, Earl, can I get you a little something? Something extra?

I checked my watch and it said 10:30, not much time to wait until her shift let off. On the screen, a team of scientists, discussing Apollo XI, the twenty-one hours and thirty-one minutes spent on the moon, the collection of nine pounds, twelve ounces of moon matter, the new information about gravitational fields, the expansion of age-old lunar theories.

Nodding at Lolo, I slipped out to the parking lot and into my pickup, switched on the radio dial, put my head back, closed my eyes. *Can't take my eyes off of you*, a song said. *You'd be like heaven to touch, I want to hold you so much*. Sweet song.

Sweet, I laughed to myself, and turned the volume most of the way down. Soon I fell into a half sleep and, right away, I was dreaming, a place at first like the television moon, an empty expanse of what became sand. A long strip of beach in the moonlight. The sand was lit up enough for me to look back and see my footsteps, how they filled up with water, caved in, disappeared. It was Pearl Harbor. I stood still, focused my eyes on the horizon, toward some sharp points of light in the distance. The longer I stood still, the heavier I felt, as if I were sinking farther and farther down, and I looked and saw that my shoes were on and soaked through and filling up with sand and ocean water that felt hot and listless. Fire in the distance grew brighter, sliced into the dark, and I couldn't look away from them, couldn't close my eyes. My head ached from the brightness and my feet sank and sank as the surf rose, to my ankles, my knees. The surf made a sound—dull, roaring, like the sound of planes and guns and explosions. The surf, singing, *at long last love has arrived and I thank God I'm alive.* I woke up, too quick, to a tapping on my car window, her lipsticked smile.

"Earl, hon," Lolo said. "You awake?" She yanked open the door, slid across the seat beside me as I rubbed sleep from my eye. Sleep, moondust.

"Let's go to the lake," she said. She touched the sleeve of my air-force jacket. "Just for old times."

~

Salute the moon, the first night we touched down on it. That's what I'd asked her out for. I rubbed the sleep out of my eyes, dropped into reverse, backed the car onto Main Street. I pushed the pedal to the floor, gave it some gas, made the tires screech. We were headed out of Inez, my favorite time of night—dark enough for the steering wheel to slide invisible through my hands. We passed by the lake, dark too, dark enough for the moon's shine to sit smack dab in the middle of the water, daring you to strip down to nothing and chase it to the opposite shore. As that dream left my head I felt alive, singing, ready for anything.

"Lolo," I said. "Give us a shot."

She reached under the seat right away, knew what I meant without having to ask. She unscrewed the bottle and took a drink herself, handed the bottle on to me.

I ended up where I always did, at the end of the dirt road through the woods, near the lake. There was a deserted house out there and I liked pulling up in the yard, just watching. The yard was full of a little bit of everything, tires, car parts, Johnson's grass, no one at home for years. I'd imagined a lot at that house, fear, loneliness, desire, the people who'd felt those things long dead, people I'd never seen. Anyone might still open the door, come out on the porch, down the steps—anyone or no one. Just waiting, not knowing, made my breath go shallow, my hands clench in my lap. It was almost like I owned the place. I'd tossed enough empty bottles out my car window there, heard them crash, pulled Lolo over on my side of the seat, pressed my lips against hers, warm, there and there, and just there.

Lolo was huddled up against the door on her side, knees drawn up in her arms, uniform skirt pulled down over her knees. On the drive out she'd turned the radio full blast, tipped the bottle back as many times as I had, sung along to Grass Roots and "Midnight Confessions." But now she was quiet, staring down through the trees.

"Cold?" I asked.

She shook her head. "No. Not cold." Her voice wasn't husky anymore. It was tired, quiet.

"Come on, Lolo," I said. I reached over for her, took her hand. It felt wrinkly from dishwater, the scar on the palm from a broken diner glass. "You sure look cold. Come on over here."

She slid over, finally, saying nothing, fit right into the crook of my arm. For so long now, we'd taken these night drives, parked at abandoned houses, behind the First National Bank, in the empty parking lots of grocery stores. We'd kissed and watched whatever moon was out and I'd gone on back to Mining Hollow, turned the sheets on my side of the bed, slept with my wife. What had my father told me, way back in Venice? Carl Wallen, failed businessman, family man, telling me, you, Earl Wallen, men make their beds. They lie in them.

This night, as I kissed Lolo Lafferty, her throat and shoulders, I couldn't stop. Eyes closed in front of her closed eyes, I saw fire at the launch pad, the trail of smoke into the sky, the far distant moon. I pushed Lolo back, farther and farther against the seat, as the radio played, song after song, and I felt that dream I'd had earlier ease up the back of my neck, take hold of me, a stranglehold. My feet were back in the sand again, sinking more and more, then my knees, then up and up, my chest, my face. I felt the whole weight of the night crush against me, the whole weight of that dream. As that dream sucked me down I looked at her lipsticked mouth and the shine of her red hair in the moonlight. She grew farther and farther away, dim and featureless and distant.

I saw Pearl Harbor again, and Rudy Hyatt, only now I took a good look at him. There was no choice. This time he was lying facing the sun, only he was faceless, his face was blown away, clean away, to bone and warm blood, blood I hadn't stopped to touch that so long ago day, to wet my hands in. The whole of that day, all the days since, Ruth and Mining Hollow, fire, houses, all my life.

I felt it, crying, making its way up from some part of me I'd rather never remember and I thought, not now. Not with her. They were playing that song again, "Can't Take My Eyes Off of You," and I pushed past the words, *at long last love has arrived, and I thank God I'm alive.* I pushed past the words, reaching for her. I reached for her, reached into the slick between her legs, reached and parted, caught hold of her as if I were dying and she could pull me back up.

All my life, caught between a fire blazing up, a fire dying away, brightness of the moon on late-night rides, moon nothing but a place of stones and dirt, airless, dead space claimed with a flag that would never ripple in the wind. That night, I believed Lolo was necessary. I needed her.

Later, with Lolo sitting on the far side again, by her door, I wanted to say, well now, honey, it'll be different this time, I'll be a free man, free as you please, and marry me, now, forever. The ribbon had fallen so her red hair covered her face. She was whispering and her voice was husky again.

"Do you love me, Earl Wallen?" she said. "Once and for all, do you?"

In the end, what saved me wasn't Lolo at all. It was the green light from a radio dial, and that's what I'll call God, radio light filling up the cab of my truck. I swear, light, gathering from the dash board, from the radio, a cloud of it. It covered me and her both, and everything, everything, was hidden, Lolo, my wanting her, myself. I stared through that light, tried to see. I climbed up on its pure waves of sound, of song, drifted out into the night air, past the truck, the abandoned house, past Lolo, past Inez, past some memory of my old man, shuffling down the hall at our house in Venice, Ohio, back from the toilet, zipping himself up, his face blank and hopeless.

"Do you, Earl," Lolo was saying. "Have you ever?"

But I was far from her, climbing up on those waves of red light and sound and radio. Where was the fire in my blood? Sweet songs, song words? The radio ones I'd wanted to sing anyone across America, to people in their forevers of home. The ones I wanted now to be sung to me, *sweet goodnight*, making me forget to remember.

ANDREW: SUMMER, 1969

My sixteenth year, I spent most of my time dreaming of the ocean. Striped umbrellas and cotton candy and hot vendors. Fireworks and bonfires at dusk by the blue, blue water. I'd run away, I told myself, sell popcorn by the box. Play in a band called the Huntington Talent Hawks in a nightclub down by the beach. Run along the burning sand, miles of shoreline. Even then I imagined him, Henry Ward, white sneakers in hand, running with me along the shore of an ocean I'd never seen.

Where that summer took me was not the ocean, but Number Nine Mine. Every morning that summer, I traveled up the road with my father, the two of us out of bed just long enough for a cup of coffee and my mother's warnings. Go to the left today, she'd say, you'll find the richest vein yet. She'd send us off with prayers, what to say just before the blackness took us in. This, she'd say. *Great and wonderful are thy deeds Oh Lord God, just and true are thy ways,* and nothing, nothing, can keep you from coming back. The taste of fried eggs and cigarettes still on my tongue, we went to the mines.

My first day, we got to Island Creek good and early. No one was there but the boss-man, sitting on his fist and raring back on his thumb, my father said. The boss, a fat man with a denim shirt with bleach spots on the cuffs. He looked me up and down the way my mother pinched roasts at the grocer's, shifted a wet cigar to his other cheek. Then he handed me my W2 and a voucher and some advice. The deeper the better, the richer the cream, if you know what I mean, he said, winking with one of his small, eyes. We set our lunch pails in the office, headed out, ready to be the first ones, the first ones down. I stood with all those other boys in the line ready to go down, Baisdens and Whitakers and Shorts, some of them I'd known in school. Their faces were still black with coal from yesterday and the day before. What'll it be today, boys, they said. *Drift, raise, winze? Up, down, across*, they said, you'll learn.

I wiped my damp hands on my coveralls, not yet like theirs, stiff with dust. My father whispered in my ear, go get them, son, this is your chance. He even sang me a little song, his. *Down*, he sang, *I'm going down to where it's dark, dark but never lonely, just full of black and cold. I'm going down where it's richer, full of black but full of gold.*

Light was so brilliant in the trees overhead I shut my eyes hard and tried to hold it in, that shine, so when I looked around me again and saw nothing but solid darkness, I wouldn't be afraid. No voices after awhile, no one saying, not here, boys, go that way. The low boy inched toward the shaft where electric bulbs first shone strong, then flickered, extinguished. Nothing, soon, but the lights on our hats, the yellows of eyes. I held on tight, counted every face beside me. Three of them. I wasn't alone.

Not until that very last minute when the blackness hit me like a damp body, a blind, my father said. And he said, let's rock 'n' roll, boys, let's do her, and I imagined a dance floor and him, long ago, cheap gold stars pasted on military issue shoes. Gone now, all he'd wanted, and here we both were, at the bottom of beyond. A beyond of sulphur and fumes. Words came out of my mouth, something about just and true and I meant God, only I couldn't think of his name. I said, it's me who's gone blind and I said it louder than I meant, and even I could hear my voice shake and a fear coiled in my gut like steal guitar strings.

Act like a man, my father told me. I didn't know what men did when they were afraid, so I shut my eyes tight and I turned and ran, boots scraping coal and rock, the sound of my father's angry voice behind me. Andrew, he said, you, boy. I ran along the tunnel, wanting the shaft to fill with light, the light of sun and air beyond this world below the earth, world of soot and hours.

As I ran toward this light, I tried to think of fire and life, I tried to think of the Holy Ghost, but I could see nothing but the thin beams from their miner's caps. There was my father beside me, the sharp slap of his hand on my cheek. But I didn't feel that at all, only inhaled the air in his palm, air smelling of burning rubber. I tasted my own blood. I gripped my elbows tight, pushed my arms against my heart until it stopped beating fast and told myself, though you think you know the meaning of being alive, you are dead, the mine is the no-light of death.

~

That night, I lay thinking of how I had learned yet one more way of dying. I knew there were other such ways. How I lay most nights, arms around myself, my man's body so familiar I ached for love, touched only myself, but dreamed of another self, a body like mine, the penis and hands and mouth. I dreamed an act so wonderful and so forbidden I could only name it sin. To think of myself, who I was or might become, who I could love or never love, was a sin. Sin, that word I turned and sucked, sweet and bitter, in my mouth.

I lay night after night that summer, holding only myself, a darkness that never seemed to end, a darkness so far back it ended only before my own birth, ended only with morning and going to the mines. At night I lay listening to the sound of an ocean I'd never seen, dreamed of a lover's face I'd never seen. Until I saw Henry Ward again.

~

Fire in the blood, they sang that morning at the end of the service at Van Lear. A bunch of Cantrells and Johnsons were down front near the altar, handkerchiefs out for the anointing. They were gathered around Ruby Dean, who lay with her fat arms stretched out, her dark eyes open, her mouth open and speaking of ladders of angels who climbed above mountains and trees and sky, danced right into heaven. Voices were singing, *fire, fire in the blood, fire in the blood.*

I sat in the back, flipped past page after page of the hymnal, hoping one of them wouldn't ask me to dance for the Lord. Dance and praise, an old lady near me said, and took hold of me with her small, powdery hands. Fire, she sang, her toothless gums parted for the high, off-key voice saying, fire. Unwillingly, I held on to her hands, sang back. *Fire in the bones.* That was when I heard him, standing near me, striking a match.

He'd come in the back, with service two thirds done and everyone already close to God and eternal life. I watched him remove his cowboy hat, edge by a pew and the group of dancers and past someone lying in the aisle. He took a seat, two behind me, rubbed at patches of dark stubble along his chin. He scraped a pointy-toed boot against the floor, spat on one finger and rubbed at a whitish scratch on his forearm.

Henry Ward had taken off from Inez at seventeen, had been gone three years, and now he was back again, back home again from Ohio or Detroit or Tallahassee, all those cities and cities where people said he'd been. A traveling salesman, some said. High fashion for businessmen. Painter of decorative murals for big city lobbies and dens of iniquity. A chain of motels with swimming pools and saunas and rooms with day-glo stars on the ceilings. A talent scout in little towns north from West Virginia to Pennsylvania. I knew right then and there Henry Ward had been everywhere, seen everything.

Fire in the bones, they sang, and I felt it course through me, a fire as alive and light as embers rising into blackness. A fire, fluttering in my chest like moths, shivering and hanging in the air, a bright something that burned up the space between me and him.

I rode on that flame, a thin, shining line of it. It had a rhythm like music, was the refrain of my own hymn, my own fire in my most secret blood. I rode out of the once dark place I had been, out of the most lonely rooms of all my life, out of Mining Hollow, out of the darkest, deep parts of the mines, straight into the center of Henry Ward. I grew closer and closer to a red and glowing thing that beat and stopped and beat. A heart. Love, it wanted to say, from the most far-reaching places of all the world where I'd never been. The heart spoke in languages I did not know, Greek, French, languages rich and dizzying and full. It said love with a caress. It was the unfamiliar and long wanted touch of hand next to hand, mouth to mouth, body to body. The heart spoke right out of the bottom of the ocean and I rocked with the sound of that word, on waves and waves of myself.

When I noticed, the church was full of voices, music, clapping. I saw Henry raise his hand high. I saw how in tongues I had spoken the truth of love and fire.

~

After the service, we went outside for the footwashing. Henry Ward, his face full sunlight, walked toward me, legs so sure of themselves in their new snakeskin boots from Detroit. You, he said, meaning he'd chosen me to be the one to kneel in front of him, take off those boots. Though the preacher said I only had to bathe one of his feet in the aluminum pan set aside for the Lord, I did both, trying to be quick so no one would notice, watching all the while the way the water drenched his skin, the way hairs on top of both his feet grew slick and pointed down, graceful waves. God said to me, *fire and quenching and fire.*

I knew that when Henry Ward knelt down to say prayers it was to a God so beautiful I could look him right in the face and touch his hair. That hair would be blue or the lightest rose, like angel hair, and I would have to be careful. It would cut into me, but I would touch it again and again.

RUTH: AUGUST 16, 1983

Then there were ghosts, ghosts of years, love, you. The dirt road up Mining Hollow turned gravel, then asphalt. More houses and a shopping center to the north, empty storefronts in Inez, pharmacy lunch counter turned fast food specials on a strip of discount stores. Bottomland let go, unkept orchards, vine covered headstones in forgotten family cemeteries. Young people long gone, north or south or west, looking for more pay, more good times. Ghosts of coal, strip mines now the way to mine. Black dust curled up and stayed behind couches and beds.

Mornings took you to the highway, to the bus, to jobs for money for them at Mining Hollow, money coal alone no longer brought. Earl coughed the black dust, wore wire framed spectacles for eyes the mines made weak. He claimed his government disability checks would bring him sleep and dreams. He dreamed even then of the big time and the time from job to job echoed songs. *Oh baby, if you loved me, the night would never be long. Baby, I'd hold you until morning and free my soul for just a song.*

Mornings, you walked out the mouth of your hollow, to the bus for Inez, ghost money jingling in your pockets. *Soap me, rinse me,*

two-fifty an hour, diner cups and saucers, how many can your rinse?
Floors to scrub, silver to polish, white shirts to bleach and iron, clean
and cleaner, dimes and nickels by the hour. Soon the highway took
you every morning to a steady maid's job at a rich strip mine home
up Van Lear, the Ward's. You soon knew that house, every corner and
cranny, light bulb and kitchen cabinet. You brought home bags of
one season out of fashion strip miner's clothes and old ladies magazines that tell you so. Clothed your son, Earl, you.

And what of love, what of hold-me-until-morning, what of
ghosts that danced away, forgotten in movie magazines? Tap shoes
striking sparks in the road, now the loneliness of fireflies. Little
Mother running, the stockinged legs all you sometimes recall.
Tobias's false teeth, gray as ash, still in a window sill glass. How you
wished for it, Saturday nights, bath in the kitchen washtub, capful of
vanilla, soaking your whole self in the scent. Ghost of you, so pretty,
so never been.

Mornings, you felt love go by on Highway 23. A coal rig loaded
down or a brand new four door bought with strip mine money.
Rushing by, showering cinder and slag or radio country, your skirts
flattened with wind. Love, a ghost on the bus to Inez. Love, ghost
over your shoulder at the new sink of suds and plates. That ghost,
love, leaning over the porch railing and calling you down to the
yard. Tobias's dreams a ghost in your dreams, four beasts full of eyes
before and behind, calling you down to the yard, a measure of wheat
for a penny, three measures of barley for a penny, see thou hurt not
the oil and the wine. At night, you brought Tobias, no, it was Earl,
rot gut whiskey and counted your change. At night, love, a ghost
you held onto in the tangle of sheets between you and him, your
husband.

Your son, your Andrew, your baby now a boy, a man, a boy. The
ghostliest of all. By day, you thought of his hands, grown, arms long,
elbows sharp. At night you lay awake and thought of ways to hold
onto the space between what that baby's body was and what it was
becoming. Catch and keep the things he dreamed, the unknown
things. You wanted to gather him up, lost ring, lost photo, lost time,

put him somewhere safe, some deep place, inside a prayer. Inside your pockets, inside the long loneliness that was you. You did not know what he thought, wanted, prayed. You wanted.

You wanted to put him back inside you, inside the belly, heart, more. He walked down the hall and whistled radio songs you couldn't name and you grew angry and afraid. Ghost slipping like water through your fingers. And so the years passed.

RUTH: 1969–1976

There were ghosts above the house.

I'd come upon them when I'd climb to the top of the ridge and walk along it and find pieces of old china, broken miner's lanterns, rusted frames of chairs, all that had been left behind. Some forgotten family cemetery took over by vines. Places they buried their own dead back then.

One spot was just a single grave. From a woman, my daddy had told me a long time ago, who gave birth to a child. A freak. Not a man nor a woman, but a union of the two, with more than one of everything, feet, hands, eyes, ears, both sets of privates. A terrible creature, an abomination. It was what come of unnatural acts, he said, laying with kin and such. So they buried it alive, said prayers over it.

Left its ghost to walk the ridge at night. You'd hear that ghost sometimes back at the house, at the windows. Trying to find comfort in the cold rush of wind down the hollow.

~

Time of ghosts, Andrew's sixteenth summer. Late July, near dark, that time of day when almost anything seemed likely to happen.

237

We were working against time, against the dry flashes of heat lightning that promised the rain we'd needed for weeks. I'd been out for hours with Earl, feeling my way, barefoot, along rows of tomatoes, tying strips of old bed sheets against the stakes, fetching bucket after bucket of tap water. The red earth felt thick and cool. I started down the row of Better Boys and Mountain Prides and felt a leftover root bite hard into my bare foot. My shoulder burned as I carried, carried.

And where was that boy, all this time, Earl wanted to know. He called first in the general direction of the front steps, then, when he got no answer, toward the trees and then the highway and the first distant headlights down the hollow. Son, where you at?

A flash of lightning, and a hollow, splitting sound, like a maul into dry hickory. Useless lightning, without a drop of rain. But with that sound, all lights vanished, the far ones from houses down the hill, toward the hollow's mouth. Behind me, the porch and the back room of our house was completely dark, not a kerosene lamp lit, not a candle.

I set the bucket down, rubbed my aching palms against my dress. Went to fetch him, inside and down the hall smelling dark, an already old scent, fresh rabbit and greens and grease and gravy.

The door to Andrew's room was ajar, and out of there came another smell, spicy and strong. Words, his, a few soft, hummed lines, the voice not a boy's, not a man's—*pretty you, he sang, that night in June, you without a name, come sing to me, bring to me, all that I'd love and soon.* He was sitting at the bureau, wearing nothing but an old cotton gown, one of Little Mother's I'd pushed back into a drawer and besides that, a string of beads, mine.

Like I was invisible, I inched forward, my bare feet wading through his cast off clothes, trousers, a belt buckle, an unlaced shoe. I stood behind him, ready to grab a shoulder or an ear. Son?

Lightning struck again, a slash of it without any sound at all, one that split the room in two neat halves, one half, all the dark and unlit corners way behind me, down the hall and into the kitchen and out into the yard and garden where I thought I could hear Earl's voice, come on down, you two, it's only rain. And the rain we'd waited for had started, tiny drops so hard they were like pellets of ice against the window. In the mirror, the other half of the world was a light of its own so clear and full of shine I hardly dared cast my eyes on it. There, all the world, my son's secret world, lit up and revealed.

In the surface of the mirror, I saw the depths of water. The surface of the mirror was the surface of the pond back at Mining Hollow. I saw down and down into green summer water, past moss and heat, into a center that was cool and clear and bright. Andrew, hair floating behind him, golden and thick with wet. He held steady, arms stroking, face raised toward the surface. Little Mother's cotton nightgown expanded with water, then floated above his head with the motion of the water, floated free and left his boy's body naked. I wanted to reach through the surface of the mirror, cover him. But there wasn't time. Another body, another boy's ghostly body, swam toward him and their fingers touched.

Son, I said, aloud now, and my mouth held fear. Andrew, I said again, and moved up behind him, grabbed a hard handful of his hair.

He looked up and I saw how the beads from my necklace were caught between his open lips. With the next flash of lightning and the next heave of the now heavy rain against the window all of that summer evening met—rain and the voice of Earl, his hard-soled boots, already in the hall, him saying, woman, where you at? Rain and my own reflection, seen now, streaks of red dirt, two sharp lines beside my mouth.

Rain and my hand against my son's face, a stinging touch of hand to skin, as if with that touch I could bring him back, the ghost of my son back from any depth of water, any secret place, any secret place at all. The shape my hand left on his check was the ghost of love, I swear it.

~

Then there were the ghosts of me, left from seven years up at Wheelwright cleaning house for those Wards. I cleaned brass and crystal and alligator high heels, vacuumed and raked the pile in the long halls where the carpet was so thick there wasn't the least sound of a footstep. Most days, I shut myself in as I cleaned, dusted and hummed in the lemon and vinegar silence filled with their ghosts, their strip mine voices. Ruth, can't you come back later? Can't you see I'm occupied right now?

One Monday, I cleaned, top to bottom, the bedrooms of those two Ward brothers, the ones who'd left Inez years back. One of the downstairs bedrooms belonged to their boy who went off to that fancy Northern city. Never wrote home.

Thankful, Mrs. Ward would say to me. You tell me, she'd say, where the thankfulness goes. It goes to automobiles, red ones, from some foreign country, too.

His room, a living testament, pictures of him and red cars on every inch of wall space, waving from red cars, standing next to red cars, racing them, towing them, in parades with them.

I cleaned those pictures, frames and glass, made them glow. The room on the other side of the hall belonged to the one who never moved farther north than Carolina. His only claim to fame was plucking chickens in an Ohio factory. His room was still a hall of fame to clean all its own, football trophies and diplomas under glass, anything to catch the dust.

At the end of the hall, I cleaned the big storage closet, took down boxes and stray coats and scarves, straightened, fixed the clutter. As I cleaned I could hear Mrs. Ward, what she'd say. She'd blot her pink lipsticked mouth, pout her lips.

Ruth, she'd say, I've put out a few garbage bags of old clothes out in the drive. My how quick fashions change, don't you think? See if some of those old dresses and slacks fit you.

I worked my way through the shiny brown fixtures in the kitchen, the fluffy green living room couches, down to the last room to clean, his room, the one far right-hand corner of the basement. His room. Full of the scent of perfumed soaps, the best bootleg, the finest catalogue order shirts. Henry Ward's room, the youngest son's, now that he was back from Ohio, or Michigan, some school they'd sent him to. Somewhere that made him different from the fat boy he had been, when Andrew was small. Shirts that rode up his middle and a gut hanging out. A fat boy Andrew snuck out of prayer meeting and school with to smoke cigars and hand rolled cigarettes.

I cleaned the picture frames on either side of his door, swept a cobweb from the ceiling. Then I turned the knob so slowly I couldn't wake him. Stepped into that room smelling of socks and sleep and cigarette ashes. Quietly, I opened drawers, pushed past shirts and vest, even checked under the bed. I was so quiet I made sure I was the ghost he never saw, the woman who cleaned and left. From the upstairs hall I could hear the jangle of the telephone and I stood still, holding my breath, hoping he wouldn't wake up.

He rolled over, went on sleeping, deep breaths, turned his face from the pillow and left the wet shape of a kiss. Asleep at three o'clock on a Monday afternoon, not undressed yet from the night before. His lips parted as I looked down into his plump, flushed face. Tiny beads of sweat clung to the corners of his mouth. Still completely quiet, I slipped the covers away from him, just as his hand twitched with some dream. His stomach rose, fell, as I lifted the front of the white shirt he'd fallen asleep in, unbuttoned a button, stared down.

Waiting to see if, inside his smooth chest, there was a heart. *Let not your heart be troubled*, Tobias had said. Or let it only be troubled by the power of the Lord, the might at the center of the earth that reaches up and up. What heart inside here? Candy heart, red Valentine box, heart on a gold chain?

But he only turned in his sleep, pulled his knees up into his arms. Then I covered him. Draped one thin, blue tie over a chair, lined his boots up with the toes pointing toward the closet, set a brush and a comb straight on the nightstand, righted and overturned glass. When I eased out of the room, shut the bedroom door with the littlest click, I could still hear him in there, sleeping deeper than ever, hard breath in, then out.

Back in the kitchen I made sure, one last time, that everything was in place, mops back in the corner, broom put away, sniffed the medicinal odor of clean I'd left. Like always, my check, ready-made, was waiting for me, stuck to the refrigerator door with a clock-shaped magnet, along with it a little note, in the handwriting of Mrs. Ward, thanks again, Ruth, and see you next week. Three neat exclamation points and a little pencil drawn smile.

~

Another day up at Wheelwright, there were the curtains to do. I took them down, room by room, window by window, washed them in the big machine in the basement, hung them up in the side yard so they'd come out, as Mrs. Ward said, when she herself was a girl. I had my serious doubts about whether a field of daisies even had a smell. More than that, though, as I stood there that morning with Mrs. Ward, I had my doubts about whether or not she'd ever been a girl, no less a mountain girl, with a mama who washed curtains on a scrub board and with a wringer washer set up in the living room, like she'd have you believe.

Mrs. Ward, that morning, was all decked out in a tight black suit, silk it looked like, with a tiny skirt that showed her chubby legs all the way up. She was standing in their recreation room, near the sliding glass doors that looked out over the swimming pool, going over the weekly list of things to do—clean out kitchen cabinets and organize canned goods, take down all light fixtures and wash them with bleach, the kind with the lemon scent, sort laundry, whites, coloreds, and I did know about the delicate things, didn't I, Ruth?

As if I didn't, after seven years of washing out her underwear and throwing away her stockings, and them with just one little picked place. But I said yes, and stood there watching her tug at her skirt and pirouette around like a ballerina in a windup music box and ask me, who was standing there in a plain cotton dress, some rolled down socks and some sneakers with the toes cut away, ask me if she looked all right to go to town to shop today, and was her suit too short, and did these heels match? She looked like a kewpie doll, her in that tight dress and pink lipstick and rouge in one spot on each cheek and her hair still in brush rollers, but I said, fine, Mrs. Ward, just fine. And looked one last time at her list of what to do, item by item as she pointed them out to me with her pointy pink nails. Especially the curtains, now, Ruth. Do them up pretty for my dinner on Friday night, won't you now, she said, as she minced out of the room, her high heels leaving indentations in the carpet.

So I took the curtains down, window by window, did them up pretty, window by window, room by room, hung them out on the clothesline, like she'd asked, to give them that fresh mountainy smell. Mountain air. And coal trucks passing her on the highway, her power windows all the way up, on both sides of her lean car. Coal trucks, them hauling heavy loads at twenty miles an hour up some windy road, trucks coughing lungsful of gray smoke as the gears shifted, raining down slag and dust, trucks bearing down hard on this road or that with load after load heavy enough to make chugholes to jolt you awake on any late night's trip back to this hollow or that, trucks belting out the smell of tar and burning oil, raining down soot. I washed Mrs. Ward's curtains and listened to them snap as they caught the wind.

I'd reached the last set of windows, those same sliding glass doors that looked out over the pool. The curtains there were off-white lace. I took down the last panel and stood there awhile, taking a body's ease, then draped the panel over my head, let it fall across my face, over my shoulders and down to my ankles, just sweeping the floor. I glanced at my reflection in the glass, my lace-covered shape. I could have been a bride, gliding in my white veil down some clean hall smelling of ammonia water, blessing the sick in some country with a foreign name, kneeling in a church-house that smelled of God and the clovery breath of angels. I pulled the curtain back, draped it over my head.

Then I looked down through the sliding glass doors, through the lace of the curtain, down to the swimming pool. I saw my son, Andrew, just coming out of the bath house at the far side of the pool. His thighs were brown with sun and wind and his fair hair blew in the wind. Then he was poised on the edge of the pool with Henry Ward behind him. Andrew raised his arms, tucked his head, dove in a clean, neat line. Henry sat, feet dangling in the blue water, watching my son.

He pushed himself off the side of the pool, waded, weightlessly, toward Andrew. I saw Henry rake through his hair with his wet fingers, saw the soft band of white above his swimming trunks as he leaned into the water, glided to where Andrew floated, the motion of the water rocking his body gently, so gently, like the swimming pool bottom and the water and their two selves could go in right there, into light whiter and whiter. When the two of them touched, the lace curtain slid back, fell to the floor.

I should have opened the window, called out into the yard, Andrew, what do you think you're doing here, get on back home, now. I didn't. I held perfectly still and only my hand shook as I lowered it next to my chest, let the curtain fall back. I watched the two of them. Andrew floated on his back and Henry Ward's cheek came to rest on his stomach. That was all. But it was like sleep, like they were one body held up by the ghost of wind and swimming pool light, one body that could go on and on into the cloudless sky and beyond and beyond. They thought no one saw.

~

After that I knew, for a long time. And not just about Henry Ward, or Earl, or my daddy, or God. None of it.

But about how everything leaves. Falls away. Skin under the eyes, face in the mirror. Love. Goes where, we can't think. I understood the old words of hymns, *time is now fleeting, moments passing.*

What I knew made me dream of rising above steps, house, roof. Of floating, just above the chimney, in the shade of the tree of heaven. When I looked down the body once mine was changed. The hair was lighter, the arms and legs slender, longer. Body of my body, my son's. His body, falling, down steps, a long stairway, a well. Down a hill into the straggly weeds of the yard. Into cold, black water, the pond at Mining Hollow.

He fell farther and farther, through silt and algae, but not to the pond's slicky bottom. The pond turned to light, to sunlight. Became the open door of a car, Henry Ward's. His open arms.

EARL: 1969–1976

Sunday mornings sometimes, half asleep, I'll hear nothing but Bible pages turning. Her, Ruth, mouthing holy words. Show me, she'll say, show me the everlasting sweet heart of the sweet Lord. December and cold enough to freeze your breath and I saw her once, fingers spread against the icy kitchen glass, held there. I could feel the tear as she pulled away, finger by finger, saying, reveal thyself, show me, who loves thee more than life. Warm her. All these years, chest against chest, feeling the exhale of prayers.

And Andrew. I wish it was that easy, me handing it to him all neat and bound up in a book with a nice cover, so he could read it, like he does all those other novels and histories of his. His own book, called, This, Son, is the Way it Will Be Sometimes. His own special book of notions to take out every time he ever needs it. Every time his shoe has a new hole. Every time under the covers looks better than out, or every midnight for the rest of his life when whiskey will work about as good as well water and when he sees every minute pass and wishes the earth would open up, a wide clean hole to China, where everybody wears silk underwear and tells him it'll be fine, just fine now.

I've wished for that, all of it. I've gambled and shot the moon, sat plenty of times outside the Inez Diner at 1:00 A.M. and waited for Lolo Lafferty with her pink lipstick saying, honey, what'll be, and where you going, after? Where, if she could have had her way? To a back street diner in the town we'd run off to? Kaylee's, that diner, ours, named after her dead mama. Her hostessing and waiting and busing, me in a chef's hat and black and white checked pants, listening to radio songs in the kitchen, *no sugar tonight in my coffee, no sugar tonight in my tea.* We'd retire on the proceeds of blue plate specials and she'd love me good, till the day I died. And this wife turned into that one would be better, after all. Prayer words turned orders back to the grill, your fries are up, Earl Wallen. Where did love go in me?

Isn't that, in the end, why we bear sons? Name to name to name, filling up the holes in the earth, keeping us anchored, filling up the holes in ourselves. My own boy, continuation of Wallen. Continuing down all the roads I'd traveled, pulling out of the same rest stops I'd slept in, turning back the same motel sheets. Filling up the same gas tank at Pappy Imes's, only continuing, this time, on that road out of Inez, past Mining Hollow and all that came after and never looking back.

~

Only the son I got was him, Andrew. Andrew Wallen. Never catch him with his work boots on at the right minute, no sir, or catch him dirtying himself up tamping the soil down. The mines took him in and spat him back out like so much bad chewing tobacco. Set him down as a stock boy at the five and dime, for awhile. Until they caught him staying late and winding up all the cheap music boxes and dancing the light fantastic behind the counter. Truck driver, service station, telephone company. What's a man for in the only the world there is?

Take that night I buried the dogs alive. He couldn't have been more than sixteen. This is not to say he was in the corner of the garden like he ought to have been, with me, at my elbow, ready to hand me the shovel. I was the one who'd stayed awake half the night watching the way that half blue tick hound crouched in the corner of the pen, belly dragging the ground. Sure, I'd seen it a dozen times before when she'd littered. She'd always dig a little hole for herself and fit her body in the middle of it, head facing the front porch.

Times before, I'd come out of the house for work, go down that way to check on something, the pole beans maybe. No matter what time it was, those times, I'd have to look right at her milky brown eyes, all that heat rising from her sides, her panting that way. But that night. It was summertime. Andrew was sixteen that year.

It was like this. I'd started out mid-afternoon, working on the truck in the shade by the mimosa tree in the side yard. Nothing particularly wrong with that engine, but you know how it is. I loved the way you could take out the plugs, check for oil on the threads or carbon on the filaments. You had control over everything that way, no one there to ask you why or say tell me what you think or ask what if, like Ruth and him always did. If an engine missed, you looked for it and sure you asked why and maybe you wouldn't find it, but you sure would put the nuts and bolts in the right places and there you had it. Working on the truck I just knew and didn't have to tell a soul what it was I knew or how.

I couldn't have asked for a better Sunday afternoon. Ruth was in the bedroom with all the curtains pulled and Andrew was lying down on the metal glider on the front porch, sleeping his life away, I guess. There wasn't a sound anywhere, maybe a little fresh, rain-smelling wind down from the hills, but everything was so still. I could hear that glider creak and sway and I thought, it's a day like that makes you thank God. When I raised my head from under the hood the shadow of a hawk crossed the sun and the electric wires hummed and I just stood there for a good little while, listening.

I'd been working an hour and a bit when I heard the sounds. There was a quick, scratching noise, then a crash, like something heaved against the chicken wire around that dog pen. Nothing peculiar, I thought, just that hound making trouble. She'd dug out more than once and it was a wonder she hadn't been shot a long time ago with the number of chicken and guinea and goose eggs she'd sucked. Altogether she wasn't worth much, not a pure blue tick, but I had sold the last ones she'd dropped at the flea market in Inez.

I picked up my socket wrench and was just tightening the valve cover when I heard another thing, a breathing kind of, a bubbly sound, air in the back of the throat of something. Then there was a long howl, like three off-key notes all at once, enough to make me want to cover my ears. Then silence. I don't know why, maybe it was because it was later by then and the sun had slipped down past the line of trees at the top of Drusilla Ridge and a wind that was down-right freeze-you-to-death was coming out of the gully back of the house by the spring, but I closed my tool box, rubbed my hands down the chill bumps on my arms and walked over that way. What I saw was enough to make anyone shiver.

That hound, I can remember it like it was yesterday, was standing in the corner of the pen in the middle of a shallow, dug-out hole, just like I'd seen it before. I'd known it was close to time for her to litter. I'd seen the way her teats had swelled and the way she'd lick at her hindquarters. But I'd never seen an animal look that particular way, not even a hog when you got ready to slit its throat at butchering time. She was huddled next to the lean-to I'd built. Her head was thrown back and her eyes were staring straight at the sun, enough to make me look too, at how white the light was. If eyes are what you'd call what I saw. The darks of those eyes were turned completely back so that what I saw were the veins, a shiny blankness like the surface of the creek where I threw my used oil. She stood perfectly still for a minute, maybe longer. I watched the edges of her lips pull back and her dry, white tongue licked and licked. She heaved her head back and there was that howl again. Not of this sweet earth, I'll tell you. I felt a shiver down my back and at the same time heard a voice behind me. What is it, Andrew asked. What's she doing?

Just hearing a human voice was enough to shake me out of the willies. Andrew and I settled back on our heels, near the lot, looking in, and I decided it was times like this and time enough for my son to be a man. I reached in my pocket, pulled out my tobacco and some papers, rolled us a couple of cigarettes. We watched that hound circle and moan. Once she rubbed her swollen sides against the fence and sank down, panting. Her eyes looked red-brown then, like blood from a nasty old cut. Andrew put his cigarette to his lips and I wanted to smile at it, him awkward as hell, but he drew the smoke in clean and quick. What'll she do now, he asked. He rocked back and forth on his heels, glanced at my face to see how I'd answer. Let's just us wait, I said.

And we did. For the first hour it was a sort of peaceful-like time and I forgot, until later, that terrible sound. I even brought us out a thermos of coffee from the truck, poured a inch of whiskey in my own cup. Andrew sat near enough the fence to reach in and pat that dog's head. Her breathing was slower and she licked the warm coffee off his hand. But that was only the first hour. After that she began to pace in a circle that got bigger and bigger. Each time she passed us I could see the way her flanks quivered. I imagined the shape of a snout, the legs, a head. And Andrew said it, how he felt something from the touch of her, something alive from the inside out. I guessed, this litter, there'd have to be as many as ten of them.

Then she stopped circling altogether and I could tell there was a change, a tenseness at the edge of her lips, a shaking in her hindquarters, like she was ready to spring. I'd just been around dogs that long. I knew. I said, Andrew, you watch out, son, but he struck his hand through the wire again, anyway, and held it there, fingers out, waiting for her to come by again and catch the scent of him. I couldn't have looked away for more than a second when I saw Andrew pull back. I saw the place, two red scratches down the middle of his right wrist. He put his hand to his mouth and sucked.

After that I knew something wasn't right. She was circling again, smaller and smaller circles, head tucked and her back legs slack, like she'd lost the good use of them. Then she fell on her side all at once, white foam oozing from her mouth. Right then I should have expected the pups to be like they were. She shuddered when each of them dropped out of her, but she didn't protest much. Not then. They fell from her, wet blue sacks of them.

I could see right away the likes of them. One of them, instead of an ear, had a deep hole in the side of its head. Another had no front legs at all and still another had two small, perfect heads. Perfect. Each of those pups was perfect in some small way I'd rather remember. That memory. The unopened eyes and their pink undersides. But they could never have lived. I heard Andrew get up and I turned to watch him as he backed away, hid himself, I reckon, back in the house, his room.

A son, they say, will raise up the name of the father. Burn his name clean on the face of the earth, make it new again. Burn that name clean down to the bones and ashes and make the dead spirit rise. Oh Jesus, Jesus, my son whispered that day.

I said to him, son, they couldn't have lived. Never, I said, as I dug a hole for them at the bottom of the garden and put them, with kindness, I swear it. But when I looked up toward the house all I saw was the way the curtain fell and hid him from me.

RUTH: AUGUST 16, 1983

You are Ruth, God has said. *She who sings glory words, kneels, prays, waits. Who dreams fire.*

She who dreams what it is that men do or say. Hands, legs, muscled backs bent in work. Them talking under the raised hood of a car, crouched on their heels on the courthouse steps, trading guns, knives, passing by in some coal rig as you walk up the road toward Inez, saying, you, there.

That man, your husband, talking in his sleep. He says words. *Go right,* he says. *Forward, explode, shatter, find. Sugar, hold me now.*

Andrew, just little. In front of the wood stove at Mining Hollow, reaching out his hand toward the red metal, saying, pretty. You thought no and then he stopped his own self just inches from the stove and looked. Where was the fire, that day? Stars off the back porch at Mining Hollow, did Andrew already have a wish? Matches in pop bottles, sticks rubbed, lightning bugs in jars, do all fires lead to one? In the church-house Sunday after Sunday, looking up at the holy light of God shining through stained glass which fire did he see? Not the sweet forever burning light of God almighty, but sunlight on hair, and taillights of some car heading down the road and watching

251

until every last red glow of it was gone. Gone, too, nights he's snuck out at bed time, then back in, later and later, to end up stretched out across the mattress, sleeping heavy like no one could wake him, his lips full and red and smelling of wine and what. Son words. In sleep, him telling about a sweet field of clover. Boy's hands move close. *Love.*

You are Ruth. You have touched the mighty wings of angels. You have gleaned, gathered, abided fast. Wife, raising up the name, Wallen. Mother, raising up the name, son. And yourself?

When you are awake now, lying awake with the night far gone, not a car on the road, not a light, not a sign of life anywhere, you are one long dream, and all around you is that dream and in you, too, and it is one you should have remembered and known the signs for.

You are now one long dream of fire.

ANDREW: SUMMER, 1980

Hell, my mother says, and quotes my dead grandfather, quotes the torments of the damned. *The smoke of their torment ascendeth up forever and forever*, she says. In hell, she says, they rest neither night nor day, they who worship the beast, his image, his name. Hell, that pit of red-hot chains and pitchforks and unquenchable fires, that after world of sin never forgotten, never forgiven. Never forgiven, the bottles of whiskey she thought Henry Ward and I would slip over the country line to buy, the nubile young bodies she thought we would have. She did not know night, those stolen hours in my father's truck down Highway 23 toward Inez, that hell of sins never named, love never blessed.

I drove those nights with the radio going full blast, playing love songs, any love song, pulled off next to the swinging bridge over the Big Paint River, a summer river smelling of dead fish and motor oil. I left the engine running and the windows rolled up tight and inside the humid truck was full of that night and cigarettes and my own breath. I jacked the music even higher, imagined the singer—a seedy Huntington nightclub has-been with an open necked polyester shirt and a gold arrow on a chain. I knew how he would smell of drugstore aftershave.

Would smell like the lovers of afternoons and afternoons, lovers, Henry Ward's and only once now mine. Clandestine encounters with truck drivers who would never touch another man like that, but might, on the odd chance we met over late night cups of coffee at wayside motels. Notes and matchbook covers and telephone numbers, strategically placed on the dash of Henry's car. Huntington barrooms and elicit two hour flings. Weekend overnighters, the perks for Henry's business engagements in this northern city or that. Hints dropped, one-night stands, the casual nature of jealousies bound to provoke a choice. My choice. A boy no more, a man but not—choose, Henry Ward has said. Choose. Run away with me. Fly. Here's the ticket, for the coast of California, San Francisco and all the winding streets. Midnight train, out of here, forever and always. Leave by night, now, now. Choose. Or not.

I cracked the window just enough, tossed out a lit butt, watched it upend and upend into the river water. That tiny flame, disappearing, pretty as a heart, one that flared up, descended, drowned without a sound.

~

Hell. That was exactly what I always thought of at Johnny Angel's, the minute I stepped into its reds, pinks, roses, colors for everything from the paper flamingos to the flaming togas worn by the cocktail waiters. Such a place, I thought, in a want-to-be West Virginia city, was a contradiction, to say the least.

At the door, that night, the bouncer, sporting a tag with the androgynous name Royce, eyed me, stamped my wrist with a tiny violet cherub wreathed in chains and wearing biker boots. Royce winked, then waved me on, a gesture acknowledging my connection, no doubt, to Henry Ward's frequent appearances at Johnny Angel's. I surveyed the room. Decor a cheap and good pretense of a tropical isle. Walls painted azure, with waves and seaweed and fish. Drinks named for lost cities, Atlantis, Pompeii, Sodom, Gomorrah. At the very center of the still sparsely populated dance floor was a grotesque reproduction of pulsating volcano. Also at the center of the floor, Rosita, sometime drag queen, wearing a slinky, orchid-covered skirt, low cut enough to show every pock mark and wisp of hair on his skeletal chest.

"Buy me a drink, Andy?" Rosita took my hand, led me to the right of the dance floor, to the bar, where we first each acquired a neon-pink lei, and a light-weight paper umbrella, which opened into the shape of a flamingo. The lei doubled as a costume, while the flamingo had multiple uses, as anything from a pseudo protection against rain to a substitute dance floor partner.

I ordered scotch for myself, a double, and a Sloe Screw for Rosita and then we settled onto bar stools to watch the night scene. Scene. I thought about the manifold meanings of the word. The dance-floor was certainly a scene from something, with the same used-up cast, Fridays and Saturdays a double bill, all of it a tawdry drama, with not much possibility of better, more exciting roles for anyone. Or scene. Already, and with it only midnight, I heard a glass crash, high-pitched weeping, some voice, one I thought I recognized, saying, come on, you can't, can't, you two bit whore, can't leave me like this. A scene I would make in about one curtain call, if Henry Ward were there, in the flesh and blood. The real scene was how the whole dance floor, Hawaiian shirted, danced a kaleidoscopic disco under the glass eye of the mirrored ball suspended from the ceiling, danced and sweated under the thin, chilly breath of the fifth rate air-conditioning, in the humid, late-night-bar air. All of it had the glittery veneer of some souvenir you'd buy at a beach side tourist trap, if only the beach were closer by than hundreds of miles. Already I felt it, that something very like boredom.

"Come on sweetie," Rosita said. "Loosen up."

Already Rosita was uncapping the tiny vial of rush, inhaling, handing it on to me, eyes euphoric. I shrugged, took two deep breaths, felt the quick flood of warmth across me face, down my arms. The room glistened, grew distant and softer, an infusion of simulated love, what Henry Ward had called an orgasm in the head, an erotic sneeze. Glancing around the dance floor, I was looking for Henry long distance, from the back of my own eyes, like looking slow motion through clear plastic, and I remembered, sadly, just how numb all of me had felt, before. How many times had we made love, had sex, fucked, rushed in and out of all of it, at a great, hazy distance? Right now, I liked it that way, the room, the dancing, the floor diamonded and sparkling and diffused. Not a sign of Henry, anywhere. I inhaled again, chased the burst of warmth with a long drink of scotch.

"Want to dance?"

Rosita looked faintly startled. "When's the last time I saw you dance, Andy?" He downed the last of his drink, held out his hand.

Rosita's palm felt soft, with an odd row of firm, rough calluses on the thumb and I held on, right out to the center of the dance floor. This, I thought, was where Henry Ward had danced. Nightly? Semi-weekly? Lately, I'd had little idea, and it certainly hadn't been with me. And when I had been here, with Henry, a dozen times, two dozen, more, who knew, I had more often spent my time curled up with a drink at the far end of the bar, looking. Just a looker, Henry often called me. To prove him wrong, I began to move, awkwardly, stiff-legged, my own peculiar dance step, one I had to admit was a bit stilted, no, that wasn't quite right, more like somebody half-drunk on a pair of stilts. Rosita handed me the rush, and I inhaled again, slowly, in each nostril, and felt my body begin to respond, its own secret warmth, languorous and quiet in the humid room, which was quickly filling up with an assortment of nightlife.

Beside me danced an elegant queen with elbow length white gloves and a sequin-studded, low cut ballroom gown. Dance with me, the ballroom queen said, and I felt myself propelled forward, to the center of movement, the dance floor lit with red, blue, yellow, lights throbbing with music suddenly louder, subduing voices, thoughts. Henry, I had come here to find Henry, and I held on to that thought, circled and moved my feet to the music, surveyed the corners of the room. Behind me was a sleazy-looking, traveling salesman type with oiled-back hair and an outdated, polyester leisure suit, dancing the twist, eyes closed. Couples danced, touching hips, arms, foreheads, holding their own tiny vials of warmth, like an embrace. I had long since lost sight of Rosita.

Dance, that was what held this room together, or was it? At the edge of the floor were college boys, dock-sidered and sockless, oblivious to the touch of anyone, any hand, any dance partner, lips rosy and moist, kissed, without shame, for the first time in full barlight. Or was it the music, DJ'd from the glassed-in cage at the top of spiral stairs at the side of the room, that held me? *Johnny Angel, you're the one that I adore, oh Johnny Angel*, they were playing that song, again, again, and I inhaled the vial again, plunged in and into the sound. Pink flamingoed umbrellas raised all around me and the music took on a new frenzy, *oh Johnny Angel, you're the, the one*, and I raised my own flamingo, looked up with the rest of them, at the swaying silver ball, glass eye shedding its light, and then at the swarms of balloons in the shapes of angels, set loose from somewhere overhead. One by one the balloons burst, sent down showers of heart-shaped confetti as the music rose, crescendoed, *you're the one that I adore, oh Johnny Angel*. Looking up, the warm rush spreading through me, the bursting angels seemed far, far away, behind some sheet of light, pink light that dimmed as I stared at it, dimmed and glazed over, became a rosy sheet of distant ice. That was it, what I was the center of, a far place of ice, and behind that ice lay all that I loved, faraway music, Saturday nights, Henry, and more that I could not name.

A hand touched my shoulder. It wasn't Rosita's.

"Care to dance?"

The voice was hoarse with cigarette smoke, made the attempt at sultriness. The face was beige, with base makeup carelessly applied over unshaven cheeks, ending sharply at the jawline, beneath which was stubbly beard. There was a peroxide blonde wig, thick red lipstick, eyelashes matted with mascara, the whole a grotesque attempt at beauty, at Mae West, a faded movie star mask over skin that seemed ashen, but familiar.

"I said, want to dance? Or don't you recognize me?"

The face bent lower, and I smelled face powder, an at first strangely familiar sweat tinged with patchiouli, one that made my heart beat faster, made me think of, what, warm afternoons and the scent of old carpet? Made me see myself, holding aloft a paper flamingo.

"I'm already dancing," I said.

"Ah, so you don't recognize me, huh?" Mae West put his hands on the hips in their tight red dress, shook his head in dismay. The one hand, now stroking the fine hairs on my forearm, that was familiar, and even more familiar, a tiny, perfect mouth tattooed on the middle finger.

"Of course I recognize you," I said, whispering, a useless hiss between my teeth, nearly inaudible beneath refrains of *Johnny Angel.*

All around me, hands disappeared beneath shirts, stroked just-encountered buttocks and thighs. How absurd that my encounter, my one unremarkable afternoon's motel fling, should make me look furtively around this room, any room for that matter, should make me think Henry, Henry Ward, when for all I knew Henry was, at this very minute, having his own furtive encounter at the same motel, in the bathroom stall at Johnny Angel's standing up on the toilet seat, who knew, for God's sake. I pulled my arm away from the blonde's hand.

"I recognized you, of course I did," I said, backing away by degrees "Said we'd have to have a drink sometime. Later."

"I'll bet you didn't." The blonde laughed, pulled a pack of cigarettes out of the sleeve of his dress, held them out in my direction. "How's about a drink? For old times sake?"

"Thanks anyway," I said. "But I was just about to meet up with someone."

"Thanks," the blonde said. "Hmm. Now what does that mean? Thanks, some other time? Thanks, but no thanks? Or giving thanks? You're a real religious type, is that it?"

"I said I was just about to catch up with someone. A friend." I moved further away into the crowd, spoke over my shoulder. "We'll get together. Soon. I've still got your number." Back turned, I was just about to disappear into the music, dancing, heat, when the blonde spoke again, his voice a little higher, coy?

"Your friend wouldn't be Henry Ward, now would it?"

I stopped, feeling light fingers, smoke, breath, on the back of my neck. "Henry?" I asked, so softly no one, not the blonde, not a soul, hardly myself, could have heard the name.

I moved closer, could smell the blonde's plastic wig. "Do you know anything about Henry?"

"Friend," the blonde said. "I've always thought that was a pretty debatable word, myself. Your friend, my friend, everybody's friend."

"I said, what do you know about Henry Ward?" I reached out, grabbed hold of gold-sequined material, twisted it.

"Darling, don't mess with my wardrobe." He pulled the fabric away. "Did I say I knew one blessed thing about your, what was it, friend? My, my, I just asked a simple question."

"What question?"

"I asked you," he said, moving his face closer to mine. "Is your pal Henry Ward?"

"What about Henry Ward?"

The blonde laughed again and his breath smelled of cigarettes. "Does your friend have these little, what do you call it, clusters of freckles on the inside of his right thigh. So romantic. Just like the Pleiades."

I was close to his face, breathed, slowly, in, out, scent of old dinners, onions, coffee.

"Or maybe I don't have the right friend at all. Let's see. Does Henry have green at the center of his left eye? A mole on his ass?"

The music grew louder, still "Johnny Angel," *how I love him, how I think of him and me*, couldn't they play any God damned thing else? My hand was clinched, and was it skin, my own, my nails biting down hard into a palm.

"Or how about his nipples? The one, do I have it right, just a wee bit bigger than the other?"

The blonde's voice grew farther away. The words grew fainter, took on a pattern, a distant shape I couldn't read or understand, swirled up and up into the ceiling full of angels and pink smoke and song words colliding, *but I just sit and wait, I'd rather contemplate, Johnny Angel*.

"The scar? The long one, the one below his arm? Near his heart?"

From far away, I contemplated Henry's pale, often plump body, the unutterable softness of stomach, the rough patches of skin, elbows, knees, the cock, ridiculously, sentimentally, a flower, the center of a flower. Now, in a swirl of words I could only distantly see, describing a body I had so loved, tasted, in a swirl of sounds that crashed into my ears, a mockery of love, I contemplated that body, saw the blonde kneeling, lips moist and red and full of lick and kiss and saying, asking, don't you want, kneeling, as if in sacrilegious prayer, before the long lost body of my lover, Henry, Henry. What had I said aloud?

"Yes, Henry, that's him. I knew he was a friend of yours." I was now holding the blonde's hand, holding on tight, and song words rose around him, washed him, submerged him, like a salt-tasting and never-beheld ocean, *how I love him, Johnny Angel, and I pray*, a long desired and unreachable sea. The night, the bar, the sea of bodies, touching bodies, almost touching bodies, never touching bodies, was a mouth, a hollow mouth to drink me in. *Someday*, the song said, and I inhaled, once, long and deep, on the tiny vial in my hand. *He'll love me*, the song said, beyond sentiment, beyond the sweet, precarious boundaries of the heart, beyond all wishing. *I'm in heaven*, I heard, and stared down hard at the blonde's hand, now encircling my wrist, taking hold of me, leading me, leading me where?

I stared down into the tiny, tattooed mouth on the blonde's middle finger and I thought, song words, I thought, *I think of him and me and how it's gonna be*. I stared down into a tattooed mouth and I saw the red, beating heart of the far away sea, the sea, of Henry, no longer Henry, maybe never Henry at all. *I'm in heaven*, I sang with the song, and stared down into the mouth and saw nothing, nothing at all. Or was it nothing? I felt myself falling, deeper than the sky, the sea, the mines of the earth, into a hollow mouth dark and unfathomably deep. I closed my eyes, felt soft, full lips touching mine. Act like a man, I had once been told. How should a man act? I drank the last of the song words in. *I just sit and wait, I'd rather contemplate, Johnny Angel.*

RUTH: AUGUST 16, 1983

In all this world there is no blood red moon, no hand of God to burn the earth away. There is you. It is through you that God speaks. *And death and hell were cast into water, a lake of fire.* This is the second death, my daddy said. The lake of fire is you. Fire and all these years coming out of you, your hollow mouth. Saying. *Repent. Unburden,* all sin. *Come clean. Start again.* Listen to it. The voice of the night.

And so you wash your hair from the rain barrel and rinse it with cologne Little Mother left, years ago. You pretty yourself, wear Little Mother's nightgown, one smelling of rose petals and dust, brush your hair a hundred strokes near the bed of your sleeping husband. You touch the mirror's thin reflection one more time, say a prayer and take the small zippered Bible. Husband, tonight angels who once came will tonight come back, reveal the holy light of love.

You stand at the window overlooking the front porch and you watch as Andrew walks down toward the road, looking behind him, checking to see if you see. You hunt the verse that says, *hallowed be,* motion to him as he opens the car door. The two of them, saying love words, promises, plans. You feel Henry Ward's hand that time he took yours and said, a fine day, and how are you? You hear Little Mother running, loose stones in the road, a car driving off. Press your palms against the window, stroke the glass until it grows thin as air.

You pray, and the air takes a scent, wild roses. Tires spin. That Ward boy, Andrew, both of them gone to Inez, down some back county road, far as Huntington. The night like seven signs of God rushes inside. Them, lips upon lips, buttons done and undone. Such echoes of touch fill you with a loneliness so awful you hold your breath to fill up your hollow chest.

When you take your hands from the window, you hear a high, sharp breaking and you know it is your heart. Your heart is in sharp glass pieces, and you think, *how I love him.* Him, God, Jules, Earl, father, son, Holy Ghost. How I love. A question and an answer and a hollowness at the very farthest, unseen center of you.

Thin and invisible, you open the cupboard, the while feeling your husband's words slip out under the bedroom door. Words starting at your bare feet, winding around your ankles, up your legs, stopping at your chest. Sleep words. *Caress, hold on, obey.* Husband words. You unwind them, think them gone, like bones dropped in water.

Taking out what you need, you go out to the porch, sit on the swing, dragging your bare feet. Very long ago, Little Mother said, you, *Ruth Blue, you've got no business out there, wet-headed, you'll catch.*

What? A voice. So long ago now, so soft under the layers of bed things washed and bodies held and good gospel truth that make up her life, hers, Ruth Wallen's, not yours, Ruth's, Ruth Blue's, that you can hardly hear. That voice. Two hollows over, years and years over. You unzip the Bible, flip through the pages, looking for prophecies— prophecies, warnings, truths. And when the thousand years are expired, it says, Satan shall be let out of his prison. And you?

Moonlight, a comb through dark, wet hair, the shivery way of this night. Cold voice of God whispering against your ankles and up.

Cold, strange weight of the shotgun across your lap.

Mouth, tasting of metal, will not make words.

But you know that with one clean shot pointed up the sky will break open. Not the opening of forbidden letters nor the opening of a wedding night, and you, crying, no. This time the opening will be the world, *fire, blessed and holy, he that hath part in the resurrection.*

You will be a bride again, a child, and farther back, so far back the world will begin again and again. Spinning earth, held still, sun's light gone gentle, hollow mouth of God breathing you in with a lover's breath. And little by little, all fierceness, turned sweet as cloves and honey. Bones, blood, you, all that you have loved dissolved by fire, made new. Ash. Light enough to float on forever and forever in the air of purification, sanctification, mystery of God. Mystery of light, quenched.

Choose, the voice says.

What choice? Had there ever been a choice? Born and raised, Mining Hollow. Arrange the arms and legs, hold on at night, give birth, wash the supper things up nice and keep the false teeth in a glass.

Choice?

Take your son with you, your pretty boy.

Rise with him beyond the burned away world. No lips and arms or hands, no lost love, no wishing. No tap shoes and sparks dying away in the road. A lightness at the brilliant center of the world. Unreachable, safe center of the sky. Mouth of God itself, lighter than love.

All your life you have waited. For love, salvation, night. For salvation. For postcards, signed Little Mother. For a song called Ruth Blue. For a blood red summer moon. You have waited through this night, so clear and full of fire that it will burn the world away to ash and nothing, leave the world a hollow palm. Palm held out, empty, waiting to be filled.

World starting over, *birth, death, birth, death,* which is first? World clean of all that has come before, all that has not come before, memory, losing, sin, photographs, mother, lover, son. Me, in a photograph's negative, doing something very ordinary, in a doorway, a cup and a spoon in my hand. Inside me bones, quiet blood, tiny crosses and the hand of God, palm down. Photograph lowered into fire, flaming up, gone, gone.

Flaming and burning to the heart, a house burned to its skeleton, its walls of ash and soot.

You stop the porch swing, hold still and listen. Nothing, not a sound, car, no birds in the tree of heaven out back by the well. You will wait until morning if you have to. You grip the shotgun, say, *oh*

Lord, I have loved in your mercy, in your kindness. You listen a very long time and when there is no answer, you shut your eyes and say, I will remember my own name. *I am Ruth, Ruth Blue.*

~

You stand near the porch railing as in the distance you hear the car. It could be a mile, but you hear it. The road seems to grow wider, longer, turn to highway and miles and miles, to an horizon you don't know. After all, you think, what will you save your son from? With your bare foot, you trace the shape of an unshaven face, sour smell of breath. Hands, any hands, not just Henry's or Andrew's, not even Earl's as they unfasten buttons, wake you, enter the unmoist places of your body. Whatsoever was not found written in the book of life was cast into the lake of fire, your daddy said. Book of life. Lost letters, hymnals, envelopes with no return address, canceled stamps on letters in a language you don't understand. Book of life, break the seventh seal. You are inside, unsaid.

As the car nears the bottom of the hill, you stand near the porch railing, lean out, listen. In the distance, you hear music, high-pitched, the cutting away of tin. You taste the metal sound. The night settles around the porch like heavy sleep, layers and layers of humid night, night and dark and all the earth in faceless shadows, white and gray and deepest black, layers and layers of earth so heavy they take your breath.

~

What will you save your son from?

The night. A black curtain of must, a place unseen and far and loveless as the forgotten insides of a pocket.

One finger moving. The slightest touch and this curtain could be pushed back.

Explosion of light, fire, brightness. You could take his hand so easily and you both could rise in the good clean light into forever and forever, with God's face seen at last, God's mystery seen at last.

Beneath the car's music, you imagine other sounds, laughter, crush of a can, cigarette ground out. The car engine shuts off, the lights dim. It rolls to a halt just before the mailboxes a hundred yards down one side of the road. There is no music at all, though you search for the least other sound, that door of Henry Ward's that needed oiling, the crunch of gravel.

Or maybe there is a sound, a hollow, distant whistling, words, hymn words. Why should we linger and heed not, those words, for you and for—mercies—his mercies—for me—mercies—mercies.

Standing next to the railing, still cradling the heavy gun, you hold your breath, all of you tensed, waiting. Arms and legs bare in the thin nightgown, your whole self is so shivery and awake the night could rub off on your skin like coal dust, leaving you so unseen you could touch the still warm hood of Henry Ward's car and remain invisible.

You wait for a sign, any sign. Words, like music you almost know, float up from the road and the parked car. *Though we have sinned, he has mercy and pardon, pardon for you and for?* For what?

You lean forward, trying to catch the last of the music sounds, but they seemed to scatter, crumble across your bare shoulders and into your empty hands as you lay the gun on the railing. The words are ashes, soot, parts of words, letters, Henry's voice, and Andrew's. How can you go home now, Henry said, and Andrew spoke back, his voice muffled. Sleep restless, Henry calls into the dark, and the car door creaks open.

~

You call down into the yard and cup your hand around your ear, feel the name, *Andrew, Andrew,* come alive. Hear it rush out of your hand, a night bird with raggedy wings darting fast and gone. The car lights come on, yellow and dim, and for just a minute you see your son, his back and his jacket collar turned up high. Andrew, you call again, but the car lights vanish in the direction of Wheelwright and then you hear no step or breath, not a sign.

You pick up the gun, brace it along the length of you arm, call, *you, Andrew Wallen, you out there, son?*

The night is a sharp, inhaled breath and you hear him feeling his way, past the pen where Earl kept his hunting dogs, past the porch, on around to the back kitchen door, with you all the while saying, son. *Answer me.*

Your heart is pounding, hard. You feel the weight of blood rich enough to burst through, spill, urgent and bright, down onto your bride's self, bare arms and smoothness of nightgown. You feel invisible, a thing of transparent skin and words, *hear me, hear me.* Andrew?

It is all your life. His.

~

By the time he goes up the steps and into the house, you are down in the yard, hidden. Your bare feet follow what might have been a trail of footsteps. You remember Bible pictures, the footsteps of God on a garden path or some desert place as you hurry around the corner of the house, toward the back door. *Hurry.* As if a hand held yours, took some of the weight of the gun, led you.

The house has only one light shining, one raised window shade, Andrew's room. You imagine rising like morning light over house and trees, over how all of Inez sleeps. Soon you will be able to rise, over this house, these houses, mountains. Soon both of you will know the morning, its light, its heavenly wonders.

~

You go up the back steps, down the hall, listen for Earl's steady breathing. Still asleep. Then you stand in the doorway of his room, Andrew's. His light flashes on and off, on and off, and as you inch the door open, you can already see his face, the kissed-looking lips.

This, you want to tell him, is the second death, is worse than death, touching someone, the hollow sound your heart makes beating against someone else's chest, what comes after that ends.

Rising to God, ash and air and forever, better than love.

~

You stand without speaking beside his bed. You see how he is still nothing but a boy, eyes open and afraid and seeing nothing but flashes of heat lightning and all the room changed by the color of night.

On his back, face to one side, away from you. Arm dangling over the bed.

Humming hymn words, softly you brush damp hair from his forehead, feel fear rise from him and see the tiny beads of sweat in the fine hairs on his cheeks.

Lightning, now, is the way he's tied the twine from the light to his wrist, the way he turns the light on and off. Fear, now, is the way his open eyes look at you as if you are a stranger, a mother he's never known. The raggedy hair hangs over his right eye and the shadows of moths cross and recross his face.

You lay the Bible on his pillow, close to his face, untie the twine from his wrist, pull the light off. Just as the light vanishes, you hear him, low words you have to lean forward to catch.

You know, don't you, he says.

Know?

How I'll never, he says. *Ever be as good as you.*

Hush, you say, and still holding the gun, you bend lower, near him, humming, come home, ye who are weary. In the dark, your mouth finds the soft, warm spot below his cheek, on his neck where a vein pulses, where you kissed him in comfort when he was a baby. You feel the blood beating that once lay inside your own self, want to draw that back into you, that gentle movement, kick, kick, I'm here, that perfect holding of a self into yourself.

You want to save him from all this dark world where love has failed, want to send him up and up and up.

Blaze of glory, save me now. *And they went up on the breath of earth,* my daddy said. *And fire came down from God out of heaven, and entered the hollow's mouth, and traveled, back and back,* to the last house in the world.

To the at last seen face of God, to that lightness where love has no name, no Ward nor Wallen nor any name at all.

You, Ruth Blue, put the gun close to him. A lover, alive with metal and promises.

Do this, the voice of God says.

And you feel his heart beating, the wildness of it, and love, and fear.

ANDREW: AUGUST 16, 1983

Ridiculous, you say, such unbounded despair, this interminable talk of heaven, mire of consciousness. You think it should be just that easy, a simple matter of choice. Consider the plethora of advice, mother-given, God-given, soul-given. Get on with your life, son. Make your bed, lie in it and sleep the sleep of the well satisfied. Choose your weapons. The good Lord? Vile affections, he says, the lust that men feel toward one another, a waste of the natural use of the women we leave behind. Foolish, these men's hands that touch, these errors of our ways. And the practical advice of the well-intentioned? Our families only spawn us, then we become men, take up men's ways and make our own decisions, leave behind all our pasts and all our memories like so much insignificant dust in the wake of a passing car. And the advice of the heart that night?

I lay there, listening, listening to that solitary beating against my pillow.

Beside me lay the gun. Blessed gift of night, she called it, before she left me alone.

The gun, a twenty-two my father and I used to take with us on Sunday afternoons. After church, or sometimes in the last hour, when some sermon went on and on, its own eternity, my father and I would go to a gully, one outside of Van Lear, one full of refuse, old washers, chairs, tires, a tangle of everything the world had left behind. We would carry that gun, head down a dirt path, ease ourselves down into the gully a dozen yards and look back up the rise where the truck sat perched at the edge of the road. I remember the gun's brace against my shoulder, the echoing explosion in the distance and the hard kick. Shoot that one, over there. Targets, the white sides of anything at all, stumps, rats scuttling, a set-up of jars. Shoot that one, that's-a-boy. I trembled, then, with the gun's heavy weight.

The explosions gave in my head now and my arms reached around myself.

Act like a man, I told myself.

I sat up in bed and looked around me, at the blank walls, the cracks fine as hairs. House before my manhood, burned to the foundations, but I remembered the sheets of on-sale paper they covered those walls with, those sheets drifting down now from the corners of the room. In the front room, praying hands on the coffee table, on the wall the dime store picture of Jesus on the cross. Lovely house, its bones and blood and heart covered over with all the trappings of home.

And if I peeled back those layers of paper and pretty pictures and plastic roses covered with dust, all the layers of years and voices and prayers, what heart would I find beating at the core?

And in myself? If I peeled back skin and bones and blood, what man there? A man who looketh not after his own household, why, he is no man. No man at all, he who looketh not at his own heart.

Gun to mouth, pull of trigger. I could do it.

A quick improvisation with the string from the light, toe in a loop, pull of trigger, release. Release of all I could not be, could never be.

I remembered the night of my sixteenth birthday, how I spent that night with my father drinking apple brandy. We stood out on the porch together passing the bottle back and forth. Three long swallows and I felt it all over. There was the fresh smell of rain. The night sang with sounds I'd never heard, strange birds in the tree of heaven out back by the well. Then he shook my hand, like I'd done something to make him proud. You, he said, will be a man soon and I want you to do these things. He slapped me on the back again and passed the bottle along with some advice on women and how to kiss them between the shoulders in just the right spot, and how, if I worked hard and saved my money, I might just be able to buy myself a coal rig or a share in the mine on Tobias's land or a deed to some Inez property where the coal would be all my own. I drank his apple brandy and then I looked through the window where I saw her sitting in the rocking chair. I saw their eyes meet. I saw how, between them, they believed that apple brandy and a Bible could make me a man.

And now, seeing my despair, she had given me a choice. Choice? You're no man in this world? Then be a man in the next.

Indecipherable, what the hand of God has written on your heart? Then look, see how God holds back the curtain of night to reveal all that is written in the book of after life.

A choice, at last, to see beyond Inez, beyond mountains and mountains and the shadows of coal, beyond and beyond to the ocean I'd only dreamed.

Bright wings of death, carry me there.

RUTH: AUGUST 16, 1983

You shut Andrew's door saying, *hush, quiet now,* son.

You lock the door from the outside, hands clinched at your sides, nails pressing into your palms.

In the hall, everything presses down and down, a held breath, Andrew's, yours, Earl's. Still, the too warm air full of Earl's cigarette after cigarette, old lard scent of last night's supper. At the kitchen door, you push your feet into a pair of Andrew's old shoes, and you are halfway there and gone when you hear the mattress springs creak and him. The covers thrown back, the feet sliding along the floor.

Ruth, he calls. Ruth?

You reach up and unscrew the kitchen light bulb, back closer to the door.

Ruth, he says again, you in there?

You turn the door knob inch by inch, can barely see his narrow, white face, the now weak, spectacle-less eyes. Then you slam the screen door and you are on the porch, looking back through the window at him, long, striped night shirt shoved into his trousers, lips full with sleep. You remember a time farther back than Andrew, a time when you might have wanted to go to him, put your body all along his in the warm bed and say, *yes.* But your choice was made a long time ago, when the blood inside you let go of Andrew, or farther back than that, when you heard the voice of God in the shadows beside the porch steps, or farther back, to you, dancing alone in a room with your own thin self.

On the top step you see him one last time as he leans against the window. He squints down into the yard. Ruth, he calls again. Andrew? Isn't there anybody home at all?

You hold your breath, blood beating in your temples. Then you turn and run, bride's nightgown thin, no covering at all, the whole night as thin as the sound of tree branches bending. You run for a good distance, eyes shut tight against all that house behind you, feet finding holds you know in the damp grass on the hill to the road, then in the sharp gravel of the roadside. You pitch into a gully at the roadside, rocks biting into your palms, your bare knees, rub your eyes until sparks of light dance, but you can still see their faces, Earl's with a two day's growth of dark beard, Andrew's pale and the surface of his skin shivery, sweating.

Their voices are asking, *where, how, tell me.*

What more can you give? You have given Earl your body's opening and opening, your son a cool kiss, gift of life, gift of night.

Listen to it, you say as you lie there for a time, eyes shut. Listen to the deep voice of God. You lie until it seems a light flashes, brilliant and exploding and joyous. Was it Andrew's room?

Oh, for the wonderful love he has promised.

And that deep voice is everywhere, above, beside, in you as you pull yourself up, walk down the road, listening all the while. Random words, *Alpha, Omega, beginning, end.* A song at the surface of your ear, time is now fleeting, the moments are passing. *Quick. Now.*

So you fill your pockets with yellow pods of deadly nightshade. Gifts, offerings, sung praises to God's at last seen face.

You don't take the highway. Not now. You climb the hill near the house, head straight over the ridge, the old way, unused dirt path, nearly overgrown with thistles and stinging nettles and honeysuckle. You skim the surface of this distance, weightless, climbing. Almost nothing in the shadows, nothing but what the partly set moon shows. Sharp fragments of old glass bottles bite through the soles of the shoes, but you move faster, fill the hollowness at the pit of your stomach with the work of moving up. By then, you are walking along the ridge, looking down on land you once knew, Leroy Johnson's, to the right, clear to the top of Abbott Mountain, and Virgil Horne's, to the left, to the top of Drusilla Mountain, and Doug Estep's pasture land beyond that. Abandoned now, the orchards, apples and peach trees, the untilled gardens, the rotting covers on well, the headstones of forgotten graves. Abandoned, sold for timber, for coal.

Come home, come home, God's voice whispers.

Soon you are at the top of the hill, the steep one above the pond at the head of Mining Hollow. All below you, Mining Hollow. You listen for distant late night radio music, car doors slamming. Far distant, a flash of green and blue and red lights from some Mining Hollow trailer, one still decorated from last Christmas. Music, too, carrying up this far from the open window of somebody's house or from the rolled down window of a car, though we have sinned, he has mercy and pardon, pardon for you and for me. Right below, tree stumps, rocks, rotting boards from an old shed. Earl once said, a long time ago, on a night when you snuck out of the house at Mining Hollow to go riding in his brand new service-man car, how moonlight could warm you, if you let it. Now, it's the wind you want next to your skin. Making its way along the top of the ridge where you breathe it, hold it in against the emptiness in you until you can't feel them anymore. Your husband, son, their faces.

Until you think of how the last light, the one you left shining in their house, has flamed up, exploded, gone. Your stomach tightens, cold and empty.

Come home, now, the night says, and you take the way down, catching handholds of roots and branches, thick vines, pushing through briars and wild hydrangea. Back of the pond, around, down that hill, until you are at the farthest corner of what used to be the yard. What used to be the house.

Chimney, decaying wood cover of the well, charred remains of walls and windows and floor. Six large stones that once held up the posts on the front porch where you brush aside dead leaves and earth, make a sitting place, reach into your pocket for the gifts you brought. Nightshade and other, forgotten things, small slivers of soap, five polished shards of glass, snarled hair from a comb.

You hold your gifts up one by one to the moonlight. Across from you on a porch-post stone are only the shadows of locusts and a handful of dust.

You hear your daddy's voice. *Do you remember that time in winter?*

Yes, you tell him, you do remember that winter, the way the world was ice, a hollowness without love.

You show your gifts one last time. The snarl of hair blows off your palm. Not the right gift, and neither are the nightshade pods that slip from your pocket and roll down into the grass. You hold tight to the other gifts and start back toward the pond. A gray smoke-shape curls around your bare legs as you set out, through the short stretch of trees.

Where the cattails are thickest there is part of the old dock Earl built, where Tobias used to fish in the springtime. You step carefully over missing boards until, almost at the end, you can see across the water. A snapping turtle dives. You lie down on the damp boards, press an eye to an opening that shows dark water stirring with moss and silvery fish. You could see down, forever if you wanted to. *Come home,* the radio song says.

You take out the two slivers of soap, toss them, and they float four or five yards from the dock, stop, spinning. Is it the very same spot you rowed out to the night after Tobias died in the fire, leaving you nothing of Mining Hollow but the yard and the pond. Beneath the spinning soap trails, you imagine toothless mouths of fishes still nibbling at the burlap sack holding your daddy's bones down there in a lonely place of moss, the place you now cast five shiny pieces of glass. They turn, light upon light, settle, softly and softly to the bottom.

You watch with all you have left, long ago angel's circle of light in your chest, hollow longing. You think, moonlight, clear, unseen God of the Abyss, God of whispers, God of light and rising, rising.

Looking down into silt and mud and river reeds, you follow a path of shine and look for God, his face, like looking into a half-empty glass, wishing, wishing it full, wishing any long ago brokenness made whole. Was that the face of God, an emptiness made full, a brokenness, whole again? Still waters stare back. Or if you look long enough, will you see an upturned face, a smile, hands reaching out, palms up?

You kiss the cold, black depths and say the words of your daddy. *Glory, abomination, pray.*

If you press your lips to the palm of God, will you taste stone, or warm, long-ago blood?

You are shaking and cold drops of sweat ease down your back. Below you, the water does not speak, has no face. God no longer whispers.

Nothing now but silence, no wind, no waves lapping against the platform, no music from Mining Hollow. You could be the last person anywhere, the last person alive.

When you touch the pond's blank face, it feels summer warm, a film of insects and stillness you push aside.

And if there is no face of God, no voice, no light behind the darkness, no rising beyond this heavy, dark world? No voice of all your life, voice saying, come, all who are weary?

You slip into this warmness and your nightgown fills and blossoms, white, night-blooming flower.

It is not a diving, but a stepping down, a weightless descent. You watch the dark, wet world pass softly by, touch you almost tenderly past broken reeds, moss and moss, past a floating, long forgotten scrap of cloth, a soleless slipper.

As you descend you pass wave upon wave of pond water, layer upon layer of silt and green, fish and the feathers of birds. There is Jules Cameron, his too-short leg and one arm treading, his camera a single flash of light that reveals the skeletons of leaves, tadpoles skimming, photographed and vanishing from broken squares of glass once called collodion. *Wave upon wave, come home, home.* Tobias, head bowed, pray, pray, his bony hand raised, striking nothing, palm closing around nothing but a dark, wet branch from a winter long past.

Layer upon layer of water, warm as sleep, forgotten as time. As long forgotten as Earl, gold stars unstuck and peeling from his waterlogged shoes, black rounds of what might have been records floating beside him, forgotten now, never, never sung. Your wet hair trails in front of your eyes as you descend and you can hardly see what you most and least want to.

Andrew, his gold hair drifting behind him as he floats, head turned and softly tilted against his shoulder, as if he is sleeping, tucked gently against a pillow. You want to reach out, touch his cheek, but you are afraid, afraid. You try to move faster against the wave upon wave, to see his face. Would that face, if you could see it, be as full of light as it was that day up at Wheelwright when you stood at an upstairs window and looked down over the swimming pool at the Ward's house? What was the thing you saw in his face that day? You refused to call it love. And if you could see it now, as he floats past and past, wave upon wave, would the thing you see in his eyes be forgiveness? Or would it be a blankness, an emptiness. Would there not be a face at all, but a mere thing, a bloated white thing, exploded away into wave upon wave of time, long past, never to be gotten back.

All of it, all the faces you once knew, vanish into water as you descend farther and farther to the bottom of the pond, that place where shadows are gathering fast, where your own deathbed is. The water-warm shadows catch at your feet, legs, fingertips. The bottom of the pond, as it touches the soles of your feet, feels slick as the inside of a mouth, as a moist palm, as just giving birth.

The face at the bottom of the pond is smooth as a stone, red-lipped, smiling, seems to look back at you. Is this, after all, the face of God, skin faded, the bare feet red as clay. Painted eye peeled away, face with a winking slyness. Is that the face of God? God you can touch, see, God of stone?

The bottom of the pond, its wave upon wave, layer upon layer, time upon time above you, is not the face of God at all. Your bride's nightgown is heavy, full of water and descent, and the bottom of the pond, bottom of the world you have known, is not a lover's face, wondrous face of God, a tenderness caught and held, rising and rising into light, good, sweet light. Oh, for the wonderful love he had promised, promised.

All, Tobias had said, *all shall have their part in the lake which burneth with fire and brimstone, which is the second death.* Where now, at last, was God's face?

Her. Oh beautiful lady of light, Little Mother, parachute silk skirts floating, one stockinged foot bare, the foot's sole white and calloused from years of dancing, dancing. Little Mother, face lit with the fire of years of sadness. All of her alight, hair, feather boa, her strong hands that once held love. Fire of sadness that will not quench nor burn away. Sorrow full face becoming pond water becoming you.

You feel yourself folding, knees into arms, holding, yourself, descending, full of water and nothing, nothing. Or is there nothing?

As you lie at the silt bottom of the pond, lungs filling slowly with the murky taste of pond water, you look up.

ANDREW: AUGUST 16, 1983

The room was filled with dozens upon dozens of moths circling the light, wings unfolded against the walls. Wings brushed the bare skin of my shoulders. White moths, brown, black, and one, a beautiful luna, its large, green wings spread wide next to the window. In this half-dark, just before morning room, all of them glowed, a dull phosphorescence.

Moths come from where? The screenless window, painted shut? Keeping out, so my mother has said, all the Godless voices of the night, leaving the room airless, sweat easing down my back, my breath coming warm, stale. From the smallest holes in the window glass, the least crack beneath a door?

I watched one of the moths, wings opening and shutting, opening, revealing a small fiery eye of orange, growing brighter and brighter.

I was at the center of this fire and I felt myself picked up, folded in, smaller and smaller, held between those wings. Together we flew toward the window, against the glass. Again, again.

Fire of desire, of all my life, held still and wanting free from the center of the world, free from this house of the holy spirit. Held between those wings, I felt the holy spirit, heard it speak.

You have not, it said, you have not yet seen God.

And so I picked up that gun, braced all its weight against my shoulder, aimed. Full of all my desire, I pulled the release, put my hand against the trigger and I said, tell me some precious, precarious truth. Show me your face.

With all my strength I pulled the trigger and felt it, the air between night and morning, felt the breath of God. Against my neck he whispered, choose, choose.

Which was God?

He said, know ye not that the unrighteous shall not inherit the kingdom, neither fornicators, nor idolaters, nor adulterers, nor effeminate, nor abusers of themselves with mankind.

I heard the breaking of glass, the rush of all the wings of the trapped moths escaping from the shattered window, and I flew there too, out and out toward the whole, light world. Riding those wings as if on the backs of angels, I hesitated only once. I looked back, held still as if all I was would never come to be, would crumble to nothing but ash and dust.

And then a voice said, surely, surely the light of God is sweet, and it's right to behold the sun.

EARL: AUGUST 16, 1983

By now you've got me figured, all right. Has-been singer and guitar player turned coal miner. Would-be song writer and radio star who stopped beside the road for a square meal and never left. Had to be coal miner who gave up and died. What good excuse do you have anyway, you ask me, to go on about it all? Some people, you say, survive wars, disasters, earthquakes in divers places. Since you son, the world has been going places. Cold War, Korea, Vietnam. Some people don't have arms or two good feet or they're blind in one eye and can't see good out of the other. And you could have picked a worse situation to settle down in. None of it's a bed of roses. Ever.

But I could tell you about beds. About lying down at night with all I'd dreamed and wished for and lost, like it was my last five cents gone through a hole in my jacket pocket. Poor you, you say. Didn't you ever pray any? There were nights I prayed. Sweet Jesus, yes.

That night, for example. Everything between itself and something else, turned inside out and backwards so no one could know the way of any of it. Light and dark, God and the earth, the truth and a lie, all of it mixed up every which way.

By now, you know more of the truth of it than I do. My wife, gone out into the night like a crazy woman and my son gone too, vanished into the Kentucky sunrise. You know more of the truth of it than me, the hows and wheres and whys. God knows you do. What you don't know is how I looked for them in all the shadows of that house.

That night I woke, dry-mouthed and sweating, from that same dream I'd had for years, the one about the war. The room was half dark and I shook myself, shook off my dream like water. In this dream, I was staring straight up into a clear sky. No, that's not right. Not clear at all. It was a dream sky full of waves of smoke so blue and familiar I ran from it, from all the spirals and wings that had caught me, held, for so many years. I was running.

No, I was waking up, waking like I always did in the room in the house. I pushed to the surface of sleep, rubbed my eyes. Heard it. The crash of gunshot. Glass breaking. Sweet mother of God, I prayed. The bed beside me was empty, the sheets gray with before dawn light.

I ran then, hitching my pants up as I went, my sock feet sliding down the hall. Down the hall, toward what looked like a light, clear and bright and sudden. While I ran, it was the same as in my dream. Me, just through the screen door that had slammed in my memory, with Rudy Hyatt following me down a wide road. Rudy, saying, come on, Wallen, just a few more yards. You'll make it. Carry that ball, son. Run. Big bellied Rudy with his big hands clapping, following me. In my dream I heard his breath came hard, only now it was my breath, and the hall of the house as long as the asphalt at Pearl Harbor had been, going on and on. Earl Wallen, the man in my dream had called after me. Wait for me. Where do we go now?

Down the hall, the door to Andrew's room was open. Wide open, and all the room beyond empty, empty as a wind died down, a breath let out. Nothing there but the floor covered from corner to corner with slivers of glass I stepped through to get to the window, a jagged hole in the middle of it. His bed was empty, too, and my shotgun was lying on the floor.

It was like my dream about running. Me, going from room to room, calling, Andrew, Ruth? In the kitchen, a pan of coffee, cold, with the grounds spilled on the stove. Broken, that glass jar with old man Blue's false teeth in it, them sitting open and pink-gummed on the floor. In the rocking chair in the front room, the Bible, open to a verse that says, the Lord God giveth them light, and they shall reign for ever and ever. I looked from room to room, back again, searching for a sign of them. Hair in a brush on the dresser, clothes, damp and streaked with mud, left on the floor. No one. Not a breath or a prayer.

In my dream I ran. Just like I really had that day in the war, never turning even once to look at who was behind me. I ended up inside a room, alone. Was it in my dream, or had it really been, me, watching a ceiling turn to fire, listening to that humming grow louder and louder. I ran fast down a long asphalt road, a road I thought I knew, one that ended up straight down to Inez. And now I was alone again, like I had been that day in the barracks room, listening to the sound of bombs. I was alone now, listening to the night, the start of morning. Alone, and who knows where the hell they were.

I guess you imagined me standing there, thinking, yipee. Thinking, yes sir, fine old times are coming. Just me and this house and the whole rest of my life and who knows what a man could do. Open him a juke joint and rent a few red dresses and a few willing women and sit out on the front porch and ladle out hard cider and just wait for the crowds. Earl Wallen, famous at last, owner of his own Starland Skatarama and Lolo Lafferty, right at his side. Pistol and matching boots, Roy Rogers and Dale Evans, skippy-ti-yi-yo. Fred Astaire and Ginger Rogers, waltzing our way to forever after. Wallen's, we'd call it. Too plain. Wallen's Roadside Wonder. Wallerama. Live it up, boys. Or me, alone, standing on the porch awhile at the house and loving it for about three days and then going to the truck and siphoning out the gas and wetting it all down real good and torching it. Scorched earth policy. Nothing left. Start all over again and good riddance.

But that wasn't how it was at all. Instead, I picked up a cold cup of coffee on the porch railing, looked down into the shadows of the yard, back at the empty house behind me. Andrew, I shouted again. Ruth? Through the handle of that cup, I looked up at the sky, like a sight aiming straight for the heart of something. Like I could see right to where God was sitting on his throne, surrounded by all the dancing angels and trumpets and celebrations and so forth.

God. That was a good one, like it always was. All of the high-sounding talk about streets of gold and celestial palaces like pie in the sky and here I was, aging would-be king of rock 'n' roll, standing on the front porch in his undershirt and yelling for his wife like a half-assed fool. Wife. There was another one. What was it old God had to say about wives? Something about rising up in the early morning before good daylight, being tireless and humble and meek. I'd gotten the humble and meek, all right, and now it looked like I'd gotten the tireless and the middle of the night, to boot. Not a creature was stirring, as the story goes. Just me, stumbling down into the yard in my unlaced boots and looking for the least sign of life.

Signs. She'd always called them that—blood on the moon, black cats and broken mirrors, the whole shebang. I could have been ninety years old and gumming my white bread and still not have believed the signs that came to me right then and there. Or the vision. You can call it that, if you need a name, an ending to all that happened that night.

I stood in the yard, light falling on me, one clear shaft of it, warm light that I reached for, took hold of. Imagine the pretty front of your church bulletin. Or one of those colored prints in your zip-up Bible. It was like that. Late night and after moon-set and I was holding out my arms and saying, yes, sweet Jesus. Or maybe not quite that much. There wasn't any front-yard salvation. No Jehovah's Witness with a suitcase to shake my hand and wish me well in my new life. But I did stand there in the dark feeling light spill over me. I shut my eyes, felt the waves and waves of it, like swimming in the ocean at night and your body and all that water meet and the lines between the two, the skin and bones on the one side and the salt and the distance on the other, the two worlds meeting in a moment that seems like forever.

Only where I was, wasn't the ocean at all of course. It was an eastern Kentucky night, the same yard as always. For that minute, that little slice of time, I saw the way it might be. Morning. The kitchen of that house behind me, that place I'd cursed and berated and stayed in, year upon year. And at the kitchen table, her. Her in an old nightgown with her long hair tumbled down, wet and threaded with moss and bits of leaves. I stood behind her, close enough to smell pond water and her cold skin. I stood close enough behind her to see the way she was next to the table, completely still, and I wanted to reach out, see if she was a haint, the walking dead, risen from a grave made of water. But I could see it, see the way she moved, ever so little, her heart beating against the table edge. Her heart beating said, this, Earl Wallen. This. This little human thing. This heart. Any heart. It's as close to God as you'll ever get. What I really saw as I stood alone in the dark of the yard was me. Me, long-suffering war hero, mourning the dead buddy he ran off and left? Mourning time and unsung songs and sweethearts he'd left behind?

No.

Me, I was the dead one all along. Dead, all the private wars for all I'd ever wanted, ever been, ever dreamed of being. War in the Pacific, war of lines crossing on road maps, roads going nowhere, war of too many lost stanzas of songs never finished, music never made real. Me, dead and with my soul floating over the whole damn world I'd wanted and could have had. In the end the only thing anchoring me to this house that was now empty, hollow, echoing.

I shouted again, louder.

Ruth.

Andrew.

Ruth? Like calling out to what kept me weighted here in this world of what I could not be. This world I was never sure I wanted.

No answer. Nothing but echoes, somebody's hunting dogs barking against the ridge, gears shifting in a truck down the hollow. Or was there nothing? As I called again, Ruth, Andrew, it was like an answer came, from the center of the sky.

A refrain, maybe.

I stood there, listening. It came to me. The reverberation of an almost forgotten chord in my fingertips. The never-written song of my own life.

The ghost of love waiting in my song-empty mouth, I set out, walking.

RUTH

You look up through layer upon layer, through the waves upon waves of faces, time, before. Light, small as a sliver of broken glass, tears through the far away surface of the black, thick water. You struggle to breathe any breath, feel the dank water hold you down as the light sends its sharp fragments farther down, far down. Will this light cut into you?

Or will you feel a hand, a warm palm touching if only you reached up?

Far off, above the surface of the pond, rising into the humid air of a late summer morning's start, you see a shape. Is this the way light begins? *Oh, for the wonderful love he has promised, promised for you and for me,* you sing with your water-filled breath.

As you rise to the surface of the pond, as you rise and rise, you sing that song of you, of all your life. Your whole life, an almost forgotten song, circles and circles above you, then like light rising, stretches up and up. Though we have sinned, this song says, he has mercy and pardon, pardon for you and for me. And you say back.

You say, *I am Ruth. She who gleans, gathers, abides fast to this world. I am wife, raising up the name of Wallen, Earl Wallen, for its* own praise among men. *I am she who the Lord gave conception, the blessing of Andrew, my son. Ruth Blue. Ruth. In secret, I sing real words of glory, kneel, pray, wait.* I listen to the voice that tells me: *follow, follow.* I praise the mighty wings of angels, touch their fierce wings. I am she who has looked for my lover, for God, in him in whose eyes grace is found. Of all sins, there is this one alone I most know: *I have wanted. I want the face, the touch, the breath of sweet God.* Even on that day, the day of my birth, I wanted. Impossible, they tell me, but it is that day of my own birth I remember best. I wanted even then.

Is that the face of God? Is it yourself?

ANDREW

Where you landed that night, after you fell back to earth, returned from the light, climbed through the window and ran into the last of that night, was the road to Florida, Henry Ward beside you, highway light and shadows changing on his face.

You left in secret, left the house and the whole coal black world whispering no. You left that place and all those things that hurt, things you would nearly forget, a time you would no longer name. You hummed as you went. You made up your own song, you sang, I am free now. Free.

You sang that one word until you believed it was true.

You left Highway 23 far behind, so far behind it became a thin red line on pages of a map you tore out and threw away.

Goodbye, you said, goodbye to forever and you tore out map pages, watched from the car's rear window as they bent and floated away.

They are your remembrances, like unto ashes, gone and gone.

Gone? Only as distant as that nonexistent scent of witch hazel. Only as distant as a song, that ghost of forever that follows you, calls out to you, lies down in your heart.

Anywhere, Henry Ward said. He said you could go anywhere at all and that meant on and on to the great unknown heart of the ocean. In the car you slept, dreaming of the sound of waves.

And so you chose what you could scarcely believe. Love.